Praise for Joan Johnston

"Joan Johnston does short contemporary Westerns to perfection." —*Publishers Weekly*

"Like LaVyrle Spencer, Ms. Johnston writes of intense emotions and tender passions that seem so real that the readers will feel each one of them."
—*Rave Reviews*

"Johnston warms your heart and tickles your fancy."
—*New York Daily News*

"A master storyteller . . . Joan Johnston knows how to spin a story that will get to the readers every time."
—*Night Owl Reviews*

"Johnston has a keen eye for quirky circumstances that put her characters, and the reader, through a wringer. Laughing one moment and crying the next, you'll always have such a great time getting to the happy-ever-after." —*Romance Junkies Reviews*

"Johnston is a writer who can combine romance side by side with tragedy, proving that there is magic in relationships and that love is worth the risk."
—*Bookreporter*

By Joan Johnston

Bitter Creek Novels

The Cowboy
The Texan
The Loner
The Price

The Rivals
The Next Mrs. Blackthorne
A Stranger's Game
Shattered

Sisters of the Lone Star Series

Frontier Woman
Comanche Woman

Texas Woman

Captive Hearts Series

Captive
After the Kiss

The Bodyguard
The Bridegroom

Mail-Order Brides Series

Texas Bride
Wyoming Bride

Montana Bride
Blackthorne's Bride

King's Brats Series

Sinful

Shameless

Connected Books

The Barefoot Bride
Outlaw's Bride

The Inheritance
Maverick Heart

Blackthorne's Bride

Joan Johnston

DELL BOOKS • NEW YORK

A Dell Mass Market Original

Copyright © 2017 by Joan Mertens Johnston, Inc.
Excerpt from *Surrender* by Joan Johnston copyright © 2017 by Joan Mertens Johnston, Inc.

Published in the United States by Dell, an imprint of Random House, a division of Random House LLC, a Penguin Random House Company, New York.

DELL and the HOUSE colophon are registered trademarks of Penguin Random House LLC.

This book contains an excerpt from the forthcoming novel *Surrender* by Joan Johnston. This excerpt has been set for this edition only and may not reflect the final content of the forthcoming edition.

ISBN 978-0-3991-7774-3
eBook ISBN 978-0-3991-7775-0

Printed in the United States of America

bantamdell.com

9 8 7 6 5 4 3 2 1

Cover design: Lynn Andreozzi

Cover illustration: Alan Ayers

Dell mass market original: July 2017

This book is dedicated to my friend
and marketing manager,
Nancy November Sloane.

Blackthorne's Bride

Prologue

SHE WAS TIED to a pole in the center of the Sioux village, naked from the waist up. What was left of her bodice was tangled at her waist above a striped muslin skirt. She still wore a pair of dusty boots. The top of one creamy shoulder was unblemished, but the rest of her back was so crisscrossed with bloody stripes that there was barely any flesh left. The blond pigtail that ran a short distance down her nape was crusted with dried blood. Her head had sunk forward, and he wondered if she was dead.

As he watched, she lifted her head and straightened her shoulders almost defiantly, emitting a harsh, wrenching sound that caused his insides to clench in sympathetic response to the excruciating pain she must be feeling. He turned his gaze to the Indian holding the bullwhip being used to torment her.

The Sioux's cheek had been laid bare almost to the bone, in a red slash very much like the ones on the girl's back. The Indian had paused briefly to note the two white men riding into camp with the reservation Sioux guide who'd brought them, but he was obviously impatient to return to his brutal work.

Marcus Wharton, the Duke of Blackthorne, turned to his guide and said, "Ask him why he's whipping the girl."

The Sioux with the bullwhip answered the question in a guttural tongue, gesturing first to his cheek and then to the girl's back, his mouth twisted in a malicious smile.

"She strike him with whip when he attack her wagon," the guide translated. "Hurt face. Knock him off pony. He punish. No one laugh at Three Crows again."

Blackthorne shared a look of disgust and disbelief with his future brother-in-law, David Madison, the Earl of Seaton. Seaton had joined him on his journey across the American West, a last desperate bid to enjoy his freedom, before he married the earl's sister, Fanny, and settled down to his responsibilities as the eighth Duke of Blackthorne.

As he stared at the scene in front of him, Blackthorne suddenly realized that he'd had his fill of adventure. He'd seen a great deal of cruelty in his twenty-five years, but nothing as savage as this.

To his horror, before he could say or do anything to rescue the poor girl, the Sioux called Three Crows sent the whip cracking toward her wounded back. The tip caught the untouched flesh at her shoulder, creating a bloody gash where none had previously existed.

The horrible cry of agony that escaped her lips had not yet died before Blackthorne was off his horse. He wrenched the whip from the Sioux's grasp and threw it away.

Three Crows pulled a knife from a sheath at his waist and stabbed at Blackthorne's belly.

Blackthorne twisted his body so the blade that would have gutted him merely ripped through his waistcoat. He kept his eyes on his foe, avoiding another slash of the Indian's knife, as he retrieved his own knife from his boot. He gripped the haft so he could stab or slice, moving in a cautious circle along with the Sioux, as they took each other's measure.

Three Crows was shorter than Blackthorne's six-foot height, with a thick, muscular body and arms. He stared with hate from eyes that were almost black, breathing hard through a flat nose and an open, thin-lipped mouth. He said something in his guttural tongue that needed no translation.

The Sioux clearly intended not just to kill him, but to cut him into painful little pieces.

The crowd that had been oddly missing while the Sioux whipped his prisoner suddenly surrounded them.

Three Crows' teeth were bared, his muscles taut, as he waited for his adversary to make his move.

Blackthorne had been told that this band of Sioux were renegades who'd fled the reservation, but who might be willing to include him in their buffalo hunt, if he traded a few trinkets with them. He realized he should have tried that road first where the girl was concerned. He and Seaton might find themselves in dire straits if he ended up wounding— or killing—this man. Not to mention how devastated his grandmother would be if he ended up getting himself killed in a knife fight before he'd married and produced an heir.

The Sioux's glinting eyes were focused intently on the knife in Blackthorne's hand.

Blackthorne suddenly realized that the Indian's gaze wasn't aimed at the very sharp blade, but rather on the intricately carved whalebone handle. He took a step back and opened his hand, so the knife lay flat on his palm.

The Sioux's eyes narrowed as he considered whether this was some ploy to distract him, so the white man could attack.

Blackthorne kept his gaze centered on Three Crows as he said to his Sioux guide, "Ask him if he'd like to have the knife."

"Blackthorne, you can't bargain with—"

He cut Seaton off and repeated in a steely voice, "Ask him if he'd like to have the knife."

His opponent looked confused, and then disdainful, as he first listened, and then replied to the guide's speech.

"Three Crows says he will take knife when you are dead," the guide interpreted.

"Tell him I'll give him the knife in exchange for the girl." Blackthorne saw the Indian open his mouth to refuse and reached into his pocket to pull out his grandfather's gold watch. He let it dangle from the watch chain so the sunlight reflected off the shimmering surface. "Along with this."

"You can't—"

"Be still, Seaton, and let the man think." He

could see the Sioux was as covetous of the watch as he was of the knife.

Three Crows glanced toward the girl, whose body lay slack against the pole. He abandoned his crouch and tucked his knife back into its sheath, then held out his hand.

Blackthorne dropped the watch into the Indian's palm, then flipped the knife and offered it to him by the carved handle.

"The girl's probably going to die anyway," Seaton hissed in his ear. "Why would you give up your grandfather's watch? And that knife goes back to the first Duke of Blackthorne. It's priceless. And irreplaceable."

Without warning, Three Crows slashed out with the knife Blackthorne had given him. He grabbed the Sioux's swinging wrist with one hand and balled his other hand into a fist that connected with the Indian's chin. He let go as Three Crows fell in a heap.

Blackthorne felt his friend edging toward him and turned to eye the Indians gathered around them. He reached down and took his knife from the Sioux's hand, then walked to the pole and used it to cut the woman free. As she fell into his arms, he let the knife drop to the ground. A bargain was a bargain. He'd promised the knife and his watch in exchange for the girl. A Blackthorne's word was as good as gold.

As her head dropped back over his arm, and he saw the damage to her face, he wished he hadn't bargained with the Sioux. He should have eviscerated him.

The girl's features were unrecognizable. Her eyes were so puffy and bruised, he couldn't tell what color they were. Her nose had been broken. Her lips were split, and blood ran down her chin. He was pleased to see dried blood under her ragged nails, proof that she'd fought back.

"Now that you have her, what do you plan to do with her?"

He turned to face his friend. "Get her to a doctor."

"The closest doctor is at Fort Laramie. It's the opposite direction from home. Considering the telegram from your grandmother saying you're needed there, I don't think we can stay around for the weeks—or months—it's going to take that girl to recover."

"Then we'll take her with us."

"She's likely got family around here somewhere. We should try to find them, instead of hauling her halfway across the world."

"Her family could be anywhere. For all we know they might be dead."

"She needs help we can't give her."

"I'm not leaving her behind," Blackthorne said, knowing his behavior was irrational but finding himself strangely unable to abandon the girl. "I want to make certain she gets the best help possible."

"Fine," Seaton said. "Can we go now? That Indian's starting to wake up. I don't want to be here when he does."

The girl moaned as Blackthorne shifted her in his arms. He brushed a strand of bloody hair away from her battered face. "It's all right," he murmured. "I have you. You're safe now."

Chapter 1

THE DUKE OF Blackthorne was sitting in a wing chair at his gentleman's club in London, drink in hand, staring absently out the window, when his best friend said, "It's the girl, isn't it? You're thinking of the waif you rescued from that savage."

"What if I am?" It irritated him to be so predictable. And embarrassed him to have his late wife's brother point out his preoccupation with a girl he'd barely known, rather than the woman who'd been his wife for a year, before she'd died bearing his son.

"It's been two years," Seaton said. "You need to forget about her. You have more important things to consider, if you want to rescue Blackthorne Abbey from ruin. You need to find a woman with means and marry her before the month is out."

Blackthorne made a face. Within a month of marrying Fanny, which was to say, within a month of his return to London from America, he'd learned that the Blackthorne estate was badly strapped. His father had made a number of risky investments that had not paid off. Then his younger brother, Montgomery, had died in a carriage race, and Blackthorne had been pressed to settle his brother's outrageous gambling debts and find somewhere for his brother's two sons to live, since Monty had died not only destitute, but a widower, whose late wife had no family.

Blackthorne had done his best to economize and had put Fanny's dowry to good use, but it soon became apparent that, without an infusion of capital, land that had been in his family for eight generations was destined to be lost forever.

He'd spent the months of Fanny's pregnancy filled with hope that she would bear him an heir to the dukedom, and with despair that he might be leaving his child an estate with only a glimmer of its former glory.

Unfortunately, things hadn't improved in the year since Fanny's death. In fact, they'd gotten worse. Now there was some doubt whether he could keep anything at all.

After his terrible experience losing Fanny and their son, he hadn't been inclined to marry again. Now circumstances demanded it. He needed a rich wife, and he needed her in a hurry.

The New York Times lay open on his lap, so he could see the text of the advertisement his solicitor had inserted in all the major American newspapers several months ago—along with the London *Times,* of course, in order to catch any American heiress who might already have crossed the pond to secure a British title in exchange for a bit of her father's wealth:

WANTED: *American heiress for purposes of matrimony to titled gentleman.*

The notice then gave the name of the Blackthorne solicitor, in an effort to make the duke's search for a wealthy bride somewhat anonymous. Not that everyone in Society didn't know the straits to which he'd been reduced. His grandmother had paraded a number of eligible English heiresses in front of him, but he'd insisted that, if he was forced to marry for filthy lucre, he wasn't going to do it among the ranks of his peers.

There was another reason he'd advertised for an American bride. Although he hadn't admitted it to anyone, he kept imagining that, somehow, the mystery woman he'd rescued all those years ago would show up again in his life.

Blackthorne thought more often than he ought to of the girl he'd nursed on the sea voyage across the Atlantic. He knew so little about her, not even her name. Perhaps that was why she'd remained so intriguing. Where was she now? How was she? He could have left her with an American family who'd been willing to take her in, but he'd refused to let her out of his sight. Why? What was it about that suffering girl that had so captivated him that he'd insisted on taking care of her himself?

Was it the courage that had kept her from begging for mercy at the sting of the lash? Was it that stubborn chin lifted in defiance of the pain the savage had inflicted upon her? Or was it the enormous strength of will that had kept her alive in spite of the terrible wounds she'd endured?

A doctor had straightened her nose as best he could, but it would always have a bump where it had been broken. Her battered face and her blackened eyes, which had remained mere slits for the balance of the journey, had left her unrecognizable. Blackthorne had feared that infection would kill her on the voyage across the sea, but she'd survived, although fever had plagued her all the way to England.

Day after day, she'd remained out of her head with pain from her ravaged back, but she hadn't complained, hadn't screamed or cried. She'd hissed when a hot cloth touched her flesh. She'd thrashed as Blackthorne held her still for the doctor's examination. Sometimes, she released a moan that was almost a sigh. He'd talked to her to keep her mind off the agony he knew he was causing, when he tended her ragged flesh.

"I've never seen a girl so brave," he'd told her as she bore his ministrations. He'd waited anxiously for her fever to break, for her to speak intelligible words, to say something—anything—to prove that what she'd suffered hadn't driven her mad.

"You have to let the physician mind the girl," Seaton had admonished him. "He knows best. You're liable to cause more damage, if you try to manage her treatment yourself."

He'd barely looked up from the girl's face, as he sat vigil beside her bunk in the captain's cabin, while the fever raged. "I bought her. She's my responsibility."

"Listen to yourself," his friend chided. "You rescued a damsel in distress. Your duties as knight in shining armor are over."

"Not until I know who she is," he'd murmured.

"What difference can that possibly make?" Seaton asked. "From the way she was dressed, it's clear she's one of the lower classes."

Blackthorne had shifted his gaze sharply to look his best friend in the eye. "That doesn't make her any less in need of my help."

"What are you going to do with her when you get her to England?" his friend demanded. "You're engaged to be married. How do you think Fanny is going to react to this wild hair of yours?"

He'd turned his attention back to the girl, who'd shifted and moaned. "Fanny will understand."

"You don't know my sister as well as you think you do."

"Go away, Seaton," he'd said in a firm, ducal voice. And Seaton had left.

Blackthorne was surprised by what the girl said when she finally spoke.

"All my fault," she muttered against the pillow. "Everything. If only they knew. All my fault."

"Surely you can't be responsible for the attack on your wagon," he'd said in a soothing voice.

She'd clutched the pillow tightly with both fists and said, "The fire. The fire."

For a long time he'd thought she was saying her back was on fire, which he could easily believe. But it wasn't that at all. She'd remained out of her head, raving and incoherent with fever, and it had taken more than a week before he'd cobbled together enough of the story, which had been revealed in bits and pieces, to understand her guilt.

She'd been referring to the terrible conflagration in Chicago three years previously, the one supposedly caused by Mrs. O'Leary's cow, which had kicked over a lantern in the barn. The resulting inferno, which had raged for three days, had burned down virtually the whole city, including this girl's home.

She'd been terrified by the flames and smoke and had hidden under her bed, making it necessary for her parents to hunt through the house for her. She hadn't replied, even when they'd pleaded for her to answer them. Her parents had finally found her, and her father had dragged her out. But by then, the bedroom doorway was blocked by fire. Her mother had tied the bedsheets together so her father could lower her out the back window. Safe outside, she'd watched her home burn to the ground with her parents inside.

He'd prodded her for her given name, or her family name, but she'd been too lost in her personal agony to respond. Apparently, she'd been orphaned. It was a mystery how she'd gotten from Chicago to the Dakota Territory, but presumably it involved travel in a Conestoga wagon, since she—and whoever was in it with her—had been attacked by the Sioux.

She'd mentioned a few names, but he had no clue whether they were relatives or acquaintances. Hetty and Hannah—always together. Miranda. Nick and Harry—again, always together. And a Mr. McMurtry. He wondered if she could be married to the man. But she wasn't wearing a ring, and there was no mark on her finger to show that she'd worn a ring that might have been removed by the Sioux.

She made two other statements relentlessly: "I

have to find them. I have to go back. I have to find them. I have to go back."

He kept hoping she would recover enough by the time they landed in England to answer all his questions about exactly who it was she had to find and where she had to go. But she was still far from well when their journey ended.

To his chagrin, Fanny was at the docks to greet him, together with her mother, who'd come along to welcome home her son and future son-in-law. Suddenly, he wasn't so sure Fanny would understand that he'd spent the entire crossing nursing a half-naked girl. Or why he'd parted with two irreplaceable heirlooms—a whalebone-handled knife and his grandfather's gold watch—to "buy" a young woman. Or why he'd insisted on nursing her himself, rather than allowing the perfectly capable physician he'd brought along to do it.

When he saw Fanny waving to him—fragile Fanny, who'd fainted at the sight of a cut on his face from a bout of fisticuffs at Jackson's Saloon—he realized Seaton was right. Fanny would never understand any of this. She would shortly be his wife, and he didn't want to start off his marriage with an unnecessary misunderstanding.

"Seaton, I need a favor," he'd said.

"Anything, Blackthorne."

"I want you to make sure that, once the girl is well, she's sent home to America."

"Of course. Consider it done."

Blackthorne had taken only one step toward the gangplank when he reversed course and hurried to the captain's cabin. He found his patient sleeping on her stomach and touched her cheek to wake her.

Her hair was still damp from fever, and her eyes looked dazed. "What's . . . happening?"

He stroked her hair, tucking a strand behind her ear as he spoke. "We've docked in London. I promise, when you're well, arrangements will be made to send you back to America. Now, I must leave you."

She grasped his hand, holding it against her cheek. "Don't . . . go."

Never had he heard a request he wanted to honor as much. But other obligations had to take precedence. He had to marry and produce an heir to the dukedom. His grandmother had insisted upon it, and he could no longer put her off.

He felt his heart twist, as he eased the girl's hand free of his own. "You'll be well taken care of, I promise. I'll make sure you have the means to find those you seek. You'll be on your way back to America as soon as you're completely healed and can stand another voyage."

She was still so weak, she was asleep almost before he finished speaking.

He leaned down to kiss her swollen cheek, which was a ghastly yellow and purple, now that the black and blue had gone away. "Sleep well, my dear."

He'd been determined not to mention the girl, in order to spare Fanny any questions about his commitment to his future wife. But on the coach ride into London, she'd asked whether he'd managed to hunt down one of the shaggy buffalo that were supposed to roam the American plains.

And it just slipped out: "I rescued a girl instead."

Fanny and her mother stared at him as though he'd said, "I not only killed a buffalo, I also sliced out its liver and ate it raw and steaming." He took one look at their faces and made up his mind not to say another word about how his American exploits had ended.

But Fanny wouldn't let it go. A sentence at a time, she coaxed the rest of the story out of him, beginning with how brave the girl had been in the face of torture.

Fanny's mother had needed a sniff of hartshorn, as he gave a greatly expurgated description of the torture the girl had endured. At Fanny's insistence, he explained how he'd given up his whalebone-handled knife and his grandfather's gold watch to buy her from the Sioux brave who'd been whipping her.

Fanny's mother harrumphed and said, "You'll be sorry someday. How could you forfeit such priceless family heirlooms for some . . . nobody?"

He explained how he'd nursed the girl on shipboard.

Fanny had slid her arm through his, leaned her cheek against his shoulder, and said, "Oh, my."

He explained how he'd left the girl—whose identity remained a mystery—behind at the docks, with instructions to Seaton that she was to be sent home to America, once she was completely healed.

"I can tell you admired her enormously," Fanny said.

"I did," he admitted. "I do." As soon as the words—in the present tense—were out of his mouth, he'd felt compelled to reassure Fanny that the girl was no threat to her. So he'd added, "All she wants is to return home and find her family."

"I'm so proud of you," Fanny said.

He hadn't expected that. "You are?"

"Your treatment of that poor girl only makes me love you more."

"It does?"

She'd looked up at him with such love that, even though her mother was sitting across from them, he'd brushed a knuckle against her cheek, causing her to blush and lower her eyes. He was glad to be home.

At that moment, Blackthorne had felt sure he was marrying the most wonderful—and most compassionate—woman alive.

Much later, he realized it would have been far better if Fanny had ranted and raged in a jealous frenzy, making it perfectly clear that he was never to think of *that American girl* again. Maybe then he wouldn't have remained entranced by her forever after.

Seaton had accused him of being obsessed. He would admit to being fascinated. By her bravery. By her sense of obligation to her family. And by all the things he *didn't* know about her. He wondered where she was. And how she was. He wondered if she'd ever been reunited with whoever it was she'd been so determined to find. He often felt saddened and frustrated by the knowledge that he was never going to have answers to his questions. That this elusive young woman was going to forever remain a mystery to him.

Most of all, he wondered why she'd never contacted him. He had no idea who she was, but surely, once she was well, she would have inquired about her benefactor. She would have been told she'd been rescued by the Duke of Blackthorne. She would have been told he'd nursed her on the long voyage from America, and that he'd provided her with the means to return from whence she'd come.

But he'd never heard a word from her. He could have asked Seaton if she'd ever mentioned him. But his pride—and his relationship with Seaton's sister—had kept him silent.

"Your Grace?"

Blackthorne turned to look at the servant holding out a silver plate that held a missive. He took the note and dropped a coin on the plate, dismissing the man.

"What is it?" Seaton asked, as Blackthorne finished reading the note and folded it again.

He grimaced. "It seems another female hoping to become my duchess is seeking an interview."

"Do you really have the luxury of refusing anyone at this point?"

"Perhaps not," Blackthorne conceded. "But I owe it to myself to take a look, before I agree to sell myself."

"And if she has a squeaky voice? Or sniffs? Or is redheaded with freckles? Or has a long nose or crooked teeth?"

"If she's rich enough to save Blackthorne Abbey, I'm willing to overlook any or all of those faults."

Chapter 2

WHEN THE PINKERTON detective finally located her, Josephine Wentworth had been a maid-of-all-work at the Duke of Blackthorne's estate in the northernmost county in England—and separated from her family in America—for two years.

"They're all alive? Miranda and Nick and Harry? And well?" she asked, when the Pinkerton informed her that he'd been employed by her eldest sister, Miranda, to find her, after she'd disappeared two years ago. "What about Hannah and Hetty? Have they been located? Are they . . ." Her throat had swollen closed with terror at the thought of what she might hear had happened to her twin sisters, who'd been left all alone on the prairie after the Sioux attack, without oxen to pull the wagon.

"All five of your siblings are alive and well," the Pinkerton confirmed. "And prosperous. In fact, Miss Wentworth, you're quite a wealthy young woman yourself."

Josie felt faint with relief that her entire family had survived, despite the calamities that had beset them. And then almost giddy at the thought of having enough money to liberate both herself and the two orphaned boys, wards of the Duke of Blackthorne, for whom she'd so often had to intervene to prevent unfair punishment over the past two years. Spencer and Clay had become the unfortunate victims of the trip wires and booby traps launched in the war between their London-born governess, Miss Adeline Sharpe, and the Scottishborn housekeeper at Tearlach Castle, Mrs. Edna Pettibone.

Mrs. Pettibone had ruled the roost for twentythree years before Miss Sharpe had shown up with the two boys in tow and insisted that she must be accorded a spot one rung higher in the pecking order at the duke's northernmost estate. Mrs. Pettibone had naturally taken umbrage at such a suggestion. By the time Josie arrived on the scene, the battle of wills was in full swing, and she had her hands full keeping the boys out of the line of fire.

Although only a small part of the ancient castle was livable, Mrs. Pettibone governed her domain with an iron fist. If the boys were underfoot—or naughty, as growing boys were wont to be—she accused Miss Sharpe of failing to control her charges. On the other hand, if the boys' clothes weren't washed and ironed to Miss Sharpe's high standards, she accused Mrs. Pettibone of failing to instruct the maids in their duties.

And that was the mere tip of the iceberg. Miss Sharpe complained endlessly about the condition of the castle, which Mrs. Pettibone was responsible for keeping in good working order. The charge of neglect was clearly unfair, since Mrs. Pettibone could hardly be held responsible for the fact that the stone structure was a broken-down ruin.

The property had been deeded to a medieval Duke of Blackthorne by King John, for the duke's assistance in taking Berwick-upon-Tweed from the Scots. As far as Josie could tell, nothing had been done since to improve it, and Tearlach had deteriorated to its current sad condition. Sheep dotted the green rolling hills that surrounded the castle and provided the income for those who lived and worked on the estate.

The Pinkerton's pronouncement that she was rich enough to escape the castle that had been her prison for the past two years seemed too good to be true. Her brow furrowed in disbelief. "I'm wealthy? How is that possible?"

"It seems your father's fortune wasn't burned up in the Great Fire after all," the Pinkerton replied. "Your uncle Stephen absconded with it. He has since been found, and most of your father's fortune recovered."

"I'm rich?" she asked again, not quite sure if she was making up the words coming out of the Pinkerton's mouth because she wanted so badly for them to be true.

"Yes, Miss Wentworth." He handed her a piece of paper and explained, "This bank draft should serve to get you back to your family in America. There's more money waiting in the bank for you there. Along with your family, of course."

"Where are they?" she asked. "Where should I go?"

"That's up to you. Your sister Miranda is married to Mr. Jacob Creed and lives on a ranch near San Antonio, Texas, with your brothers, Nicholas and Harrison. Your sister Hannah is married to Mr. Flint Creed and lives on a ranch near Fort Laramie in the Wyoming Territory."

Josie couldn't believe Hannah had married again. Hannah's first husband, Mr. McMurtry, had died of cholera during their journey from the Chicago orphanage, where they'd been living, to Cheyenne, in the Wyoming Territory, where Mr. McMurtry had planned to open a store. Josie had already opened her mouth to ask whether the two Creeds—Jacob and Flint—were related, when the Pinkerton said, "The Creed men are brothers."

Josie wondered how two of her sisters could have met and married brothers living so far apart, but that could wait until she saw them again and could hear their stories in person. "And Hetty?" she asked anxiously. Hetty had been struck in the shoulder by a Sioux arrow during the attack on their wagon. All this time, Josie had worried and wondered whether Hetty had survived her wound.

"Your sister Henrietta is married to Mr. Karl Norwood and lives in the Bitterroot Valley in the Montana Territory."

"No one lives near anyone else," she cried in consternation. "How can they bear it?" They'd been a caring, close-knit family. Now, not only were all her sisters married to men who were strangers to her, but they resided at such vast distances from each other that visiting must be next to impossible.

"Do you know if they've been able to get back together anytime in the past two years?"

The Pinkerton doffed his black derby and ran a hand through his hair before replacing the hat and tugging it down low on his brow. He cleared his throat and said, "I believe they've been waiting until you could be located, before they attempted to reunite the family in one place. I have orders to escort you to London and make sure you have no trouble making arrangements to return home."

Josie felt ashamed that she hadn't tried harder to get back to her family in America. But she couldn't figure out a way to take Spencer and Clay with her, and she wasn't willing to leave the two persecuted boys behind. They'd needed her as much—or maybe more—than her siblings. Besides, she'd had no idea how to locate her sisters and brothers, or even whether any of them were still alive. Now it seemed the Wentworths would all be together again someday.

But that day was going to have to wait awhile longer. First, she had to rescue Spencer and Clay from the clutches of the dastardly Duke of Blackthorne, whose neglect had allowed two unhappy women to make the lives of their charges miserable.

Josie had been the one to suggest that Miranda leave the rest of them behind at the Chicago Institute for Orphaned Children, so she could become a mail-order bride in Texas. She'd hoped Miranda might marry a man who had a large enough home that they could all go there to escape the cruel headmistress, Miss Iris Birch.

But after Miranda left the orphanage in the dead

of night—sneaking Nick and Harry out the door along with her—she'd never been heard from again. Josie and her older twin sisters hadn't known for sure whether Miranda and the boys were alive or dead.

During the three months after Miranda left, the beatings from Miss Birch had gotten worse, and Josie had pressured Hannah to become a mail-order bride as well, in order to escape Miss Birch's wrath at Miranda's middle-of-the-night escape with their two brothers. Hannah had married Mr. McMurtry, and the three remaining sisters had ended up on a wagon train headed to the Wyoming Territory.

That journey had ended in utter disaster. They'd been lost on the prairie when Mr. McMurtry died of cholera, and shortly thereafter, the three girls had been attacked by a marauding band of Sioux. Mercifully, most of what came after her capture was a painful blur. Josie had no memory of being rescued from the Sioux village. She wasn't sure at what moment she'd realized she was safe, that she'd been saved from the savage who'd taken her captive. She'd felt the sway of the bunk in which she lay and smelled the salt air and heard the men above deck singing sea chanties as they worked and realized she was on a ship. Her whole existence had narrowed down to the rough timbre of a soothing male voice, the touch of gentle hands, and the excruciating pain of having her wounds treated.

She had only one vivid memory: the spoken promise of her rescuer that she would be sent home and given the means to find her sisters. It was a promise he hadn't kept. All the kind treatment in the world by the Duke of Blackthorne—the man she'd discovered was her supposed savior—couldn't make up for that bitter betrayal.

Instead of being shipped home to America when she was well, she'd been sent off to Tearlach Castle, a few miles from the Scottish border, and had become a virtual slave. She intended to have an answer from the duke's own lips someday, as to why he'd broken his promise.

Meanwhile, the housekeeper had made Josie's options clear: either wash dishes, sweep floors, cook, empty the grates, keep the lamps clean, haul coal, polish silver, do needlework, make beds, wash and iron laundry, weed the garden, and help keep "those pesky boys" out of the way, or be kicked out to starve without a roof over her head.

Josie had written numerous letters to the Duke of Blackthorne, but she'd gotten no response. Which made her wonder whether they might have been intercepted by Mrs. Pettibone. So she'd sent a letter through one of the shepherds and got no response. And finally, through a traveling peddler, with the same result.

At that point, she'd concluded that the duke had gotten all the letters she'd sent and simply ignored them. It was a case of out of sight, out of mind. She'd been an interesting diversion, nothing more.

When she'd felt strong enough, Josie had tried to run away, only to discover just how far Tearlach Castle was from Berwick-upon-Tweed. She'd walked for two days and hadn't seen another living soul. No stagecoach traveled the closest road, and even assuming she could find a port where she could take ship for America, she had no way to pay for her passage.

Her hate and resentment of the Duke of Blackthorne had grown, as she'd realized the true extent of her captivity. He'd rescued her from the Indians, only to make her a prisoner in one of his poorer estates, which he never visited.

Her circumstances had been bearable, but her heart ached for the duke's nephews. When she'd arrived, Clay and Spencer were only four and six. Their situation reminded her most of what her two younger brothers, Nick and Harry, had suffered at the hands of Miss Birch at the orphanage. Mrs. Pettibone found her two charges a nuisance and a burden and made sure they knew it. And Miss Sharpe was as strict as she was quick to punish for a fault.

It would have been bad enough if the two mistreated boys had been the children of poor relations. But Josie had discovered they were *Lord* Spencer and *Lord* Clay, the orphaned sons of the Duke of Blackthorne's younger brother, Lord Montgomery Wharton.

Josie found the boys' abandonment as outrageous as her own, and she made it her business to make their lives easier. She spent as much time with them as she could, taking them for nature walks that gave Miss Sharpe a break and keeping them out of the way of Mrs. Pettibone as best she could. In short, she'd done everything in her power to make their childhoods more fun. She couldn't have loved them more if they'd been her very own brothers.

Josie was jerked from her reverie by a tug on her skirt and an eight-year-old voice saying, "Josie, come quick! It's Clay!"

"What's happened?"

"Mrs. Pettibone caught him stealing an apple tart in the kitchen. She's running up the stairs after him, and Miss Sharpe is in the schoolroom, where Clay likes to hide. You know what that means."

A shiver of foreboding skittered down Josie's spine. "Excuse me, please," she said to the Pinkerton. "Don't leave! I'll be back."

Then she turned and followed Spencer, as he scampered away toward the stairway in the hall.

Chapter 3

JOSIE RACED UP two flights of cold stone stairs to the third floor, where both she and the boys had their rooms, Spencer a step ahead of her. The perpetually hungry boys often purloined food from the kitchen. Spencer was rarely caught; Clay, not nearly so clever or so fast, almost always was.

The door to the schoolroom was open, revealing a familiar tableau. Mrs. Pettibone had a fistful of Clay's shirt clutched in her hand and the six-year-old was standing on tiptoes to avoid being strangled by the muslin at his throat.

"Stealing food again! What did I tell you would happen the next time? Do you remember? Or are you too feebleminded to recall?"

"If punishment should be meted out—" Miss Sharpe interjected.

"*If? If?*" Mrs. Pettibone said in outrage. "Are you suggesting you condone this behavior?"

"Mrs. Pettibone—" That was all Josie got out before the rail-thin woman rounded on her.

"Don't bother pleading for mercy," she snapped. "This insolent brat has been asking for a whipping, and he's going to get it."

"No one is going to discipline my charges but me!" Miss Sharpe retorted.

Josie took another step into the room, putting herself between Miss Sharpe and Mrs. Pettibone, and announced, "I just wanted to let you both know that this is my last day at Tearlach Castle."

Mrs. Pettibone was so perturbed by Josie's statement that she released her hold on Clay, who slumped to the floor and then scuttled away on hands and knees to hide behind Josie's skirt.

The housekeeper found the boys a trial and Miss Sharpe a constant irritation, but she hated Josie with a passion. For someone as lowly as a maid-of-all-work, she considered Josie far too proud and interfering. Mrs. Pettibone would have dismissed her within a day of her arrival, when Josie had first interceded on behalf of Spencer and Clay—coincidentally, on the side of Miss Sharpe—but it turned out that she didn't have the authority. The Duke of Blackthorne had apparently banished Josie to this remote prison with no hope of parole. The maid and the housekeeper had waged a war of words and wits—and Josie had walked a tightrope between the housekeeper and the governess—ever since.

"You can't go anywhere," Mrs. Pettibone said vindictively. "Blackthorne won't allow it."

"The duke no longer controls my destiny," Josie replied. "I'm leaving today to rejoin my family in America."

"With what funds?" the housekeeper inquired, one bushy white brow arched in disdain.

Josie had been paid next to nothing in the two

years she'd worked at the castle. She lifted her chin and said, "My family provided money for my passage."

Josie found the scowl on the housekeeper's face immensely satisfying, but she hadn't contemplated the effect her words would have on the two boys. Or rather, on Spencer, since Clay didn't seem to understand the significance of what she'd said.

"You're going away?" Spencer asked, a horrified look on his face.

"Good riddance," the governess muttered, since Josie's defense of the two boys had caused her to be the bane of that lady's existence as well.

Josie brushed the dark hair in need of a cut out of Spencer's eyes in a gesture as loving as it was necessary. "I'm afraid I must." She wanted to reassure Spencer that she would be back to rescue him and his brother as soon as she could, but she didn't want to reveal her plans to the spiteful housekeeper or the possessive governess, either or both of whom would surely intervene, if they could, to ruin Josie's chance of separating the boys from their uncaring uncle.

"We'll just see what His Grace has to say about this," the housekeeper muttered. As she strode past Josie, she pointed an arthritic finger at Clay and said, "Don't think you've escaped your punishment, you pestilential rodent. The moment Miss Wentworth is gone, you'll have your comeuppance."

Spencer put his narrow-shouldered, eight-year-old body between his brother and Mrs. Pettibone and said, "You'll have to go through me first."

The housekeeper glared at the defiant boy. "That can be arranged."

"Over my dead body," the governess growled.

Josie would have felt a great deal better about leaving, if the governess had been as much interested in protecting the boys as she was in squelching Mrs. Pettibone's pretensions.

Josie quickly turned the two boys away from Mrs. Pettibone and Miss Sharpe and headed them toward the door. "I would appreciate your help packing."

She ushered the boys down the hall to the small room she had to herself, since none of the other maids wanted to associate with someone who was so clearly a trial to both housekeeper and governess. The instant they were all inside, she shut the door and leaned back against it. Then she took the two steps necessary to gather one boy in each arm and pull them close.

"I didn't want to say so in front of Mrs. Pettibone or Miss Sharpe, but I'll be back as quickly as I can, and when I come, I'll have the necessary blunt to take you both away from here."

"You're leaving?" Clay said.

She bent down on one knee so she could look into Clay's confused gray eyes. Clay had always been slow to understand, and Josie knew he would always need someone to take care of him. "I must, dearest. But I'll be back."

Clay clutched her around the neck and cried, "Don't go, Josie! Please. Don't go!"

Josie held him close as he sobbed. She glanced up at Spencer, whose blue eyes welled with tears that he scrubbed away before they could fall. From his dejected appearance, he didn't believe she'd be back, that this was goodbye forever.

Spencer looped a comforting arm around Clay's shoulders and said in a voice that trembled with emotion, "Let her go, Clay. Josie needs to pack."

Josie freed herself from Clay's grasp and crossed the room to retrieve a cloth traveling bag from the bottom of her wardrobe. "I *will* be back," she said to Spencer. "As soon as I can convince the duke—"

"Nothing you say is going to make a difference," Spencer said bitterly.

"I'll make him listen to me. I'll make him understand—"

"Even if he listens," Spencer argued, "I'll bet you a golden guinea that he won't let us go anywhere with you. Not that I have a guinea, or I'd have loaned it to you long before now, so you could escape this place."

"There must be some way—" Josie began.

"Uncle Marcus has forgotten all about us!" Spencer cried. "It's as though we fell down a well and disappeared from the face of the earth."

"I intend to correct that," Josie promised, stopping to give the distraught boy a reassuring hug. The sad truth was that she had no idea how she was going to convince the toplofty Duke of Blackthorne that he should allow his nephews to trot off to America with her. She only knew that she wasn't going to leave these two boys prey to the callous whims of the feuding housekeeper and governess.

Once Josie was packed, the boys followed her

downstairs to the kitchen, where she'd left the Pinkerton. "I'm ready," she announced.

She turned to say a last goodbye and realized her throat was too thick with emotion to speak. Tears filled her eyes and made their stricken faces difficult to see. She swiped at her eyes, then bent down on one knee to embrace the two boys one final time.

"Be good while I'm away," she croaked. "Don't give Mrs. Pettibone an excuse to confront Miss Sharpe."

"She doesn't need an excuse," Spencer muttered.

"I know," Josie said, holding him tight. "Just do your best to stay out of her way."

She kissed the tears from Clay's cheeks, then rose and leaned down to kiss Spencer on the forehead. As her lips touched his skin he jerked backward. "You don't have to leave! If you cared about us, you'd stay."

Josie gasped at the virulence in his voice. "That isn't fair! I have to go."

Spencer put a supportive arm around Clay, who'd started crying in earnest, and said, "Then go! Get out! We don't need you. We don't need anybody. We were fine before you got here, and we'll be fine when you're long gone."

"Spencer, I know this seems—" She stopped speaking because Spencer had grabbed Clay's hand, torn open the kitchen door, and run outside, dragging his younger brother behind him.

Josie turned to the Pinkerton and said, "I have to speak to them, Mr. . . . What is your name?"

"Thompson, miss."

"I have to explain that I'm coming back, Mr. Thompson. They don't understand that I have to leave."

She'd only taken two steps toward the kitchen door when the Pinkerton said, "The sooner you go, Miss Wentworth, the sooner you can return, if that's your intention."

She stopped in her tracks, realizing the truth of his words, then turned to him and said fiercely, "I *am* coming back."

"If you say so, Miss Wentworth." He picked up her bag from the floor, where she'd dropped it to say farewell to the boys, and gestured toward the door. "Shall we go?"

Josie looked around the kitchen one last time, remembering all the potatoes she'd peeled, all the dishes she'd washed, all the silver she'd polished— even though His Grace had never shown up to use it. She was done being the Duke of Blackthorne's servant. It was time to confront the man and make him pay for his dishonorable behavior toward her—and the two boys who'd had the misfortune to become his wards.

Chapter 4

"JAKE! COME QUICK!" Miranda Creed carefully settled her eight-months-pregnant body into a chair in the kitchen, hugging a telegram to her chest that had just been delivered to their ranch outside San Antonio.

A moment later, her husband appeared in the kitchen on the run, their one-year-old son, Will, tucked under one arm, and his four-year-old daughter with his first wife, Anna Mae, straddling his hip. Miranda's two younger brothers, Nick and Harry, along with Slim, her husband's father-in-law, who rode in a wheeled chair, trailed close behind.

"Is it time?" Jake asked, setting the two children down at her feet. "Should I fetch the doctor?"

"You all right, Missy?" Slim asked anxiously.

"Mama, are you okay?" Anna Mae cried, tugging at Miranda's apron.

"Mama hurt?" Will said, trying to climb into her lap.

"What can I do, Miranda?" twelve-year-old Nick said, hovering beside her chair.

"Is the baby coming?" six-year-old Harry asked, leaning his hands on her leg.

"The Pinkertons found Josie! She's coming home!" Miranda said, a grin splitting her face from ear to ear. She reached out to tousle heads of hair and leaned to kiss little ones, before pulling Will onto what was left of her lap.

All the Wentworths had light-colored hair, but Anna Mae had her late mother's dark brown hair and eyes, and baby Will had Jake's black hair to go with sky-blue eyes that matched her own.

The wheezing cough that had plagued Harry at the orphanage when he was a baby was long gone, but Nick's unruly cowlick remained to remind her of days gone by. The elder of her two brothers had sprouted like a Texas tumbleweed and, like that native plant, seemed always to be in motion, his twelve-year-old voice cracking as it wavered from boy to man.

For the past two years, Miranda's cup had felt full to overflowing, but the liquid within had never been entirely sweet, not with the unexplained disappearance of her youngest sister always there to remind her that her family was not complete.

But Josie had been found at last and was on her way to Texas at this very moment. Miranda's heart felt so full of joy it was hard to contain it.

Jake slid an arm around her shoulders and leaned down to kiss her hair. "I'm so glad for you, sweetheart. I know how much you've worried about your missing sister."

"Josie's really been found? No fooling?" Nick said.

"Mr. Thompson sent this telegram," she said, picking it up from the table where she'd dropped it and waving it in the air. "He found Josie working as a maid at a place called Tearlach Castle in England. He's putting her on a ship bound for Charleston today. She should be here within a matter of weeks."

"Just in time to greet the new baby," Nick said with a grin.

Miranda reached for the edge of her apron to swipe at the tears streaming down her cheeks. "I'm so happy!" she said with a laugh that ended in a sob.

"All right, all of you, go play outside," Jake ordered. "Give your mom a little time to herself."

Jake no longer made the distinction between mother and sister where Miranda's brothers were concerned. For all practical purposes, Miranda had been a mother to both Nick and Harry since they were small children.

There was no grumbling from anyone, since it was a beautiful spring day, and they all had chores that were apparently going to go undone because they'd been ordered to go play.

Miranda felt Jake's hands sliding under her arms to stand her upright, and realized he'd taken her place in the chair before he lifted her into his lap.

"I'm too heavy, Jake," she protested.

"Not for me. Let me hold you," he whispered, his arms tightening around her.

She leaned her head against his shoulder and sighed, a soft exhalation of relief and joy. "I can hardly believe it," she said. "I was so afraid . . ."

In two long years, all the Pinkerton agency had been able to discover about Josie was that she'd been bought from the Sioux who'd captured her by the Duke of Blackthorne, who'd paid for her with his gold watch, which one of the Pinkertons had recovered.

With that much information, it should have been simple to find her sister. But Josie seemed to have disappeared from the ship that brought her to England. The Duke of Blackthorne had been inaccessible, and inquiries to the duke's solicitor had provided no information about anyone named Josephine Wentworth. No further sign of her sister had been found in England. She'd simply disappeared.

Miranda wondered how Mr. Thompson, one of the many Pinkertons she'd hired and sent out across the country—and around the world—had located Josie at last. Although, it didn't really matter how she'd been found. The important thing was that she *had* been found.

"I want to send word to Hannah and Hetty. I want them to be here when Josie arrives."

"I know you've been as anxious to reunite with your other sisters as you have been to see Josie," Jake said. "But perhaps you should wait to have everyone come until after the baby arrives, and you've had time to recover your strength."

"The sheer bliss of having my family around me will be all I need to keep me well," Miranda assured him. "Please, Jake. I have to tell them she's been found. They've been as worried as I have about Josie. *Two years*. That's forever! I wonder what she'll look like, how she'll have grown. I can't wait to hear what's happened to her and why she didn't return to us sooner."

"Very well, love. Write down what you want in the telegrams to Hannah and Flint, and Hetty and Karl, and I'll make sure they get sent."

"You don't mind if I ask my sisters to come as soon as they can?"

"I'll add my entreaty to yours," he said. "I guess it's about time you and your sisters got back together and met each other's husbands and families."

"Don't forget to invite *both* your brothers," Miranda said. "Ransom won't want to miss out on this reunion."

Somehow, some way, Miranda's sister Hannah had ended up married to Jake's younger brother Flint, who co-owned a ranch in Wyoming with Jake's youngest brother, Ransom.

"Your mother will be ecstatic to have her family back together," Miranda said.

Jake scowled. "I hope you're not suggesting I invite *her* husband to this reunion."

After Jake's father had died in the Civil War, Jake's mother, Cricket Creed, had married a man named Alexander Blackthorne, who'd quickly claimed what should have been Jake's inheritance. Jake had refused to move farther than Three Oaks, land that sat, like an irritating chicken bone in the throat, smack in the middle of Blackthorne's vast— and growing—Bitter Creek empire.

"You know your mother won't want to come

without her husband and their twin boys. You have to forgive Alex someday for marrying her."

"Why?" Jake demanded.

Miranda put a hand to his cheek, feeling the muscles in his jaw flex as he gritted his teeth. "Because you love your mother, and you don't want to make her unhappy."

He made a disgusted sound in his throat before admitting, "All right. Fine. I'll invite the son of a bitch. But I don't have to like it. And I can't guarantee what Flint and Ransom will do or say when they lay eyes on him."

"Thank you, Jake. Let's let their wives worry about their behavior."

Jake snorted. "I suppose they're being led around by their noses by the women they love, just like I am."

Miranda caught his nose between two fingers and giggled. "As if you do anything you don't want to do, just because I ask it of you."

She let go of his nose when she saw the look in his eyes.

"You know I'd kiss that rotten son of a bitch, if it would put a smile on your face," he said seriously. "I love you, Miranda. I bless the day you walked into my life."

"Even when I showed up with two little boys you weren't expecting?" she said breathlessly.

He nodded, then lowered his head and kissed her as tenderly as she'd ever been kissed. "Even with those two little brats in tow."

"Jake!" She jerked back at his description of

Nick and Harry, and then saw the teasing light in his blue eyes, before they crinkled with laughter.

"Oh, you! You know you love them."

"I do," he admitted. "I mourned when those outlaws burned Three Oaks down. I never imagined anything could replace it—even with all your inherited millions. I had no idea that love was the thing that made Three Oaks a home. And we have more than enough of that to go around."

"Oh, Jake." Her eyes welled with tears, and she felt his warm lips on her cheek, kissing away the first one to fall.

He lifted his head and added, with a cheeky grin, "I also have to admit, I'm damned grateful you insisted on a house so big that we'll have plenty of room for everyone who's bound to show up here over the next couple of weeks."

Miranda laughed. She laid a hand on her belly and said, "Now, if this little one will just cooperate, and wait until everyone arrives before she—"

"Or he," Jake interjected.

"Makes an appearance," Miranda finished, as though he hadn't interrupted. "I promised Anna Mae a sister, if you'll recall, and I intend to keep my promise."

Jake nuzzled her neck below her ear. "But I promised your brothers another brother."

Miranda chuckled. "Well, I suppose if either of them doesn't get their wish, we'll just have to keep on trying."

Jake's hands slid up to cup her breasts. "Well I, for one, will be happy to oblige."

Miranda turned her head so her husband's mouth

could find hers, but their kiss was interrupted when Jake released his breath in an *oomph* and sat up straight.

"That little dickens hit me! With fists like that, it has to be a boy."

Miranda put her hand on her belly where the kick had originated. "Our little girl is just anxious to join us." She leaned close until their lips almost met and whispered, "Or maybe it'll be both."

Jake reared back. "What makes you say something like that?"

"You know twins run in my family. Admit it, I'm twice as big as I was with Will."

"You look beautiful to me."

She laughed. "I wish I could believe you."

He met her gaze and said, "You're the most beautiful thing I've ever seen."

Miranda leaned her head against her husband's chest, because the look of love in his eyes made her throat swell and her heart ache. How lucky she was to have found him! It had been terrifying to come all the way from Chicago to Texas to become a mail-order bride. It all could have turned out so very wrong. Instead, she'd married a strong, loving man who was a wonderful father to both their children and her brothers.

"Time for you to rest, sweetheart," Jake said, standing up, shifting her in his arms, and holding her close.

Miranda's eyes slid closed. She tired so easily these days. She hadn't been feeling well, but she didn't want to worry Jake, so she'd kept her inability to keep food down a secret. Whether he wanted to admit it or not, she'd gotten much larger around the middle with this pregnancy. Was it twins? She worried that two small babies would have a harder time surviving than one large one. On the other hand, one very large baby might be a lot more difficult to deliver.

"Don't forget to send the telegrams," she murmured as he settled her in their bed.

"I won't forget."

She felt him spread a blanket over her, before he leaned down and kissed her forehead. The last thing she remembered was the door closing with a quiet *click* as he left the room.

Chapter 5

JOSIE WAS SITTING near the fire at the Hare and Hound, a pub near the London docks, the Pinkerton across from her, when she overheard a conversation between two gentlemen at the next table.

"The duke is completely pockets to let. If he doesn't find a rich wife within the month, he's going to lose everything."

The word "duke" had caught her attention, but she was still only half listening, when the other gentleman said, "I heard he's advertised both here and abroad seeking an American heiress."

Josie was startled to realize that, if everything Mr. Thompson had told her on the endless train ride from Berwick-upon-Tweed to London was true, she qualified as "an American heiress."

"I heard Blackthorne's turned down at least a dozen girls. Too conceited. Too loud. Too brassy. Too bossy."

Both men guffawed at the last pronouncement, apparently imagining the haughty duke being pussy-whipped by a woman he'd been forced to wed.

Josie froze in place. *Blackthorne* was seeking an

American heiress? He *had* to marry? And in the next *thirty days*?

"Time to go, Miss Wentworth," Mr. Thompson said, rising from the table.

"Not yet," she said. "We have something to discuss."

The Pinkerton eased back into his chair. When she said nothing, he asked, "Is there something else I can do for you, miss?"

"Yes, Mr. Thompson, there is. You can find out the truth of the matter those gentlemen were just discussing."

"You mean whether the Duke of Blackthorne is, in fact, seeking an American bride? The answer is yes, he is. He needs a rich wife, and he's too proud to seek her among his peers."

Josie smiled. "I guess I shouldn't be surprised that you were listening. Or that you know the answer to my question."

He smiled back. "A Pinkerton never sleeps."

Josie huffed out a breath. There it was. The answer to all her problems. She could offer the duke her inheritance to release the Lords Spencer and Clay Wharton into her care. Surely he would be happy to have the means to save his estate without the burden of a wife. Before she could change her mind she said, "How would I manage an introduction?"

The Pinkerton looked startled. "To the duke? For what purpose?"

"I want him to release the two boys you met at Tearlach Castle into my care. I'll happily give him my fortune in exchange."

Mr. Thompson steepled his fingers under his whiskered chin. "Are you aware of the precise amount of your inheritance, Miss Wentworth?"

Josie made a face. "I suppose it's not enough, is that what you're saying?"

"No, miss. It's substantial. More than a million, I should say."

Josie gasped. "Dollars?"

"Pounds, miss."

Josie's heart was beating a fast tattoo in her chest. "That should be enough, wouldn't you say, to induce him to give the boys to me?"

The Pinkerton chuckled. "I suppose it depends on how much value he puts on his nephews."

"None at all, from what I've seen over the past two years," Josie retorted. She glanced down at the plain gray dress and black half boots she was wearing, then lifted a hand to the braids wrapped tightly around her head, which Mrs. Pettibone had insisted she employ to restrain her blond curls. "I can't meet the duke looking like this. Do you think I could obtain the funds to dress myself properly?"

"I don't see why not, miss. I'd be glad to act as an intermediary for your meeting with the duke, if you wish."

"Thank you, Mr. Thompson. That would be wonderful!"

"Don't thank me yet," he replied. "The duke may already have chosen a bride."

"That doesn't matter."

The Pinkerton quirked a brow, and Josie explained, "Even if he's secured one fortune, surely he wouldn't turn down another."

Mr. Thompson looked doubtful. "There's no understanding the Quality, miss. Sometimes what they do makes no sense to anybody."

"I can't disagree with that. I need to see a modiste and a hairdresser. I don't want to look like a supplicant, even though that's what I'll be."

Josie parted ways with the Pinkerton, who left her with Miss Harriet Brownlee, the most expensive dressmaker in London. Harriet spoke French to her assistants and English to Josie, which consisted primarily of *tsk, tsking* about her clothing and hair.

Josie was careful not to give the modiste or her assistants the opportunity to see her back. She insisted on undressing and dressing herself in private. The terrible wounds she'd suffered two years ago had long since healed, but her back contained rivers of mutilated flesh that she couldn't look at without shuddering. She still felt pain on occasion, if she jerked and the scars pulled. But once she was dressed, there was no way to tell that, once upon a time, she'd been savagely whipped.

Miss Brownlee brought in a hairdresser, because she didn't want Josie leaving her establishment wearing one of her fabulous frocks with the hair of a washerwoman.

When Miss Brownlee and the hairdresser, Monsieur Pierre, were done, Josie could hardly believe what she saw in the mirror. Sparkling blue eyes set in a heart-shaped face, a dainty nose sprinkled with freckles, full lips, and even white teeth—which was when she realized she was smiling with delight at the transformation in her appearance.

"Why, I'm . . ."

"Stunning," Miss Brownlee said with a satisfied smile.

"*Magnifique,*" the French hairdresser added, kissing his fingertips.

"You look devilish dashing, Miss Wentworth," one of the assistants, to whom Miss Brownlee had spoken in French, said with a cockney accent.

Miss Brownlee lifted a disapproving eyebrow, and the girl disappeared behind a curtain.

Josie had grown up as the daughter of wealthy parents, so once upon a time, she'd been used to nice things. But it had been five years since the Great Fire of 1871 had killed her parents and sent her and her siblings to the Chicago Institute for Orphaned Children. Since then, she'd worn home-made muslin dresses and had her hair cut by her sisters.

The long-sleeved, powder-blue silk taffeta dress designed by Miss Brownlee buttoned to Josie's throat, then followed her form to the waist. The skirt fell in folds to the pleated hem. Matching silk-covered buttons lined the bodice from throat to waist, and embroidered flowers decorated the sleeves at the wrists. Miss Brownlee had provided ivory kid high-top shoes that buttoned up the sides. Josie's hair had been trimmed so bangs swept away from her face, and a small satin bow held her hair at the crown, leaving shiny blond curls falling onto her shoulders.

She'd grown nearly three inches in the two years since she'd come to England, and she was taller than average. At eighteen, her face and form had fulfilled the promise of the beautiful young woman she'd once been destined to become. The only visible hint that she'd been badly beaten about the face was a slight bump on the bridge of her nose.

"A gentleman is waiting for you in the parlor," Miss Brownlee said, gesturing Josie in the right direction. "Are you sure you don't want more than one gown?"

"One is all I'll need," Josie said with certainty.

"I'll dispose of the garment you wore on your way here."

Josie smiled wryly. That had been her very best Sunday dress. But those days were behind her. She would keep enough of her inheritance to get herself and the boys back to America. Surely she would be able to stay with one of her sisters until she could find work to support herself.

Josie never considered marriage. There was no way to hide her scarred back from a husband, and she couldn't imagine anyone not becoming nauseated at the hideous sight. She would die inside, if a man she loved cringed from her. Better not to put temptation in her path. Better not to fall in love in the first place.

"Good heavens."

Josie grinned at the Pinkerton's shocked expression, then twirled around, so he could look at her from all angles. "I take it I pass inspection."

"I'll say, miss." He put a finger in his shirt collar to pull it loose. "Near took my breath away, you did."

"Thank you, Mr. Thompson. Were you able to make arrangements for me to see the duke today?"

"Wasn't easy, but luckily, he hasn't made his choice yet, so his solicitor said yes to your request."

Josie was suddenly nervous and realized she hadn't acquired a fan or a purse to keep her hands busy while she was with the duke. "Excuse me." She turned and headed back into the dressmaker's salon. "Miss Brownlee?"

"Have you forgotten something, Miss Wentworth?"

"I need a handkerchief."

Miss Brownlee pulled a delicate, lace-trimmed hanky from her pocket. "You're welcome to this one. Is there anything else I can do for you?"

Josie took the handkerchief, smiled, and said, "That's all. Thank you. For everything."

As she turned and left, she was already wringing the handkerchief like a washrag. How many times had she used a washrag on those two dear, dirty faces? More times than she could count. Soon the duke's nephews would be hers to take care of forever after, and it would be deep copper baths and soft cotton washcloths, instead of a wooden tub and a worn-out rag.

"Hang on, boys," she whispered. "I'll be there soon to take you away. And we'll all live happily ever after."

Chapter 6

BLACKTHORNE KNEW HIS solicitor was only doing his job. Nevertheless, he felt more and more like a hapless fox being run to ground by baying hounds. He kept a tight hold on his temper as he said, "Your message sounded urgent, Phipps, so I'm here. But I meant what I said this morning. I don't want to see any prospective brides today."

"Forgive me, Your Grace, but if you intend to read the banns for three weeks before the wedding, you have less than a week to make your selection. This young woman is scheduled to return to America shortly. If you don't speak with her now, the opportunity may be lost."

Blackthorne turned his back on his solicitor and leaned both palms against the mantel in his study. Even though it was May, it was a chilly day. Unfortunately, the crackling fire did nothing to warm his frozen heart. It had been a year since Fanny's death, but he wasn't ready to take another wife.

It had been hard—impossibly difficult—watching Fanny die a day at a time. He'd believed he loved his wife on the day they married, but he hadn't realized how his feelings would deepen over time, as they lived their days together and made love at night.

At first he hadn't realized Fanny was sick. She'd simply asked to be excused from her wifely duties on occasion, stopped attending every party to which they were invited, and no longer hosted dinners.

Then she'd gotten pregnant. Her sparkling green eyes could have lit up a ballroom, she'd been so happy. He'd been pleased and proud, chest puffed out like a strutting cock—until the doctor told him that he'd warned Fanny her body couldn't support the extra burden of a child, that the consumption that was daily stealing her strength would likely take advantage of her pregnancy to kill her.

Blackthorne had been stunned to discover that Fanny was in such poor health. He'd been furious when he learned she'd endangered her life by keeping him in the dark about the effects a pregnancy would have on her body. He'd confronted her, using his most daunting ducal voice, and demanded, "Why didn't you tell me you were ill? Why would you allow me to get you with child, when it's so dangerous for you? I don't understand. Explain it to me, please."

She'd looked into his eyes, a tender smile on her face, and said, "I want to give you a son. I want to leave you this gift."

"I'd rather have you!"

She'd stepped into his arms, and they'd closed around her, as though he could keep her safe by holding her tight. He'd wanted Fanny a thousand times more than he'd wanted an heir. He'd told her his younger brother's boys could inherit for all he cared.

One of them still might. Fanny had died along with their son, who'd been stillborn.

Blackthorne realized he hadn't seen his nephews for some time, but he trusted the arrangements his wife had made for their care. He'd confirmed with his solicitor that they were being well taken care of at Tearlach Castle, where they had room to run and play in fresh country air.

His conscience niggled at him over the fact that he hadn't visited them, or had them visit him, for more than two years. He'd assuaged it with the knowledge that he'd had two very good reasons—first, Fanny's illness, and then, working night and day to keep the estate afloat in a sea of debt—for abdicating their care and supervision to a governess.

Unfortunately, nothing he'd done had brought him back to solvency. Marriage to a wealthy woman was his only option. And since he had no intention of loving his mail-order bride—some American trading her money for the title of duchess—he'd been putting off the necessary nuptials.

He gave a long-suffering sigh. "All right, Phipps. I'll speak to the girl. How old is she? Who is she?"

"She's eighteen, Your Grace."

Blackthorne wasn't that much older than Miss Wentworth, only twenty-seven, but he would rather have married someone who'd lived in the world awhile. Who knew what fantasies of life as a duchess the girl had concocted?

Phipps ignored his groan and continued, "She's

an orphan, so there will be no parental interference."

Blackthorne made a dismissive sound in his throat. One less hurdle to leap. "And her fortune?"

"More than enough to meet your needs."

He hadn't allowed himself to think about his bride's looks. Beggars couldn't be choosers. He'd been more concerned about temperament. About kindness. About having someone he could abide interacting with for the rest of his life.

When he'd been married to Fanny, there had been no question of seeking physical pleasure with another woman. But he wasn't sure what to expect with a bride who was marrying him merely to become a duchess. He would need to consummate the marriage, of course. But he had no idea whether the woman would want to continue marital relations.

He'd wanted children with Fanny. He wasn't so sure how he felt about having children with a wife who'd been forced upon him. There was also the issue of whether she wanted to have children with him. They would have to work through those issues over a lifetime together.

He had the choice, of course, of letting Blackthorne Abbey fall into ruin. Of having all his estates sold off to the highest bidder. Of having the dukedom become a shell that consisted of a title, the entailed, crumbled-down Abbey, and little else.

Blackthorne sighed. He'd gone over his options in his head endlessly without ever coming to any good answer for what was best. He was willing to try marriage to a stranger and attempt to make the relationship work. That seemed the lesser of two evils.

But he wasn't hopeful. He wasn't optimistic.

His opinion was likely colored by the candidates he'd interviewed so far. He'd been surprised by how many young—and much older—women had responded to his advertisement in the American papers, especially since he'd required them to come to him, rather than going to America himself.

He hadn't set limitations on who might apply, which meant he'd seen a great many women who were unsuitable for one reason or another. He rubbed a hand across his eyes, dreading the coming meeting. He might as well get it over with.

"Tell her I'll see her at four o'clock this afternoon."

"She's here right now, Your Grace, waiting for you in the Garden Room."

Blackthorne could hear the hounds baying again. He looked for some way to delay the interview, but he was already dressed for company in a plain black frock coat and trousers, a white shirt, a gold brocade vest, and a four-in-hand tie. On the other hand, his black hair needed a cut, and although his valet had shaved him that morning, when he rubbed a hand across his chin, he felt the beginning of whiskers. On the other, other hand, spending time on his appearance would only delay the inevitable. If the girl was already here, there was no sense keeping her waiting.

The Garden Room had been Fanny's idea. She'd added windows to the backyard-facing wall and put in a garden that brought the outdoors inside.

He'd done his part by making sure there were always bouquets of fresh-cut hothouse flowers for her to enjoy as well.

The garden behind the house had been left fallow since Fanny's death, and he'd never bought another flower. The Garden Room seemed empty without the profusion of colors and scents—and without his wife. He'd met every candidate there, because it allowed him to compare their behavior with his memories of Fanny in the same space.

"Wait for me here," he said, then added cynically, "I won't be long."

Phipps raised a judgmental brow, probably because he realized that Blackthorne had every intention of dismissing this woman as quickly as he had all the others. "Very well, Your Grace."

Blackthorne marched down the hall of his mansion on Berkeley Square and nodded curtly to the footman standing by the door to the Garden Room. The servant opened the door and the duke entered, stopping just inside to wait for the door to be closed, before he moved farther into the room.

The woman had her back to him. She was staring out the tall windows at the street below, and even though she must have heard the door open, she hadn't turned around.

He observed a fetching feminine silhouette and the most beautiful golden curls he'd ever seen, spilling down her back. He waited with bated breath for her to turn around. Would the face match the form?

"There's an altercation on the street," she said,

ignoring him and taking another step toward the windows.

Right away, her behavior was different. He crossed the room in several long strides and looked to see where she was pointing. In the street below, a carter's horse had fallen to its knees. The carter was whipping the animal in an effort to get it back onto its feet.

"We have to help!" she cried.

Before he could speak, she grabbed his hand and headed for the door. Her gloved hand was small and engulfed by his. She gave a slight tug but seemed confident that he'd follow her. He still hadn't gotten a good look at her face, just the hint of a strong chin and an upturned nose—with a pair of spectacles perched upon it.

She didn't wait for him to open the door, just pulled it open herself and headed out past the startled footman, who stared goggle-eyed at the duke being led like a naughty boy toward the front door of the house.

The butler had more warning than the footman, and the front door was open when they arrived. The girl led him through it and down the steps to the street. He'd gotten a glimpse of startling blue eyes—the same color as her dress—when she glanced over her shoulder to make sure he was still following, even though she had hold of his hand.

She had the face of an urchin, with freckles dotting a peaches and cream complexion and lips the color of berries. But the formfitting bodice and tiny waist of the fashionable gown revealed an appealing, womanly figure. It seemed her only flaw was a bit of nearsightedness. The wire-rimmed spectacles did little to hide a pair of enchanting blue eyes.

Blackthorne wasn't sure whether he was more astonished or amused by the girl's precipitous behavior. She seemed to have no idea of proper protocol in the presence of royalty, but he found it refreshing that she didn't seem awed by his title.

She released his hand when they reached the carter, who was still whipping the horse.

"Stop that this instant!" she ordered.

The carter looked startled to hear a female voice admonish him, but his jaw dropped when he turned and saw what was obviously a lady standing with her hands on her hips in front of him. "This is my horse. I'll whip him if I please."

"If you insist, I'll buy him from you," the girl said.

Blackthorne could see where this was headed. The carter would ask an outrageous price for the animal, and the girl would pay it. She obviously had a soft heart, but he wondered about her common sense.

"He's a good horse," the carter said.

"He's underfed and overworked," the girl responded pertly. "I'll give you ten guineas."

The carter snorted. "He's worth fifteen."

"He's on his knees," the girl replied. "If you can't get him up, he'll be worth a lot less than ten to the butcher."

The duke felt a twinge of admiration as he watched her haggle. She might be too softhearted, but at least she wasn't a dupe.

The carter pursed his lips and eyed the broken-down horse. Then he held out his hand. "Ten guineas, milady, and he's yours."

The girl froze and then turned to stare up at him. "I don't have a farthing with me. Would you? Could you please pay the man?"

Blackthorne smiled at her audacity. Then he reached into his coat pocket for a leather purse and dropped ten guineas into her white-gloved palm. She smiled up at him, and his heart jumped.

Then she turned and laid the coins in the carter's hand. Before his fist had closed, she'd crossed to the horse and was on her knees beside its head, petting its neck, and crooning to it. A moment later, she'd coaxed the animal to its feet.

"Would you mind unharnessing him?" she said to the duke.

Blackthorne was amused again. Did she think dukes went around harnessing and unharnessing vegetable wagons? Apparently, she did, because she turned her attention back to the spavined horse, as though it were the most natural thing in the world for the Duke of Blackthorne to be unharnessing a carter's broken-down nag.

Outwardly, his visage was stern, daring anyone in the street to remark on the outlandish situation in which he found himself. But inside he was chuckling. Inside he was grinning from ear to ear.

Chapter 7

WHILE SHE'D BEEN focused on saving the carter's horse, Josie had been able to ignore the duke's overpowering maleness.

Once the two of them were back in the Garden Room, the horse having been temporarily dispensed to the duke's stable, she was suddenly very much aware of Marcus Wharton's height. *Tall.* The breadth of his shoulders. *Massive.* The cut of his jaw. *Rock-solid.* And the force of his gaze. *Blue steel.*

She felt very much like the youngest and most bookish of the Wentworth girls and very little like a worldly, wealthy heiress, intent on getting what she wanted from a man who might very well be unwilling to give it up. She pushed her glasses up over the slight bump in her nose with a gloved forefinger. What on earth had possessed her to drag the Duke of Blackthorne out onto the street? She'd come here to negotiate a business deal and had succumbed to a combination of nerves at the prospect of facing the man and compassion for the horse.

The duke was the one dabbing sweat from his forehead with a monogrammed handkerchief, but

Josie was having trouble catching her breath, as though she were the one who'd unharnessed the nag, rather than the duke.

She was here to convince Blackthorne to put his nephews in her care in exchange for her fortune. She believed him to be uncaring enough of their welfare to be glad of her offer.

At first, she'd been anxious that he might recognize her, but she bore little resemblance to the battered creature he'd rescued. She'd considered using a false name when she met with him, but the Pinkerton had discovered from Blackthorne's solicitor that he'd had no previous dealings—none at all—with anyone named Josephine Wentworth. He really had forgotten all about her!

Josie had been incensed all over again at the thought that, instead of spending the money to send her home, the duke had dumped her at one of his faraway holdings and completely wiped her from his mind—along with his nephews.

The fact that he'd helped her rescue the broken-down horse suggested he wasn't completely heartless. Maybe she'd misjudged him. Maybe there was some other reason he'd ignored the two boys. Maybe it would be sufficient to bring his nephews' plight to his attention.

The impudence of her original plan—to buy the boys with her inheritance and take them back with her to America—suddenly struck her, making her breathing even more labored. Alone in this barren room with the duke, she felt like a helpless lamb who'd come face-to-face with a ravenous wolf. She wondered if the feeling of being trapped had anything to do with the fact that Blackthorne stood between her and the door.

A picture of Spencer and Clay appeared in her mind's eye with welts on their calves and palms, the result of Mrs. Pettibone's war against the governess. That pitiful image gave her the strength to lift her chin and ball her gloved hands into tight fists in the folds of her skirt.

She was about to speak when the duke said, "I understand you're here to apply for the position of duchess."

His low, rumbling voice reminded her of those painful days on the ship, when he'd coaxed her to hang on to life. But that was another lifetime ago. Josie took a breath to contradict him, but he'd already continued speaking.

"I think you're exactly what I've been seeking. My solicitor will explain the terms of our agreement. It will be up to you whether we continue marital relations once the union has been consummated."

Josie was flustered by such plain speaking. Her clenched fists unfurled and rose to cover her cheeks, as she sought to hide her blush. But she was appalled by the duke's assumption that any woman would agree to marry him because of who he was, without even the courtesy of a proposal.

She lowered her hands, which quickly curled back into tight knots behind her skirt. "Do you plan to propose? Or have you assumed I'll accept, even before you've made your offer?"

The duke looked taken aback. "I presumed—"

"Yes, you did, Your Grace," she interrupted. "I

never said I was here to apply for the position of duchess."

"You didn't?" His brows lowered. "You aren't?"

Josie hadn't expected the duke to be interested in her as a prospective bride, so she hadn't considered becoming the Duchess of Blackthorne as a possible means of taking the boys under her wing. But why not?

Because he's a thoughtless, unkind human being, who's ignored his nephews for the past two years.

He saved the carter's horse.

You *saved the carter's horse. He came along because you gave him no choice.*

He saved *you.*

Well, yes, that's true. But he broke his promise to send me home. He made me an utter slave at one of his estates and forgot I was alive.

So here's your chance to repay the man for his perfidy. You could show him how it feels when someone makes a promise—for instance, to love, honor, and obey—and then breaks it. You could marry him, and then, when he least expects it, abandon him the way he abandoned you.

Josie turned her back on the duke and stared out the window at a garden that seemed as untended as the duke's nephews, giving her the chance to think without being distracted by Blackthorne's steady, penetrating gaze.

It suddenly occurred to her that, if she married the duke, she would become Spencer and Clay's aunt. She would be able to bring them to live in the duke's home, where they belonged. Eventually, if the duke cared as little as she believed about the boys—and a wife he'd married merely for her money—she would be able to take them home with her to America.

If you marry the duke, you'll have to lie with him. He'll see your back. He'll know at once—or at least suspect—who you are.

All the better. He should know from the start how I feel about him—when it's too late to do anything about it. He'll be stuck for the rest of his life with a wife who despises him.

But you'll be stuck with him, too! The duke will never divorce you. Even if you return to America, you'll always be tied to him.

Josie pursed her lips at the dilemma she faced. To save the boys, she was considering marriage to a man she didn't like or admire, let alone love. On the other hand, she'd never planned to marry, because of her disfigurement. Her back was a dreadful thing to see, something no man would ever want to touch. So it wasn't as though by marrying Blackthorne, she'd be giving up a chance of finding her one true love someday.

Besides, if their marriage was like most Society marriages in England, she and her husband would see very little of each other. And, the icing on the cake, she would have the experience, at least once in her life, of knowing what it was like to be a woman in a man's arms. If the duke was virile, perhaps she would even conceive during that single encounter. Because she'd never intended to marry, Josie had never let herself imagine having children of her own, but that possibility had considerable appeal.

Blackthorne had foolishly agreed to leave the issue of "marital relations" up to her, so she would be the one deciding whether or not they repeated whatever happened between them on their wedding night.

So why not marry him?

Josie turned back around and discovered that, in the interim, a suspicious frown had been carved on the duke's chiseled face. She realized she needed to distract him from asking why she'd come here, if not to become his bride. She didn't want to give him any inkling that he was being cleverly manipulated into this marriage, so that she could both have her revenge against him and rescue his nephews.

"I came here to see for myself whether marriage to *you* would suit *me*," she said.

The frown disappeared, and a smile teased at his lips. "What have you decided?"

"I'm willing to listen to your proposal, Your Grace."

He took several steps to close the distance between them, and it took all Josie's courage to stand her ground. When he stopped, he was no more than a foot from her, close enough that she got a whiff of his cologne and a musky, though not unpleasant, odor that had likely resulted from his recent labor unharnessing the horse.

She was close enough to see the tiny black lines radiating from his pupils into his startling blue eyes. To see the beginning of a dark beard shadowing his cheeks and chin. To see the satanic curve of his dark brows. She resisted the urge to reach out and shove the single black curl off his forehead, as she'd done so often with Spencer and Clay.

Josie realized she was holding her breath and carefully let it out, so the duke wouldn't realize how powerfully she'd been affected by his closeness.

Then he focused his eyes on hers and spoke.

"I'm not sure what you want to hear, Miss Wentworth. I don't love you, and I have no doubt the feeling is mutual. I need your wealth to save my estate. In exchange, you will become the Duchess of Blackthorne, and you, and any children we may have, will forever after be royalty."

Josie appreciated his frank speaking and decided to be equally frank. "I understand my inheritance will become yours upon our marriage. I will need some funds of my own." She was taking no chance that she would end up without the financial means to bring the boys from Tearlach Castle to wherever she and the duke ended up making their home, and then on to America.

She saw the cynicism overtake his eyes and mouth before he replied, "You can speak to my solicitor and name the amount you will need for a quarterly allowance. The rest, I'm afraid, must go to repaying debts and repairing the estate."

"Very well," she said. "I don't love you, and you don't love me. Let us say merely that we agree to marry for our separate personal reasons. Shall we shake on it?"

The hint of a smile was back. When he reached

out, she set her gloved hand in his and became aware of his very human warmth, which didn't fit with her image of him as someone so coldhearted that he would pawn off the care of his nephews on a housekeeper and a governess.

"You Americans—"

"Stick to our agreements," she said archly, as she pulled her hand free.

"I hope you'll agree to stay with my grandmother while the banns are read in church over the next three weeks. That will give you the opportunity to get acquainted with her, and for us to spend time together before we're wed."

Josie was very much aware that Spencer and Clay were essentially dodging bullets on a battleground every day that she was separated from them. "Must we wait for the banns to marry?"

The duke raised a surprised brow. "I thought you would appreciate time to plan a wedding at St. George's, so all of your relatives and friends could see the spectacular catch you've made."

"I have no family or friends here in England to attend the wedding. Is there a way we can do this sooner?"

"We can be married tomorrow morning with a special license, if that's your wish."

Josie swallowed painfully over the sudden lump in her throat. "Tomorrow?" Knowing she had only a day before she became the duke's wife made what she'd agreed to do seem very real.

"Or we can wait three weeks and marry at St. George's."

Waiting wasn't going to change anything. The

sooner they were wed, the sooner she could rescue the boys. "Tomorrow, then."

She looked into the duke's blue eyes and felt as though she were tumbling into a bottomless well. Her stomach turned upside down, and she suddenly felt dizzy. She lowered her gaze and clasped her gloved hands together to steady herself. How was she ever going to make it through the wedding? And the wedding night?

"I would like you to meet my grandmother, the Dowager Duchess of Blackthorne, before the nuptials tomorrow morning. Is there anyone you would like to invite to the wedding?"

Josie thought of the Pinkerton detective, the only person she knew in London, but realized Mr. Thompson's attendance would raise too many questions she didn't yet wish to answer. She shook her head.

"My solicitor didn't lie," Blackthorne muttered. "You don't have any connections."

"No," she said. "I don't. I think now I should meet with your man."

"Very well. I'll take you to him. Phipps is working in my study. Once you've finished your business, I'll escort you to my grandmother's townhome."

Josie self-consciously poked her glasses up her nose. She hoped she hadn't made a terrible mistake. It wasn't too late to back out. She could simply walk out the door and try some other means of rescuing the boys.

The duke set his hand on the small of her back to aim her toward the door, and a frisson of feeling skittered down her spine. She edged away, resisting the urge to lean into his touch, afraid he would feel how her flesh was ridged with scars beneath the cloth.

Josie grudgingly admitted to herself that she wanted that wedding night. She wanted that once-in-a-lifetime chance to be held in a man's arms. She wanted to become a woman in the duke's bed.

She just had to figure out how to keep him from getting anywhere near her naked back.

Chapter 8

"GRANDMAMA, I'D LIKE you to meet Miss Josephine Wentworth of America, my intended bride."

Josie curtsied. She knew that much of proper behavior toward royalty. But she couldn't have spoken to save her life. She was completely tongue-tied, knowing she was in the presence of the Dowager Duchess of Blackthorne.

Blackthorne's grandmother sat near the window in the sitting room of her townhome with the sun streaming down on her, making her upswept hair shine like silver. She was so petite the wing chair seemed to engulf her, yet her rigid back and regal pose, with one hand on a black cane set before her, made her seem daunting.

Nerves had Josie wringing the lace handkerchief Miss Brownlee had given her. The thought of those two unhappy boys she hoped to save was all that kept her from running to the docks and taking the first ship back to America. She knew when she was unwelcome, and the Dowager Duchess of Blackthorne was *not* happy to see her.

It was one thing to believe in your heart that no one person was better than any other, simply because of his birth. It was another thing entirely to stay calm in the face of someone as intimidating as the dowager, especially when she was marrying the woman's grandson under false pretenses.

Josie gritted her teeth in an effort to stop her chin from quivering and tucked the wrinkled handkerchief into the edge of one glove, as she met the dowager's arrogant gaze.

To her dismay, when she spoke, she ended up stammering, "I'm g-g-glad to m-m-meet you, Your G-G-Grace."

The dowager turned a baleful eye on her grandson and asked, "Is that a permanent affliction or—"

"No, Your Grace," Josie interjected. And then realized she'd committed another faux pas by interrupting. She swallowed over the irksome knot of fear in her throat and said, "Excuse me, Your Grace, but this has all been very sudden. And very overwhelming."

The dowager ignored her and asked Blackthorne, "Did you rush the girl into this without giving her a chance to reconsider?"

"No!" Josie said, bringing the dowager's attention sharply back in her direction. She squared her shoulders as her gaze collided with the older woman's piercing blue eyes, and said, "I *want* to marry your grandson."

"I'm not surprised," the dowager replied. "This must be a dream come true for you."

Josie flushed at the contempt she heard in the dowager's voice. Blackthorne's grandmother thought she was a grasping American, trading coins for a British title. Josie yearned to tell her the truth, that

she was marrying Blackthorne to rescue his mistreated nephews, but she didn't dare give away the
truth before she and Blackthorne were well and
truly wed.

"Grandmama."

The single word, spoken by the duke in a soft,
firm voice, caused the dowager's lips to purse, as
her blue eyes locked with those of her grandson. In
a similarly quiet voice she said, "I expected you
to choose a woman of equal rank and heritage, a
woman worthy of your name."

"Miss Wentworth is doing me the honor of becoming my wife," he replied. "As my future duchess, she's entitled to your respect. I insist upon it."

The dowager raised a finely arched brow. "You
insist?"

Josie watched the two proud peers of the realm
face off and wondered who would give in first. The
dowager suddenly turned to Josie, without a hint
of capitulation, and said, "You will be my guest for
dinner tonight."

Josie couldn't imagine how she was going to
swallow a bite of food past the giant lump in her
throat and searched for a way she could politely
refuse. She would much rather have a plate of food
sent to her room—a room anywhere other than in
the dowager's home—and avoid further interaction
with either the duke or the dowager duchess before
the wedding. "I would love to, Your Grace. However," she shrugged and smiled, "I have nothing
appropriate to wear."

The dowager slid an incredulous look toward her

grandson, then met Josie's gaze again. "Why is that?"

"I was scheduled to return to America this morning, and my baggage was already loaded on shipboard. I have no idea where my trunks are at the moment," she said, feeling the heat rising on her cheeks at the lie.

"One of my granddaughters should have something that will fit you," the dowager said.

Josie looked at Blackthorne in astonishment. "You have sisters?"

"Two of them. Twins," Blackthorne said. "They live here with my grandmother."

If the duke had a grandmother and sisters living in London, Josie wondered why his nephews had been relegated to some faraway estate. Since she wasn't supposed to know of Spencer's and Clay's existence, she didn't ask. But it was one more black mark against the duke.

"Where are the girls?" the duke asked his grandmother. "I expected them to be here to meet Miss Wentworth."

"Lark and Lindsey attended a picnic this afternoon at Kensington Gardens. You can't expect them to drop everything whenever you interview another potential bride. Especially since you've been so dismissive of every female you've met so far." She added in an undertone, "Including some very proper ladies I've introduced to you myself."

Blackthorne's lips thinned and a muscle in his jaw bunched.

His grandmother must have recognized he was at

the limit of his patience, because she added, "I expect the twins to be home at any moment."

As though they'd been summoned, Josie heard two female voices laughing and chattering beyond the door. A moment later the parlor door flew open and two identical girls with black curls, bright smiles, flushed faces, and flashing blue eyes appeared arm in arm. The twins were tall, with shapely figures—definitely not schoolroom misses.

Josie guessed the girls were somewhere between seventeen and twenty, since they had to be at least seventeen to be out in Society, and by the age of twenty, most girls were married and lived with their husbands. They were dressed at the height of fashion in the exact same peach-colored princess sheath, with stylish straw bonnets tied under their chins with matching peach ribbons.

"Good afternoon, Grandmama," one of them said, untying the ribbon and removing her bonnet.

"Good afternoon, Marcus," the other said, following her sister's lead and letting the bonnet swing from her hand by the grosgrain ribbon.

"Who's this?" they both said together, their eyes focused on Josie.

"This is the young woman your brother intends to marry," the dowager announced.

Josie expected the same disdain she'd gotten from Blackthorne's grandmother. She couldn't have been more wrong. The two girls tossed their hats onto a nearby sofa and came rushing toward her, embracing her from both sides.

"I'm Lark," one twin said.

"I'm Lindsey," the other said.

"It's so nice to meet you," they chorused.

Josie smiled back, laughing along with them, because they seemed so entirely attuned to each other, just as her own twin sisters, Hannah and Hetty, were. "I'm Josie," she said, responding with her first name, since they'd used their own. She saw a pinched look appear on the dowager's face and presumed it was because she'd introduced herself using her nickname, rather than her entire proper name. Or maybe it was the devil-may-care way the girls had abandoned their hats and embraced a perfect stranger, surely not the ladylike behavior the dowager must expect from her granddaughters.

Which gave Josie some hope.

If these girls could grow up with the duke and the dowager as their role models and still be so friendly and outgoing, maybe there was a way for her to survive and thrive as a member of this family.

Josie searched for some difference between the two English girls, something that would allow her to tell them apart. Her sisters Hannah and Hetty looked identical, but the differences in their behavior—Hannah was far more confident and forward, Hetty far more silly—made it possible for her to easily discern who was who.

Then Josie saw something that stunned her, something she knew would make telling the duke's sisters apart far more simple than it should have been. The twin named Lark had a scar across the left side of her neck, as though it had been sliced with a knife—or cut with a whip. She glanced at the other twin and was shocked to see that she had the same scar, but on the opposite side of her neck.

Josie wondered how they'd ended up with scars so similarly located. Had they been involved in some mishap? Or was it mere coincidence that the twins had mirror-image scars? In any case, she had the clue she needed to identify them.

"Miss Wentworth needs a gown to wear to dinner tonight," the dowager said to the twins. "Please take her upstairs and see what you have on hand that Miss Pope can alter to fit her."

"Gladly, Grandmama," Lark said.

"Come along, Josie," Lindsey said.

They looped their arms through hers and hurried her toward the door. She pulled them both to a stop and freed herself so she could turn and curtsy to the dowager. "It was a pleasure meeting you," she said, flushing again at this second lie. The meeting had been more traumatic than enjoyable. She turned to the duke and said, "I presume you will also be at dinner?"

"Of course. I want you to meet my best friend, David Madison, the Earl of Seaton. I've asked him to stand up with me at our wedding tomorrow."

"Tomorrow?" There was no mistaking the horror in the dowager's voice. To emphasize her displeasure, she rose imperiously to her feet. "What sort of foolishness is this? A rushed-up wedding for the Duke of Blackthorne? Unthinkable!"

"I'm sorry to break the news to you this way, Grandmama," Blackthorne said. "But neither Miss Wentworth nor I care to wait for the banns to be read. I've obtained a special license, and we'll be married tomorrow morning." He held up a hand to stop his sputtering grandmother from protesting further as he added, "At St. George's. You and the twins are invited, of course."

"And your bride?" the dowager said. "Who will stand by her?"

"There is no one, Your Grace," Josie said. "I'm an orphan. My sisters and brothers are scattered across America with no opportunity to come here within the three weeks it would take to read the banns. So, you see, there's no reason to wait."

The dowager shot a frigid look at her grandson. "There's propriety. And tradition. And honor. And courtesy to one's family." Then she turned her cold blue eyes on Josie. "You said your trunks are missing, and you have nothing to wear tonight. What, pray tell, were you planning to wear to your wedding tomorrow morning?"

"I . . ." Josie hadn't thought about a wedding gown. "I suppose I will have to find my trunks." Which meant she had to contact Miss Brownlee and have her make a wedding gown, if such a thing could be accomplished in so short a time.

"You will stay here tonight," the dowager said. "My dressmaker, Miss Pope, will take care of the matter, as soon as she finishes altering whatever you will be wearing to dinner tonight." She turned to her grandson and said, "I wonder if you've thought about the time needed to plan a wedding breakfast to introduce your wife to Society."

Josie saw the perturbed look on the duke's face. Obviously, he hadn't considered the need for a wedding breakfast but apparently realized, once it had been pointed out to him, the necessity for it.

"How long would you need to plan such an event?" he asked the dowager.

Josie could almost see the wheels spinning in the dowager's head, wondering how much time she would need to change the duke's mind about marrying some uncouth American girl.

Before the dowager could speak, Blackthorne said, "I'm willing to postpone the wedding for a week, Grandmama, if that's agreeable to Miss Wentworth, in order to give you time to plan a wedding breakfast. But the wedding will remain a family affair."

Josie was afraid that even a week was going to give her too much time to reconsider and regret what she was doing, but it seemed the best compromise she was going to be offered. "A week would give us time to become better acquainted," she said.

"I suppose I can manage a wedding breakfast in seven days," the dowager conceded. She glanced at Josie. "And have a wedding gown made for Miss Wentworth."

Josie opened her mouth to protest the dowager's high-handedness, but the older woman said, "It will be my wedding gift to you." Under her breath, Josie heard her mutter, "At least you'll look like a proper Blackthorne bride."

The twins rejoined her and Lark said, "We'll stand beside you, Josie." She turned to her brother and asked, "You won't mind, will you, Marcus?"

"I think that's a very kind gesture," he said. "If Miss Wentworth is agreeable. Miss Wentworth?"

Josie could hardly see the duke through the sudden rush of tears in her eyes, and her throat ached too badly to speak. She wouldn't have to stand at the front of the church alone. She would have these two young ladies, who reminded her of the family she missed so terribly, to stand up with her.

She managed a wobbly smile and croaked, "I think that would be lovely."

Chapter 9

JOSIE CONSIDERED TELEGRAPHING her sister
Miranda to inform her that she wasn't going to be
arriving as scheduled in Charleston. In the end, she
decided it didn't make sense to say anything, until
she knew just how late she would be. Besides, she
would have bet good money that Miranda had sent
for Hannah and Hetty, who would already be on
their way with their families to Miranda's home in
Texas. She was in no hurry to tell everyone she was
a duchess—and married to a scoundrel—until all
the Wentworths were together again.

The wedding had been delayed a week, but that
gave her more time to plan her escape with the two
boys. Once she was the duke's wife—and the boys'
aunt—she would be on her way to America as
quickly as she could find a ship to take them there.

Meanwhile, Josie thought it best to keep herself
aloof from the duke. She didn't want any sort of
emotional involvement with him, because that
would make it more difficult to leave when the
time came. It quickly became apparent, when he
invited both of his sisters and his best friend along
on every outing during the following week, that he

was as committed to keeping his distance from her as she was from him.

Unfortunately, having Lark and Lindsey and the Earl of Seaton along ended up having the exact opposite effect from the one she believed the duke had intended. The two girls inevitably traipsed off with Seaton, leaving her alone with her future husband.

Josie had her arm looped through Blackthorne's as they observed an Indian elephant at the zoo. Her fiancé's great height and broad shoulders made her feel small and protected, even though she was a tall woman. She was aware of the scent he wore, something that smelled like the woods. And she could feel his eyes constantly on her, when he should have been paying attention to the wild animals they'd come to see.

She searched her mind for something to say in the unbearable silence that had fallen between them once Seaton and the twins had gone in another direction. It seemed safer to confine her conversation to the beasts in cages, rather than the one standing next to her, so she said, "That elephant seems rather large to be confined in such a small space."

"I agree. It seems cruel to pen up a wild animal in such a way."

She waited for Blackthorne to elaborate, but he didn't. He merely walked a few paces farther, bringing her along with him, to observe a ragged-looking bear pacing within the iron-barred cage in which it was confined.

"I've felt a lot like that bear over the past year," he said.

She looked up at him in surprise. "You have?"

He shot her a sardonic smile. "Constantly searching for a way out, with no hope of escape."

"What is it you're seeking to escape?"

"Debt, I suppose, primarily."

Again, she waited for him to elaborate, but he didn't. What else was he hoping to escape? Even what little he'd admitted was more frankness than she'd expected from him. "Your debt will become a thing of the past within the week," she pointed out.

"Thanks to you." He sounded more cynical than grateful.

"But you'd rather not be married, if you could help it." She made it a statement rather than a question.

"I lost my wife a year ago to illness. I couldn't do this—marry again—if there were any obligation for affection on either side. It's fortunate we each have something else to gain from this marriage."

It seemed one of the other things he couldn't escape was grief. Josie was glad she was getting out of this marriage as quickly as she could. Glad that she was the woman marrying him, and not some other heiress who might have hoped someday to earn the duke's love. Apparently, he had none to give.

The lion opened its jaws and roared, startling her into jerking backward and wrenching one of her scars. She bit back a cry of pain, but Blackthorne must have believed the lion had frightened her, because his arms closed around her, and he pulled her close, murmuring, "There's no danger. He can't escape."

Any more than you can, Josie thought. Nevertheless, she appreciated Blackthorne's offer of comfort. She became aware of her breasts pressed against his muscular chest, of his cheek against her hair, and the way their bodies fit together so perfectly. She was surprised when he abruptly released her and took a step back. She looked up to see what might have caused him to let her go and saw the two vertical lines that had formed between his brows and the look of confusion in his eyes.

"Is something wrong?" she asked.

"Nothing." Except his voice was curt and his shoulders were stiff and his jaw was taut.

Josie was irked because she had no idea why Blackthorne was acting so strangely, when he'd been so kind only a moment before. It occurred to her that she was better off seeing him as the ogre she knew him to be, rather than as the nice man who occasionally emerged from the shadows. She had to remember that they were using each other to achieve their separate personal ends, which didn't require them to like each other.

"Shall we join my sisters?" he said. "I believe it's time we headed home."

He offered his arm, and she took it again, refusing to look into his blue eyes, which she found especially attractive. She might have saved herself the effort, because Blackthorne kept his gaze focused on the caged animals to their right. She aimed her gaze at the three people who were walking on their left, a short distance away. Which was when she noticed something peculiar. Seaton kept glancing surreptitiously toward the twin on his left. Which one was it? Lark or Lindsey?

In the next moment, the twin on the right drew his attention, and Josie watched as the twin on his left shot a look at him that was equally furtive.

Why, they're attracted to each other! But neither seems willing to reveal his or her interest in the other.

What she couldn't figure out from this distance was which twin had caught Seaton's interest and was attracted in return to the earl.

"Your sisters are lovely young women," she said. "Are either of them being courted?"

"Not at the moment," Blackthorne said, turning at last to look at her. "One of the benefits of your fortune is that I'll be able to dower them again."

"Again?"

"My father stole their dowries and spent the money," he said flatly.

"Oh."

"In any case, I'd rather they take their time and look around before they fix their interest on any one man."

Josie opened her mouth to ask Blackthorne if Seaton had mentioned his interest in one of the girls but closed it again without speaking. Surely, such a good friend would speak to Blackthorne before he courted one of the duke's sisters. She was determined to discover which sister had caught Seaton's eye, but by the time she turned back around, the twins were walking toward them arm in arm with each other. Seaton followed behind, and it was impossible to tell which girl had previously been standing on his left.

"What do you think of the zoo, Josie?" Lark asked as they approached. "Isn't it thrilling?"

Josie wouldn't have used that word. "Terrible" was more like it. Maybe it was her experience of being a captive and unable to escape a horrible situation that made her so empathic to the caged animals' plight. She couldn't remember feeling this way when she'd gone to the Lincoln Park Zoo in Chicago with her parents, when she was ten.

She was spared from answering when Lindsey asked her brother, "Can we stop for ices on the way home?"

"Your grandmother is expecting us. She asked me to be sure Miss Wentworth arrived home in time to have a fitting for her wedding gown, before we go to the theater this evening."

Josie wondered if Lindsey had asked to stop somewhere because she wanted more time with Seaton, but whatever her reason, she accepted her brother's response without a fuss.

Blackthorne left Josie at the door to his grandmother's townhome without any gesture of affection. He merely bowed to her and got back into his carriage, where Seaton was waiting for him. The twins each took one of her arms and dragged her upstairs to the guest room she'd been given in the dowager's townhome, where Miss Pope, the dowager's dressmaker, was waiting for her.

Having a wedding dress made for her was a serious trial for Josie, because she felt the necessity of hiding her scarred back from Miss Pope and her assistant. She didn't want anyone revealing her secret to Blackthorne before they were wed, for fear it would raise questions she'd rather not answer—like why she was marrying him without revealing that she was the woman he'd rescued from the Sioux.

Having her body measured had been a trial, because she refused to undress completely for the seamstress. Even now, she insisted on trying on the completed gown behind a screen.

"Are you sure you don't need some help, Josie?" one of the twins asked. Josie still couldn't tell their voices apart, but she assumed it was Lark speaking, because Lark was the sister most likely to put herself forward in every activity.

"I'm fine," Josie said. "Except for a few buttons I can't reach."

Before she knew it, one of the twins—Lark, as it turned out—was behind the screen with her.

Josie gasped and turned her back away from the girl. She was wearing a chemise, but she wasn't sure how noticeable the raised scars might be under the thin cotton. She held the dress together behind her with both hands as she demanded, "What are you doing back here?"

"Helping you, of course. You don't have to be shy. You're beautiful, you know. Your spectacles don't detract from your stunning blue eyes or your flawless skin or your silky hair or your very attractive feminine curves. My brother is a connoisseur of women. He waited a very long time—almost too long—before he chose you. But I can see what he likes so much about you, even beyond your good looks."

Josie was embarrassed into laughter by the effusive compliments. "What is that?"

"You don't kowtow to him," she said matter-of-factly. "You stand toe-to-toe with him and speak your mind."

"And no one else does?"

She shook her head. "Everyone's too busy trying to please the Duke of Blackthorne to object to anything my brother says or does. He's used to ruling the roost. I suspect he isn't quite sure what to do with you," she said with a cheerful grin.

"And that's a good thing?"

Lark nodded. "Absolutely. Marcus needs a challenge."

She tilted her head like a curious bird and asked, "Are you going to let me help you button up that dress?"

Josie reluctantly turned her back to the girl, holding her breath, hoping against hope that the marks on her skin were concealed sufficiently beneath the cotton chemise.

A few moments later, the dress was buttoned up, and Lark said, "All done. Turn around and let me see how it looks."

Relieved that the girl seemed to have noticed nothing amiss, Josie turned back around and said, "Thank you."

"You should thank Miss Pope. That dress is stunning. Marcus is going to be knocked off his feet when he sees you coming down the aisle."

Josie smiled. "Let's hope not. I need him standing there to say his vows."

Lark laughed. "I suppose you do. May I ask a question?"

"Anything."

"What happened to your back?"

Josie's heart skipped a beat. She'd thought she was home free, that Lark hadn't noticed anything unusual when she'd buttoned up Josie's wedding gown. What should she say? How could she best keep the girl from mentioning what she'd seen to her brother? Josie's mind was racing, and she forced herself to take a deep breath and let it out before she spoke.

"What do you mean?" Josie realized as soon as the words were out of her mouth that pretending ignorance wasn't going to work.

"Where did you get those horrible scars on your back?" Lark said in a quiet voice.

Josie's face blanched. She couldn't actually touch most of the ridges on her back with her hands. She could trace the ones on her shoulders and the ones lower down, but the ones in the middle were beyond her reach. She could see them in the mirror, so she knew they were ugly, but she hadn't realized they would be quite so noticeable through a film of cotton.

"Please don't say anything to your brother." Josie heard the panic in her voice, and tried to calm herself by threading her hands together and holding them tightly before her in a way that seemed to beseech Lark's help. "The scars are from a childhood injury. I conceal them because they're hideous. Please don't say anything about my back to anyone, including your sister, and especially your brother. I know how hard that will be, but this is my secret to keep. And now yours, too."

The concern in Lark's eyes made Josie feel sick to her stomach. It was bad enough deceiving Blackthorne. She hated lying to his sister as well, but she didn't know what else to do. Josie waited for some confirmation from Lark that she was willing to do as Josie had asked.

She got a jerky nod before the girl spoke. "All right," Lark said. "I'll hold my tongue. But I don't see how you're going to hide those marks on your back from Marcus after you're his wife. I mean . . ." Her voice trailed off as she shrugged and held out her hands, as though her point was obvious.

Josie knew exactly what she meant. What would happen when she and Blackthorne were in bed together as man and wife? Wouldn't her husband's hands be all over her, including on her back?

Of course they would, if she and Blackthorne were married for fifty years or so. But Josie planned to be gone from England long before Blackthorne got a good look at her without all her clothes.

"Let that be my problem," Josie said.

"All right," Lark agreed with a skeptical shake of her head. "Once Miss Pope checks your gown to make sure it's perfect—and it is—I'll be glad to undo all those buttons."

Josie set a hand on Lark's shoulder. "Thank you for keeping my secret. Let me know if I can ever return the favor."

She waited a moment, wondering if Lark was the

sister interested in Seaton, and whether she would share that information with her. But Lark remained silent.

Josie squared her shoulders, smiled, and said, "Well, let's see what Miss Pope has to say." She stepped out from behind the screen to the *oohs* and *aahs* of Lark's sister and the approving nod of the dowager's dressmaker.

She met Lark's gaze over her shoulder and saw that her eyes had narrowed speculatively. Josie kept the wobbly smile on her face with an effort. She would just have to hope that Lark was as discreet as she'd promised to be. Otherwise, this whole marriage business could be over before it ever got started.

Chapter 10

BLACKTHORNE WAS AWARE of his grandmother's probing gaze focused on him as he paced her sitting room, waiting for Miss Wentworth to make her appearance for their engagement at the theater that evening. Rather than have the dowager remark on his restless behavior, he forced himself to stop in front of the crackling fire and put his hands out, as though they needed warming.

Actually, he was already so warm he would have been more comfortable without his coat, and he wouldn't have minded loosening his tie as well. The girl made him jumpy. Uneasy. Edgy. And for the life of him, he couldn't understand why.

Maybe it was this forced evening alone with his soon-to-be bride. The dowager had insisted that he be seen at some public gathering with his fiancée at least once before their wedding.

She'd given him a choice between a musical evening hosted by one of her cronies and a night at the theater. He'd figured the theater would bring him into contact with the fewest people to whom he would need to be effusive about the merits of the woman he'd chosen to marry, since he planned to arrive late and leave early, and visitors could only stop at his box during the interval.

To his chagrin, he was more eager and excited to be spending time alone with Miss Wentworth than he'd expected—or wanted—to be. He'd been surprised to discover, over the past week, how much he enjoyed his fiancée's company. Young misses weren't exactly his cup of tea.

But so often, when Miss Wentworth spoke, he found himself agreeing with her, as he had this afternoon at the zoo. It was unusual to hear a young woman voice such an unpopular opinion. He suspected her forthrightness was a result of growing up in America, where people spoke their minds more freely. It was one more reminder that she was completely unimpressed—and undaunted—by his royal title.

Miss Wentworth also seemed to have a great deal of common sense. She'd worn a hat at the zoo to keep the sun off her face, but there had been no concoction of fruit or flowers on it. Her dress had been almost plain, with simple buttons down the front and a fitted bodice and waist that had prompted him to remove the garment in his imagination and take the feminine assets he found beneath it into his willing hands.

Because Miss Wentworth had seemed so level-headed, he'd been more amused than irritated when she'd squeaked and turned to him for succor when the lion roared. When he'd taken her in his arms, she'd fit perfectly there, her chin reaching his shoulder, her brow level with his mouth.

It would have taken no effort at all to let his hand

drift into her silky blond curls, something he'd been yearning to do, or to press his mouth to the soft skin at her temple. The temptation had been there to touch, but he'd resisted it. He'd meant what he told her. There was no room in their marriage for emotional attachments—on either side.

What he'd found most disturbing was his physical desire for the woman he planned to wed. What magic web had this slip of a girl spun in the brief time he'd known her to make him want her so badly? The need to kiss her, to hold her, to thrust himself deep inside her, had become intolerable. He'd never experienced anything like it. Not with Fanny. Not with any woman since. Whenever he was with her, he found himself in an excruciating state of arousal. He swore under his breath as he realized that just thinking about her had accomplished that dreaded result.

His wedding couldn't come soon enough. Once he'd had Miss Wentworth, the froth would be off the beer. The bloom would be off the rose. He'd be satiated and satisfied, and this unbearable longing would be over and done.

Miss Wentworth came tripping into the room wearing a robin's-egg-blue evening gown, a smile on her face that revealed bewitching twin dimples, her wide-spaced blue eyes open and unguarded behind the ridiculous spectacles perched on her upturned nose, and said, "Good evening, Your Grace."

His heart jumped. And then pounded hard in his chest, as though he'd been running in place the fifteen minutes he'd been waiting for her. His body sprang to agonizing life, reminding him that he was no more than a savage beast, determined to mate with the most alluring of its kind. He felt a flare of embarrassing heat in his chest and neck and prayed it wouldn't spread to his cheeks, where his grandmother could see and remark upon it later. He had to clear his throat to reply, "Good evening, Miss Wentworth. Are you ready to go?"

"Yes. I've never been to the theater."

"Never been?" the dowager interjected. "Why not?"

Miss Wentworth looked flustered for a moment before she said, "I mean, not in London. Of course I've been to the theater in America."

Blackthorne realized he had no idea how long his fiancée had been in England, or even why she'd come here in the first place. The subject had never come up. Maybe he should ask a few more questions of his bride, before they were tied together for the rest of their lives.

But he was in no hurry to discover her secrets. From the moment Miss Wentworth had taken his large hand in her small one and dragged him out into the street to unharness some carter's nag, he'd known there was something about her that was out of the ordinary, something about her he wanted to examine at greater depth, something that might take him a lifetime to uncover.

He'd seen and spoken to a great many prospective brides. The moment she'd lifted her chin and met his gaze from behind her gold-rimmed spectacles, bringing him up short for failing to offer her a proper proposal he'd known: *This is the one*.

Marrying someone was a financial necessity. He was glad he'd found a woman, just in the nick of time, who he thought might suit him. It was galling to admit that he was beginning to crave having her in his bed.

He held out his arm for her to take. "Shall we go?"

She curtsied to the dowager and said, "Good night, Your Grace."

"Don't be late," the dowager said, pinning him with a stare that made him feel like a gauche boy.

He shot her a quizzical look, wondering why she'd considered the admonition necessary. He had no intention of spending any more time with Miss Wentworth than it took to drive to the theater, see the play—something by Sheridan or Shakespeare, he wasn't sure which—and return her to the dowager's townhome. Since he was a grown man, not a ten-year-old child, he didn't see the need to explain or excuse whatever he decided to do during his evening with his intended bride. So he said nothing, as he escorted his fiancée from the room.

Miss Wentworth sighed with pleasure, as she settled into the seat of the ducal carriage and ran her fingertips over the plush blue velvet. He felt his whole body tense, as he imagined her hands roaming his flesh with that same sound of satisfaction. He bit back a groan, as he seated himself on the luxurious seat opposite her.

The silence in the carriage soon became uncomfortable. Not to mention rife with sexual tension, at least on his part. "Why did you come to England?" he asked at last.

"My being here is more accidental than intentional," she replied.

He waited for an explanation, and when none was forthcoming said, "Accidental?"

"I began traveling with my sisters, but we ended up going in different directions. I landed in England."

Her answer told him little and left him with a dozen questions. "Tell me about your family."

"I have three older sisters and two younger brothers scattered across the American West. My sisters are all married. My brothers live with my eldest sister. I miss them all terribly. Why don't your unmarried sisters live with you?"

"My sisters required a female to teach them everything they needed to know to get along in the wider world. With my mother gone, that person became my grandmother."

"Why not have your grandmother come live with the three of you, rather than sending them off to live with her?"

He frowned, unsure what she meant. "My grandmother prefers to have a home of her own. My sisters love Grandmama, and it keeps her young to have the two girls underfoot. Besides, I've always been there for my family whenever they needed me."

"Don't you miss seeing them every day?"

Was that blame he heard in her voice? Rebuke? Censure? *How dare she! Did she know who he was? What he was?*

He bit the inside of his cheek to cut off the critical words that sought voice. This girl—woman, he corrected himself—was very shortly going to be his wife. There was no sense getting off on the wrong foot with her. Instead of speaking, he forced himself to consider what she'd said.

Had he missed his sisters while they were growing up? Perhaps. A little. But he'd been too wrapped up in grieving Fanny's death, and in wild behavior when he'd realized all was lost, to think of anyone else but himself for the past year. He hadn't considered—until this moment—how selfish that behavior was. He'd shifted the burden of his sisters' upbringing to his grandmother, and he'd delegated his nephews' care to the governess in whose charge they'd been left. What kind of man did that make him?

He looked resentfully at the woman sitting opposite him. Where did she get the audacity, the effrontery to confront him about his behavior? He had no intention of letting his wife dictate right and wrong to him, any more than he allowed *anyone* in his life to dictate *anything* to him. Just who in bloody hell did she think she was?

Miss Wentworth looked at him with her head tilted like an inquisitive bird, her eyes shining in the softly lit interior of the carriage, her full lips inviting his kiss.

He bit back an oath at the carnal direction his thoughts had suddenly taken. Was Miss Wentworth to be excused of every insult to his character and person because he wanted her body?

Fortunately, at that moment, they arrived at the theater, and he was neither required to answer nor allowed the opportunity to give the scathing reply that had come to mind.

Miss Wentworth was enthralled by the play. It was one of Shakespeare's comedies, *A Midsummer Night's Dream*. She confessed to having read the play, but she'd never seen it performed. She was fizzing with excitement during the interlude, like an exploding bottle of champagne.

"The performance is wonderful! Are the actors always this good?"

He found her enthusiasm contagious. "I don't know how they usually perform. I don't often come to the theater."

"Oh!" She put a gloved hand to her mouth in shock. "Why not? How can you resist? I would come all the time, if I could."

She looked up at him hopefully, as though seeking his concurrence in returning to the theater sometime soon. In fact, he'd rarely come because Fanny wasn't interested in the theater, and he had other, much better uses for the ladybirds he'd spent time with after her death. "We'll see," he said at last.

She didn't beg or plead with him. She merely got a certain look on her face that told him she would be back here—with or without him.

Blackthorne was jolted by the thought that Miss Wentworth didn't just have opinions about zoo animals. She had opinions about the theater. And about his behavior toward his sisters and grandmother. She not only had a great many opinions, she seemed entirely willing to share them. She might not have a royal title—yet—but she seemed

to have definite ideas about what she wanted and
no compunction about telling him.

Fanny had left all the decision making to him.
Except for concealing her illness, he couldn't think
of any choices she'd made without consulting him,
and she'd always deferred to his judgment. How
difficult was it going to be to get along with someone, day in and day out, whose opinion he was
expected to consider before choosing a course of
action?

And Fanny had never, ever been critical. Miss
Wentworth had already suggested he was a self-
centered son of a bitch. She hadn't said those precise words, but he'd understood what she'd meant,
right enough. He couldn't change what he'd done
in the past. And he wasn't sure he wanted to change
his behavior in the future.

Neither his sisters nor his grandmother had complained about their living situation. So why was he
feeling so guilty? What was it about Miss Wentworth that had him reconsidering his conduct? She
was marrying a royal duke, a peer at the very top
of the realm, with no one except the king himself to
call him to account. He'd be damned if he was
going to let some barely-out-of-the-schoolroom
American girl shame him into changing his behavior.

He didn't say another word to her, determined to
show her his displeasure.

When the performance was done, she chattered
on effusively about the play, seemingly unaware of
his continuing silence. Which made him wonder if
he was always this surly, so she simply expected

this sort of behavior from him. He found her lively face beguiling. He found her busy hands, which she used to demonstrate her points, fascinating. He found her lips, as she chided him, entrancing.

His body surged to exhilarating life. Even as he sat there angry and unyielding, he yearned to taste and to touch. And he could hardly wait for the day—and night—of his wedding.

Chapter 11

JOSIE'S WHOLE BODY was trembling, and she couldn't get it to stop. St. George's was impressive enough to make her feel overwhelmed, but not since she'd been a captive among the Sioux had she felt so frightened and alone.

In the Sioux village, although she'd fought to live, she'd known her likely fate was death. The brutal whipping had been excruciating, but she'd known there would be an end to it. But once she'd spoken vows with Marcus St. John Wharton, Eighth Duke of Blackthorne, she would be tied *for the rest of her life* to a man who'd both attracted her with his looks and repelled her by his selfish behavior.

Josie was grateful for the presence of the two girls standing to her left, but it simply wasn't the same as having her own family there to support her. She'd been separated from her sisters and brothers for two interminable years, and now she was committing to even more time in England—enough to establish her right to take Spencer and Clay with her when she finally returned to America.

Knowing she intended to leave Blackthorne as soon as the opportunity arose to grab his nephews and run, made what she was about to do even more of a travesty. Which might be the source of the terrible tremors making her shake like a leaf in a storm.

Blackthorne hadn't indicated by so much as a glance in her direction that he'd noticed her difficulty. He'd merely taken a firm grip on her hand early in the ceremony and hadn't let go. Which could be interpreted as an effort to provide comfort . . . or a desire to keep the golden goose from taking wild flight.

Blackthorne gently squeezed her hand, and she realized the cleric must have asked her a question requiring a response. Josie fought back panic as she replied in a whispery voice, "I will?"

The bishop shot a look at the duke, then cleared his throat, before frowning down at her.

Josie realized she'd phrased her response as a question and quickly said, in a stronger voice, "I will."

She heard the bishop's voice again, and then Blackthorne replying in his rich baritone, "I will."

She had no ring for her husband, but to her amazement, the duke removed her glove and slid a ring on the fourth finger of her left hand. Josie's eyes went wide at the sight of the enormous, square-cut ruby. She was even more amazed that the ring fit so well, and suddenly realized that she now had an explanation for Blackthorne's strange caress of her hand after the pre-wedding dinner for close friends hosted by his grandmother last night, one of the few times in his company when she'd been without gloves. He'd been estimating her ring size! He must have employed some jeweler to work through the night, because the ring slid onto her finger as though it had been made for her.

Josie gazed in dismay at her hand, where the ruby sat like a horrific weight on her guilty soul. She would have to leave behind this ring, which was obviously some kind of family heirloom, when she left her husband. She couldn't begin to imagine its value. It must also have a great deal of personal meaning, if he'd hung on to it through all his financial difficulties. Then she looked up and met Blackthorne's gaze.

She hadn't expected concern. Or kindness. Which only made the knot in her throat tighten further. She turned her gaze back to the bishop, who was making the sign of the cross, she presumed to signal the end of the formal ceremony.

"Josie."

The unexpected use of her nickname by the duke, in that soft, coaxing voice she recognized from the ship, startled her into looking at him. That soft voice might as well have been the screech of a mountain lion, freezing her in place for the kill, because she couldn't move, couldn't gasp, couldn't do anything except stare at him, mesmerized.

He bent slowly, giving her time to turn her face away. But Josie was entranced, not quite believing what was about to happen. She was going to be kissed. For the very first time. By the duke. On the mouth.

Her eyes slid closed, and she felt his grip on her

hands tighten, as she waited breathlessly—her lips pursed as she'd practiced in the mirror at the orphanage, when none of her sisters were looking and could laugh at her—for their mouths to meet.

She waited, but his lips never reached hers. She opened her eyes to peek at him, to see what was taking so long, and saw a slight furrow between his brows, before his head began moving downward again. She quickly closed her eyes, waiting for something she wanted to be wonderful—and feared would miss the mark.

Josie hadn't met anyone, other than the duke, whom she'd wanted to have kiss her, although Miss Birch's fourteen-year-old son had tried often enough. Josie had been quick enough on her feet to escape Freddy's grasp, and then had cleverly adopted the practice of wearing spectacles—with clear glass— to dissuade him from pursuing her. It had worked. Sadly, all the reading she'd done by candlelight and firelight over the past few years now made spectacles a necessity.

She wondered if her glasses would be in the way when the duke kissed her.

Josie was so busy reminiscing that she was caught off-guard when Blackthorne's lips brushed softly against hers. She felt a definite tingle all the way to her toes and found herself leaning toward him, not wanting the kiss to end. She heard him take a hitching breath, as his mouth closed over hers once more.

Josie felt his tongue pressing between her lips and jerked backward, staring up at him in shock, as her hand, the one heavy with the weight of his ring, came up to touch her lips. A belated quiver ran through her, as her body reacted to the duke's sexual provocation.

She saw color rise on Blackthorne's cheeks and wondered whether he'd felt anything like what had just happened to her, or whether he was embarrassed that she'd turned away, when he'd tried that thing he'd done with his tongue. She decided it must be something married people did and wished now that she'd let him finish what he'd started.

Josie opened her mouth to apologize and closed it again. Saying anything at this point would only make the situation worse. They had a whole day to get through before the wedding night, including a wedding breakfast—which was really lunch—hosted by the dowager at the duke's residence, where Josie would be introduced to a wider group of Blackthorne's friends.

Josie wanted a wedding night, but that had meant finding a way to successfully conceal her scarred back from her husband. She was glad for the one week delay of the wedding, because it had taken all that time to come up with something she thought might work. She didn't want Blackthorne to feel her scars, because she didn't want to give the duke any warning that she had a grudge against him, before she'd punished him for everything he'd done to both her and his brother's sons. He would have the rest of his life to consider his selfish actions once they were gone.

A moment later she was whirled around by the shoulders and hugged by Lark.

"Welcome to the family," Lark said, smiling broadly.

Lark let go so Lindsey could hug Josie, and they both said, almost in unison, "It's going to be wonderful having another sister!"

"Thank you," Josie replied, grateful for the reprieve from Blackthorne's attentions and tittering like an idiot with nervous laughter at their enthusiasm. "I'm looking forward to having two more sisters."

Blackthorne, meanwhile, was being congratulated by his best friend. Josie liked the Earl of Seaton, who'd told her to call him Seaton, since all his friends did. "Blackthorne and I were brothers-in-law for a short while, but we've been best friends forever. I'm hoping you and I can be friends, too."

Seaton was a few inches shorter than the duke, slender, with chocolate-brown hair and grass-green eyes. *No wonder one of the twins is attracted to him,* Josie thought. Which led her to wonder if Seaton's sister, Blackthorne's first wife, had possessed equally good looks. She felt a sudden spurt of jealousy and realized she was being ridiculous, since Fanny had been dead and buried for a year.

When she shot a surreptitious glance at the duke, his eyes looked bleak, making her wonder if the fact that he was still mourning his first wife's loss might have added to his willingness to enter a loveless marriage of convenience.

"Josie, you're not listening!"

Josie felt her cheeks being framed by one of the twin's hands and reached up to gently remove them. "I guess I was woolgathering."

."About what, I wonder?" Lark said with a cheeky grin.

Josie wasn't about to answer that question. She smiled and said, "Wouldn't you like to know!"

Both twins laughed, and Josie lowered her gaze demurely, as though they were right in their gleeful assumption that she was already anticipating her wedding night.

She'd learned a great deal about the Wharton girls during the past week. They were as playful and innocent as kittens, closely watched and protected from the darker side of life. Neither twin seemed to have any inkling that their brother had once rescued a girl who'd nearly been whipped to death. And both seemed completely unaware of the dire financial straits into which their family had been sunk. Perhaps the dowager had funds that had kept the girls from realizing the desperate financial problems their brother had solved by marrying her.

Several times, one or the other had seemed intent on speaking to her alone, but the twins seemed inevitably to arrive in a room and leave together, as though some invisible string tied them together.

It had been necessary for Josie to pretend that her trunks were on their way back to America, so she could have an entire wardrobe appropriate to her new station made during the week prior to her wedding. The twins had been on hand, eager to help, when the dowager's seamstress measured her for both her new wardrobe, which Blackthorne had insisted upon purchasing, and her wedding gown, which was a gift from the dowager.

"Oh, Josie, I'm so envious," Lark said when Josie had her final fitting for her wedding gown. "I can't wait till I walk down the aisle."

Lindsey had arched a dark brow and said, "Do you have someone in mind with whom to make this walk?"

Lark had flushed and answered, "No. I was merely dreaming of the future."

Josie thought she had her answer for which twin might have an eye for Seaton. She might have inquired further of Lark, but she was never able to speak with the girl when Lindsey wasn't around.

The elegantly simple gown Josie had worn for her wedding was made of white satin in honor of Queen Victoria, who'd made the trend popular when she'd chosen to wear white at her wedding to Prince Albert. Josie's gown had lace insets at the throat and sleeves with satin-covered buttons at the wrists. The waist was fitted, with luscious folds of satin falling to the floor in back in a short train.

An infinite number of satin-covered buttons down the back might have created a challenge for the groom on his wedding night, except Josie had no intention of offering Blackthorne the chance to undress her. She planned to be wearing something far less enticing when he arrived in her bedroom to consummate the marriage.

Josie had piled her golden blond hair onto her head to diminish the number of curls she had to contend with if it rained. She'd rarely pulled her hair up to expose her nape over the past two years, because a thin scar showed above even a high collar. She hadn't realized how naked and exposed she would feel simply leaving her neck bare. By the time she'd conceded her discomfort, it was too late to go back and start over again.

"We need to sign the register," the duke reminded her, putting a hand to her elbow and urging her toward the bishop's office at the back of the church.

"We'll meet you at the house," Lark said to her brother.

"Don't be too long," Lindsey said with a wink.

Josie wasn't sure what the wink was for. She looked up at Blackthorne and saw he was chuckling and shaking his head at his sister.

Then it dawned on her that Lindsey believed her brother was hoping to have a little time alone with his bride. Perhaps to kiss her again?

Josie kept her head lowered to hide the hot blush that rose on her cheeks as they entered the bishop's chambers. The churchman must have been delayed, and she could feel the tension growing between herself and the duke, as they stood silently in the austere room. She was painfully aware that they were alone. And that she was Blackthorne's wife.

Josie wondered if the duke would actually take advantage of this moment of privacy to kiss her again and realized that that was a foolish thought. It was surprising that he'd kissed her at the altar. Now that he had, why would he want to kiss her again, especially after she'd pushed him away?

"You look quite fetching today."

The words were spoken so softly that Josie almost thought she'd imagined them. She felt the duke's forefinger tip her chin up until she was looking into his striking blue eyes.

"The gown your grandmother's seamstress made for me is certainly fetching," she agreed.

"I wasn't admiring the gown. I was admiring you."

Josie self-consciously reached around his hand and poked her spectacles up her nose. "You were?"

His lips curved in the beginning of a smile. Then he looked deep into her eyes and said, "I was."

Josie felt her insides squeeze into a tight ball. All the oxygen she'd breathed in was suddenly caught in her chest, so it felt like she might explode. A frisson of feeling scurried down her spine, and her toes curled inside her shoes.

Blackthorne's gaze was suddenly focused on her lips, as he lowered his head. Josie felt almost dizzy with the knowledge that he was going to kiss her again. She wondered if he would do that thing he'd done before, and put his tongue in her mouth. She'd liked the little bit of it she'd experienced before she'd panicked. She'd only drawn away because she hadn't expected what he'd done. She was willing to try it again and see if it proved to be as pleasant as it had seemed like it might become.

The duke's lips had nearly reached hers when someone behind her loudly cleared his throat. Flustered, she was startled into stepping backward, while the duke slowly raised his head, not acknowledging in any way that he'd been about to kiss his bride.

The bishop was standing in the doorway. "Are you ready to sign the register now, Your Grace?"

"We are," he replied. "You first," he said to Josie. Her hand trembled as she signed her name. She quickly stepped back and handed the feathered quill to the duke, who dipped it once more into the inkwell and signed his name with a flourish.

"Are we done here?" the duke inquired.

"Yes, Your Grace," the bishop said. "May I add my congratulations on your wedding?"

The duke was already ushering Josie from the room as he replied, "Yes. Thank you."

Josie was surprised to find Blackthorne's grandmother and sisters waiting for them at the front of the church, since the girls had suggested they would meet us later at Blackthorne's mansion.

"Is there some problem?" the duke asked, his voice filled with concern. "I thought you would be on your way by now."

"It's pouring rain," the dowager replied.

"You won't melt if you get a little wet," the duke said with an indulgent smile.

"You go ahead," the dowager said. "We'll wait until the deluge slows down."

"Suit yourselves."

Josie should have known from the way the twins were huddled together laughing, that they weren't going to encounter a typical English rain.

And they didn't.

Chapter 12

BLACKTHORNE TOOK ONE step outside and staggered when a strong gust of wind hit him. His new bride gave a cry of consternation as the powerful draft caught her train and lifted it like a kite. He now understood the dowager's reluctance to leave the church, and the twins' giggles. Those two mischief makers could have warned him that, when he opened the church door, he'd be facing gale force winds and torrential rain.

A servant stood nearby on the church porch, struggling with a black umbrella turned inside out by the storm. Clearly there was no way to get from the porch to the carriage without getting drenched.

Blackthorne grimaced. He couldn't bear the thought of stepping back inside and making polite—and assuredly awkward—conversation with his family in the church vestibule until the maelstrom abated. And it was clear the servant's umbrella would never recover from the indignity forced upon it. So he did something entirely uncharacteristic and utterly fanciful.

His bride gave a delighted shriek, as he swept her off her feet and into his arms. She clung to him, and he held her close as he ran down the church steps. The servant dropped the umbrella and rushed ahead of him to open the door to his carriage and put down the steps. He practically threw his bride onto the closest seat and followed her inside, dropping onto the seat opposite her, as the servant put up the steps and slammed the carriage door behind them.

They were both drenched.

His new wife sat there in her soggy dress with her sopping hair for only a moment, before he was treated to burbling laughter, a sound as happy and soothing as the brook running over stones at Blackthorne Abbey.

She was pointing at him and laughing so hard she could barely get a word out. "Your . . . hair. Your . . . eyelashes. Your . . . chin."

He shoved his wet hair back off his brow, then took a hand to his face, swiping off rainwater and wiping it on his trousers.

"You're in no better shape," he replied with a laugh. Instead of letting her repair her own misfortunes, he shifted himself to the seat beside her. He tilted her chin up, so he was looking into her laughing face, and realized it was amazing she could see him at all, with her spectacles so doused with rainwater. He slipped them off, so he could dry them with his handkerchief.

Once they were in his hand, he looked across at her laughing face and felt his heart stop. Only for a beat or two, but it must have stopped, because it felt as though he'd been struck by the proverbial bolt of lightning.

His bride wasn't just pretty. She was stunningly beautiful.

Maybe it was her willingness to laugh at a situation he knew would have sent any other woman of his acquaintance into hysterics. Maybe it was her willingness to laugh at *him,* as though he were a mere mortal man and not the formidable Duke of Blackthorne. Or maybe it was seeing her amazing blue eyes for the first time out from behind the glass that had slightly distorted them.

He turned immediately back to the task of removing the rainwater from her spectacles, disturbed by what he'd discovered. How could he *not* fall in love with her? She possessed many of Fanny's good qualities—kindness, a concern for others, a lack of vanity—and a few Fanny hadn't possessed—most significantly, forthrightness and a willingness to speak her mind.

And she was far more beautiful.

Blackthorne felt ashamed for making the comparison. It was unfair to Fanny, whose loss he still felt intensely a year after her death. He realized he would have to guard himself against anything so ill-advised as an infatuation with his new wife.

By the time he was done drying his bride's spectacles, her laughter had died, but he could still see amusement in her eyes. She shoved her wet bangs aside, but raindrops clung to her eyelashes.

"Close your eyes," he said in a voice that was strangely hoarse.

"What?"

"Just close them."

He dabbed at her eyelashes with his handkerchief. And then he succumbed to temptation and kissed her. With hunger. With desire.

He felt her hands at his shoulders, as though to push him away, but they slid around his neck instead. And he realized she was kissing him back. With awkward eagerness. With guileless enthusiasm.

While his tongue sought a willing haven in her mouth, his hands traced the tempting contours of his new wife. There was no telling where things would have ended, if he hadn't dropped her spectacles.

The sound of shattering glass brought them both to their senses. She pulled away, staring down at the debris on the floor of the carriage, and then back at him, with horrified—he could think of no other word to describe the look—eyes. As though she'd betrayed some other lover. As though she'd committed a cardinal sin. As though she'd done something worthy of shame.

She covered her mouth with her hands and said, "Oh. Oh, no." Then she lowered her gloved hands, folded them primly in her lap, and turned her head to look out the window.

He'd been shaken by their kiss, but he was even more shaken by her reaction to it. What was going on in that head of hers? Was he wrong about her innocence? Did she love some other man? Why had she seemed so upset by her behavior? It was only a simple kiss.

Except there had been nothing simple about it. The soft weight of her breast had filled his free hand, and that kiss, which had involved teeth and tongues, had been a sensual, lascivious thing, a carnal prelude to sex.

He retrieved her broken spectacles from the floor and said, "I'll have these repaired today."

She didn't say "Thank you." She didn't say anything, or look anywhere but out the window, leaving him to think about his bride in silence.

Blackthorne reclined on the plush seat of the ducal carriage wondering what the rest of his life would be like, now that he was married to this strange American girl. Unusual. Unconventional. Unpredictable, for certain, if the past week turned out to be in any way typical of the next fifty years.

He couldn't help thinking of Seaton's reaction to his decision to marry Miss Wentworth, which his friend had expressed at the table after their pre-wedding dinner last night. The two of them had been enjoying a glass of brandy, the women having adjourned to the sitting room.

His friend had startled him by saying, "I thought in the end you'd give up everything before you married anyone."

"Why on earth would you think that?"

"Because you've had this hope—this dream—for the past year that the woman you saved in the Dakota Territory would miraculously reappear. I'm sorry, for your sake, that you never saw her again. Maybe then you could have closed that chapter—no, that single sentence—in your life, once and for all."

Because Blackthorne had denied his infatuation with the girl so many times in the past, he didn't bother protesting. But his gut had churned at the thought of giving up forever the forlorn hope his friend had put into words.

"Based on the poor quality of her clothing," Seaton continued, "your rescued maiden obviously didn't have the wealth to solve your financial woes. It's probably a good thing her whereabouts remain a mystery. Imagine the disaster if you'd decided to do something so foolish as to marry her. You'd have lost everything. As it turns out, this American girl—this Josephine Wentworth—is something out of the ordinary."

"She is that," Blackthorne had agreed, as an image of his future bride—leaping up like a jack-in-the-box from the dowager's dining table—rose in his mind's eye. "I should have anticipated something like what happened at dinner, I suppose. After all, she was raised in an egalitarian society. Still, it was a surprise."

Seaton chuckled. "You mean hopping up to serve the turtle soup? I thought your grandmother was going to choke on her wine."

"I was impressed with the reason the future Duchess of Blackthorne gave for helping Grandmama's elderly footman."

"That the tureen looked heavy? That she could easily serve, if he would hold the bowl?"

Blackthorne realized he was grinning. "To be fair, I was half out of my own chair when Soames tripped on the carpet as he entered the room and nearly dumped the soup in her lap."

Seaton chuckled again. "I thought her excuse for leaving her own bowl empty was priceless."

"That she'd once had a pet turtle, and couldn't

possibly eat anything that reminded her of Murtle? Definitely priceless."

They'd both laughed. Guffawed, in fact.

But there was nothing funny about what he'd felt at the altar, as he'd stood beside his bride. He glanced at the woman who was now his wife, but her face remained determinedly aimed out the window of the coach.

When she'd looked up at him at the altar with those summer-sky-blue eyes, shaking like a lost soul, he'd wanted to protect her, to shield her from hurt and from harm. He'd taken her hand and felt the enormity of the obligation he was accepting for the second time in his life.

It had been unsettling to admit that he didn't love the woman who would be his wife. He'd taken solace from the fact that he found her endlessly entertaining, since she was constantly doing the unexpected. It was disconcerting to realize that, ever since he'd met her, he'd been continually surprising himself with his *own* behavior, which was anything but normal—at least for him.

Whatever had moved him to kiss his bride at the altar, in front of his grandmother and Seaton and the twins? He would never hear the end of it from any of them.

That kiss . . .

It must have been sympathy or empathy or God knew what that had made him do something so uncharacteristic for the reserved Duke of Blackthorne, with a bride he barely knew. He'd wanted to laugh—or was it cry?—when she'd answered the bishop's question with that whispery, "I will?"

When his turn came, he'd felt shaken by the hopeless knot in his throat. He'd been relieved when he'd managed to speak without his voice cracking.

He suddenly realized what it was he'd seen on her face at the altar that had caused him to lift her chin and lower his head: desolation.

Which made no sense. He glanced again at the back of his wife's head, as she stared out the window. She was getting what she wanted, wasn't she? As his duchess, she would live the rest of her life at the height of Society in London—and for that matter, the world. She could lord it over all of her American friends. What did she have to be sad about?

Which made him question why she'd married him, if it hadn't been to purchase a royal title. But what other possible motive could she have had for giving up her fortune and marrying a perfect stranger, someone she'd known for a single week? Which made him wonder, not for the first time, why she'd been in such a hurry to get married. She would have married him a day after meeting him, if his grandmother hadn't intervened.

Blackthorne's mouth turned down. He had the awful feeling that Josephine Wentworth had put something over on him. But it was hard to conceive of a nefarious plan being hatched by someone as artless as his American bride.

As he'd lowered his head to kiss her at the altar, she'd closed her eyes and pursed her lips in a way that convinced him she had very little experience at such things, which was as it should be. He'd been very much aware of her vulnerability, her trust in him to keep her safe, and her belief, however naïve, that he would never hurt her.

Knowing that the vows had been said, knowing that it was too late to undo what he'd done, he'd felt an uneasiness he hadn't expected. Guilt? For what? She'd consulted with his solicitor. She was well acquainted with the terms of their agreement. She already had her very generous first quarter's allowance in hand. She was going into this with her eyes wide open, even though they'd been shut at that moment.

Then she'd peeked at him, checking the progress of their kiss. He'd realized he had to go through with it or embarrass both her and himself. So he'd brushed his lips lightly against hers. And felt his whole body quiver in response.

He'd tried to end the kiss, but she'd leaned into him, and he hadn't been able to resist the urge to continue the experiment, to see if he could determine what it was about kissing this uncommon girl that made all his senses suddenly come alive.

He'd wanted to taste her, so he'd slid his tongue along the seam of her lips seeking entrance. She'd opened her mouth, more from shock, he now believed, than anything else, but before he'd gotten the chance to satisfy his curiosity, she'd jerked away. He'd had the distinct impression that, if he hadn't been holding on to her, she might have fled.

It was the wonder in her eyes when she'd looked up at him afterward that had brought home to him how much power he had to wound her.

Something he'd apparently done when he'd kissed her just now in the carriage.

He noticed her gloved hands were knotted tightly in her lap. He worried that, as unworldly as she was, Josephine Wentworth Wharton harbored some starry-eyed expectation of romantic love that he could never fulfill. He had no intention of falling in love with his mail-order bride. In his opinion, their marriage-for-the-sake-of-money precluded it. Besides, after the unbearable pain of losing Fanny, he wasn't sure he could ever give his heart so freely and fully to another woman.

However, their recent kiss—in all its carnality— gave him hope that they might at least share the pleasures to be found in the marriage bed. Assuming he could make of his wife a willing partner. That seemed doubtful at the moment, although the thought of seducing his bride made their wedding night something he eagerly anticipated.

He darted a look at Josie and realized she hadn't stopped looking out the window since he'd released her from that kiss. He would have given a great deal to know what was going on in that pretty little head of hers. He pursed his lips ruefully, in no doubt that when the time came, she would tell him exactly what was on her mind.

After he'd welcomed her to his home and introduced her to his servants, they had to entertain their guests at their wedding breakfast. Except, he thought wryly, *his* home was now *their* home, and *his* servants were now *their* servants.

As the carriage drew up to the front steps, Blackthorne wondered how well his American bride would cope with greeting a multitude of servants and meeting so many of his titled friends. His lips quirked. Whatever happened, it was bound to be out of the ordinary.

After being hurtled from church to carriage through gusting winds and lashing rain, his new duchess could very well have ended up looking like a drowned rat. But her wedding dress was only a little the worse for wear, and her blond hair had dried in soft curls around her face. Blackthorne realized she must have ironed her hair to get it to straighten. That led him to wonder what all those blond curls would look like spread out on a pillow around her face.

He cut off the direction his thoughts had taken. Time enough to think about such things once night had fallen. Right now, he needed to break the ice, to avoid any awkwardness between them when they left the carriage and encountered the line of servants that would be waiting inside to greet them.

The carriage suddenly stopped.

"We're here," he said.

"Oh, dear." She turned toward him, her eyes wide and frightened, and he found himself reaching out to clasp her hand.

"Don't worry. You'll do fine."

"After last night . . . The dowager said . . ."

His grandmother had left his bride in no doubt that she disapproved of her behavior at the supper table the previous evening. She'd admonished Josie to behave better—more like the duchess she would be—at the wedding breakfast.

He squeezed Josie's hand reassuringly, but she continued staring at him, gasping air like a rabbit run to ground. He brushed his thumb across her lower lip, forcing her to release it from between her teeth. "I promise no one in my household will distress or discomfit you."

If they did, he vowed to himself, they would have him, at his most forbidding, to answer to.

"I like your curls," he said with a smile intended to ease her anxiety.

"Oh!" She reached up to touch her hair and appeared dismayed when she felt the tendrils about her face. "I must look a fright."

"You look . . . fine." He stopped himself from saying "beautiful," or even "lovely." Both words had come to mind. It wasn't safe to think of Josephine Wharton, Duchess of Blackthorne, in those terms. She was merely the mail-order bride he'd married to save his estate. She didn't love him. He didn't love her. And if they were both smart, things would stay that way.

But he had no idea how he was supposed to get through his wedding night—with a wife he found incredibly beautiful and entirely lovely and completely desirable—without losing his heart.

Chapter 13

JOSIE WAS CONFUSED by her behavior in the carriage. How could someone who'd reviled the Duke of Blackthorne for the past two years have enjoyed kissing him? And she hadn't just enjoyed the experience, she'd reveled in it! She felt ashamed of herself. How could she have been so easily seduced by a handsome face and a reassuringly tender touch?

Put in those terms, she could understand why she'd succumbed to Blackthorne's spell. It wasn't the handsome face; it was the reassuring touch. It had felt so wonderful to lean on someone else, to grasp Blackthorne's strong hand and know it was there to support her, even if it was only for a few moments at the altar. Once their vows were spoken, that hand was presumably there, along with that support, for the rest of her life. It was a heady feeling, to say the least.

She hated herself for being such a ninny, forgetting every bad thing the duke had ever done to his nephews—or to the girl he'd rescued—because he knew how to kiss a woman so her knees turned to jelly and her thundering heart felt as though it might burst.

Josie had been astonished by Blackthorne's unexpected behavior on the steps of the church. The proud, remote figure who'd taken her hand at the altar was not the same man who'd scooped her into his arms and raced helter-skelter through buckets of rain to the ducal carriage. Seeing Blackthorne's hair plastered to his face with rainwater, seeing it drip from his nose and chin and eyelashes, had suddenly made him seem human. She wasn't sure whether he'd smiled first or she'd laughed first, but both of them were soon overcome with mirth.

Then he'd removed her spectacles, and something had happened. Their humor had dissolved as he stared at her, his eyes revealing wonder and what she finally—and stunningly—realized was desire. Her whole body had felt taut, as though she were being held captive by strong, invisible bonds. She'd waited, her breath coming in short pants, for whatever came next.

What happened next was that she realized *she* was human, too. That she was as susceptible as the next silly miss to a rake's seduction. It made no difference that Blackthorne was her husband. He was still a virtual stranger, and that kiss had been . . .

Wonderful.

Josie chided herself for focusing on the feelings the duke's kiss had evoked, rather than the audacity of the man who'd provoked them. She was an innocent bride. That kiss had been . . .

Beyond anything I ever thought a kiss could be.

When her spectacles splintered on the carriage floor, Blackthorne had broken the kiss. And she'd suddenly realized that his hand was cupping her breast. She'd stared down, watching as his thumb brushed across the satin, where the shape of her aroused nipple was clearly visible, causing her to shudder with pleasure. She'd pulled away abruptly and angled her body toward the window, staring out at the people hidden under black umbrellas on the rain-splashed London streets.

Josie caught her lower lip in her teeth. She was remembering Blackthorne's mouth moving on hers and his hand cupping her breast. She couldn't believe how much that kiss in the carriage had affected her. Or how much she feared—and yes, also desired—the wedding night to come.

How could Blackthorne be so understanding and reassuring to a bride who was a virtual stranger and so unkind and uncaring to his nephews? Where was the selfish ogre who'd ignored her written pleas to rescue his brother's sons from the untenable situation in which they found themselves? It seemed her new husband had two different faces.

Luckily for her, Josie had seen them both. Maybe the behavior she'd found so appealing was temporary, and Blackthorne was only being nice until the marriage was consummated, and he had the golden goose well and truly caged. Josie had made up her mind, as the carriage pulled up in front of Blackthorne's mansion in Berkeley Square, to be on her guard, to watch and wait, in order to better gauge whether the duke's current kindly attitude would last.

Blackthorne had explained before the wedding that she would be meeting his servants when they arrived at his home for their wedding breakfast.

She hadn't expected them to be lined up directly inside the door, wearing stiffly starched uniforms and crisply ironed aprons appropriate to their ranks within the household.

Josie thought back to all the times she'd been condescended to when neighborhood gentry had stopped by Tearlach Castle. As a maid-of-all-work, she'd been beneath their notice. Growing up in America, her feelings about equality had been bred into her, skin and bone. It was the character of a person that mattered, not his birth. She had a golden opportunity to put her beliefs into practice when she greeted the duke's staff.

Blackthorne slid her arm through his, patted her hand, and said, "This is my wife, Josephine Wharton, Duchess of Blackthorne." He then gestured toward the line of servants and said, "My household is ready to serve you in whatever way you may want or need."

Josie slid her arm free and walked up to the first man in line and held out her hand for him to shake.

"Hello," she said, giving the portly balding man her most engaging smile. "What's your name?"

The servant looked at her hand and sent a glance toward the duke, before taking her hand, bowing stiffly, and announcing, "I'm Fairfax, the butler, Your Grace."

"It's so nice to meet you, Fairfax." Josie smiled more broadly to ease the tension she could see in the butler's shoulders, but a visible look of relief crossed his face when she released his hand and moved on to the next person.

A middle-aged, florid-faced woman curtsied and

said, "I'm Mrs. Rooney, the housekeeper, Your Grace."

"So nice to meet you, Mrs. Rooney. I hope we can be friends."

"Oh. I couldn't possibly—" The housekeeper looked toward Blackthorne for help.

Josie turned to face him as well. "Is there some problem?"

The duke pursed his lips thoughtfully before he said, "If that is my wife's wish, you must follow her lead, Mrs. Rooney."

"Oh, no!" Josie said, turning back to the housekeeper. "You must do what feels comfortable to you. I only meant I would welcome your friendship."

The housekeeper's lined brow furrowed more deeply at that suggestion.

"*Friendship,* Your Grace?"

That question, spoken with bewilderment, made it clear to Josie that she would be fighting an uphill battle convincing the duke's servants to treat her like an ordinary person. She turned to peruse the line of footmen and lesser servants, and found all of them gawking at her as though she were some rare bird the duke had brought home that had begun squawking in Turkish.

Josie sighed inwardly. It was going to take time to change the ingrained habits of a lifetime. She would have to show the way. But her personal overtures could wait for another time, when the duke wasn't standing there looking imposing and daring his servants to show his new bride any disrespect.

She greeted several footmen and as many maids before she reached the last person in line, a young girl who blushed as she announced, "I'm Gretta. Your maid. Your Grace." The girl was obviously young and overwhelmed by the position she'd assumed.

Josie glanced at Blackthorne, whose face was void of emotion. She bit back the need to argue that she'd never had a maid and had no idea what to do with one. She suspected this was the work of Blackthorne's grandmother, who'd been appalled when Josie admitted that she dressed and undressed herself, sewed her own clothes, and curled—or in her case, ironed—her own hair.

Instead she said, "Would you mind if Gretta took me to my room? I would like to repair my appearance before the guests arrive."

"Of course. I'll knock at your door and escort you downstairs in time to greet everyone."

"This way, milady. I mean, Your Grace," the girl corrected herself with a blush. She took off, only pausing long enough to curtsy to Blackthorne, before hurrying toward the staircase.

Josie followed after her, head held high, refusing to acknowledge her husband as she passed by him. She reminded herself that her stay here was temporary. It didn't matter if she ended up as isolated and friendless in this house full of servants as she'd ever been at Tearlach Castle. Once she had custody of Spencer and Clay, she would be on her way back to America and a happy reunion with her family.

Josie was not entirely surprised that her bedroom had a door connecting it to the duke's bedroom, but she was dismayed to discover that there was no lock. She wondered if Blackthorne planned to wander into her bedroom at will. That would never do. She would have to make it plain that she needed privacy.

"Don't you wish to change, Your Grace?" Gretta asked.

Josie shot the maid a chagrined smile. "I haven't anything else up to the occasion." The dowager's seamstress had promised her elaborate wardrobe would be ready soon, but she'd been focused on finishing Josie's wedding gown.

Gretta opened a cupboard filled with beautiful dresses for all occasions. "What about one of these, Your Grace?"

"Those can't be mine."

"But they are," Gretta insisted. "They were delivered today. I ironed them myself."

Josie gaped at the cupboard full of elegant clothing—far more than she'd ordered from the seamstress. Obviously, the dowager had been at work again. She crossed to examine them and found a yellow princess sheath that reminded her of a field of daffodils. She was glad to see it buttoned up the front, so she wouldn't need her maid's assistance. She wasn't willing to show anyone the scars on her back, especially not a maid who might gossip to the rest of the staff.

"That will be all, Gretta."

"You don't want help dressing? Your Grace?" she added belatedly.

"Thank you, Gretta, but I can manage on my own." Josie waited for the girl to leave the room, then locked the door behind her. She turned to stare at the door between her room and the duke's. Surely he wouldn't enter without knocking. Nevertheless, she stepped behind a dressing screen in a corner of the room to remove her wedding gown—not without a little difficulty—and don the dress she'd picked from the cupboard.

That done, she sat down at the dressing table, leaned close enough to see without her spectacles, and peered at herself in the mirror. She took a deep breath and let it out. She'd made it through the wedding. She was pretty sure she could hold her own over the next couple of hours with Blackthorne's titled friends. But a herd of buffalo was trampling through her stomach as she contemplated the night to come.

Josie had decided to wear something to bed that would discourage the duke from disrobing her completely. The garment she'd come up with contained enough material to keep him from discerning the raised scars on her back. She'd coaxed the dowager's seamstress into making her a blousy flannel gown that tied at the throat and had long, full sleeves, claiming she was always cold at night in England. Then she'd personally added additional layers of cloth inside the back of the gown. She only hoped that would be sufficient to do the job.

The knock on her door was almost a relief. Josie jumped up and opened it, then took an involuntary step backward.

The duke had changed out of his morning coat into a dark blue velvet frock coat and buff trousers, along with a brilliant white linen shirt. But he looked no less imposing. And no less attractive.

"Are you ready?" he asked, lifting a dark brow.

"Yes. Only . . ."

"Is something amiss?"

"There's no lock on the door connecting my room to yours." Josie waited for the frown she expected to form, but Blackthorne merely said, "I hoped there would be no need for locks between us."

Apparently, there had been no need for a lock when he'd been married to his first wife. Josie struggled not to give in to his subtle pressure to leave things as they were. "You agreed I would be making the decision whether you may enter my bedroom again after tonight. Or not."

A smile flickered on his lips and was gone. If she hadn't been watching his face closely, she would have missed it. She held her breath, wondering whether he would allow her a lock to ensure the privacy she sought.

"Very well. I'll have a lock installed tomorrow."

Of course she had to receive him in her bed tonight. But tomorrow, and every night after that, she had the right to refuse him. And would. She didn't want to get any more physically—or emotionally—involved in this marriage than she already was.

Her husband held out his hand. "Shall we go and greet our guests?"

She took the offered hand and let him lead her downstairs, where they formed a receiving line at the door to the ballroom. The dowager and Blackthorne's twin sisters arrived early and disappeared into the ballroom, but Josie didn't recognize another soul for the next hour. She smiled until her jaw ached.

"Sorry to be so late," Seaton said as he shook Blackthorne's hand. He grinned at Josie and said, "Nice to see you again, Duchess."

Josie found herself grinning back. "I'm so glad to see a familiar face."

"I think you're nearly the last to arrive," Blackthorne said. He turned to Josie and added, "The rest can greet us inside. Shall we join the festivities?"

Josie heard annoyance in his voice, but decided it was due to the amount of time they'd been forced to stand without moving, rather than anything she'd done. She lifted her chin, ready to face the throng, and headed into the ballroom, which was redolent with fresh-cut flowers. Everyone was clustered around a table holding a towering wedding cake and plates stacked high with finger sandwiches and other delicacies.

"Is there some reason why no one is eating?" she asked.

"They're waiting for us to cut the cake." Blackthorne led her to the table past guests who curtsied to the duke and his new duchess.

Josie felt her face heating with embarrassment at obeisance she didn't believe she deserved. She managed to smile and nod her head, while she hung on tight to Blackthorne's arm.

When they reached the table, he picked up the knife beside the cake and turned to meet her gaze. "I believe we should do this together."

Josie put her hand over his as he slid the knife into the lowest level of the three-tiered, intricately decorated cake. A smattering of applause greeted this accomplishment. Josie let go of the knife and began pulling off her right glove.

She saw Blackthorne watching her, confusion written large on his features.

She grinned, then reached out with her bared hand and broke off a hefty piece of the slice they'd just cut. She held it up in front of his mouth. "Open."

To her surprise, he did. She shoved the piece of cake into his mouth, laughing merrily at the sight of the Duke of Blackthorne with a ring of frosting surrounding his lips.

The assembled group gasped and then tittered.

"I presume this is one of those peculiar American customs," he said as he picked up a cloth napkin to repair the damage.

"Yes, it is," she said, still laughing.

"And is turnabout fair play?"

"What?"

Before Josie realized what the duke had in mind, he slid a confining arm around her waist, then grabbed a chunk of cake with his opposite hand and brought it up to her mouth. "Open."

Josie saw the mischievous twinkle in his eyes and opened wide. Laughing and choking, she swallowed as much of the cake as she could. She used her ungloved hand to collect the frosting from around her mouth, then held up the forefinger on which most of it resided, offering it to the duke.

Josie heard a humming sound, like a hive of bees,

in the distance, but everything had ceased to exist except the two of them. The duke's eyes crinkled at the corners, and she thought she might easily lose herself in those two enticing blue orbs.

He took her hand and brought it to his mouth, his eyes locked on hers, then opened his mouth and sucked the icing from her finger. Josie felt the wetness of his tongue all the way to her belly . . . and beyond.

A moment later, the dowager appeared in Josie's peripheral vision.

"Marcus." With that single utterance of his name, she made it clear that the duke's behavior was not up to her standards.

Josie was the recipient of a veiled look of contempt. She knew she shouldn't care what the dowager thought, but her throat was suddenly tight, and her stomach churned. She became aware again of the guests in the ballroom, who were talking low to each other and shooting sideways looks in her direction.

Josie eyed her husband. A duke's behavior was above reproach, no matter what he chose to do, but apparently hers was not. Josie glanced at the dowager long enough to see the pinched look on her face and decided she wasn't in the mood for whatever criticism the duke's grandmother might make of her antecedents, her looks, or her behavior.

"Come now, Grandmama," the duke began. "You must admit a bridegroom is entitled to some leniency on his wedding day."

Josie took advantage of Blackthorne's distraction

to murmur, "Excuse me, please," then turned and walked away.

She had no idea where she was going. She knew very few people in the room, and although she searched for the Earl of Seaton, she didn't see him. She discovered the doors to the balcony were open to let in fresh air, now that the storm had passed and the sun was out again, and she quickly slipped outside. The balcony was empty, and she crossed all the way to the rail and stood there looking down at the fallow garden, wondering how long it would take flowers to grow once she planted them.

Which was when she spied a figure dressed all in black, standing behind an evergreen bush looking up at her. She gasped and would have backed away, except the figure took off what she realized was a bowler hat and waved it at her. The Pinkerton! Josie realized Mr. Thompson was gesturing for her to come down. Of course he couldn't show up at the door and announce himself.

The boys! Something had happened to Spencer or Clay. Or both. Josie left the balcony in a headlong rush, then realized how strange it would look if she were seen running through the crowd at her own wedding breakfast. She glanced toward where she'd left Blackthorne, but he wasn't there. The dowager was engaged in conversation with a woman her age, and the twins had joined a group of young girls.

Josie glided along the wall, hoping to avoid speaking to anyone. Nevertheless, one or two ladies stopped her along the way. She did her best to respond intelligently before moving on, aware every second that disaster might be looming and wondering how she was going to be able to help the duke's nephews, if they were in trouble.

She discovered a side door to the ballroom and slipped out and down the stairs, hoping she could speak to the Pinkerton and be back before anyone—especially Blackthorne—noticed that she was gone.

She never saw the stealthy figure watching her as she left the room.

Chapter 14

FLINT CREED SAT at the kitchen table of their ranch house with his wife, Hannah, each of them holding one of their children in their lap, watching her read a telegram that had just been delivered. He hadn't planted the seed for their two-year-old daughter, Lauren. She'd been sired by Hannah's first husband, Mr. McMurtry. But Flint didn't love his daughter one bit less than their son, Billy, who'd been born a few months ago.

Flint blessed the day he'd come across Hannah Wentworth McMurtry, whose yellow dress had caught his eye as he'd ridden hell-for-leather across the prairie. At the time, he'd been desperate to find a woman in the Wyoming Territory—any woman—he could marry, to take his mind off the fact that he was in love with the exquisitely beautiful lady who was engaged to marry his brother.

Neither he nor Hannah had married the other with quite honorable intentions. Hannah had needed a father for her unborn baby. He'd needed a wife to distract him from the woman he loved. Flint had never imagined he would come to care for both his wife and the child of another man so much that he would gladly give his life for them. Having a son with Hannah had merely been honey on the cornbread.

The beatific smile on Hannah's face—which created dimples in both her cheeks—made his heart beat faster. He suspected the telegram contained news that she'd been waiting to hear for a very long time, but he asked, "What does it say?"

Billy had pulled the paper out of her hand and was chewing on the edge of it, when she replied in a breathless voice, "One of the Pinkertons has found Josie."

Then she laughed, a sound that reminded him of the robins in spring. He felt his heart swell with hope that, at long last, the shadow that had clouded her blue eyes for the past two years would finally disappear.

His wife had never forgiven herself for not being able to rescue her two sisters, after their Conestoga wagon had been attacked by renegade Sioux. Hannah had watched her youngest sister being carted away over the back of an Indian pony without any way to save her. She'd left her wounded sister, Hetty, behind in the wagon to go for help and had wandered for days without water or food or enough clothes to protect her from the cold.

When Flint discovered her, she'd been on death's doorstep and had no memory of exactly who she was or where she'd come from. By the time her memory returned, and they made it back to the wagon, her wounded sister had disappeared, and Josie's trail was too cold to follow.

Fortunately, Hetty had been located by the Pinkertons in the Montana Territory nearly two years ago. But the guilt Hannah felt over Josie's disappearance had kept her from ever being completely happy.

"It seems my little sister was in England all this time," Hannah said with a rueful smile. "She's on a ship bound for Charleston. Miranda wants us to come to Texas, so the whole family can be there when Josie arrives at Three Oaks. Can we go, Flint?"

"Texas is a long way off," he replied. "You know I need to get some hayseed in the ground before it's too late." He was among the few cattle ranchers who planted hay to feed his cattle through the bitter Wyoming winter. It had proved to be a sound economic decision after a series of blizzards piled up ten-foot drifts and left other cattlemen with decimated herds that had starved in the snow.

"It isn't just about seeing Josie," Hannah cajoled. "I miss Miranda and Nick and Harry. My sister invited Hetty, too. If my twin comes, all the Wentworths will be reunited at last. I won't be able to bear it if they all show up at Miranda and Jake's home, and I'm not there."

Flint wore a severe expression, even though he had no intention of denying his wife the chance to see her family all in one place again. It was sweet to know that whatever he decided, Hannah loved him enough to consider his wishes first and foremost. And because she always wanted what was best for him, he made it a point to do everything he could to ensure her happiness.

"Are we going on a trip?" Lauren asked.

Flint ruffled the nearly two-year-old's auburn curls, a final gift from Mr. McMurtry, and said, "We're going to Texas, sweetheart."

The smile on his wife's face was so dazzling, it made his heart leap. "Thank you, Flint. Oh, thank you!"

He leaned over to kiss her lips and saw Billy's hand reach out to pat his mother's cheek.

"Where's Texas?" Lauren asked.

"It's where your uncle Ransom and I came from."

"Oh, my goodness, Flint!"

"What's wrong?"

"I just realized you'll have a chance to see your brother Jake and your mother—"

"And my stepfather," Flint said, his lips flattening.

"Is he really so bad?"

At that moment, the kitchen door burst open, letting in a swirl of icy wind, along with Flint's younger brother, Ransom.

"Are you going?" Ransom demanded, clutching what was clearly a crumpled telegram in his hand.

Flint raised a surprised brow. "You don't want to go?"

"Jake never said a word about us coming back to Texas before now," Ransom said. "It's got to be that wife of his who put this wild hair up his ass."

"Watch your language," Flint said.

Ransom grimaced, glanced from Flint's scowl to Flint's kids and wife and said, "Sorry, Hannah."

"You should be sorry for maligning my sister," Hannah retorted. "She only has your best interests at heart. Don't you want to see your eldest brother again? Or your mother?"

Ransom's face looked tortured. "Yes, but—"

"But you can't stand to be anywhere near your stepfather." Hannah looked from one brother to the other and said, "Are you two grown men going to let your hate for that sorry son of a bitch keep you from seeing your family again? That seems a bit shortsighted to me."

Flint's dark eyebrows rose nearly to his hairline at Hannah's irreverent description of Alexander Blackthorne. He met his brother's gaze and grinned. "She's right, you know. We've let that sorry son of a bitch dictate to us for far too long. Hannah and I are going. Why don't you and Emma come along?"

Flint knew the source of the indecision in Ransom's eyes. Emma hadn't been well since she'd miscarried their second child, another little girl.

"Emma could use a change of scenery, don't you think?" Flint said.

"And Jesse would love having other children to play with," Hannah added.

"I'm not sure Emma's strong enough to make the trip," Ransom hedged. His wife, who'd grown up pampered in the home of her military father, had never been as healthy, or as capable of managing the sorts of surprises the wilderness threw at a woman, as Hannah.

"Emma's stronger than you think—or than she thinks, for that matter," Hannah said. "She'll go if you let her know it's something you want to do. And you do want to see your family again, don't you?"

Ransom heaved a huge sigh. "All right. Yes. I would like to see Mom again. And catch up with Jake. Just keep that sorry son of a bitch out of my sight."

"It's settled, then," Jake said. "We'll all pack up today and head for Cheyenne tomorrow to catch the train."

"We're going on a train?" Lauren said, eyes wide with wonder.

Flint met his wife's eyes and said, "All the way to Texas."

Chapter 15

LADY LARK WHARTON hoped no one had noticed the flush that rose on her cheeks as the Earl of Seaton shot a cheerful—but dismissive—smile in her direction, after making his manners to her grandmother. It didn't seem to matter that she was seventeen and considered a catch on the Marriage Mart. As far as David Madison was concerned, she was merely his best friend's little sister. Even worse, he never greeted her as though she were an individual, but only as one of a matching pair. It was always, "How are you two doing today?" Or, "How are you young ladies?" He lumped her together with Lindsey as though they were indistinguishable.

But Lindsey wasn't in love with him. Lark was.

The earl was the same age as her brother, and Lark was certain, now that Marcus had married again, that Seaton would begin looking for a bride of his own. She intended to be that woman.

Her task would have been a lot easier if Fanny were still alive. In the year Fanny had been her sister-in-law, Lark had spoken to her often about how attractive she found the earl. Fanny had been amused by what she called "your youthful infatuation with my brother." She'd been certain that fifteen-year-old Lark would forget all about Seaton when she saw how many beaus presented themselves to meet a duke's sister, once she was finally "out." Nevertheless, Fanny had promised that, if Lark was still interested in the earl once she turned seventeen, she would help her young sister-in-law gain her brother's attention.

Fanny had been buried nearly a year before Lark's seventeenth birthday arrived. Now, if she wanted Seaton to notice her, she was going to have to manage it on her own.

It was far easier to make the decision to try and engage the Earl of Seaton's feelings than to actually do something about it. First of all, it wasn't easy to get the distance from her twin to act independently. Grandmama had insisted that they spend several weeks apart each year, but otherwise, she and Lindsey did everything together. Lark loved her sister and hated the thought of any sort of separation. At least, she had before she'd fallen in love with Seaton.

Second, her grandmother kept a close eye on both girls and seemed to be aware every second of every day exactly where they were, what they were doing, and with whom.

Third, Seaton spent a great deal of his spare time with her brother. Arranging to be alone in the same room as her prospective groom when he came to call wasn't easy. Although, during Marcus's honeymoon period, surely he would be spending more time with his wife, leaving Seaton at loose ends.

Finally, and most importantly, Lark had no idea how to flirt with someone who still saw her as the child he'd watched grow up under his nose. How did a woman get a man to fall in love with her? How did she let him know she wanted to spend the rest of her life with him?

If Fanny were alive, she would have posed those questions to her. But Fanny wasn't around, and although Lark had once or twice opened her mouth to ask Josie what she should do, she didn't know Marcus's fiancée well enough to confide in her. What if Josie told Marcus that Lark loved his friend? There was no telling what her brother would do. And Lark would be appalled if Seaton learned of her interest in him through her brother.

Worst of all, she found it impossible to discuss the subject with her twin. She could tell that Lindsey suspected she was hiding something, but Lark refused to divulge what was bothering her. The look on Lindsey's face when she'd refused to reveal her secret had been hard to bear. Lark had almost crumbled and confessed the truth. But the sudden lump in her throat had kept her from speaking at once, and by the time she'd swallowed past the painful thing, Lindsey had already reeled and left the room.

There was no help for it. Lark was simply going to have to manage this quest on her own. And there was no time like the present to begin.

She edged closer to Seaton and overheard him say to his friend Viscount Burton, "Now that Blackthorne is married, I have some business to attend to in Northumberland. I'll be leaving at the end of the week, taking the early train on Friday. I should be able to make the trip to Berwick-upon-Tweed by rail in a day each way, assuming the train is on schedule. Even presuming another day away for business, I could easily be back in time to join your hunting party next week."

At the mention of Berwick-upon-Tweed, Lark's gaze searched the ballroom to locate her friend from school, Stephanie Court, whose family had an estate near that city on the northernmost tip of England. If she needed an excuse to be on that train with Seaton at the end of the week, Stephanie could provide it. Her friend had already told her that her family planned to leave London on Friday as well.

All Lark had to do was tell her grandmother that Stephanie had invited her to travel home with her family, and that she wanted to make this one of her yearly excursions without Lindsey.

Lark felt her stomach twist at the thought of lying to her grandmother. But desperate circumstances required desperate actions. She needed Seaton to notice her before his heart became fixed on some other woman. A day-long train trip each way would give her plenty of time to charm him. And she was sure, even if Stephanie and her family hadn't yet arrived home when she made the journey, that she could manage to stay as a guest at their estate in Northumberland.

Lark didn't allow herself to think about all the lies she would have to tell, or the dangers she might encounter by traveling so far by herself. Her entire future was at stake.

But she needed to know the exact train the earl

was taking, so she could be on it. "I couldn't help overhearing that you have travel plans," Lark said, smiling at Seaton as she tried to calm her galloping heartbeat.

Lark was watching closely, so she saw the barest hint of irritation in Seaton's green eyes as he turned to acknowledge her, as though a child had interrupted a grown-up conversation.

"My business has already been postponed for far too long. I'll be catching the seven o'clock train on Friday morning from King's Cross." He chucked her under the chin and said, "Will you miss me?"

He seemed to realize what he'd done only a moment after his fingertips touched her chin. It was a gesture more appropriate to a seven-year-old than a seventeen-year-old. He drew his hand back awkwardly and said, "I beg your pardon, Lady Lark."

Lark wanted to curl up under a rug somewhere and die. She could feel the heat on her cheeks, but running would only compound the problem. She managed a wobbly smile, and looking up at him through a sudden film of embarrassed tears said, "To answer your question, yes, I will miss you."

Then she turned and marched away, with all the dignity she could muster, to find somewhere to cry in earnest, all the while muttering under her breath, "Damn and blast! Can't the man see I'm not a child? I'm a grown woman. Just give me seven hours alone with him, and I'll open his eyes to the truth!"

It was only later that it dawned on her, *He knew it was me.* She'd never been quite sure that Seaton could tell the difference between her and her sister, because he was careful never to speak to either of them individually. *Probably just a lucky guess,* she decided, feeling entirely uncharitable toward the man she loved.

Her mind was already working on a plan to get herself on that train with Seaton. She had barely a week to arrange everything. She had to convince her grandmother that she'd gotten an invitation to visit her friend and then pack, all the while keeping both the Courts and her grandmother from finding out the truth. She just *had* to manage it somehow. This opportunity was too perfect to pass up.

Lark was halfway across the room when she realized that she would need to make arrangements to meet up with Seaton on the train. Otherwise, she might have trouble finding him, especially if he had a private cabin. She didn't want to have to hunt him down. It was another half hour before her chance came to speak to him again. She managed to "accidentally" step in front of him as he was crossing the room. She looked up as though surprised and said, "Oh, it's you. It turns out I won't be missing you after all."

He raised an inquisitive—and suspicious?—brow. "You won't?"

She flipped a black curl off her shoulder as nonchalantly as she could. "It turns out I'm traveling on the very same train."

"You are?"

Lark nodded. She could feel her chin begin to tremble at the recklessness of what she was about to do. With any luck, her brother would be gone on his honeymoon before Seaton had a chance to mention their coincidental plans to take the same train to Berwick-upon-Tweed. "I'll be traveling with a friend and her family who've been visiting in London and are returning home to Northumberland. I'll be their guest for a little while."

"Lindsey isn't traveling with you? I didn't think one of you went anywhere without the other."

"Recently, we've begun spending time apart each year," Lark replied breezily. She was surprised that, for the second time, he'd identified her correctly.

Even though she and Lindsey both had distinctive scars on their necks, most gentlemen of their acquaintance couldn't tell who was who. They kept forgetting which side of whose neck bore which scar. She wondered if Seaton had simply guessed right, again, expecting her to correct him if he'd been wrong.

"I'll look forward to having tea with you in the dining car at ten," she said. Before he could say yea or nay, or do more than gape at her, Lark turned and strolled away. She intended to do a lot more than have tea with Seaton. If she had her way, they would spend the better part of the three-hundred-and-fifty-mile trip in each other's company.

It took her only a breathless minute to find Lindsey and admit, "I need help."

She started to blurt the truth, but at the last minute realized that if she told the truth—that she would be on her own with Seaton on the train—it was likely her sister would demand details she preferred not to share. Instead she said, "Stephanie invited me to come spend a week with her in Northumberland. I want to go, but they're leaving Friday morning, and I'm not sure I can talk Grandmama into letting me go on such short notice."

She saw the pain in her sister's eyes when she realized Lark hadn't included her in the visit, but that lasted only a moment before Lindsey said, "I'll add my entreaties to yours. Surely that will be sufficient. Shall we go to her now?"

"Not now." Lark didn't want her grandmother to discover from the Courts, who were present at the wedding breakfast, that she hadn't actually gotten an invitation to visit. "Grandmama has enough to deal with at the moment. But tonight, after all the guests have gone, I would appreciate your help convincing her to let me go."

Lark felt lower than one of the fishing worms Seaton had once dangled to frighten her, as Lindsey gave her a hug and said, "Consider it done. You'll be on your way to Stephanie's house bright and early Friday morning."

Chapter 16

JOSIE WAS NEARLY frantic by the time she surreptitiously made her way to the empty backyard of Blackthorne's mansion. She held up her skirt and stayed on the stone path that led to the back gate. Although the storm had passed, the garden had become a giant puddle of mud.

She met up with the Pinkerton behind a tall evergreen bush that concealed her from anyone standing on the balcony and looking down into the garden. "What's wrong?" she asked anxiously. "Are the boys all right?"

"Sorry to worry you, miss—I mean, ma'am—but you never said how I should contact you, and I thought you'd want to know that both boys have measles."

"Are you sure it's just measles and not scarlet fever?" The symptoms were similar, but scarlet fever was much more dangerous, and she wasn't convinced Miss Sharpe would be willing to admit it, if she couldn't distinguish between the two. "I need to see them."

Mr. Thompson was already shaking his head. "I wouldn't advise it, ma'am."

"Why not?"

"Has the duke discovered yet who you really are?"

Josie shook her head.

"As far as the ladies know, Josephine Wentworth is on her way to America. If you return as the Duchess of Blackthorne, the ladies are sure to inform the duke that you were employed at Tearlach Castle as a maid-of-all-work. Is that something you want him to know?"

Josie made a face. It would certainly raise questions she wasn't ready to answer.

"The boys can't travel anyway, sick as they are. I have someone keeping a close eye on them. I'll let you know how they fare. I presume you'll be making arrangements soon to have them transported here?"

Josie caught her lower lip worriedly in her teeth as she considered the Pinkerton's question. "I'm not sure. I need to find out where Blackthorne intends for us to make our home. Then I can have the boys join us. Thank you for coming, Mr. Thompson."

He bobbed his head and touched a finger to his hat. "You're very welcome, ma'am. And may I offer my best wishes on your marriage?"

"Thank you. I—" Josie stopped in mid-sentence when she heard someone coming. She glanced around the bush and gasped when she realized it was Blackthorne. If he discovered the Pinkerton, he was sure to ask questions that would be difficult to answer. By the time she turned back to tell Mr. Thompson to disappear, he was already gone. She gritted her teeth in frustration when she realized Blackthorne's interruption had caused the Pinkerton to exit through the back gate without arranging a way to stay in contact with her in the future.

"My grandmother pointed out that you were missing from your own wedding breakfast," Blackthorne said as he approached. "What are you doing out here?"

Josie hesitated, uncertain what to say. She settled for something that could have been the truth. "The flowers in the ballroom are beautiful, but also a little overwhelming. I needed some fresh air."

"I thought I heard voices. Was someone here with you?"

Had he seen the Pinkerton? Josie wished the sun were not so bright. There was no way to hide the flush rising on her cheeks as she lied, "I was alone until you arrived."

Blackthorne's eyes narrowed, but he didn't argue with her. Instead, he surveyed the muddy patch that was all that remained of what had once been a garden. "This place needs a woman's touch. Unfortunately, you won't have a chance to turn your hand to making this garden what it was in the days my wife—my late wife—gave it her attention."

"Why not?"

"Because we won't be here."

"We won't?" He *must* have seen the Pinkerton. Then she saw the impressions of the Pinkerton's shoes in the mud and realized Blackthorne must have seen them, too. But those footprints might have been made by anyone at any time after the storm. Surely that didn't prove she'd met up with someone. Josie had the feeling Blackthorne was suspicious, but unsure, and was making up his mind as he spoke. "Where will we be?" she asked in as normal a voice as she could muster.

"Blackthorne Abbey, the hereditary seat of the Dukes of Blackthorne, ceded to the first duke by Henry II. It lies about forty miles south, in Kent."

If it was south of London, it was forty miles farther from Spencer and Clay. "I would rather stay in London."

"Now that I have the funds to do the work, I want to oversee the repairs to the Abbey myself."

"Repairs?" Josie asked. An image of the shabby interior of Tearlach Castle rose in her mind's eye. "Is it habitable?"

"Barely," the duke said through tight jaws. "At least, it was the last time I was there. I'm afraid my father didn't put a farthing into the Abbey during his tenure as duke, and it wasn't in the best shape when he inherited it."

Josie realized that if Blackthorne Abbey turned out to be a moldy heap of stones, it might not be a fit place to bring the boys. "How long do you expect the repairs to take?"

"It's been seventeen years since I spent any appreciable time there. I went away to school when I was ten and only came back for short visits thereafter."

"Perhaps it would be wiser for me to remain here while the repairs are ongoing," Josie suggested.

The duke shook his head. "The Abbey will be your home, too. In fact, we'll be spending far more of our time in Kent than in London. You should be present to help make decisions."

Josie was surprised that Blackthorne intended to involve her in the decision making, but perhaps if she were there, she could ensure the repairs were done as quickly as possible, so the boys could the sooner be brought to live with them. "Very well. When will we be leaving?"

"Tomorrow morning. After breakfast."

As he stared down at her, his eyes became heavy-lidded, reminding Josie that she still had a night of deception to get through. It dawned on her that, if they left first thing in the morning, she would have little time or opportunity to contact the Pinkerton and make arrangements to stay in touch. Surely Mr. Thompson could figure out where she'd gone and let her know how best to contact him.

Josie was startled from her thoughts when the duke led her farther behind the bush. He took her right hand in his and began pulling her wrist-length glove off her left hand, one fingertip at a time, not an easy thing to accomplish with the enormous ruby ring she had on underneath it. She stared at his long, strong fingers, wondering what he had in mind.

She wasn't left in suspense long. Once the duke had her glove off, he turned her hand palm up. His hot breath touched the center of her palm a moment before his lips, and she felt a shiver race up her arm, then down her center, all the way to her toes. "Oh."

Josie felt dizzy, and her knees were suddenly wobbly. She reached out with her remaining gloved hand to steady herself against the duke's chest. What she knew was living muscle felt as hard as stone. She stared at him in surprise. She hadn't expected someone with a title, rather than an occupation, to be so fit.

"You seem distracted," the duke said. "Is something wrong?"

Josie pulled her bare hand free and tugged her glove from Blackthorne's grasp. She turned slightly away from him, so she wouldn't be mesmerized by his blue eyes, and began pulling the glove back on. "Nothing's wrong." She flashed him a reassuring smile. "It's my wedding day. What could be wrong?"

Except, she didn't quite manage to get the second sentence out without it catching in her throat. And she couldn't quite keep the panicked look from her eyes. *Everything* was wrong. That's what was wrong. Her family wasn't here. She'd married a man she barely knew and, as soon as the sun fell, must allow him intimacies she could hardly imagine.

The boys were sick, and she knew Mrs. Pettibone and Miss Sharpe were likely at odds over how best to care for them. Tomorrow she would be moving even farther away from the duke's nephews to a home that might very well end up being a hovel. And who knew how long it would be before she could bring Spencer and Clay to live with her and finally find her way back to her family in America?

Josie fought the ache in her throat and blinked hard to stem the tears that threatened. She didn't want Blackthorne to see her discommoded and wonder why she was so upset, when she'd supposedly achieved her heart's desire by marrying a duke and becoming a duchess. But when she looked up, his features were blurred by a haze of tears.

She fought the arms that surrounded her offering comfort, but he didn't let go. She forced herself to stand still within his embrace, but she couldn't keep her body from trembling.

His low voice rumbled in her ear. "There *is* something wrong." His arms tightened around her, and somehow, the firm embrace settled her nerves, and the shaking stopped.

"I miss my family," she admitted. That seemed the easiest and best explanation for her tears and gave away none of her secrets.

"This has all been very sudden," he agreed. "But it's done now."

She waited for him to suggest they postpone their wedding night. But the offer didn't come, and she didn't have the courage to suggest it herself. She was certain he had no idea she intended to run off with his nephews. More likely, he wanted to be certain the marriage couldn't be repudiated on the basis that it hadn't been consummated, if they found themselves at odds in the future. If there was one thing she'd learned in her eighteen years of living, it was the fact that it was better to address an unpleasant task than to put it off until later.

She felt her lips curve and realized that, although the night to come might be awkward, it might also be a great deal less than unpleasant.

"Are you calm now?" he asked.

"Yes. You may release me."

Blackthorne kept one arm around her waist as she took a step back. She looked up and saw his gaze was focused intently on her face, as though to discern her thoughts. She lowered her gaze, knowing it might suggest that she had something to hide, but she wasn't ready to face the duke's penetrating blue eyes. Instead, she set her hand on his arm, and said, "Shall we go back inside?"

"Not quite yet."

Josie was startled into meeting his gaze again. What she saw caused her breath to catch in her throat.

Chapter 17

HIS WIFE WAS lying to him. Someone had been in the garden with her. Blackthorne was almost sure of it. But who? And for what reason? He'd been so glad that he could acquire the funds he needed, along with a beautiful face and an intriguing personality, that he hadn't asked why, if Josephine Wentworth was willing to spend a fortune to impress her friends and relatives with a royal title, she'd agreed to marry him with so little fanfare and with not one person she knew present. She *must* have some ulterior motive for becoming the Duchess of Blackthorne. He simply had no idea what it could possibly be.

He had no fortune of his own, so she couldn't be planning to steal from him. And if she had a lover, why marry someone else? His misgivings led him nowhere. Unfortunately, none of his suspicions kept him from finding his bride as enticing as she'd been the first moment he'd laid eyes on her. He'd led her back inside without another word being spoken between them, but it hadn't been a comfortable silence. His wife was turning out to be quite an enigma.

The rest of the day had seemed interminable, most likely because he spent it anticipating his wedding night. The guests left in trickles and drabs, but they were all gone by the time darkness fell. After an awkward, almost silent, private supper with his bride, he escorted Josie to her room and asked how long she would need to ready herself for his visit.

She shot him a look that told him a hundred years would be too soon. He watched the pulse throb in her throat before she finally said, in the same whispery voice that had struck her at the altar, "Half an hour."

Blackthorne paced the length of his bedroom yet again, wondering how much longer he had to wait before the half hour had passed. He missed his grandfather's watch. He glanced at the ormolu clock on the mantel and saw, to his relief, that twenty-eight minutes had come and gone since he'd left her at her door. He felt unaccountably nervous. It wasn't as though he hadn't done this before.

He shuddered when he remembered how difficult his wedding night had been with Fanny. She'd *loved* him, yet she'd been reluctant to allow him the liberties of a husband. He believed Fanny had eventually learned to enjoy their lovemaking, but she'd never relished it as he did. He couldn't imagine what the coming night was going to be like, when he'd only known the woman he'd wed—and planned to bed—for a single week.

Except, Josie was as different from Fanny as night was from day. He hadn't been tempted to kiss Fanny at the altar. He hadn't carted her through a rainstorm and laughed about it afterward. And he hadn't kissed her with abandon on the way to their wedding breakfast.

But comparisons weren't fair. Fanny had been raised to be a proper English lady, a model of decorum, whose impeccable behavior was permanently restrained and reserved. Blackthorne doubted his American wife had a reticent bone in her body.

After they'd returned from the garden, Josie had smiled and nodded to everyone who'd attended their wedding breakfast, without a single protest. She'd laughed with his sisters and listened attentively to his grandmother. She'd even chatted for a few moments with him.

But he'd been certain that, in spite of her constant smile, she'd been preoccupied by whatever had been troubling her when she'd escaped to the garden. His wife was in some kind of trouble. He wasn't sure how he knew that, but he didn't think he was wrong. Josie was a good actress. He just wished he knew what role she was playing.

He tightened the belt on the paisley silk Sulka robe he'd donned to spare his bride's modesty. He'd bought it in New York, a last stop before heading home to be married to Fanny, after he'd rescued the girl from the Sioux. He wondered where that wounded waif was now. He felt a lingering regret that he'd never heard from her again. Where she was—or who she was—no longer mattered. Whatever hope there had been of perhaps finding her and getting to know her had died with this forced wedding to someone else.

How different this wedding was from his first!

For one thing, there would be no honeymoon. Instead of sailing the Aegean, enjoying decadent dinners in Paris, and viewing antiquities in Rome, as he had with his first wife, he and Josie would be spending their time refurbishing Blackthorne Abbey. It dawned on him how unfair that was to his bride.

But Josie hadn't grumbled about—or even mentioned—the missing honeymoon. Which was another one of those anomalies that made him wonder and worry about his new wife.

Blackthorne glanced at the clock again and saw it was now thirty-one minutes since he'd left Josie. He crossed to the door between their rooms and knocked. He waited, his pulse unaccountably racing, for his bride to invite him inside.

And waited.

He reached for the doorknob but realized he needed—wanted—his wife's permission to enter her room. As he stood there contemplating whether to knock again, the door opened. The only light in the room came from the fire, which had been built up in the fireplace. Shadows loomed everywhere else.

He stifled a laugh when he saw what Josie was wearing. The white flannel nightgown had a bow at the throat that was tied up tight. The blousy sleeves covered her arms to her wrists, and the heavy winter material left nothing but the tips of her bare toes showing on the Aubusson carpet. His breath caught in his throat when he focused his gaze on the glorious golden curls tumbling across her shoulders.

"I was in bed waiting for you," she said. "I didn't think about having to let you in."

He saw the pale-pink silk sheets on the bed were rumpled, saw the indentation of her head on one of the pillows, and felt an immediate flare of pure animal lust.

She must have sensed his reaction, because she took a step back, gasped, and put a hand to her throat.

He took a step toward her, and she took another step back. He grinned wolfishly. "At least you're headed in the right direction."

She glanced over her shoulder and apparently realized that in a few more steps she would be backed up against the bed.

"I'm a little nervous," she admitted, lifting her chin and standing her ground.

"Me, too."

She looked flustered at his admission. "At least you've done this before."

"Not with you."

Rather than backing up any more, she headed for the fireplace across the room, where she held out her hands toward the flames. "I can never get over how cold it is in England in the spring. It reminds me of—"

He wasn't sure whether she'd stopped speaking because she didn't want to finish her thought, or because he'd crossed the room to stand behind her and had cupped his hands around her shoulders. He realized he didn't give a damn what she'd been about to say. He wanted to kiss his wife.

She resisted only a moment before she allowed

him to turn her around, so she was facing him. He didn't pull her close. He had the feeling that if he did, she would resist. Instead, he used a forefinger to tip her chin up. Her gaze remained cast down, so he said, "Josie, look at me."

She raised her gaze almost defiantly to meet his, but her breathing was erratic, and he could see the pulse leaping in her throat.

He slowly eased an arm around her waist and realized she must be wearing some sort of undergarment beneath her nightgown. He'd felt a layer of something beneath the gown when he'd touched her shoulders, but there was so much additional fabric between his hand and her back that he couldn't feel the heat of her flesh. That was a problem he could solve later. Right now, he wanted to taste her mouth.

He took his time lowering his head, giving his wife the chance to turn away. Her face remained upturned, and at long last, her lips met his. And clung.

Blackthorne felt ravenous but reminded himself of her behavior when she'd kissed him in the carriage. Naïve. Uninitiated. He must take his time. He must be gentle. Ever so slowly, he slid his tongue into her mouth, seeking the honey inside, while he clutched a handful of her silky hair to angle her head. He kissed her until he couldn't catch his breath and then kissed her some more. He teased her lips with his teeth and waited for her tongue to seek his mouth. But she seemed content to let him do the tasting.

He felt her struggling and reflexively tightened

his hold around her waist, until he realized she was only trying to get her arms up around his neck. Once she did, their figures were welded together from breast to hip. Her hands tentatively slid up to caress his cheeks, to trace his ears, to scratch their way uncertainly up his nape into his hair.

His body caught fire.

Blackthorne broke the kiss to look into Josie's eyes. He was confused—but delighted—by her behavior. He'd been prepared to counter reticence and restraint. He hadn't expected his wife to be so willing. He didn't quite believe what was happening between them.

And he didn't quite trust her to be honest with him.

Her pupils were huge, her lips swollen from his kisses, her cheeks flushed, and her breathing was even more irregular than it had been when she'd admitted she was anxious about what he might want to do with her—or to her—on their wedding night. She couldn't be faking those responses.

He pulled the bow loose at her throat and undid several buttons, before pressing his lips against the flesh at her throat beneath her ear and sucking lightly. Her head fell back, and her moan of pleasure caused his shaft to throb.

Blackthorne knew that the first time could be painful. But his insistent body made it impossible to think about anything except putting himself deep inside her.

He scooped Josie into his arms and carried her to the bed, laying her head on the pillow so her hair flowed out like a golden halo around her face in the firelight. He untied his sash and yanked off his robe. Her eyes turned into saucers in the few moments she had to view his nakedness, before he covered her body with his own. He shoved her gown up far enough to reveal her naked belly and spread her legs apart with his knees, leaving her open to his thrust.

"Wait! Stop!"

Her fingernails clawed at his forearms, but her protest had come too late. He was already past the barrier that confirmed her virginity, already seated deep inside her wet warmth. He paused then, and looked at her face in the shadows. Her eyes were luminous. Mysterious. And filled with pain.

She whimpered, and he said, "Shh. The worst is over."

He remained still, although his body pulsed with the need to move inside her. "Shall I stop?"

It would probably kill him if she said yes. But the necessary broaching of his bride had been accomplished. The marriage could no longer be invalidated on that basis. He hated the suspicion that had brought that thought to mind and forced it out of his head.

He saw the struggle on her face before she said, "You're not done?"

He felt the smile coming before it appeared on his face. "No. There's more."

She lifted a brow in question, and he said, "I've yet to spill the seed that creates a child. Shall I continue?"

She hesitated, then nodded.

He'd wondered if his mail-order bride would be

willing to bear his child. Apparently she was. He was surprised. And surprisingly pleased.

"Very well," he said. "Let us continue."

He lowered his head and softly kissed her while their bodies were joined. His tongue mimicked the thrust of his shaft within her body, and he groaned as he felt her hips rise to meet him. Her fingers dug into his back, sending a shiver through him, while his hand found its way inside her nightgown to her naked breast, to pinch and to play.

Blackthorne had nothing with which to compare what followed. Josie's legs came up to circle his hips, and she clung to him as though he were the only person left in her universe. The sounds she made drove him to greater heights of excitement, and he kissed and bit and sucked every part of her he could reach.

It was a time out of time. He hadn't expected his bride to be so responsive. He took the chance of touching her more intimately than he might have dared, finding the bud that would truly make her flower, and restraining his own climax until he felt her body begin to contract and shudder around him.

Her eyes, which had been heavy-lidded, opened wide with wonder, and she made a wrenching, guttural sound that provoked an equally animalistic response from him. Her hips arched high beneath him, and he plunged so hard and deep that her body was forced across the satin sheets. Even so, she met him thrust for thrust. Until finally, his head fell back, and he uttered a harsh, primeval sound, as he spilled himself inside her.

Chapter 18

JOSIE FELT TRIUMPHANT. She'd coupled with Blackthorne, perhaps creating a child, and still managed to keep her identity a secret. She'd resisted when Blackthorne attempted to remove her nightgown, and it had remained on. Nor had he remarked about the additional layer of material she'd sewn into her gown, which had made it difficult—impossible?—for him to feel the raised scars on her back. They were well and truly wed, and her husband had no idea who she really was. She'd managed everything perfectly. So she couldn't understand why—as she lay there with Blackthorne's weight pressing her into the feather bed, her heart beating a fast tattoo, her lungs heaving—stupid tears kept welling in her eyes.

Josie still couldn't quite believe he'd fit inside her, or that so much pleasure would follow the brief pain of penetration. Fear had made her cry out, but by the time she'd spoken, it had been too late. And what had followed . . .

She'd never imagined anything like the shuddering pleasure she'd found in Blackthorne's embrace. The rasp of his beard against her flesh. The silky texture of his hair as she grabbed handfuls of it to encourage his mouth to keep on doing magical things to her breasts. The taste of him, as she tried her first shy forays into his mouth with her tongue. The play of muscle and bone, as she wrapped her legs around his naked flanks. And the exquisite pleasure that had caused her to writhe beneath his touch, when he'd caressed a place on her body she hadn't known existed.

What had happened between them was something inexplicable. Something soul-shattering.

Was it like that for everyone? Her sister Hannah hadn't seemed in any hurry to repeat her wedding night with Mr. McMurtry. How could her sister have resisted lying with her husband, if this was how it felt?

Josie realized suddenly what might be causing her tears. When she'd agreed to marry the Dastardly Duke, she'd conceded that she would have to consummate the marriage. Therefore, she'd been determined to enjoy the one night of lovemaking she would ever experience. She'd known that making love to Blackthorne after that would be dangerous, because she planned to leave for America with the boys as soon as she could manage it, and she couldn't afford any emotional ties that might arise and interfere with her plans.

Unfortunately, Josie had loved making love with the duke. She wanted to do it again. And again. But if she did that, pretty soon she'd be making excuses for his behavior. There was no excuse for his neglect of his nephews or his abandonment of her. He had to be punished. The boys had to be saved.

Which meant she had to avoid a repetition of the glorious wedding night she'd just experienced.

Since she couldn't escape to cry alone, Josie settled for turning her face away from the duke, as tears began streaming down her cheeks.

A few moments later, Blackthorne slid off of her onto his back. She immediately turned onto her side away from him, curling herself into a tight ball.

"Are you all right?"

She forced back a sob and rasped, "Why wouldn't I be?"

"It sounds to me like you're crying."

Josie sat up, glowering at him, as she swiped at her eyes. His hair was tousled, his eyes heavy-lidded, and his beard-stubbled face looked more relaxed than she'd ever seen it. "I've just been through the most harrowing week of my life. I think that deserves a few tears. Of relief, if nothing else."

"Harrowing?"

"How would you describe everything that's happened to us in the short time since we met?"

"Exhilarating."

"Ha!" she muttered. "That shows what you know."

He sat up, pulling the sheet across his lap when he caught her staring with curiosity at the part of him that had been recently joined with her. "Granted, the past week has been a whirlwind of activity, but look at everything we've accomplished. The dukedom is saved. And you're a duchess."

She snorted inelegantly.

He sighed. "We'll be heading to Blackthorne Abbey early tomorrow morning, so I suggest we both get some sleep." He plumped the pillows behind his head and began settling the linens more comfortably around him.

Aghast at what his behavior seemed to imply, Josie clutched the bedsheet to her chest and said, "I hope you don't intend on sleeping here."

"Is that a problem?"

"You have a bed of your own."

He arched a suggestive brow. "Would you rather join me there?"

"I'd rather sleep in my own bed by myself," she retorted. "You said the choice was mine whether—"

"Whether we ever make love again. Yes, that's true. I didn't agree to separate accommodations. I expect to spend my nights sleeping in the same bed as my wife."

"That's outrageous!" Josie sputtered.

"Believe me, I can resist your charms."

That statement was even more outrageous, as far as Josie was concerned, but she didn't bother saying so. If Blackthorne insisted on sleeping in the same bed with her, she wouldn't be able to discard the uncomfortable camouflage she'd donned to conceal her scarred back. She'd never have a moment's peace, knowing that he might walk in on her at any moment and discover the truth.

In desperation she said, "Very well. We can share a bed. But not yet. Please. We're still strangers. We need time to get to know each other first."

He frowned. "How long is that going to take?"

"I don't know."

"Another week? A month? Six weeks?"

None of those sounded like enough time to Josie. But the longer she could put off the inevitable, the better. Grasping at straws she said, "Until we finish the repairs at Blackthorne Abbey."

He eyed her askance. "That could take months."

Josie realized she'd accidentally stumbled onto the perfect solution to a completely different problem. If Blackthorne wanted her in his bed, he'd be more inclined to hurry the renovations, which suited her purposes perfectly. The sooner the Abbey was whipped back into shape, the sooner she could bring Spencer and Clay to live with them, and the sooner they could make their escape.

"Very well," he said. "We'll sleep separately until the renovations are complete. Or until you invite me back to your bed."

"That isn't going to happen."

"I won't argue the point."

He seemed to think she would give in to temptation. He was wrong. He had no idea how determined she could be. She'd survived three years at the Chicago Institute for Orphaned Children. She'd survived a grueling trip across the American prairie in a Conestoga wagon. She'd survived an Indian attack and the torture that followed. And she'd survived two years of exhausting work, assigned by a housekeeper who hated her.

She could survive marriage to the Duke of Blackthorne.

She watched as Blackthorne rolled off the edge of the bed and stood naked, revealing a broad, sculpted back, a narrow waist and hips, muscular buttocks, and long, long legs. He grabbed his robe from the floor and pulled it on, hiding the male beauty she'd been admiring. Once he had the sash tied, he turned to face her again.

"My name is Marcus. I'd like to hear you say it."

Josie grimaced. She needed to keep the Dastardly Duke at arm's length. Calling him by his first name seemed to halve that distance. "Your friends call you Blackthorne," she hedged.

"My family calls me Marcus."

She would call him "Marcus," she decided. But every time she did, she would remind herself that he was—and always would be—the Dastardly Duke. "All right, Marcus. I've called you by your name. Are you satisfied?"

He dropped his palms onto the bed and leaned over far enough to kiss her on the lips.

Her heart leapt with joy before she could stop it.

He grinned and said, "Very satisfied. Good night, wife."

He strolled across the room, out the connecting door, and into his own bedroom without another word.

Josie growled, just like the Shetland bitch that roamed Tearlach Castle had, when she'd tried to take away its dirty old bone. Blackthorne could try his best to steal her heart, but he would never succeed. Not when she was guarding it tooth and claw. The Dastardly Duke could kiss her all he wanted. He would never get past her defenses, because she would never give up the fight.

Chapter 19

THE EARL OF Seaton had committed a great wrong against his best friend, although he'd done it with the best of intentions. He'd kept a secret from Blackthorne for two long years: He'd known where the American girl was all along. Now that Blackthorne was married to someone else, Seaton was on his way to Northumberland, at long last, to send her home.

Seaton had watched his friend's fascination with the American woman he'd rescued grow into something close to obsession during the voyage across the ocean. He was relieved when, at the last possible moment, Blackthorne had asked him to take over the responsibility for keeping the girl safe while she recovered and then sending her home to America.

He'd arranged to have the injured girl taken to an inn close to the docks and provided a doctor to oversee her care. Then he'd gone to see his sister, glad to know that the American would never become a threat to her happiness. Only to discover, to his horror, that Blackthorne had confessed everything!

"I have a favor to ask," Fanny had said, once Blackthorne left them alone in the sitting room of their widowed mother's townhome.

"Anything," he'd replied. "You want that bloody girl shipped back to America immediately? Done. I'll send a doctor along with her to—"

"I don't want the girl sent back at all."

His jaw had dropped to the floor. Or would have, if it hadn't been connected at the joint. "What?"

"I'm dying, David."

"You don't know that!" he'd snapped back. He'd seen the pain in her eyes and felt his heart wrench. Without their mother's knowledge, he'd helped her consult the best doctors in London. They'd all told her the same thing. Her consumption was irreversible. If she took care of herself, she might have a year—or two—to live. He couldn't fathom how she could accept her fate without fighting harder against it. "You can't die, Fanny. I won't let you."

"You can't stop what's going to happen any more than I can."

"When are you going to tell Blackthorne?"

"I . . . can't tell him."

"He deserves to know."

She'd shaken her head. "You know as well as I do that he would marry me even if I told him I had only a month to live. But he would suffer terribly every day of that month. This way, he can be happy—we can be happy—for however long I have."

"Why are you so interested in what happens to the American?"

"Because Marcus seems so captivated by her."

"I'd think that would make you want to be rid of her as quickly as possible."

She'd smiled mischievously. "I do want to be rid of her, at least, for the present. But I don't want her gone permanently. If you send her back to America when she's well, Marcus will likely never see her again. He's going to need someone when—"

"Don't say it, Fanny. Don't mention your dying to me again. I can't bear it."

She'd risen from the wing chair where she was sitting and crossed to where he stood near the crackling fireplace and held him close, whispering in his ear, "The sooner you accept the inevitable, David, the easier it will be." Then she'd looked into his eyes and said, "I want that girl to be here in England, so Marcus has someone to love when I'm gone."

"The girl may want nothing to do with him," he'd protested.

"She can't help but love Marcus. He's a very lovable man."

He'd laughed at her logic. But she'd been implacable. She would take over care of the girl from David. She would make all the arrangements for the American's stay in England through Seaton's solicitor, to keep Blackthorne in the dark, and Seaton was not to worry his head about the matter again.

He'd acceded to his sister's wishes and, to protect himself from accidentally giving away her secret to his best friend, had made it a point not to learn the girl's name or where she'd been sent. Thus, when Blackthorne asked him about her, he could honestly say he had no idea where she was or what she was doing.

When Fanny's health had begun failing, she'd sent a note asking him to come visit her at a time when Blackthorne wasn't at home. She'd looked so frail carrying Blackthorne's child it had made his heart ache. She'd laid her cold, dying hand in his and said, "The American is at Tearlach Castle."

"Isn't that where Blackthorne's nephews are staying?"

"It is. It hasn't been easy keeping him away. I've made several excuses for us not to visit Spencer and Clay—primarily the effect such a long journey would have on my health, and my desire to have him nearby during my confinement—but I've been assured by the governess I hired that the boys are well and happy. It won't be long before they'll be back in Marcus's care."

Seaton winced at the reference to her failing health. She'd been radiantly happy when she'd discovered she was pregnant, but he could see the toll the baby was taking on her body. He only hoped she would live long enough to hold her child in her arms.

"I needed to keep the girl somewhere I could be sure Marcus wouldn't accidentally run into her," she'd explained. "Tearlach is so far away, it isn't easy to visit."

Blackthorne had mentioned he missed his nephews, but Seaton hadn't realized his sister was the one keeping his friend from visiting them—or them from visiting him. But Seaton could easily understand why his sister had chosen Tearlach Castle as the place to hide the girl, since it was so far from London, just a few miles from the Scottish border. "How is the American faring?"

"She's completely recovered."

"How did you get her to stay, once she was well?"

She'd smiled that very same mischievous smile he'd seen more than a year before, when she'd talked about her plans for the injured girl, and admitted, "I made sure she didn't have the where-withal to leave. I've also intercepted her correspondence, both to Marcus and to her family in America."

"I had no idea you could be so devious."

"I know I haven't been fair to her, but it won't be long, no time at all, really, before I'm gone. Then she can make the choice to stay in England with Marcus . . . or go home."

He'd opened his mouth to beg her not to speak of how little time she had left to live and shut it again when he saw the tears brimming in her eyes, biting his tongue to keep from saying what he really thought of her silly machinations.

What Fanny had done seemed not only unfair, but unkind, which wasn't at all like her. She seemed to think the result justified the means. His sister's illness must have left her feeling very desperate to be so unscrupulous toward another human being.

Seaton doubted whether Blackthorne or the girl either one would be willing, when the time came, to fall in with Fanny's plan for them to meet, fall in love, and live together happily ever after— Blackthorne because he'd be grieving, and the girl because she'd be celebrating her freedom to return from whence she'd come. It was absolute fantasy, a preposterous plot from one of the romance novels his sister devoured. But he was willing to do anything that gave his dying sister peace of mind in what he was coming to accept were the last few months of her life.

Fanny continued, "I understand, from the governess I hired to take care of Marcus's nephews, that the American has become very attached to the boys. In fact, Miss Sharpe said she's become a bit of a nuisance, interfering in their care. That's a good sign, don't you think? It must mean she has a generous heart. Marcus will need that when I'm gone."

He'd shaken his head, unable to believe his sister could be so matter-of-fact about the end of her life, and so naïve about the girl's willingness to forgive and forget. "What you've done won't endear Blackthorne to her. He promised he would send her home."

"It's up to you to explain the truth," she said. "I expect you to make it clear that *I* was the one who made the arrangements to keep her in England."

"What if she demands to be sent home at once? What do I do then?"

"Use your best judgment. Hopefully, she'll at least want to speak with Marcus, to thank him for rescuing her." She smiled and said, "I trust Marcus to take things from there. I would be very surprised if that girl ever returns to America."

He'd been too sunk in grief to think about the American immediately after Fanny's death. Before he could comply with Fanny's wishes and reveal what she'd done, Blackthorne had confided, on a night when they'd both drunk too much, the dire nature of his financial circumstances.

Seaton had realized, long before Blackthorne admitted it to himself, that his friend would need to marry well to recoup the calamitous losses incurred by his father and his brother. Based on the poor quality of the American girl's clothing, and the fact that she'd been traveling by wagon rather than by train across the prairie when she'd been captured, he was convinced that she didn't have the resources to save his friend.

Unfortunately, Blackthorne's fascination with the girl had never waned. Seaton had thought it entirely possible that Blackthorne might avoid making the alliance with an heiress he needed to save his estate, if he discovered the woman he'd rescued was still in the picture. So, to save his friend from making a disastrous mistake that could lead to his financial ruin, he'd never told Blackthorne that the girl he'd rescued was still in England. That in fact, the girl Blackthorne had never been able to forget was never any farther away than Tearlach Castle.

But Seaton hadn't immediately sent the girl back to America, either. He'd left her exactly where she was, because sometimes miracles happened. If, by some chance, Blackthorne was able to restore his fortune, Seaton had wanted to be able to fulfill his sister's request to reunite Blackthorne with the waif he'd rescued.

As it turned out, his friend had married an American heiress. Seaton was now at liberty to send the American girl back where she'd come from. He'd done nothing to change Fanny's instructions to his solicitor following his sister's death, which meant the girl had remained exactly where Fanny had put her for safekeeping—but for a far longer period than Fanny had ever intended. It had taken three months for the girl's back to heal sufficiently for her to leave London. In a perfect world, the girl's subsequent stay at Tearlach Castle would only have lasted the brief six months his sister had lived after that, before she died giving birth.

But Fanny's plan had gone terribly awry. She hadn't counted on Blackthorne's grief. Or his financial woes. Consequently, what had been meant to be a short delay in returning the girl to America—assuming Blackthorne's infatuation was merely that—had become a full two years.

Poor girl, Seaton thought. It was past time he sent her home.

It was still important that he know as little as possible about the American, because now, more than ever, Seaton didn't want to slip and give away the truth. If—when—Blackthorne indulged his need to talk about her, Seaton wanted to be ignorant of her situation.

All he had to do was show up at Tearlach Castle and ask to speak to the American who worked there as a maid. He would let her know that arrangements for her return to America were being made through his solicitor.

Seaton planned to apologize for the delay in fulfilling the promise to send her back to America, without bringing Blackthorne into the discussion. With any luck, she would simply be happy to go back where she'd come from, and he could return home and forget any of this had ever happened.

He was keeping his fingers crossed that everything would turn out all right, but deep down he knew, the same way he knew green apples made one sick as a dog, that something was bound to go wrong.

Chapter 20

THE TELEGRAM WAS dated several days earlier than the day it reached Henrietta Wentworth Norwood in the Bitterroot Valley, about as far west as you could get and still be in the Montana Territory. "Karl," she said, clutching the missive to her chest, as she closed the door on the messenger who'd delivered it. "Miranda sent me a telegram."

Karl, who was serving breakfast to their eighteen-month-old twin girls, Charlene and Caroline, handed two bowls of oatmeal to his twelve-year-old stepson, Griffin, who set the food in front of two brown-haired, brown-eyed little girls, while Karl crossed to take his wife in his arms.

He still couldn't believe a man as plain-featured as he was could be married to a woman as stunningly beautiful as his wife. Even more amazing was the fact that she loved him as dearly as he loved her.

"I guess Miranda finally has some news about Josie," he said.

"Maybe they found her." Hetty's blue eyes were filled with both anxiety and hope.

"Why don't you read the telegram and find out?" Griffin suggested with a laugh.

Hetty shot Karl a terrified look that spoke volumes. Her greatest fear was that word would come that Josie had been found all right—found planted six feet under. The longer Josie was missing, the worse Hetty's foreboding had grown.

Karl caught his wife's stricken face between his two large hands and pressed a comforting kiss on her lips. "Read it, before you weep."

Hetty laughed nervously and pressed her forehead against Karl's chest. "You know me too well."

Karl knew the unendurable guilt Hetty had suffered, as a result of the disaster that had befallen her and her two sisters on the trail. His wife blamed herself for every bad thing that had happened to the three of them since.

Against Hannah's advice, Hetty had flirted with two men at the same time, not realizing that in the West, jealous battles were settled in ways far more deadly than she could have imagined. In the confrontation she'd caused, both men had ended up dead. Even worse, she and Hannah and Josie, and Hannah's husband, Mr. McMurtry, had been forced to leave the safety of the wagon train and travel on alone.

Shortly thereafter, Mr. McMurtry had died of cholera, Josie had been stolen away by the Sioux, and Hetty had been left behind at the wagon, while Hannah went for help. It was only by the grace of God, and the ministrations of a Chinese man named Lin Bao, that Hetty had survived the arrow wound in her shoulder.

Bao had come across Hetty's wagon while returning to the Bitterroot Valley from Cheyenne, after picking up Karl Norwood's mail-order bride and her two children, Grace and Griffin. When Karl's mail-order bride was accidentally killed, Hetty discovered that Grace and Griffin weren't really the woman's children. In fact, it was Grace who'd written all the letters from his intended bride to Karl. The young girl been looking for a way out of the terrible life she and her brother had led in Cheyenne.

With Bao's help and encouragement, seventeen-year-old Hetty had stepped into the shoes of Karl's much-older mail-order bride. They'd decided to tell Karl the children were several years younger than the thirteen and ten years old they actually were, while she would pretend to be their mother.

Karl hadn't been fooled. He'd known his bride wasn't twenty-eight any more than he was a cornstalk, and the children had looked too old for their ages and neither like each other nor their supposed mother. But he'd never seen a woman as breathtakingly lovely as Henrietta Wentworth when she smiled and twin dimples appeared on her cheeks. And he liked children enough to take on the two she'd brought with her.

So he'd married Hetty. And—except for the brief period when an endless spate of lies had come to light—never been sorry. In fact, they'd all been amazingly happy, especially after Grace met one of Karl's loggers, Andy Peterson. His stepdaughter and the Texan had married last summer and were living in a house he and Andy had built not far down the road. Everything would have been picture perfect, except for the shadow of guilt that hung over his wife, keeping their life under the wide-open Montana skies from being absolutely cloudless. He hoped the telegram contained good news. He wanted his wife to be as wholly happy as he was himself.

Hetty was still holding the telegram clutched against her breasts, her eyes closed as though in prayer.

"Why don't you read it, Mom?" Griffin said.

She opened her blue eyes, which looked bleak. "What if it's bad news?"

Karl *tsked* and countered, "What if the news is good?"

At that moment, the door opened with a bang and Grace stood there with the spring breeze ruffling her red curls. Andy was only a step behind her. "I saw the messenger leaving," she said breathlessly. "What's happened? Has Josie been found?"

"That's what we're all trying to find out," Griffin said. "Mom hasn't opened the telegram yet."

"Open it, Mom!" Grace said. "I know it's good news. It just has to be!"

Hetty shot another desperate look at Karl, who gave her an encouraging smile, revealing the overlapping front tooth that she'd said was one of the reasons she'd fallen in love with him.

"All right," she said almost angrily, tearing the telegram open and quickly perusing the contents.

Karl felt his heart stop when he saw her face scrunch up and heard her sob. "Hetty?"

She looked at him through eyes shiny with tears, but the wobbly smile—and the enchanting dimples that suddenly appeared in her cheeks—told a different story. "Josie's been found! She's on her way from England to Charleston right now. Miranda wants all of us to be there when Josie arrives at Jake's ranch. We're going to be together again at last!" She scanned the telegram and frowned. "This is days old! We need to leave right away, if we're going to be there in time."

"Are we really going to visit Aunt Miranda?" Griffin asked.

Hetty's heart was in her eyes as she asked, "Karl? Can we go?"

Karl loved his wife for salving his pride by asking, but the truth was she had a fortune of her own to cover the cost, if she wanted to make the trip. The logging business Karl had come to the valley to start had faltered, and he and Andy had been making plans to buy a herd of cattle and drive it north, to provide beef for the valley's growing population.

"I wouldn't miss a chance to see the infamous Josephine Wentworth in person," he said, pulling Hetty into his arms and hugging her tight. "Besides, a trip to Texas will give me and Andy the perfect opportunity to get our cattle business started."

"Then we're all going?" Grace asked, glancing at her husband over her shoulder.

"Why not?" Andy replied.

Grace threw herself into his arms. "I can't wait to meet Mom's family and see where you grew up."

Griffin hooted and said, "We're going to Texas!"

Caroline banged her spoon on the table and said, "Tex-as!"

Charlene mimicked her twin, and the two ended up chanting, "Tex-as! Tex-as! Tex-as!"

Karl laughed and said, "I guess it's unanimous. How soon can everyone be packed?"

Chapter 21

JOSIE'S HEART SANK to her toes when she got her first look at Blackthorne Abbey. She had the example of Tearlach Castle to show her how run-down a medieval dwelling could get. And Blackthorne's estimate of "months" to repair the crumbling walls and bring the overgrown landscape back under control seemed optimistic.

Although it was called the Abbey, for the monks who'd once lived there, Blackthorne's ancestral home was, in fact, a gray stone castle. It had turrets—towers raised above the castle wall to give a view of the valley below, and crenels—the gaps between the stonework at the top of the castle wall, through which defenders would have fought. It even possessed a foul-smelling moat.

Josie fought a welling of despair as the carriage that had brought them from the railway station passed over the drawbridge and under the portcullis— a strong oak grille that had once protected the gate against attack—and then through another gateway to the middle bailey. Beyond this unkempt court-yard stood the stone keep itself, a building several stories high with majestic, arched mullioned windows that must have been added sometime over the past few centuries.

"When Henry II created the first Duke of Blackthorne, the Abbey housed twenty knights and their retainers," Blackthorne said. "The bed the king slept in when he visited is still here. It's a massive thing, with a carved footboard depicting some knight decapitating his enemy in battle."

Josie shuddered. "I wouldn't think that would encourage a peaceful night's sleep." Her gaze slid from the broken-down castle to Blackthorne's face and remained there, caught by the glow of excitement in his eyes. He was apparently seeing the castle as it used to be, in valiant days gone by, not as it was.

He turned his head to speak directly to her, and she flushed at being caught staring. Josie lowered her gaze to her hands, which were tightly knotted in her lap. She couldn't imagine why she felt so edgy. Except, if the exterior condition of the Abbey was any guide, the necessary repairs inside might take far longer than Blackthorne was willing to wait to return to her bed—or she was willing to wait to bring Spencer and Clay to live with them.

It had occurred to her that she might bargain away one thing—the duke in her bed—for the other—his nephews safe at the Abbey.

"The Abbey is full of ancient armor, including shields and swords and pikes, and a dank dungeon full of grisly torture devices," he continued. "Once upon a time, the dungeon even boasted a skeleton. It finally got decently buried a couple of generations ago."

Josie found the duke's enthusiasm infectious and realized he was reliving a happier time in his youth, when he might have imagined himself as a heroic knight fighting with all those medieval weapons and then putting his enemy to the sword.

"The monks created a myriad of secret passages in the walls leading to almost every room in the castle, including the dungeon," Blackthorne continued. "My brother and I . . ."

He paused and stared out the window. She watched him swallow hard before he continued, "Monty and I got locked in the dungeon once. We were there for three days before our father found us. He whipped me, because I was the elder. I was. By a year. He said I should have known better.

"He didn't take into account the fact that I'd gone looking for Monty because he'd disappeared, and his governess was going to suffer for it. Monty shut the door to the dungeon and locked us in because he didn't want to spend the morning studying. He said he'd rather die first. We very nearly did."

When Blackthorne turned back to her, he had a bittersweet smile on his face. "Monty was charming and funny. Somehow, he never ended up getting punished." His voice hardened as he added, "It was a mistake I don't intend to make with my own children."

Josie thought she was glimpsing that "other" Blackthorne again, the one who could abandon his nephews. "You intend to punish your children regularly?"

"I intend to discipline them," he corrected. "My

brother was never held accountable for anything he did wrong, so he felt no sense of responsibility for his actions. He left a great deal of hurt and harm in his wake, and he died an unnecessary death that left his sons without a father to guide them."

Or an uncle willing to pick up that burden, Josie thought.

"Your brother left children behind? Where are they now?"

"My nephews—Spencer is eight and Clay is six— are living in the country, where they have plenty of fresh air and room to play."

That was a bucolic description that bore scant resemblance to the truth, Josie thought. Did the duke truly not realize the nerve-wracking circumstances in which his nephews were living? Or was he painting a rose-colored picture for her benefit?

Josie had a sudden shocking thought. "If your brother's children are six and eight, and he was a year younger than you, he must have been no more than a boy when he was wed."

Blackthorne's lips twisted wryly. "Monty was eighteen. His wife was a girl of sixteen. She was nearly six months gone when the girl's widowed father discovered she was with child and came to see my father. He allowed the marriage because she was from a noble family, and because Monty swore he loved her.

"Unfortunately, my brother's infatuation with his child bride didn't last much past the birth of his heir. His wife died of influenza shortly after his second son was born—with the cord wrapped around his neck. As a result, Clay will likely always need someone to care for him. By the time Monty died, his wife's father had passed away, which left me in charge of my brother's children."

Josie wondered if Blackthorne knew how much Spencer loved—and leapt to the rescue of—his less able brother. "Why don't they live with you?"

A shadow crossed his face, and Josie wondered what had caused it. Guilt? She hoped so, for his sake. That might mean he had a heart. That might mean he had tender feelings, even if they hadn't been much in evidence. He should be ashamed of abandoning the girl he'd rescued, of not caring enough to make certain she'd been returned to her family in America. He should be ashamed of forgetting his nephews, of leaving them to fend for themselves in the care of a resentful governess and a bitter housekeeper.

He shot her a puzzled look. "I wouldn't know what to do with two young boys, other than what I'm doing now."

You could love them and care for them! Josie bit back the words, because they would reveal far too much. "You could as easily hire a governess to take care of them in London as anywhere else. At least then you'd know they were safe and secure. And they'd know you love them and care for them."

The duke frowned at her. "I don't appreciate your insinuation that I *don't* love them or care for them. I'm doing everything my father ever did for me and Monty."

"And you believe that's enough? When was the last time you saw them?" Josie challenged.

"I—"

Josie figured he'd cut himself off because, as she well knew, he hadn't seen them for more than two years.

He continued, "There were good reasons why I couldn't visit them recently. Or have them visit me. Besides, I get regular reports on their condition."

"From whom?"

"My solicitor."

"From whom does he get his reports?" Josie persisted.

"How should I know? Someone reliable, I'm sure."

"How sure are you? For all you know, your own flesh and blood could be wearing rags, stealing scraps from the table, and sleeping in the attic."

"You're being ridiculous."

"Am I?" Josie could feel the blood rushing through her veins, sending a flush into her cheeks. Spencer and Clay's situation wasn't that bad, but it could have been, for all Blackthorne knew. "How long since you've seen your nephews in person? How long since you've spoken to them? How long since you've played with them or read to them or hugged them or—" Josie cut herself off when she saw the look of shock and incredulity in the duke's eyes but then decided to finish what she'd started. "Or told them you loved them?"

"Where is all this coming from?"

"I just think . . ."

He made a sound in his throat. "I believe I understand. You're concerned for my nephews because you know what it's like to be without parents. I assure you, Josie, Spencer and Clay have not been abandoned."

"But—"

"I can see I'll have to prove it to you. I'll arrange for them to visit us, once we've restored the Abbey."

It dawned on Josie that Blackthorne might have given her the perfect opportunity to retrieve the boys from Tearlach Castle sooner than she'd hoped. "Why not have them brought here now?" she suggested. "That way, you'll be able to ask them yourself about their living conditions—whatever they are," she hurried to add, since she could see the objection forming on his lips.

The carriage stopped before an oversized wooden double door hung on huge brass hinges that appeared to be the entrance to the Abbey.

"Why don't we take a look inside before we make that decision?"

Josie was ready to argue further, but the footman had already opened the carriage door. Blackthorne stepped out, then held out his hand to help Josie down. As she set her foot on the stone flags, she made up her mind that, unless Blackthorne Abbey was a total ruin, she was going to plead for Spencer and Clay to be allowed to come live with them as soon as they could be safely transported from Northumberland.

She expected the duke to let go of her hand when she reached the bottom stone step, but he held on and headed up the half dozen steps to the door. It was hard to imagine the duke was nervous, but after all, it must be difficult to see his boyhood home in such a terrible state.

The footman raced ahead of them to open the door, but it was stuck. Blackthorne let go of her hand and lent his muscle to the effort, and the right-hand door creaked open enough to allow them inside, scraping on stone as the top hinge sagged.

Blackthorne shook his head in apparent disgust, then reached out a hand to her. Josie realized he must be dreading what he might see inside and needed her support to face whatever he found. She clasped his hand and followed him into the Abbey.

No stream of servants came running. In fact, the place looked empty, unless someone was hiding in the standing suits of armor on either side of the entrance. Cobwebs draped the chandelier in the central hallway. A grand stone staircase covered by a tattered rug spread upward before them, while streaks of sunlight fought their way through windows overgrown with ivy.

Blackthorne stood inside without moving. Josie had never seen such a ravaged look on a person's face. Something terrible must have happened to him here. He'd mentioned his father several times, but not his mother. What had happened to her? Or to his father, for that matter? How had they died? Had this home been the site of some family tragedy? Was that why he'd spent so little time at the Abbey as a boy?

Their footsteps on the stone floor echoed off the tall ceilings as he drew her down the hall to a library, with its three walls of shelves crammed with musty books. He hesitated only a moment before he led her past two separate drawing rooms filled with furniture with clawed legs (which was all she could see, since they were covered with dusty sheets), a dining room with a table that seated sixteen, and a gallery containing portraits of what she presumed were past Dukes and Duchesses of Blackthorne.

He didn't pause long enough for her to pose the question. His eyes roamed each room as though he were looking for something. Or someone. He apparently didn't find whatever it was he sought, because he kept moving.

Josie got only a glimpse of a chapel with six pews made colorful by the light from stained-glass windows, before they arrived at a kitchen that looked as if nothing had been cooked there for a hundred years.

"I thought you said you lived here as a child," Josie said.

"I did."

She shook her head in disbelief that anyone could have used such an antiquated stove and brick oven. "Where are the servants?"

"I had to let most of the household staff go a year past."

Josie's heartbeat ratcheted up a notch. "All of them? You don't have a housekeeper? Or a cook?"

"A number of candidates for each position will be here this afternoon. I thought you might want to choose the staff yourself."

Josie was pleased that she would have an opportunity to select the household help she would be supervising, but she was also surprised. "I expected to find a flock of servants who'd been here all their lives."

"The housekeeper passed away three months ago, and I didn't have the heart to replace her. The butler is around here somewhere. I thought we'd see him before this. I consider Harkness to be family. Six generations of Harkness men have worked at Blackthorne Abbey, and Harkness has been overseer here for the past year."

At that moment, a stooped gentleman with pure white hair came down a set of back stairs to the kitchen, bracing himself against the stone wall all the way. When he reached the floor, he straightened as much as he could and said, "Your Grace, it's good to see you."

"And you, Harkness. You haven't aged a day since you took me over your knee for stealing tarts from Cook."

The duke was grinning, and Josie realized the ancient retainer must be even older than she'd imagined.

"I apologize for not being here to greet you, Your Grace," Harkness said, "but the mice have—"

"You have mice?" Josie croaked past a fear-constricted throat. "Upstairs? In the bedrooms?" She was terrified of the flesh-eating rodents. Mice and rats had been the bane of her existence at the orphanage. It had been her job every morning to empty the sickening traps that contained the vermin, bound there by their squashed limbs or snapped necks.

"They should all be gone now," Harkness reassured her. "I found a tabby who's turned out to be quite a mouser. Fitch, I call her. I wanted to make sure your rooms were salubrious before bedtime, so I set Fitch to work."

Josie wished she could be certain they were all gone. She was glad she wouldn't be subjected to mice in traps, but she wasn't sure she would be any happier finding one in Fitch's mouth.

"Are you all right?" Blackthorne asked.

She shuddered. "I hate vermin!"

"I'm not crazy about them, either," he said with an indulgent smile.

She wanted to say more but bit her lip to keep from speaking. She was supposedly an heiress. Where would an heiress learn so much about rats and mice? So she held her tongue. But she made up her mind to get herself a cat and keep it in the bedroom at night. Cats hadn't been allowed at the orphanage in Chicago any more than Mrs. Pettibone had allowed them inside Tearlach Castle. Josie had always wondered what it would be like to have a kitten to pet and to pamper. Maybe, at long last, she would have that experience, now that she would be the one making those sorts of decisions.

It dawned on her that she was going to have a lot of opportunities to do things she'd never done and to have things she'd never had. Josie couldn't quite imagine what that sort of freedom might be like.

"Shall we take a look upstairs?" Blackthorne said, gesturing back down the hall toward the main stairs.

"I can't wait." He shot a look at her, and Josie realized she hadn't done a very good job of keeping the cynicism out of her voice. But what she expected to see upstairs was more rot in the linens, thicker dust on the furniture, and heavier mold on the dank stone walls.

She preceded Blackthorne up two flights of stairs but stopped once she reached the top, so he could direct her one way or the other down halls that led in opposite directions.

He gestured her down the hall on the right and led her to the corner room. Inside, she found tall windows draped with rotted red velvet curtains trimmed in gold braid and a fabulous rug, with images of the Crusades, on the stone floor. What little of the glass windowpanes were visible through ivy revealed rolling hills that ended in a brook that ran across the valley, which then rose to forests as far as the eye could see.

Most of the room was taken up with the huge mahogany bed King Henry II had supposedly slept in, which was covered with a moth-eaten, gold brocade counterpane. Josie couldn't resist the urge to see the scene Blackthorne had described in the carriage. She edged around to the side of the bed to take a look at the carving, which was only visible when one was lying in bed.

A chill ran down her spine as she studied the brutal images. She hadn't expected the medieval battle to look quite so lifelike. Or the death of the knight to seem quite so ruthless.

She glanced at her husband. Having run her hands over his broad, powerful shoulders and muscular arms, she could easily imagine Blackthorne being capable of that sort of ferocity.

Except, the current duke had nothing to fight except mold and decay.

Blackthorne smoothed a hand along the top of the footboard as he said, "This is the master suite." His hand trailed off as he crossed to a door and opened it. "This will be your room."

Josie was careful not to brush against her husband, as she crossed into the bedroom connected to his, but she wasn't quite successful. She bit back a gasp when her breasts brushed against his chest as she squeezed past him. She stepped farther into the room, determined to ignore her body's sensual response to even that slight touch.

She forced her breathing to slow as she surveyed her bed, which was surely fit for a queen, although no famous one had apparently slept there. The counterpane was emerald green to match the moth-eaten green velvet curtains trimmed in gold fringe.

"There *is* a lock on this door," he said as he crossed into her room and pulled the door between the two rooms closed.

Josie could see a skeleton key in the lock. He pulled it free and crossed to hand it to her. She drew the inference from the tone of his voice and the distaste with which he handed her the key, that the door might have been locked in the days when his mother and father had occupied these rooms.

She closed her hand around the key, took a deep breath, and said, "How long ago did you lose your mother?"

"I was ten."

That was about the same time Blackthorne had said he'd left the Abbey as a boy. Josie waited for an explanation of how his mother had died, but it didn't come. So she asked, "What happened?"

"She disappeared."

Josie hadn't been expecting that. "What do you mean?"

"I mean one day she was here, and the next day she was gone."

"Gone where?"

"Your guess is as good as mine. My mother wasn't a happy woman. My parents fought often and loudly. My father didn't trust her to be faithful, so he kept her immured in the Abbey. But he was often gone. She detested being left by herself so much of the time, but there was no possibility of divorce. After the twins were born, she drank too much and slept the days away. I imagine she finally got her fill of the situation—and us—and left."

Josie heard the underlying pain in his admission. She couldn't imagine how any mother could leave her children behind, no matter how difficult the marriage. Her parents had been happy together, so she had nothing with which to compare the awful relationship her husband had described.

"So your mother may still be alive?"

He shrugged. "Anything is possible." He crossed to stare out the window through a small space where no ivy blocked the view. "When my father died—he overdosed on laudanum—I hoped she might contact me. But she never did."

He turned back to face her and continued, "Even if she isn't dead, nothing remains of her now but memories of shouting matches and shattered wine goblets that I'd rather forget."

Josie crossed to him and slid her arms around his waist, laying her cheek against his chest and holding him close. It took a moment before she felt his arms close around her.

"I'm so sorry, Marcus. So very sorry."

Josie understood a little better why her husband might have left his nephews to languish. He certainly hadn't learned from his own parents how to nurture a growing child. Maybe she could do some good before she left. Maybe she could teach the duke how to express the love for his nephews he'd insisted he felt.

And if the duke does love them? Should I leave them in his care when I return to my family?

What if something came up as soon as she was gone, and he abandoned them again?

Josie couldn't bear to think of the two boys alone and unhappy, but she had family of her own she ached to see. She caught her lower lip in her teeth, as she struggled with the difficult choices ahead of her, and realized she was putting the cart before the horse. The first thing to do was reunite the boys with their uncle and see how he behaved with them.

It suddenly dawned on her that, even if she somehow managed to get the duke and his nephews together, she had another problem.

How could she keep her prior relationship with the boys a secret? Realistically, it was impossible. Spencer might be willing and able to keep a secret. But Clay would surely slip.

So where does that leave me?

Josie released a breath of air she hadn't realized she'd been holding. When the boys came, she would tell Blackthorne the truth about herself. She would also tell him why she didn't trust him to take care of Spencer and Clay. She would explain, in a way he could understand, why they would be far better off living with her.

What if he doesn't really love them, but refuses to let me take them away with me?

Josie suddenly became aware of Blackthorne's steady gaze, curiosity clear on his face, and realized she must have been silent—lost in her thoughts— for quite some time. As she looked into his piercing blue eyes, she decided that, in the end, she had no choice. If Blackthorne didn't love his nephews, and he balked at letting her take them with her when she left, she would simply have to steal them.

Chapter 22

AFTER HER EXPERIENCE with Mrs. Pettibone, Josie was determined to find a housekeeper for Blackthorne Abbey who loved children and could stand to have them underfoot, since she hoped to have Spencer and Clay living with her soon. She'd been speaking with candidates for three hours and hadn't yet found the right person for the job.

Then Miss Harriet Carpenter stepped into the sitting room.

Josie figured the young woman was only a few years older than she was herself. Miss Carpenter's plain, navy-blue princess sheath, which was of good quality, but worn, her perfect posture, her frayed gloves, the tinge of pink in her alabaster cheeks, and her worried, dove-gray eyes suggested that she was more used to doing the questioning than to being questioned. Josie looked at the information she'd been given and realized Miss Carpenter had applied without references.

"Please be seated, Miss Carpenter," Josie said, gesturing to a tattered brocade wing chair across from the claw-footed sofa on which she sat.

The newest applicant settled herself on the edge

of the chair, her hands folded in her lap. Before Josie could ask the first question, Miss Carpenter said, "I know I'm young for this job, but I've managed a household in the past, Your Grace, and I promise I will work hard to please you."

She bit her lip to keep herself from saying more, and Josie could see it was taking a great deal of effort for the young woman not to fidget. She was tempted to hire Miss Carpenter on the spot, because she saw a great deal of herself in the woman sitting across from her. But she'd been desperately hoping to find a housekeeper who had more experience than she did in managing such a huge estate.

"Where have you worked in the past?" she asked.

The tinge of pink in Miss Carpenter's cheeks became a rosy flush. "I managed my father's manor before . . ." She stopped and glanced out the window, swallowing hard before she turned back to Josie and said, "Before I was forced to leave."

She didn't explain the circumstances that had "forced" her to leave, but Josie could easily imagine what might have happened. Miss Carpenter's father had likely died, leaving her without means. English law distributed all property to the closest male relative, and it was entirely possible that whichever male had inherited her father's estate had not been willing to support her.

"As you can see," Josie said, gesturing toward the dilapidated furnishings in the room, "everything here needs a great deal of work."

"I'm used to hard work, Your Grace."

"How would you feel about having children underfoot?"

Miss Carpenter sent a pointed look toward Josie's waist. "Are you . . ."

Josie settled a hand over her womb. "I'm not expecting." Although there was still the possibility that Blackthorne's seed had taken root. "The duke has two nephews, six and eight, who may be—who *will* be—coming to live here shortly." Somehow she was determined to get them here.

"I love children. I grew up with three younger sisters and had the care of them all my life. My greatest sorrow is that I had to abandon them when I left home."

Josie felt her sympathy, and empathy, for Miss Carpenter growing as she learned more about the young woman's situation. She, too, had left family behind. "Where are your sisters now?"

"They live with an aunt, Your Grace."

Not *our* aunt. Just *an* aunt. Were her siblings related to the aunt, but not her? Or had the aunt sent her out to earn her own living? Josie wondered if Miss Carpenter dreamed, as she had for years, of being reunited with her family someday.

"You're hired."

The look of astonishment on Miss Carpenter's face made Josie smile.

"I am?" The young woman blinked quickly to hide what might have been tears and added, "Your Grace?"

Josie rose and crossed the room. By the time she got there, Miss Carpenter was on her feet and composed again. "I think the first thing we have to do is dispose of all this formality. Please call me Josie. May I call you Harriet?"

"Of course, Your Grace."

"Of course, *Josie*."

Miss Carpenter's smile reached her gray eyes, which crinkled at the corners. "Of course, Josie. Please call me Harriet."

Josie felt a sudden qualm at what the duke would think when he saw how young, and arguably inexperienced, their new housekeeper was. Not to mention the fact that Miss Carpenter came without references.

He'll think his duchess is a fool. That she isn't responsible enough to be put in charge of such an important decision. That she allowed her emotions to take over, rather than using reason to make her choice.

Josie gritted her teeth. It didn't matter what Blackthorne thought. What was important was to create a safe, happy home for Spencer and Clay, which made Miss Carpenter a perfect addition to the duke's household.

"Where would you like me to start?" her new housekeeper asked.

Josie chewed her lower lip while she thought, uncertain exactly where to put Harriet to work, and then had a brilliant idea. "You can finish up these interviews." Josie counted off on her fingers the different kinds of help she needed. "With luck you can find us a good cook, a few maids, some footmen, a gardener, and whoever else you think might be necessary to help us put the house and grounds in order."

"Wouldn't you rather choose those people yourself?" Harriet asked hesitantly.

"If you've managed a household in the past, you're one step ahead of me," Josie admitted.

"Very well," Harriet said. "What about a steward? And someone to manage the stables?"

"I believe the duke will be selecting people for those positions." But she wasn't sure. "I'll check with him and let you know."

The first thing Josie did was go to her room and change out of the dress she'd put on to impress the help. There was work to be done, and she was itching to start. She wrapped a scarf around her hair, much as she'd done when she was a maid-of-all-work, and put on the apron she'd brought from the kitchen to cover the simplest dress she now owned.

Then she went to work in the duke's bedroom, where there was no chance she'd be seen by the stream of prospective servants being interviewed by her new housekeeper. It was enormously satisfying to see the gleam appear on tables and chests as she wiped away decades of dust.

Once she'd cleaned Blackthorne's room, she headed back into her own. It looked considerably lighter than it had when she'd changed her clothes just a short while ago. Then she realized the reason why. One of the windows was now completely clear of ivy. Harriet really was a wonder, she thought, if she'd already put a gardener to work.

When she went to the window to observe the man, it wasn't a gardener standing on the ladder perched three stories high against the Abbey wall.

It was her husband.

Josie turned and ran down the stairs, passing a startled young woman with a broom in her hands,

who barely had time to curtsy before Josie was past
her and out the front door. She nearly ran into the
ladder that had been set up across the main entrance. She stepped around the ladder, at which
point a spray of ivy landed on her head. She jerked
sideways, more startled than hurt, then ducked out
of the way of another falling sprig, shading her
eyes against the glare of the sun, as she confirmed
what she'd seen through the upstairs window. The
Duke of Blackthorne was, indeed, trimming the ivy
away from her bedroom window.

She resisted the urge to shout at him, fearing he
might lose his balance. Speaking in as normal a
voice as she could muster in her winded condition,
she called up to him, "Isn't that a job for our new
gardener?"

"Do we have one?" He focused his gaze on her,
and a quizzical look appeared on his face.

She reached up to brush aside a strand of hair
being whipped across her face by the wind and
realized she was still wearing a scarf on her head
and an apron over her dress.

He'd taken off his jacket, opened his shirt at the
throat, rolled up his sleeves to reveal strong forearms, and was holding a large pair of garden shears,
which made her feel a little better about her own
attire.

"We'll surely have someone to do this sort of
work by tomorrow," she replied.

He shot her a boyish grin. "I didn't think this
could wait. I want you to see the sun rise in the
morning. I presume we'll have maids by tomorrow
as well, but judging by that scarf on your head and

that apron you're wearing, you seem to have made yourself busy cleaning."

"I was just an ordinary person the day before yesterday," she pointed out. "On the other hand, I didn't think dukes indulged in manual labor." She realized she'd discounted her wealth in that statement. Heiresses probably didn't spend a lot of their time cleaning. But he didn't seem to have noticed her gaffe.

Blackthorne started down the ladder, and she took a step back to give him room, once he reached the ground. His shirt was damp with sweat, and she was aware of a not-unpleasant masculine odor as he dropped the shears on the tall grass beside the stone walk. "I wasn't complaining," he said as he tugged the scarf off her head and let it swing from his hand. "But I can't guarantee the neighbors won't be appalled by my new duchess's appearance."

"You're the one up a ladder half undressed, for anyone passing by to see."

He grinned, and she felt her stomach do a strange flip-flop. Unconsciously, she took another step back, as though to escape some web that threatened to entangle her.

"They expect outrageous behavior from me."

"Why is that?" she asked, aware that she was having trouble catching her breath.

He reached out and tucked a flying curl behind her ear, his knuckles lingering as they brushed her cheek. In a low, quiet voice he said, "We Blackthornes are known to be a scurrilous lot."

"It would have been nice to know that *before* I married you."

He laughed and tweaked her nose, then tossed her the scarf, which she caught in the air, as he bent to retrieve the shears. "I'd better get back to work. Call me when you have some food on the table."

Josie stared at his broad back, followed by his buttocks and thighs, as he headed back up the ladder, then realized what she was doing and hurried back inside.

Chapter 23

JOSIE COULDN'T BELIEVE she was married to the man sitting to her right at the head of the dining table. The duke had dressed for supper, and it was hard to believe that this arresting man, in his formal attire, was the same one who'd spent the day in a blousy white shirt and tight-fitting pants cutting ivy from the windows.

She felt unaccountably nervous and searched for something she could say to break the silence that had fallen between them, as they waited for dessert to be served. She finally came up with, "Harriet is a wonder."

"Oh?" Blackthorne replied. "Miss Carpenter, you mean?"

He hadn't criticized Josie for putting herself on a first-name basis with the housekeeper, but he'd refused to call Harriet anything other than Miss Carpenter. Josie continued determinedly, "Harriet found the cook who made this wonderful meal."

Blackthorne merely lifted a dark brow, which was the same reaction he'd had when he'd first been introduced to their new housekeeper. Josie had been relieved to see that Harriet's chin remained up when she'd met the duke, although the young woman hadn't been able to control the blush that rose on her cheeks. "I know she's young," Josie said, feeling the need to defend her choice, even though the duke hadn't attacked it.

"She's a veritable babe in the woods," the duke agreed sardonically.

"I like her."

"That's important," the duke conceded.

"Yes, it is." Josie wanted to argue, but Blackthorne wasn't giving her much of an opening. She'd been feeling increasingly on edge the closer they got to the end of the meal, which was to say, the closer they got to bedtime. Would he escort her to her bedroom door? Would he kiss her good night? Would he ask if he could join her? If he did, what would she say? She was tempted to say yes. Oh, how she was tempted!

"What are your plans tomorrow?" Blackthorne asked.

"There are dozens of things in the house that require my attention. Did you have something else in mind?"

"I'd like to show you the estate and perhaps visit a few of our neighbors. Can you ride?"

She wasn't as comfortable on horseback as her twin sisters, but as a child, Josie had always enjoyed riding. "That sounds wonderful. And yes, I can ride. Do we have horses?"

"I had a few mounts transported here by train. They arrived late this afternoon."

"Good." Josie was about to ask which neighbors he planned to visit, when the newest footman set a bowl in front of the duke. "It's a trifle," she said. "I'd never heard of such a thing before I arrived in England. I didn't know what you liked, but I thought—"

"It looks delicious," Blackthorne said, cutting her off.

Josie realized she'd been babbling. Dinner was clearly almost over. The duke was planning to spend the day with her tomorrow. But what about tonight? Did he have plans for her tonight?

"You aren't eating yours," the duke pointed out. "Don't you like it?"

"Honestly? It's not a favorite of mine. Too many different flavors all mashed together." A trifle contained sponge cake brushed with raspberry jam and then soaked with sherry, interspersed with some kind of fruit—in this case, strawberries—as well as custard and whipped cream, served in a glass dish, so all the layers were visible.

Josie watched as Blackthorne devoured the dessert. When his tongue lapped up a tiny bit of whipped cream beside his mouth, she shivered, remembering where he'd used that tongue on her.

She watched as the duke set down his spoon and arranged his napkin on the table. She'd taken only one bite of her trifle, but she didn't think she could get a second bite past the sudden knot in her throat. She set down her spoon and dabbed unnecessarily at her mouth, before setting her napkin beside her plate.

"Shall I leave you alone to have a brandy?" she asked. "Or a cigar? Do you smoke?"

He smiled. "I do enjoy brandy and a cigar now

and then. But I would rather have your company right now."

"Oh."

"Shall we go into the library? I can as easily have a brandy there. Perhaps you would like to read for a while before we retire."

Anything that postponed bedtime sounded fine to Josie. "Yes, I would."

She was half out of her chair by the time he got there to move it back for her. He reached for her hand to help her stand, even though she'd been getting out of chairs by herself all her life, and she reluctantly put her hand in his.

Once she was on her feet, he crooked his elbow and pulled her hand through it, so they were walking side by side. She was aware of a woodsy smell that she found pleasing and wrinkled her nose. She didn't want to be pleased by anything about the Dastardly Duke. "Good evening, Harper," she said to the footman who opened the dining room door for them.

"Good evening, Your Grace."

"How are you tonight, Stanley?" she asked the footman who opened the library door for them.

"Very well, Your Grace."

Once they were alone with the library door closed behind them, Josie turned to Blackthorne and said, "I think you intimidate our new servants."

"That's certainly not my intention."

"Nevertheless, I thought I had Harper and Stanley convinced it was perfectly all right to call me Josie. Yet, in your presence, they reverted to that blasted British formality."

Blackthorne chuckled.

"It isn't funny!"

"What you don't seem to understand, my dear, is that the consequence of a servant in England is raised by the consequence of those whom they serve."

Josie frowned. "I don't understand."

"It's far more prestigious for my footmen to be in service to the Duke of Blackthorne and his duchess than to plain old Marcus and Josie."

Josie shook her head and muttered, "I will never understand the English."

The duke chuckled as he poured himself a brandy, while Josie perused the bookshelves, which were filled from top to bottom with still-dusty tomes. She would make it a point to put one of the maids to work in here in the morning.

"Is there something I can help you find?" he asked, as he turned with his filled glass in hand.

Josie had been a voracious reader most of her life. As a child, her parents had bought her so many books, her room was overflowing with them. The orphanage had possessed a surprising number of books donated after the Great Chicago Fire of 1871, and she'd read them all. On her ill-fated journey by Conestoga wagon to Cheyenne, she'd read by the campfire at night, devouring books from a wagon-load of them being carried west by a teacher and his son.

She recognized many books in the Abbey library that she'd read but just as many that she hadn't. A smile broke across her face when she found a large collection of Charles Dickens's works. "Oh, my goodness!"

She ran her fingers across the spines, removing dust so that she could more easily read the titles: *Oliver Twist, The Pickwick Papers, Nicholas Nickleby,* and her favorite, *A Christmas Carol.* She trailed her fingertips across the cherished novels, her heart caught in her throat, hoping against hope that she would find the two titles she'd heard so much about, but which she hadn't yet read. "Oh! Here's one of them!"

"One of what?" the duke asked as he moved to her side.

Reverently, she pulled out the copy of *Great Expectations.* "I've wanted to read this novel forever." She turned to him with a rueful smile. "Well, ever since I started reading Mr. Dickens, anyway."

"When was that?"

"In the orphanage. After my parents died. A girl who came to live there had a copy of *A Christmas Carol.* It was the first Dickens novel I read."

He frowned. "You lived in an orphanage?"

Josie realized her mistake. She'd admitted her parents were deceased, but she hadn't explained the horrible circumstances she and her siblings had lived through after their uncle had stolen their inheritance and sent them off to live in an orphanage. Their utter destitution had caused her sisters to seek new, more hopeful lives as mail-order brides.

"We were too young when my parents died to take care of ourselves. My uncle decided an orphanage was the best place for us."

She didn't explain that they'd been stuck there

for three years before they discovered that their uncle had stolen their father's fortune and left them to languish. Josie realized in that moment how much Blackthorne's heartless abandonment of his nephews mirrored the behavior of her uncle, who'd turned out to be a villain indeed. No wonder she'd sympathized with their plight!

She was startled out of her dark thoughts by Blackthorne's next question.

"You said you'd found 'one of them.' What's the other Dickens novel you want to read?"

She was happy to have the subject changed and answered, "*A Tale of Two Cities.*"

He recited, " 'It was the best of times, it was the worst of times . . .' "

Josie shot a look at him. "What is that?"

"It's the way the book starts."

"You've read it?"

He nodded.

She turned back to the shelves, unable to contain her excitement. "Is it here somewhere?"

"I'm afraid not. I took it with me to Town the last time I was here—a long time ago. I have no idea where it might be now."

"Oh." Josie couldn't keep the disappointment from her voice.

"It might be in my library in London. Shall I write to my housekeeper and have her take a look?"

Josie held *Great Expectations* tightly against her bosom, hoping against hope that the other novel could be found. "Would you?"

"Of course. Would you like to sit for a while and read?" He gestured her toward one of two worn leather chairs facing the fireplace, and once she sat down, seated himself in the matching chair next to her.

She opened the book and began to read but couldn't concentrate because she could feel her husband's eyes on her. She kept reading the same paragraph over and over. Finally, she looked up and said, "I can't read with you watching me."

He smiled. "I was admiring the way your blond curls pick up the light from the fire."

She frowned. "It's just hair."

He didn't argue, merely reached out and brushed a tumble of curls behind her shoulder.

Josie shivered at his touch. She felt irritated without knowing why. She closed her book and said, "I think I'll wait to start this until I have more time to read."

"Very well." He set his glass on a side table and rose, then held out his hand to her. "Shall we retire?"

Josie set her hand in his, because it would have been rude to ignore it, and allowed him to help her to her feet. She kept the book under her arm, causing him to ask, "Are you going to take that with you?"

"I thought I would, if it's all right." She hesitated, then added, "I like to read in bed."

He lifted a dark brow.

Josie felt a blush heating her cheeks. His look suggested that he might have something far better for her to do in bed than read, if he were allowed to join her. She let him lead her upstairs to her bedroom door, then pulled her hand free and turned to him. "Good night, Your—" She stopped herself, met his gaze and said, almost defiantly, "Marcus."

He smiled, and gave her a tender look that reached all the way back inside his eyes, before saying in a rumbling voice that reverberated through her body, "Good night, Josie."

Josie stood there for a moment, until she realized she was waiting for him to kiss her. Appalled at her behavior, she shoved open her door, scooted inside, and closed it behind her. She leaned back against the door with her eyes squeezed closed and let out a ragged sigh.

She must have wanted his kiss, since she'd stood there, like a nincompoop, waiting for it. What was wrong with her? Her husband wasn't a good person. Why did she find herself longing for his touch? She would never understand herself.

Josie pulled the book out from under her arm and stared at it with delight. At least she had a good book to keep her company for the evening. As she changed into the frilly white nightgown the dowager had intended for her to wear on her wedding night, she admitted she wouldn't have minded being made love to again. If only Blackthorne were a better person. If only he'd kept his promise to return her to her family. If only she believed he was a man she could trust.

A good book was a much safer alternative than the duke's lovemaking. She could probably read a great deal of *Great Expectations* before sleep claimed her. With any luck, it would distract her from unwelcome memories of making love to the Dastardly Duke.

Chapter 24

JOSIE REARRANGED THE lovely nightgown trimmed in lace around her, then settled into the pillows stacked behind her, so she could read comfortably. Despite how engaging she found the book, her thoughts kept skipping to the man in the next room.

Had she locked the door? Surely she had. It was too cold to get out of bed, walk over there barefoot, and check. Besides, the duke wouldn't come in without knocking first, and if he did, she'd simply tell him to go away.

Or maybe not.

Josie was confused by her feelings, especially her disappointment that Marcus hadn't tried to kiss her good night. Not to mention her willingness to make love to him again. She consoled herself with the knowledge that if he had kissed her, he might have wanted to do more than that.

She pursed her lips in disgust when she realized she would gladly have welcomed him into her bed, especially when she knew full well that any further physical relationship with the Dastardly Duke would only complicate her life.

After reading a few chapters, her eyelids kept sliding closed, and Josie knew she ought to set her spectacles aside, extinguish the lamp, and go to sleep. She had a long day of hard work ahead of her tomorrow, but she was enjoying the story and wanted to read just a little more.

Her eyes fluttered open when something tickled her chin, and she realized the maid must have turned out the lamp and banked the fire after she'd fallen asleep. The open book had fallen to her side. She turned her gaze toward the window, marveling at the moonlight streaming in through windows the duke had cleared of ivy. He'd told her he wanted her to be able to see the sunrise in the morning. She wondered if he'd had any idea how beautiful the moonlight would be.

Josie felt another tickle and brushed at whatever it was. Her fingertips bumped into something furry, something sitting on her shoulder, something that squeaked as she flung her hand across the top of her nightgown to remove it. But tiny claws were caught in the lace collar of her nightgown, and the agitated animal began scratching frantically at her flesh in an attempt to break free.

A rat! It was a huge, hairy rat. And it was going to bite into her flesh at any moment!

Josie screamed in terror and sat bolt upright, just in time to see a small brown mouse go flying toward the foot of the bed. She shoved at the covers with both hands and both feet to get free of the sheets, and leapt out of bed to get away. She heard the mouse's claws skittering along the wooden floor beyond the carpet and shrieked at the thought that it might be heading back in her direction. She didn't even realize where she was going, until she met the duke coming through the doorway between their two rooms to meet her.

"Josie? What's wrong?"

She was trembling too hard and feeling too terrified to respond. She threw her arms around his neck and pressed her body tight against his, which was clothed only in a nightshirt. His hands tightened around her as he said, "I have you. You're safe."

She kept gasping, trying to climb up his body, because she couldn't stand the thought of her bare feet on the frigid wooden floor, where they might be discovered by the carnivorous rodent, until at last, he reached down and lifted her into his arms.

He started to carry her toward her bed and she cried, "No! Not there."

Without a word, he turned and headed back into his room. He tried setting her down on his bed, but she wouldn't let go of his neck, so he slid into bed beside her, pulling her close. Tears were streaming down her face, and she was shuddering at the memory of how close the awful flesh-eater had been to her face, to her throat, to her *ears*.

Josie burrowed her face against her husband's throat and pressed her body against his as tightly as she could. She couldn't get close enough, and begged him, "Hold me tighter."

His arms were already around her, and she felt them tighten. But it wasn't enough. She needed to escape the memories, she needed to escape the past, she needed . . . escape.

"Come inside me. Now," she pleaded, dragging at his nightshirt to pull it away from his hips.

He tore his nightgown off over his head and threw it aside, then pulled her nightgown up to her waist, as he turned her onto her back. Then he drove himself into her to the hilt. His mouth came down to cover hers, and Josie thrust her tongue inside to taste him, as she grasped handfuls of his hair to hold him close. As he levered himself away, she arched her hips to meet him, desperate to maintain the closeness between them.

She ceased to think, aware only of the strength of his arms, the smooth planes of his muscular chest, and the taste of brandy in his mouth. She heard his guttural groan of satisfaction, and reached her own crest of passion, as their bodies sought the oxygen to support them in extremity.

Suddenly, she was flying, completely divorced from her corporeal body, in some ephemeral heaven that she sought to hold onto, but which fled almost as soon as she recognized it for what it was. Then she was sliding into sleep, totally enervated, unable to keep her eyes open even a second longer.

When she awoke—moments later? hours later?— she was aware of being held in the duke's arms. And that he was awake. "I . . ." She hid her face against his shoulder, unsure how to explain her behavior.

"I've read *Great Expectations*," he said wryly. "I don't remember any horrifying passages. What scared you so badly?"

Josie was afraid to admit the truth. It was such a

silly fear. But she had to tell him something, so she said, "A mouse."

He laughed and pulled her snug against him. "A mouse sent you screaming from bed in terror?"

She shoved at his shoulders and said, "Have you ever been bitten? Or seen someone whose flesh has been eaten away in the dark of night?"

"No," he said, putting enough space between them that she could see the frown between his eyes. "I haven't."

"It isn't a pretty sight."

"I take it you *have* been bitten. Or seen someone whose ear has been eaten away?"

She nodded jerkily. "My youngest brother, Harry, had part of his ear chewed off by a mouse at the orphanage. He was wrapped tightly in blankets as a baby to keep him warm and couldn't get his hands free to save himself. His screams brought my eldest sister, Miranda, to the rescue. I got there when she was tearing the mouse free from his ear." She shuddered. "It wouldn't let go."

"There were a lot of mice at the orphanage?"

She nodded, then ducked her head under his chin to hide her face from him. "I've hated mice ever since. When I woke up and found one sitting on my shoulder, I . . . panicked."

She felt his hands smoothing their way across her back outside her silk gown and stiffened in his embrace.

His fingertips were tracing the raised scars from the torture she'd suffered two years ago. First one. And then another. And then another.

She tried to bolt, terrified at the thought of his seeing her mutilated back, but he held her tight, so there was no hope of escape.

His body was tense, his voice low and harsh, as he asked, "What happened to your back, Josie?"

Chapter 25

BLACKTHORNE'S HEART WAS beating so hard his chest hurt. "Answer me! What happened to your back?"

She remained silent, but he could hear her panting in the dark.

"Take off that gown and show me your back."

"No," she whispered, adding in a frightened, quavery voice, "Please. Don't . . ."

Blackthorne held on to his wife's wrist, tugging her resisting body after him as he left the bed, ignoring the nightshirt that lay on the floor, as he headed—heart in his throat, anger at her deception building—for the stream of moonlight that could be seen through his bedroom window.

When he reached it, he slung her around so her gowned body collided with his naked one, then reached up and caught the two sides at the front opening of the gown and ripped the flimsy silk in two. Before she could do more than gasp, he yanked the gown back from her shoulders all the way to her waist, binding her arms and exposing her naked back.

He inhaled a sharp breath and felt gooseflesh rise

on his arms, as he stared at the slashing scars that crisscrossed her flesh. She was breathing in frightened gasps as he angled her body toward the window. The moonlight suddenly revealed the horror of what had been done to her. He reached out hesitantly with the balls of his fingers to trace the largest scar—from the deepest wound—and felt her flesh quiver beneath even that gentle touch. His belly curled in on itself in sympathetic pain and his heart pounded as though he were a child running in fright.

His brain was swirling with questions for which he needed answers. *Where had she been? Why was she here? Why had she married him?* But his throat was too raw and swollen to speak.

The raised scars looked startlingly white in the moonlight. He could still see each one as they'd looked when he'd tended her on the ship.

His wife whimpered like a wounded animal as he traced the scar that ran from just under her arm, across her back, all the way to her hip, and then followed the one that angled from her nape to a spot just under her right breast. He knew each slash intimately. He remembered them as though he'd seen them yesterday. He touched the last, devastating cut she'd received, the one marking in blood what had been virgin flesh.

He could still hear the sound of her scream that long-ago day, as the whip cut into her shoulder. He could still see each deep gash dripping with bright red blood. He shuddered at the memory of her pleading moans not to hurt her anymore, as he'd treated her infected wounds. And he would never forget the sound of her raspy voice, begging him to let her die.

Blackthorne realized he was trembling, and that his breath was coming in harsh breaths as rapid and uneven as hers.

He'd married the woman he'd rescued in the Dakota Territory, the woman he'd fantasized about for two years. He was holding her in his arms. Where was the joy he should be feeling?

Swallowed whole by confusion.

Why hadn't she said something before now? What the hell was going on?

Blackthorne turned his wife so he could see her face again. Her chin was tilted mutinously upward, and her eyes burned with strong emotions he could easily identify but didn't understand.

Contempt. Loathing. Scorn.

He felt unaccountably hurt. Why should the woman he'd rescued loathe him? What had he ever done to offend her?

Blackthorne could feel the resistance in his wife as he drew her back toward the bed, the urge to be gone from his sight. He kept waiting for her to speak, but her lips were pressed so tightly together, her mouth had become a thin, obdurate line.

He seated himself on the bed, draping a sheet over his aroused body, disgusted with himself for desiring her despite everything. He dragged her down beside him, holding tight to her arm, lest she escape.

He swallowed over the painful lump in his throat and demanded, "Why didn't you tell me who you are? Why did you marry me?"

Her lips turned down in something that looked like revulsion, and her body stiffened, as though she couldn't bear his touch.

He felt another jab of hurt and resisted the urge to shake the answer out of her. His jaw tightened, and he gritted his teeth in frustration.

She must have realized he was at the end of his tether, because she said in a voice dripping with disdain, "I don't know what you're talking about."

He laughed, but it was a bitter, ugly sound. "I tended your back myself. I recognize the scars. The deepest one, from your right shoulder to your left buttock. The sliver under your left shoulder blade. The short one along your side. The one that curls over your shoulder. The one on your nape. I know them all. Intimately."

Her mouth was open as she sucked air, and her eyes looked panicked. Good. Maybe she would give up this ridiculous game she was playing and explain herself.

"And I recognize the names, my dear." There was nothing tender about the endearment. It was spoken with all the fury—and hurt—he was feeling.

Her eyes narrowed. "What names?"

"Miranda. And Harry."

The blood left her face. He wasn't sure how he could tell, considering the fact that her skin was already deathly pale in the moonlight.

She opened her mouth to speak, but nothing came out.

"Is there something you want to tell me?"

She looked him right in the eye and said, "No, Marcus. Nothing."

She ripped herself free of his astonished grasp and ran for the open door to her bedroom. He got tangled in the sheets, but even so, he was only a step behind her when the door slammed in his face and he heard the key turn in the lock.

He pounded the door with his fist and roared, "Open the bloody door, Josie."

He waited for her to shout back at him, but he was met by nightmarish silence. He gnashed his teeth, fighting the urge to throw his shoulder into the wooden barrier and break it down.

He wasn't just enraged because she'd been lying to him from the moment he'd seen her in London. He was also furious because, even now, knowing how she'd deceived him, knowing in what low esteem she seemed to hold him, he still wanted her with his whole being. Even while he'd been questioning her about her deceit, he'd wanted to caress her breasts, to taste the flesh at her throat, to thrust himself deep inside her.

He couldn't believe the infernal, captivating, irritating, unbelievably desirable woman had managed to make her escape without offering an explanation for where she'd been for the past two years, or why she'd come back to London and married him.

His fist was poised to bang on the door again, but he realized he didn't want to give her the satisfaction. He grabbed his nightshirt from the floor where it had fallen and pulled it on over his head, as he stalked toward the door leading to the hallway. If he stayed in his bedroom, he didn't trust himself not to do something stupid, like tearing the door that separated them off its hinges.

If he was right about what he'd discovered, he'd married the American girl he'd been obsessed with for two years. But it wasn't exultation he felt at the knowledge. Oh, no. Far from it! He felt like a fool for not immediately recognizing her.

Surely, Miss Josephine Wentworth must have known, when she'd shown up on his doorstep, that he was the man who'd rescued her. So why hadn't she admitted the truth from the start? Why had she continued to keep her identity a secret after they were married? What was the point? What was it she wanted from him? What did it all mean?

He headed downstairs in the dark, realizing as he did so that, although he hadn't lived here in years, he knew—and loved—the Abbey well enough to traverse it with only moonlight for his guide. He was unsure where he was going, until he arrived in the library and saw the decanter of brandy. He poured one for himself and drank it down in a single gulp. He poured himself another before sinking into the leather chair before the last embers of the fire.

If she'd lived in an orphanage after her parents died, where had she gotten the fortune she'd given him to become his duchess?

That was another mystery to be solved. Josie had been wearing homespun clothing and work boots when he'd rescued her. What was an heiress doing all by herself in the middle of the Dakota Territory?

Blackthorne could hardly believe the woman he'd married was the battered girl he'd rescued. He didn't know what he'd expected his American waif to look like when her face finally healed, but physically, there was nothing of his wife that reminded him of that bloody, beaten girl. Except, there was that slight bump on her nose that could have been the result of a break. Were the gold-rimmed spectacles part of her disguise? Or did she actually need them?

If he hadn't discovered the scars on her back, which he now realized she'd purposely concealed from him on their wedding night, he would never have suspected anything. Blackthorne shook his head in disbelief, as he considered how little he knew about his wife. Why hadn't he asked more questions?

More to the point, why hadn't she simply admitted she was the girl he'd rescued when he'd confronted her tonight? In fact, why hadn't she admitted the truth during that brief interview before she'd married him? Did she feel some sort of obligation to marry him to repay him for saving her life? Had she wanted to salve his pride by marrying him without revealing her identity, so he wouldn't refuse to accept her charity?

If so, what was that scorn he'd seen in her eyes all about? Why had she married him, if she despised him?

Blackthorne chuffed out a breath of air. He'd been obsessed—that wasn't too strong a word—with the mysterious girl he'd rescued for a very long time. He'd admired her courage, but he'd never been "in love" with her. Although, he might be lying to himself about that. Perhaps it had been necessary to mislead himself because of his previous obligation to marry Fanny.

And now? What did he feel for the woman who was his wife?

Anger at her deceit. Frustration at her unwillingness to explain herself. And, God help him, desire.

Miss Josephine Wentworth should have told him who she was. She should have given him the opportunity to refuse her benevolent offer to rescue him in return. Was that why she disliked him? Because she'd felt obligated to marry him?

Blackthorne had been willing to sell himself to the highest bidder, because he'd believed that whoever married him would be getting something in return for the money she brought to the table. Now he realized why Josie hadn't cared if her family or friends were in church to see her triumph. She hadn't wanted his title in return for her money. She'd merely wanted to repay him for his kindness.

That didn't explain the contempt toward him that he'd seen in her eyes. In his entire life, no one had looked at him with such loathing. No gentleman would have had the courage to offend him in such a manner.

She had.

Did he have it all wrong? Was there some other reason, something he knew nothing about, that had motivated her to marry him? Why did he have the awful feeling he'd been tricked?

Blackthorne's gut churned. Whatever Josie's motives, the two of them were bound together for life. Their marriage could only be undone by an act of Parliament, and even then, one or the other of them would have to plead guilty to adultery or some equally heinous moral crime.

He wished Seaton were here. He'd never directly inquired of his friend what he'd done about returning the injured girl to America, and Seaton had never offered the information. He hadn't wanted to know, because nothing could ever come of his brief interaction with the girl, since he was engaged to marry Fanny. Maybe Seaton would be able to fill in some of the very large blanks in the information he possessed about his wife.

Blackthorne remembered Seaton saying he would be out of town for a few days but, try as he might, he couldn't remember his friend naming any particular destination. He would send a letter to Seaton's London residence and hope he returned soon.

Meanwhile, how was he going to deal with his wife? He'd planned to show her the estate tomorrow and visit with neighbors and tenants. Well, why not? She was still his wife, whether she was the girl he'd rescued or not. And until he had some explanation for her behavior, he wasn't letting her out of his sight.

Chapter 26

BLACKTHORNE'S WIFE GLANCED at him across
the breakfast table with wary eyes. He hoped she'd
had as restless a night as he'd had. She hadn't spoken a word since she'd said, "Good morning," simply ate her eggs and toast and sausage, putting the
burden on him to solicit answers to the questions
he'd asked last night. He decided to wait and let
her worry.

"We'll be visiting our neighbors and meeting a
few tenants today as planned. I presume you have
a riding costume."

She nodded.

"I'll meet you in the library when you're ready."

She rose and left the table without a word, arriving in the library a surprisingly short while later,
dressed in a forest green riding habit that emphasized her slender waist and generous breasts, both
of which he could remember holding in his hands.
A tiny velvet hat was perched saucily forward on
her brow, and a red feather brushed her petal-soft
cheek, which had rested on his heaving chest after
they'd coupled last night.

She walked ahead of him to the stable, her hips

swaying, golden curls cascading down her back, reminding him of how her silky hair had fallen across his shoulders.

He found himself becoming aroused and tried to think of something vile, like fish guts, to erase the vivid memories of his lovely wife writhing passionately beneath him in bed.

The groom led their saddled mounts out of the stable as they arrived.

"Oh, how beautiful!"

Blackthorne was surprised to hear Josie speak with such animation, until he realized she was speaking to the horse. Nevertheless, he couldn't help feeling pleased that she liked the bay Thoroughbred he'd intended as a wedding gift for her. He'd imagined this moment, when his wife would see the mare for the first time, and he enjoyed seeing her dimpled smile. He hadn't imagined he would also be feeling resentful that she didn't seem to like him as well as she did the horse.

Josie ran her hand down the mare's sleek neck, then looked up at him from beneath dark lashes and asked, "What's her name?"

"Tumble."

She laughed, a sound that sent tremors of desire down his spine. "How did she get a name like that?"

"Apparently, Tumble made a practice of leaping sideways whenever she saw her shadow and dumping her rider."

She shot him a questioning look. "That doesn't sound friendly."

"The problem's been mended," he assured her,

"but she already answered to the name, so I didn't change it."

He assisted her into the saddle, feeling mollified that his wife was making an effort to be cordial, then mounted his chestnut. "All set?"

"Ready as I'll ever be. I'm looking forward to meeting your neighbors and tenants." She flushed and corrected, "*Our* neighbors and tenants."

That comment suggested she planned to stay around. Did she? Or was that one more example of her ease with deceit? Everyone he'd ever cared about had left him—his mother, his father, his brother, his wife. He had no reason to expect anything different from the American he'd married—that is, if he allowed himself to care for her.

Experience had taught him a hard lesson, but he'd learned it well. His mother had walked away. His father had killed himself. His brother hadn't actually committed suicide, but his reckless behavior had been the direct cause of his death. And his wife had known she was ill and deprived him of sharing a few more months or years with her by concealing her illness and getting pregnant. He wasn't about to allow his emotions to become involved with a woman who'd been lying to him since the moment she'd come back into his life.

He would bed his wife to get an heir—if she ever let him near her again—but he would never give her the chance to rip out what was left of his heart. He sat up straighter in the saddle and forced himself to look at Josie merely as the woman he'd married to save his estate and further his bloodline. He'd given her his name and the title of duchess.

He owed her nothing more. But there was no reason not to be civil. He made his voice as cordial as hers had been and said, "I'd like to show you around the estate before we call on anyone."

"Lead the way."

Blackthorne couldn't help wanting her to like what she saw. He loved the hills and valleys, the oak forest where deer were allowed to roam without being hunted, and the brook that ran across green vistas that had been in his family for eight generations. He'd played pirate here with his brother, and it was land he wanted his own children to roam.

He was surprised by that thought when, prior to his marriage to Josie, he hadn't cared whether it was his own children or his brother's who inherited Blackthorne Abbey. It also made him wonder why Josie had come into his bed a second time—even if she had been frightened by a mouse—if she detested him so much.

"Are you ready to answer a few questions?" he said abruptly.

"I'd rather enjoy the beautiful surroundings. How could you bear to live in noisy, crowded, stinky London, when you had all this waiting for you here?"

He laughed at her description of one of the most cosmopolitan locales in the world. "Stinky?"

"Malodorous, if you will. But stinky fits."

He conceded her point with a nod and a rueful smile. Despite the broom boys who did their best to collect animal waste, the sharp, acrid odor of manure and urine from horse-drawn carriages made London reek in the summer.

She took a deep breath, straining the buttons in her bodice—and his fitted buckskins to their limit—and let it out with a loud sigh. "If all this had been mine, I would never have left."

"You're forgetting the terrible condition of the Abbey."

"It won't be long before it's restored. Would you ever consider staying at the Abbey year round?"

"I haven't made up my mind yet about that." He wasn't going to admit anything to her. He had to be in London part of the year to sit in the House of Lords. And he had social obligations and friends who made their homes in Town. Part of his year would certainly be spent in London. He still wasn't sure whether the bad memories from his childhood would interfere with his desire to live at the Abbey.

"One of my ancestors built a glass summer house at the pond where the brook ends," he said. "Would you like to see it?"

"Is it safe to ride at more than a trot?"

He pointed toward the sunrise. "Can you make out the cart path across that field?"

She tilted her head, causing the feather to caress her cheek, then pointed toward two indentations that ran across the overgrown field, where wheels had compacted the grass. "Is that it?"

"That's it."

"I'll race you to that big oak on the other side!" She kicked Tumble, who bolted into a gallop, nearly throwing her out of the saddle. She merely laughed, seated herself more firmly, and leaned forward over her mount's neck, as she raced away.

He was only a moment behind her, spurring his horse to a gallop and easily catching up to her. She shot him a crooked smile, then urged her horse to greater speed.

His heart was in his throat. Was she always this reckless? What if some obstruction had been placed on this path during the years the Abbey had been abandoned? She would end up dead, and he would never get an answer to his questions.

"Slow down!" he yelled at her.

"And let you win? Never!" She leaned closer to her mount's neck, her golden curls flying.

He considered reaching out and grabbing Tumble's reins, but once upon a time, the horse had been skittish, and he had no idea how the mare would react. He gritted his teeth and raced ahead of his wife. That way, he would encounter any obstacle first, and take whatever fall resulted himself.

But there was nothing blocking their way except overgrown grass. He reached the oak first and was already out of the saddle and waiting for Josie when she arrived with a huge grin on her face, as though it had all been a great lark.

"That was wonderful! I'd forgotten how much I love riding neck-or-nothing on horseback."

He reached up and grabbed her by the waist, yanking her out of the saddle, and then had no idea what to do with her. He felt like shaking her within an inch of her life, but that would have meant letting go of her waist to grasp her shoulders, and if he did that, she would likely bolt as fast as Tumble had.

He tightened his grip on her waist and said, "I told you to slow down."

"I don't like taking orders."

"I'm your husband."

"Exactly," she shot back, her blue eyes flashing like rippling water in the sun.

"What does that mean?"

"It means I'm a grown woman, and I'll make decisions for myself."

He could hardly believe what he was hearing. "Is that some quaint American custom?"

"You married the wrong woman if you expected me to be some docile creature doing what she's told."

He held on to his temper and said through tight jaws, "Even if what I'm asking you to do is for your own good?"

"Especially then! I have a mind and a will of my own. I can decide whether I want to take a risk—"

"As your husband, I'm responsible for your well-being," he interrupted.

"As a wife, I don't intend to have my every move controlled by some tyrant."

If he hadn't had his teeth clamped together, his jaw would have dropped. "Tyrant?" The word came out sounding like he had gravel caught in his throat.

Her eyes focused intently on his face, searching for something, although he had no idea what. "You're responsible for altering the course of my life."

"I—"

She put her leather-gloved fingertips on his lips to silence him, and he felt her touch all the way to his belly. "Whether you intended it or not, I've been separated from my family for the past two years. I married you because . . ."

He waited with bated breath to hear what she had to say, but she must have changed her mind about completing her sentence, because she finished, "It doesn't really matter why I married you." She tried to retreat, and when he held on, turned a baleful look toward his hands, which were clutching her waist.

Reluctantly, he let go, and she took a step back.

She met his gaze again and continued earnestly, "The point, as I'm sure you've realized, is that we *are* married. Tied together forever. And I intend to be the one who charts the course of my life from now on."

His cheeks felt hot. Who did she think she was? He was her husband. Her lord and master. "What about the vows you took in church? Don't they mean anything?"

"Which ones?"

He could feel his heart pounding crazily in his chest. "To honor and obey."

"What about the loving and cherishing part? Are you planning to fulfill *those* vows?" she countered. "Tit for tat, Your Grace."

Although it infuriated him to admit it, she had a valid argument. He'd had no more intention of loving and cherishing her, when he'd spoken those vows in church, than she'd apparently had of honoring and obeying him.

She turned her back on him, effectively ending the conversation without conceding anything, and collected the reins that had dragged on the ground while the mare chomped on the tall grass. "I will need your help to remount."

"Haven't you forgotten something?"

She halted and glanced at him over her shoulder. "I don't believe so."

"What about my prize for winning the race?"

She angled her body toward his and lifted her chin. "We didn't agree on a prize."

"Since I won, I get to choose."

Her lips thinned, and her eyes narrowed. "I'm listening."

He was tempted to ask for a kiss. But he could tell she wouldn't freely give it, and he didn't want to take it by force, even though he badly wanted it. Forever, which was how long they were tied together, was a very long time. He could be patient.

"I'll take your feather."

"What?"

"The feather on your hat. I'll take it as my prize."

He wasn't sure whether she was disappointed or merely confused, but she reached up and unpinned her hat, pulling the red feather free of its mooring, then pinned the stripped hat back on her head, before crossing to him and holding out the feather. "Your prize. Fairly won."

Was she suggesting he might *cheat* if given the opportunity? His wife's behavior was outrageous!

And he had never felt so invigorated, so awake and aware and . . . alive.

Their gloved hands touched as he accepted the

feather. She glanced at him with a startled look in her eyes, and he knew that she'd felt it, too. Some spark had passed between them. He could tell it disturbed her. It disturbed him as well, but he'd be damned before he'd let her see the effect she'd had on him.

He knew a great deal about women—about their wants . . . and their needs. It shouldn't be too difficult to tame his American wife and bring her to heel. He'd have her eating out of his hand in no time. Just see if he didn't. She'd learn the meaning of "honor and obey" if it was the last thing he ever did.

Chapter 27

JOSIE SIGHED WITH pleasure as she settled on a stone bench inside the summer house, which was situated on a hill above the pond. The glass walls collected the sun's heat and made it warm inside, something she appreciated after spending half the morning riding the boundaries of Blackthorne's estate in the brisk spring air. "I wonder which fair maiden asked her knight in shining armor to build this wonderful refuge from English weather?"

Blackthorne's lips pursed. "I don't think this house goes back that many generations."

"I only meant that some duke must have loved his duchess a great deal to go to all the trouble of building something so whimsical out here in the middle of nowhere."

"If you say so."

Josie wasn't going to argue with him, not when they'd managed to spend the rest of the morning after their confrontation in agreeable conversation. The subject of taking orders hadn't come up again, but neither had her husband issued any orders he expected her to follow.

The thought of letting Blackthorne manage her

life, after turning it upside down, had raised her hackles. Perhaps, if she hadn't known she would be leaving him soon, she would have tried negotiating the matter. But for the little time she was going to spend in her husband's company, she intended to do exactly as she pleased.

Josie kept waiting for Blackthorne to ask where she'd been for the past two years. She was in a quandary about what to answer. Should she tell him the truth? Or wait for him to discover it himself? Obviously, someone had been keeping secrets from him, if he didn't know where she'd been. Therefore, it might not be that easy for him to figure out that she'd been living at one of his poorest, most remote properties.

On the other hand, if she told Blackthorne where she'd been, he would know she was acquainted with his nephews, and she wasn't sure she could keep her anger at his treatment of them from showing. She didn't want to give him any hint that she was planning to remove the boys from his guardianship. Or, heaven forbid, give him any inkling that she intended to leave him in the not-too-distant future.

Josie realized her hands were knotted in her lap, and she was chewing anxiously on her lower lip. She glanced up and saw Blackthorne watching her intently. She slowly let go of her lower lip and eased her hands free of each other before rising and straightening her skirt. "I would love to stay here longer, but I know you want to visit a few people this morning."

He crossed to the open doorway, but instead of

going through it, he leaned against the portal, so his body blocked her escape, and stared into the distance. "Fanny and I visited the Abbey a couple of times early in our marriage. She loved this glass house. She said it warmed her cold bones. At the time, I didn't know she was ill, or that her illness made her feel cold all the time."

Josie was astonished that Blackthorne had mentioned his late wife. She wasn't quite sure what to say. "I can see where a place like this would be a comfort to her."

"Fanny couldn't ride horseback, so she needed me to drive her here in a horse-drawn cart. Most of the time, I was too busy with estate matters to accommodate her."

Josie was even more confused by Blackthorne's admission that he hadn't been much of a knight in shining armor to his fair maiden. Was that a warning to her that she shouldn't expect special consideration either? Or an admission that he wished he'd been a better husband?

"I'm sorry for you both."

"I don't need your pity," he snapped, turning to glare at her.

"It wasn't pity, it was sympathy." She took a few steps forward, so she could put a hand on his arm, and felt the muscles bunch under the cloth. "It sounds like the burdens you faced on the estate kept you from spending as much time as you might have wished with someone who was shortly going to be taken from you."

He stared at her gloved hand. "I wish . . ."

Josie waited, but he never finished the sentence.

He turned abruptly, so her hand fell free, and they were facing each other. "I don't intend to make the same mistakes with you that I made with her. There was something else I never did with Fanny in this glass house."

She raised her gaze to his face too late to realize what he had in mind.

He slid one arm around her waist and pulled her snug against his muscular frame, while his other hand palmed the side of her face and tilted it upward.

Before Josie could protest, his mouth had covered hers. She'd been expecting violence. What she got was a gentle assault on her senses, an exploration of her mouth that sought both to give—and take—pleasure, while his hand threaded into her hair and angled her head back to give him better purchase. She was caught off-guard and found herself sucked into a whirlwind of unsettling emotions. Her mind protested, even as her body responded to the press of his rock-hard chest against the pebbled tips of her breasts.

The male hand at her waist slid down to press her hips into the space between his widespread legs, and Josie became aware of the heat and hardness of her husband against the part of her where it was meant to fit.

Abruptly, he let her go and took a step back.

Josie stared up into his hooded eyes, her shocked mouth half open to draw breath to heaving lungs, her body awake and aware—and wanting—from head to toe. "What . . . ? Why . . . ?"

What had happened? Why had he stopped?

He reached out and gently tucked a golden curl behind her ear. "I didn't want to have any regrets, in case we never come back here again."

She'd told him she loved this summer house. Why would he think they would never be here again? Unless he had plans to abandon *her*. It was a possibility Josie had never imagined in her wildest dreams. She was the one planning to run away at the first opportunity. Had Blackthorne planned to restore the Abbey and then leave her behind in that gray stone mausoleum while he returned to his frivolous life in London?

She stared at him wide-eyed, wondering what was going on behind those inscrutable, heavy-lidded blue eyes. She reminded herself that it didn't matter what *he* had planned, because *she* had plans to take both herself and his nephews away from here. Nevertheless, she found herself wondering how long Blackthorne intended to hang around and fix up the Abbey. Maybe he only intended to stay long enough to get her started on the renovations before he disappeared.

That was good, wasn't it? She would be free to come and go as she pleased. She could leave whenever she liked and retrieve Spencer and Clay and board a ship for America.

"It's time to leave," he said, holding out an arm for her to take.

She slid her arm through his, her lower lip clamped tightly in her teeth. She couldn't understand why she was so upset by what she'd intuited from Blackthorne's kiss. Or rather, what he'd said before and after the kiss. She should be glad he was leaving her. So where was this sinking feeling in her stomach coming from?

Josie eyed Blackthorne askance. His features revealed none of the confusion she was experiencing herself. What game was he playing? And what should her next move be?

He helped her to remount Tumble, then mounted himself, simply throwing himself into the saddle without using the stirrups, as she'd seen American cowboys do. She couldn't help admiring his strength and agility. If only he had a better character to go along with his physical attributes.

"My tenant, Mr. Moreland, and his wife and five children live on the way to Squire Cartwright's home," he said. "I think there's time to visit both families before luncheon."

The Morelands seemed to be a happy family, even more so when Blackthorne promised he would repair a roof that had been leaking for quite some time. Josie thought Mr. and Mrs. Moreland did a little too much ducking and bowing to both her and the duke, but she hoped she'd made Mrs. Moreland feel more comfortable before they finally left.

The five children, all girls, ranged in age from three to twelve. She'd promised each of them a hair ribbon, to be delivered on her next visit. Josie smiled as Mrs. Moreland, who was well into her sixth pregnancy, ducked her head one last time, before they mounted their horses and rode away.

"They're blessed to have five beautiful children and another on the way," Josie said, once they were out of earshot.

"With any luck, he'll get a son this time, to help him in the fields."

Josie bridled at Blackthorne's insinuation that sons were more desirable than daughters. She realized it might start an argument, but she couldn't keep herself from saying, "If necessary, daughters can do as much physical labor as sons."

She'd certainly done her share of work during her trip across the prairie from Chicago to Cheyenne. It had been her job to collect the buffalo dung and any wood she could find along the way and fill up a sling carried under their Conestoga, to be used to build the fire in the evening.

Blackthorne frowned. "Girls? Work in the fields? It isn't done."

"It is in America."

"This is England, in case you've forgotten. Women have a role to which they're born. Most have no wish to step out of it."

Josie stared back at him, unwilling to concede the point. So what if he thought she was an odd duck? He'd better get used to it. She wasn't going to be around here long enough to change her feathers. The sooner she got back to America, where men were happy—and even grateful—to have their wives carry their share of what was an enormous load of work on the frontier, the better.

Rather than argue, she said, "Tell me about Squire Cartwright."

"His family has been on the same land for as many generations as mine. The Cartwrights raise milk cows and corn. The squire's wife bore him twelve children, but only three are still living. The two boys are at boarding school, and their daughter is married to a baron in the next county."

"What happened to the rest?"

"Three died in the first year from childhood diseases. Two died in farm accidents. One drowned. And three died of smallpox."

"How do you know all this, if you haven't been living at the Abbey?" And if he knew so much detail about a family he hadn't lived near in years, why hadn't he been aware of what had happened to her, or to his nephews?

He smiled. "Harkness. He's kept in touch over the years, letting me know what's going on in the neighborhood."

Josie wondered if Blackthorne realized what he'd revealed with that admission. It was one more sign of how much he loved the Abbey. He'd apparently been starved enough for information about his boyhood home to commit to memory everything he'd been told about it. How else could he know— and remember—so much about one of his many tenants' lives? No wonder he'd been willing to marry a perfect stranger to save it.

It was also more evidence that he didn't value his nephews—certainly not as much as he did the Abbey. Otherwise, why didn't he know every little detail about *them*? It made her all the more determined to take the boys with her when she left.

The squire and his wife didn't do as much bowing and scraping as the Morelands, but Josie was very much aware of the enormous distance English folk put between a duke and his minions. It helped to explain why Blackthorne expected her to fall into line.

They didn't stay long, because it was close to lunch time, and they didn't want to impose on the Cartwrights to feed them. They arrived home a little after noon and rode directly to the house, where a groom was waiting to take their horses.

Josie had just patted Tumble's neck and was ready to dismount, when she felt Blackthorne's hands at her waist to assist her to the ground. She braced her hands on his shoulders to steady herself, but Tumble unexpectedly edged sideways, and she fell forward, so their bodies collided. He grabbed her around the waist and staggered backward as he lowered her to the ground.

When he was steady again, he met her gaze with a smile on his face and a twinkle of mischief in his eyes. "We have to stop meeting like this."

For a breathless moment, she thought he was going to kiss her. And realized, to her horror, that she *wanted* to feel his lips against her own.

Josie took a quick step aside, pulling free of Blackthorne's embrace. "I enjoyed the ride," she said. "Thank you for taking me."

"It was my pleasure."

At that moment, two servants managed to get the front door to creak open. Harkness stepped through and onto the porch, a missive in his hand.

"Your Grace, a telegram arrived while you were gone."

Josie was astonished when he handed the missive to her, rather than Blackthorne. "Are you sure this is for me?"

He gave her a look that told her he wasn't the kind of butler who made that kind of mistake.

"Thank you, Harkness."

She took the telegram and then stared at it, afraid to open it. What disaster had befallen her family that they'd needed to send her a telegram? She felt sick to her stomach, and the copper taste of fear rose in her throat.

"Aren't you going to open it?" Blackthorne asked.

She shot him a look of desperation. Through most of her childhood, she and her sisters had felt DOOMED to a terrible life. Now, at a time it seemed disaster might have been averted, she'd received this telegram.

The paper was still trembling in her hand when Blackthorne took it from her. "Shall I read it?"

She nodded, unable to speak because of the knot of fear in her throat.

The duke read:

Your Grace,

Received word today that everyone has arrived safely.

Your obedient servant, T

"Who is 'T'?" Blackthorne asked in a gruff voice. "And where is it everyone has arrived?"

Josie wondered why Mr. Thompson had openly sent her a telegram. It was vague enough that Blackthorne hadn't been able to decipher its meaning, and yet, it was a clear reminder that her family was anxiously awaiting her return. Time was running out. She had to give the boys time to get over the measles, but then she needed to grab them and go.

She didn't realize how long she'd been silent until Blackthorne said, "Is this another secret you've been keeping from me?"

"My time in England was over and my family was expecting my return, when I heard you were looking for a wife. They don't know I've stayed. They don't know I've married you."

"Or that you're not returning?" he said, a brow lifted in question.

"Certainly, any plans to reunite with my family have been delayed until a more opportune time."

"You mean, when we can both go, and you can show off the royal duke you've snagged for a husband?"

Josie bit her tongue rather than snap the retort that came to mind. Instead, she smiled and said, "Naturally."

"Who is 'T'?" he repeated.

"A Pinkerton detective."

His eyes widened in surprise. "Why did you need a detective?"

She wasn't about to tell him the man had been hired by her sister to find her. "I wanted to know more about you, before I committed to marrying you."

His lips compressed. "And did you satisfy your curiosity?"

"I married you, didn't I?"

She lifted her skirt and headed up the stone steps

without another word. *Let him stew on that for a while*. She wondered if there was some other message Mr. Thompson had intended for her to receive by revealing himself to the duke. Was there some other emergency he hadn't wanted to state in the telegram? But surely, if the situation had been dire, he would have made a point of meeting with her face-to-face. She had to assume the telegram meant no more than it had said.

Her family was waiting for her. It was time to grab Spencer and Clay and go.

Should she leave a message for the duke, telling him why she'd married him? Should she answer his unanswered questions?

Why not leave him in doubt? About her. About everything. Why not let him suffer, at least a little, for the two years of hell she'd been put through? It was the very least he deserved.

Chapter 28

JOSIE MADE SURE the bedroom door between her room and the duke's was locked that night, as she made plans to sneak away from Blackthorne Abbey the following morning. She still found it hard to believe she hadn't locked it that first night. But she wasn't making that mistake again.

She spent a restless night trying to sleep and finally gave up at dawn. She dressed, collected her carpet bag, and glanced one last time at the door that separated her room and the duke's. Then she quietly opened her bedroom door, stepped into the hall, and gently pulled it closed behind her.

She was creeping down the hall on her way to the stairs, when she heard a woman crying. She told herself that what happened at the Abbey was no longer her concern, but she only took three more steps before she reversed course, dropped her carpet bag next to the wall, and headed down the hall toward the heart-wrenching sound.

When she arrived at the housekeeper's bedroom door, she knocked softly. The sobs stopped abruptly, but the door remained closed. "Harriet?" she whispered.

The door opened a crack, and one swollen, reddened eye and a tearstained cheek appeared in the sliver of dawn light. In a choked voice, Harriet said, "Good morning, Your Grace."

"May I come in?"

Josie saw the reluctance on the housekeeper's face to involve her employer in whatever was causing her so much distress. "I would like to help."

"No one can help, Your Grace."

Josie realized that, in her anguish, Harriet had reverted to more formal address, instead of using her name. "I'd like to try."

The door opened farther, and Harriet stepped back to allow her inside. Josie was appalled to realize how bare the room was of any adornment. Apparently, Harriet owned nothing of her own, or hadn't unpacked whatever she did have during the few days she'd been in the duke's employ.

Harriet crossed to the bed and slumped down on it, the graceful posture of the applicant for the housekeeper's job wilted by whatever unbearable weight she was carrying. The chair that provided the only place to sit was positioned in the far corner of the room, so Josie decided to sit next to the distraught woman instead.

Harriet's body tensed as Josie joined her, and she looked confused by a duchess's willingness to insinuate herself in something that arguably was none of her business.

Josie decided to take the bull by the horns and simply asked, "What's wrong, Harriet?"

Tears leaked from Harriet's eyes and dripped

down her cheeks. She covered her mouth as another sob broke free.

Josie slid an arm around the other woman's shoulders and said, "It's all right, Harriet. Everything will be fine. Please, tell me what's happened."

"It's my sisters," Harriet choked out. "Their aunt, Lady Gertrude, no longer wants the burden of caring for them. They're being sent to an orphanage. It's an awful place, where they'll be cold and hungry all the time. And there's nothing I can do!"

Josie shuddered. She remembered all too well the three years of hunger and deprivation—and the beatings with a birch rod—that she and her siblings had suffered at the Chicago Institute for Orphaned Children. She wouldn't wish that fate on anyone, let alone her housekeeper's family. "I'm sure something can be done."

"Even if I had the funds to care for them somewhere else, my sisters are Lady Gertrude's wards. I'm powerless to help."

"We'll see about that," Josie said, her chin coming up pugnaciously. "You forget you're now part of a duke's household. Surely Blackthorne has enough influence to wrest your sisters from this contemptible woman's grasp."

"Why would the duke bother with my family's problems?"

"Because his duchess will insist upon it," Josie said with an encouraging smile, standing and turning to grab Harriet's hands, before drawing her to her feet. "Now get up, wipe your eyes, and leave everything to me."

The look of hope in Harriet's eyes brought a

lump to Josie's throat. There was no way she could leave today, she realized. She had to convince Blackthorne to help, and since she didn't trust him entirely, she would need to remain long enough to ensure that Harriet's siblings found a place to live.

She was halfway to the door when she turned back and asked, "How old are your sisters?"

"Emily is ten, Georgette is nine, and Anna is six."

"Hmmm." Josie's lips pursed thoughtfully.

"Your Grace?"

"I was hoping they might be old enough to be employed at the Abbey, but that won't work. Never mind. I'll figure something out."

She turned again to leave, then stopped once more to ask, "Where does Lady Gertrude live?"

"Seven miles west of the Abbey, on a small estate she bought with funds left to her by her late husband."

"So the duke could be there and back with the girls in a day?" Josie asked.

"Yes. I was hoping to be able to visit them on Sundays, but the orphanage where they're being sent is too far away for that."

Josie waved her hand to allay the anxious look on Harriet's face. "Your sisters will never see the inside of an orphanage, if I have anything to say about it."

Josie hurried back down the hall, retrieved her carpet bag, and hid it under her bed. Surely she could resolve Harriet's problem within the next week and then be on her way. Once the high-and-mighty Duke of Blackthorne made his desires known, Lady Gertrude would likely fall all over herself to please him.

All she had to do was convince Blackthorne to intervene.

That didn't turn out to be as easy as she'd hoped. All morning, Josie felt like she had an itch she couldn't scratch. She kept waiting for precisely the right moment to approach Blackthorne with her request. But it never arrived.

He spent the morning in the study with his new steward, going over renovation plans for the Abbey and discussing long overdue repairs he planned to make on his tenants' homes.

Mr. and Mrs. Robertson, another of Blackthorne's neighbors, came by to visit shortly before noon and stayed for lunch.

Once they left, Blackthorne was called outside to advise the gardener on several landscaping decisions. When he didn't return after an entire hour, Josie went hunting for him. She didn't want the sun to set before she had the issue of Harriet's siblings resolved.

She found Blackthorne in the stable loft. The place smelled of hay and harness and manure, and dust motes drifted in the sunlight. She put a hand above her brows to shade her eyes, as she leaned back to gaze up at him. "What are you doing up there?"

"Come see."

Josie made a face as she stared at the ladder leading to the loft. She'd dressed to please Blackthorne that morning in a fitted day dress and a pair of buttoned-up high-heel shoes, none of which would be easy to climb in. However, if she joined him, there was little chance of being interrupted, and nowhere he could easily escape before she'd made her plea for help. She grabbed the closest rung and headed up.

Blackthorne was waiting at the top and slid his hands into her armpits to lift her the last little way. She was breathless from the climb, and felt a frisson race down her spine at the feel of his hands in such intimate proximity to her breasts. Once she was steady, he let go of her and took a step back. The air caught in her lungs when she took a good look at him.

His sleeves were rolled up to reveal strong forearms, and his blousy white shirt was open at the throat, where she could see sweat rolling down in streams, making the thin cloth cling to his broad chest. Sunshine poured in from the open loft doors. No wonder he was hot. She was feeling quite warm herself.

"What did you want to show me?" she asked.

He took her hand and led her to a corner, where a stack of hay had been hollowed out to form a nest. "This."

"Oh!"

"It seems Fitch has been busy doing more than chasing mice."

Fitch lay in the nest of straw with four sleeping kittens at her side. Josie dropped to her knees to get a closer look. She glanced up at Blackthorne and asked, "How old are they?"

"I'd say about five weeks. They'll be old enough to leave their mother soon."

"How will they get down from the loft?"

He shrugged. "I imagine Fitch will teach them."

Having just climbed the intimidating ladder, Josie asked, "How do you suppose she gets up here?"

He shrugged again. "I have no idea."

Josie desperately wanted to cuddle one of the kittens, but she wasn't sure how Fitch would react. "Do you think she'd let me hold one?"

He dropped to one knee beside the cat. "Let's see."

The first thing he did was to stroke Fitch's side. When the mother cat allowed that without protest, his large hand circled the one kitten that was different from the others, which were black-and-brown, and lifted it away. Fitch watched him carefully but didn't try to scratch or bite.

Josie settled herself down in the straw as Blackthorne handed her the taffy-colored kitten. She held it up to observe its adorable face and then aimed a grateful smile at him. She could hardly believe she was holding a kitten at long last. She stroked its forehead as she cooed to the little animal, "You're about the cutest thing I've ever seen. I think I'll call you Dusty."

"I take it you're planning to keep that one."

"Yes," she said, making the decision on the spot. The kitten should be old enough to leave its mother within the week she'd given herself to get Harriet's siblings settled, and she could take it with her when she left. "Can we move Fitch and her kittens inside to my room? She can keep the mice away, and I'll be able to enjoy all the kittens before they find new homes. Besides, I don't like to think of one of them getting too adventuresome and falling from this height."

He didn't look entirely happy about having a family of cats in the house. "I suppose that would be all right." He grinned and added, "But I can't say I would mind if you found yourself fleeing another mouse and ended up in my arms again."

Josie felt the heat on her cheeks. She didn't know what to say, so she said nothing. But the fact that Blackthorne was teasing her suggested he might be in a good frame of mind to help her with Harriet's problem.

"I have a favor to ask." She met his gaze and realized his eyes were focused on what she was doing. Josie suddenly realized she was rubbing the kitten's soft fur against her cheek and lowered the tiny animal back to Fitch's side, before turning to face her husband.

"What can I do for you?" he asked.

Since he was still down on one knee, she put a daring hand on his thigh. "It isn't something for me. It's something for Harriet."

He cleared his throat. "The housekeeper?"

She talked fast, because the look on Blackthorne's face suggested that his patience for talk was fast disappearing. "Harriet's three sisters are going to end up in an orphanage, if we don't help."

"What do we have to do with Harriet's siblings?"

"The girls are wards of their aunt, and Lady Gertrude has decided she doesn't want to take care of them any longer. I thought you might be able to persuade her to let you take over their guardianship."

"Why would I want to do that?"

"Because orphanages aren't the best place to raise children who have a family member willing to care for them. Harriet loves her sisters. She's been distraught that she can't do anything to change their situation. I told her you would do what you can to make their lives better."

He put a hand over hers where it lay on his thigh, making it possible for her to more easily feel the rock-hard muscle beneath her fingertips. She became aware of the heat of his body and the not-unpleasant smell of a hard-working man. "I presume you've figured out a way I can do that?"

"Well, no, actually." She resisted the urge to pull her hand free. She needed to keep Blackthorne close until she got his help. She focused her gaze on his and said, "I thought you might be able to come up with a way to get Harriet and her sisters back together."

Josie realized when she finished speaking that she hadn't actually thought this out. She should have figured out a solution to the problem herself, before confronting Blackthorne. Or several solutions, to give him a choice of how to help.

"I'd be willing to donate a portion of my allowance every quarter to support them." Although, she wouldn't actually be here to do it, she could have a solicitor arrange for the funds to be transferred from wherever she ended up.

"That won't be necessary," he said, his thumb caressing the top of her hand where it lay on his thigh.

Josie shivered, even though she wasn't the least bit cold. "It won't?"

"Do you remember the gatekeeper's cottage I showed you at the entrance to the property?"

Josie remembered the one-story stone house, because it had seemed a waste that no one was using it. "Oh, Marcus! The girls can live there with Harriet. What a wonderful idea! And with the allowance I provide—"

"It might be better to increase Harriet's wages enough for her to pay for the care of her sisters, so it doesn't seem like charity."

"You're right. She does have a great deal of pride. That will work much better." However, having a place for Harriet's siblings to live and money to feed them didn't entirely solve the problem, so she said, "Can we go now and talk with the children's aunt? I don't want the threat of living in an orphanage to be hanging over their heads even one more day."

"All right," he said with a laugh. "If you insist."

"Thank you, Marcus. Thank you! I have to tell Harriet the good news. She'll be ecstatic!"

Josie was feeling pretty ecstatic herself and pulled her hand from beneath Blackthorne's, so she could throw both of them around his neck. The impetus of her move caused the duke to lose his balance. He tumbled backward laughing, pulling her along with him, rolling over so she ended up lying beneath him in the straw.

Josie's joyful smile faded as Blackthorne slowly lowered his mouth to hers. The heat of the sun, the scratchiness of the straw, the weight of his body on hers, with his hips cradled between her thighs, all combined to make the soft touch of his lips on hers the most sensual experience she'd ever had in her life.

The kiss went on. And on. Josie could feel the hard length of Blackthorne's manhood and realized that in a moment he would be making love to her.

She turned her face away to break their kiss and said, "Marcus. We have to stop."

"Why?" He kissed her throat. "No one will disturb us here."

Unfortunately, he was right. But it was the very worst time of the month for her to be doing this, and she didn't want to take the chance of becoming pregnant. That would only complicate everything. "We need to leave soon, if we're going to retrieve Harriet's sisters today."

He was nibbling on her ear and stopped long enough to say, "This won't take long."

She shoved at his shoulders. "I don't want to do this now."

He lifted his head and looked at her with eyes that promised her pleasure. "Does that mean you'll want to do it later?"

She avoided the question, because what she wanted and what she was willing to allow herself were two different things. Besides, she was confused again. Blackthorne's willingness to help the housekeeper's sisters didn't jibe with his unwillingness to have his nephews living close by. Who was this man? Where was the ogre she knew him to be?

"Please, Marcus. Not now."

He levered himself off of her and stood, then reached down to help her to her feet.

She ducked when he reached a hand toward her head, until she realized he was merely picking straw from her hair. "Oh. Thank you." She stood still while he removed several more pieces, taking the opportunity to brush some straw from his shoulder.

"I will need to bathe and dress before we can leave," he said, "but I presume you still want to make the trip to visit Lady Gertrude today?"

"I do. I'm going now to tell Harriet the good news. I'll be ready to leave whenever you are." She didn't fight the urge to rise on tiptoe and kiss him on the lips. She quickly turned and lowered herself onto the ladder, smiling at Blackthorne until she was too far down to see him anymore.

Chapter 29

BLACKTHORNE WONDERED WHO was taming whom. Over the past week, he'd allowed a cat and her kittens to set up house in his wife's bedroom. He'd cleaned and furnished the gatekeeper's cottage and installed three young girls with a governess to watch over them during the day, so his housekeeper could be available to continue her work at the Abbey. And he'd made a special trip back to his tenant's home with Josie, to deliver a colorful selection of silk ribbons to Mr. Moreland's daughters, which she'd personally woven into each delighted child's hair.

And he'd done it all to please his wife.

Blackthorne had found himself reveling in the enchanting smile that appeared on her face in each instance. For the kittens. For their housekeeper's sisters. For the little girls receiving their silk hair ribbons. He'd waited for her to turn that dimpled smile on him. He'd yearned for it. And been left wanting.

Blackthorne couldn't imagine any duchess of his acquaintance concerning herself with a few flea-bitten cats (which she'd divested of their fleas), or the housekeeper's kin (for whom he'd been named guardian), or hair ribbons for a tenant's children (which he'd driven her into town to personally select). His wife was turning his world on its ear. She seemed to care about everyone and everything at the Abbey. Except him.

He hadn't noticed at first that Josie was avoiding his company, because they'd both been busy over the past week in their separate spheres of activity. He'd spent hours every day locked in his study with his steward. She spent her days supervising the housekeeper and the cook, searching the attic for treasures and figuring out what needed to be ordered to bring the kitchen into the nineteenth century. He was stunned when it dawned on him that she was only speaking to him in response to questions he addressed to her.

He'd thought relations between them would improve after the intimate moments they'd shared in the loft. But he and his wife were further apart than ever. He wasn't sure what had gone wrong. He'd spent every night sleeping by himself, having discovered, after surreptitiously checking each evening, that the door between his bedroom and hers was locked.

He paced the floor of his bedroom for the umpteenth time, wondering if it was worth the effort to check the door tonight. And if it was locked? Was he going to knock? Was he going to ask his wife— beg her—to let him in?

He'd be damned before he did any such thing! To hell with her. If she didn't want him, that was her loss.

Blackthorne untied his Sulka robe and threw it onto the foot of the bed, then buttoned his night-shirt the rest of the way up the front. He shoved both hands through his hair, leaving it standing on end, as he went over everything that had happened between them since their marriage, wondering what he could have done differently.

Why hadn't he pressed his advantage in the loft? He'd felt Josie's pulse racing in her throat, seen her eyes glazed with passion, watched her desire rising. Why had she stopped him? What was it about him that she found wanting?

He'd always thought that getting to know the girl who'd captured his heart with her courage would be a dream come true. It was turning out to be more of a nightmare.

He'd been the soul of patience, not pressing Josie for explanations he felt he deserved. Where had she been all this time? Why hadn't she admitted who she was when she'd applied to be his bride? And why had she married him, especially when she didn't seem to particularly like him?

Blackthorne put a hand to his chest. He'd never realized a heart could actually, physically ache with hurt. After all the disaster in his life so far, he hadn't believed he would ever let himself get close enough to anyone to suffer this kind of pain again. But then, he'd never imagined ending up married to someone he admired but who, apparently, had such a low opinion of him.

And it wasn't just his heart she'd trampled. Josie's rejection of him—and his lovemaking—had touched his pride. When he'd married Fanny, he could have had his choice of any female he wanted with the mere crook of his finger. When he'd decided to marry a mail-order bride, he hadn't cared one way or the other what she thought of him, or whether he ever bedded her again, once they'd consummated the marriage.

So why was he obsessing about Josie now? Why was he pacing on the other side of her bedroom door like a stag in rut?

The simple answer was that he wanted her to like him. He wanted her to want him. What he didn't understand was why it mattered to him. How had she managed to get under his skin in such a short amount of time? How had her opinion come to mean so much to him?

Blackthorne realized that, if he didn't get out of his bedroom, he was liable to do something stupid. Like breaking down the door and ravishing his wife.

He headed downstairs and only realized when his bare feet left the scruffy Aubusson carpet on the stairs and landed on the cold stone floor below, that he hadn't bothered to put on any slippers. He also hadn't bothered to bring a lantern with him. He ended up in the library, where he knew he would find a decanter of brandy on an end table.

He poured himself a drink and slumped down in one of the two chairs facing the fire to contemplate the state of his life.

Why hadn't he asked Josie those all-important questions about where she'd been all this time, and precisely why she'd married him? What was he waiting for? What was he afraid of?

He'd just swallowed the last of his brandy when he heard a commotion and realized someone was banging on the front door. He looked down at the nightshirt that was all he was wearing and grimaced. He hadn't even stopped to put on his robe before he'd left his bedroom. In London, his butler would already have answered the door, but he wasn't sure Harkness could even hear the noise, let alone get to the door before whoever it was gave up and went away.

It suddenly occurred to him that no one would have come to the Abbey at this hour of the night unless it was some sort of emergency. Blackthorne leapt up in alarm, swearing bitterly when he stubbed his toe in the dark. He hastened to the front door, his heart in his throat the whole way, and swore again when the door stubbornly refused to open. He finally managed to free it and found a man standing before him bathed in moonlight.

It took him a moment to recognize the messenger's livery. When he did, fear rose in his throat and choked him into silence.

Chapter 30

SEATON HAD TAKEN precautions to ensure that Blackthorne wouldn't discover he'd traveled to Northumberland and ask what business he had there, all of which might come undone, because Lady Lark was making the long journey north on the same train. The last thing he wanted was for her to find out what Fanny had done and tell her brother. He would need to be careful what he said to her when they met for tea.

He arrived at precisely ten o'clock in the dining car, as they'd arranged, and was surprised to find Blackthorne's sister sitting at a table all by herself, without a friend or a maid or a chaperon in sight. She smiled in welcome when she saw him and shifted her shoulders back as she straightened in her chair.

He forced his gaze away from the fashionable fit of her bodice, which emphasized her feminine assets, toward the expected cherubic face. Except, he discovered that the once-full cheeks had thinned, the wide-set blue eyes were framed by very long, very black lashes, and the once-pouty mouth had developed into surprisingly kissable lips.

Seaton couldn't take his eyes off his best friend's sister and realized he needed some distraction, or he would soon be in no condition for decent company. As he settled himself opposite her at the table in the dining car, he said, "Where are Mr. and Mrs. Court and their daughter?"

Her smile got even brighter, if that were possible. "In London, I imagine."

Seaton was confused. "They're not here with you?"

"No." Just that one word, with no explanation.

"You're traveling alone?"

"Yes."

He glanced around the dining car. "Where's your maid?"

"Visiting her mother in Devon."

"Are you telling me that you're on this train all by yourself?"

"Of course not!"

He felt relieved, until she added, "I'm here with you."

He felt his heart take a giant leap and grabbed the edge of the table to steady himself. "What's going on, Lark?" He realized he'd called her by her first name, without the title he'd begun using over the past year to keep her at a distance.

She looked at him with round, innocent eyes and announced, "I've decided to have an adventure."

"On a journey that can't be completed in a single day? Alone in the company of a single gentleman? Your brother will kill me—after he forces us to marry."

She had the grace to blush, the minx. When she

was younger, he'd admired Lark for her willingness to try anything. While Lindsey had run screaming when he'd threatened her with fishing worms, Lark had stood her ground.

But she was no longer a child, something he'd become painfully aware of during the past year. He'd been philosophical the first time he'd become aroused in her company. She'd been shoved against him at a crowded garden party, and her breasts had accidentally been crushed against his chest. That had caused a very natural, very predictable male response.

He'd told himself the same thing would have happened no matter who the woman had been. The problem was it didn't happen with Lindsey, when the same sort of mishap occurred later that same day, and not once with Lark's sister in the three months since.

Only with Lark. And always with Lark.

He was aware of her whenever she came into a room, but he'd schooled himself to ignore her presence. Blackthorne's sisters were barely out of the schoolroom, and he was nowhere near ready to marry. Besides, he had no intention of losing his heart to any female. Not for a long, long time. Waiting for Fanny to die—and watching Blackthorne suffer through her illness—hadn't just been difficult, it had been a nightmare from which he didn't think he would ever awaken.

He could understand why Blackthorne had been willing to marry without love the second time around. Love hurt. He was in no hurry to have a wife who might die in childbed or fall sick from some other illness. Or to have a child who died at birth, taking its mother along with it.

So he was particularly concerned by the fact that he now found himself in the uncomfortable—unbearable—situation of being the chaperon for a young lady to whom he was sexually attracted.

There was no question of sending Lark off on her own. He owed his protection to his best friend's little sister, even if time spent with Lark was going to play havoc with his body and seriously challenge his self-control.

"What am I supposed to do with you?" he demanded in a severe voice.

"Enjoy my company?"

He wanted to laugh but forced a ferocious frown onto his face. "This won't do, Lady Lark. We need to get off this train at the next station and—"

"No. Please."

The look of entreaty in her eyes stopped him in mid-sentence. He stared at her, perplexed.

"It was difficult enough to make the decision to do this," she said in a voice that trembled. "It would be too humiliating if you drag me home like a wayward child."

"Why *did* you do this?" He couldn't fathom why she would engage in such risqué behavior.

She chewed on her lower lip, and he felt himself thinking that he'd like to be doing that. Which caused the response one might have expected. He gritted his teeth and shifted in his seat. And waited for her to explain herself.

"I'm no good at this," she muttered.

"At what?"

She spread her hands helplessly. "This."

He still had no idea what she was talking about. "Where were you planning to stay when we arrived?"

"At the Courts' home, of course."

"How were you planning to get there?"

"I suppose I'll hire myself a carriage." She hesitated, then looked up at him from beneath lowered lashes. "Unless you're willing to escort me."

"You expect me to change my plans to accommodate this foolish prank of yours?"

She met his gaze squarely. "I know how thoughtful you are, Seaton. And I know you and Marcus had adventures when you were young," she said earnestly, "so you must understand why I wanted to spread my wings and do something I've never done before."

It didn't hurt his ego to be called thoughtful. And of course he understood her desire to break free of the shackles her grandmother put on her behavior. The dowager was a fierce guardian who took her duties seriously. He could imagine how a free spirit like Lark might chafe under such restrictions. "How did you evade your grandmother's eagle eye?"

"She believes I'm being watched over by the Courts."

"You lied to her?"

She nodded but didn't look contrite. "I had no choice. It was the only way to escape."

"You can't hope to keep this from her indefinitely."

"Why not? She believes I'm with the Courts, who only come to London to shop once a year. By the time she discovers what I've done, I'll be a matron with four children at my knee."

He grinned. "Four?"

"Two girls and two boys, if you must know."

"That will keep your husband very busy." The words were already out of his mouth before he realized how provocative they sounded.

She looked him right in the eye and said, "I hope so."

Seaton slid a finger around his collar, which suddenly felt like a noose. Was Lark suggesting that *he* should father those children?

"Will you help me?" she asked.

"We have a long journey ahead of us," he said at last. "We can decide what to do once we arrive at our destination."

The smile she gave him made his heart skip a beat. Seaton realized there was far more at risk on this journey than Lady Lark's reputation. He had to be very careful not to be caught in parson's mousetrap. There were good reasons why he didn't want to be married. He'd do well to keep them in mind for the hours he spent on the train with his best friend's little sister.

Chapter 31

IT HAD NEVER occurred to Lark that the train wouldn't run on time. She'd expected to arrive at Berwick-upon-Tweed early enough to have supper with Seaton before he dropped her off at the Courts' home. Instead, the train pulled into the station long past midnight, following an endless delay caused by the need to replace a missing rail. They were lucky the engineer had noticed the problem in time to prevent a terrible accident. It had been necessary to back up to the nearest town and send for the supplies that were needed to make the repair.

Lark felt hot and tired and cranky. The cough she'd thought was merely something caught in her throat had persisted, and even gotten worse. Her eyes were watering, and her nose had started to run so much that she'd used up not only her own hand-kerchief but Seaton's as well.

"I don't see how I can show up at the Courts' home in the middle of the night. Everyone will be in bed," she explained to Seaton. "I'll have to get a room in town for the night."

"Your brother will kill me," Seaton muttered.

"After he stands me before an altar with you by my side."

Lark would have felt more guilty, if getting Seaton to the altar wasn't the main reason she'd come on this adventure. "I've stayed at an inn before."

"With your grandmother and your sister and an abigail or two, I have no doubt," Seaton said curtly. "What is the innkeeper going to think, when I ask for a room for a single young lady with no chaperon in sight?"

Lark blushed. When he put it that way, it made the situation sound licentious. "Maybe I could be your sister."

"Traveling without a maid for respectability?" he said, arching a disdainful brow.

"Then I'll have to be your wife."

Seaton choked on whatever it was he was about to say and had a coughing fit before he could speak again. "Are you suggesting we stay in the same room? Together?"

"I trust you not to take advantage."

"That's big of you. Where do you propose the two of us should sleep in a room with a single bed?"

Lark pursed her lips in response to what she considered an idiotic question. "If you give me a pillow and one of the blankets, I can sleep on the floor. I've done it before, when Lindsey and I made a tent of our bed linens and pretended we lived in a harem in Arabia."

Seaton rolled his eyes, then lowered his head in defeat. "I will sleep on the floor, of course."

Lark blinked to clear her blurred eyes and pressed

Seaton's handkerchief against her runny nose. "Then we're going to share a room?"

"Against my better judgment. Just let me do the talking."

Lark slid her arm through Seaton's as they entered the closest establishment to the train station, a place called the Black Swan, and tried her best to look like his wife.

"I'd like a room, please," Seaton said when the sleepy innkeeper showed up in response to a bell that rang when he'd opened the door, adding belatedly, "for myself and my wife."

Lark gave the innkeeper her most brilliant smile. "We're newlyweds."

She heard Seaton moan softly beside her.

"Then you'll be wantin' the bridal suite," the innkeeper said with a grin.

"That's not necessary," Seaton replied in a quelling voice.

"Surely you want the best room in the house for your bride," the innkeeper said. "It's only a little more blunt than a regular room."

Lark figured the bridal suite was likely larger than the run-of-the-mill room, and they would be needing the space to make a bed for Seaton on the floor. "Please, darling?" she said, fluttering her eyelashes in a way she'd seen Lady Frockman, her grandmother's crony, do when she wanted something from her husband.

Seaton made a sound in his throat that could have been a groan or a moan, but was definitely disturbing, since it suggested he wasn't pleased with her interference. "Very well, my dear."

It might have been thrilling to hear Seaton call her "my dear" for the very first time, if she hadn't also discerned the sarcasm that accompanied the cherished address. She felt so hot and so very, very tired. She just wanted to lie down on cool, dry sheets and go to sleep.

Seaton took the key the innkeeper offered, listened to his directions for how to reach the room, then pulled his arm free of hers, as he picked up both his bag and hers, and headed up the stairs.

The bridal suite turned out to be on the corner at the end of the upstairs hall. Seaton opened the door and lit the lamp, before gesturing her inside.

All she could see was the enormous bed that took up the entire room. There was barely room to walk around its edges. A small dressing table and chair had been crammed in one corner, but it was clear where the occupants of this room were expected to spend their time. Lark gulped and turned wide eyes on Seaton, whose lips had thinned to nothing.

He dropped both their bags on the floor and said, "I'll be staying downstairs in the taproom, of course."

"What is the innkeeper going to think when you show up downstairs again?"

"That I need a drink," he said flatly.

She pressed Seaton's handkerchief to her nose, which was dripping again. "We could share the bed."

He barked a laugh that didn't sound the least bit amused. "I will remain downstairs by the fire. I may not get any sleep, but at least I'll be warm."

"David, it's silly to spend the night sitting up in a

chair when you can be comfortable in bed." She saw his eyes widen at her use of his first name and flushed. Her slip had only made the situation worse.

"Comfortable?" he snarled. "In bed with a single young lady to whom I'm not married? My best friend's sister, in fact? Are you really so naïve, Lady Lark?"

She coughed, then took a step closer to the bed and began pulling the pillows from under the counterpane and arranging them down the center of the bed. "We can make a barrier. We're both adults and—"

"That's questionable," he interjected.

She continued without acknowledging the jibe. "And I trust you to respect my person."

"It isn't done. Traveling alone was bad enough, but this will put you beyond the pale. Your grandmother—and your brother—will want to know where you spent the night. They're sure to discover I've hired a single room, after telling the innkeeper we're man and wife. What you're suggesting simply won't do. If I stay in the taproom, I won't have to lie to your brother about sleeping in the same bed with you."

"Marcus won't think the worse of you," she argued.

"Your brother knows me rather too well," Seaton said. "He's seen me with enough young women to know my tastes."

Lark was suddenly alert, staring intently into his warm green eyes which, she admitted, looked troubled. "And I match the sort of woman to whom you're attracted? Is that what you're saying?"

She was surprised to see him flush. Which was when she noticed the dark beard growing on his cheeks and chin. And that his suit was rumpled and his hair in disarray. She'd never seen him look quite so disheveled. Or quite so alluring.

Lark took a step closer without realizing what she was doing and saw his gaze focus on her mouth for a moment, before it shifted back to her eyes. She hoped they didn't look as red and swollen as they felt. He gazed into them as though he couldn't get enough of looking at her, as though he would be happy to continue what he was doing for the rest of his life. So she was taken aback by the words he spoke, in a voice that was harsh and cross.

"I have no desire to be married, Lady Lark. Not now, and not for a very long time, if ever. So the sort of young lady to whom I'm attracted, while she might be a joy to look at, like you, and have black silky hair and sapphire eyes, like you, does not expect a ring on her finger, like you. She's satisfied with a few pounds or a few baubles."

Lark had been protected from the world beyond her grandmother's parlor, and it took her a moment to register what Seaton had said. She couldn't believe he'd spoken to her about something that was no part of her world. She wasn't sure how to reply. She wasn't sure how to react. The only thing she could think to say was "Oh."

He must have seen her shock, because he continued, "I never intended to speak so frankly, but it's better that you understand why it's imperative that I keep my distance."

Lark saw the chagrin on his face, as he realized what he'd admitted. "So you *are* attracted to me."

"Whether I am or whether I'm not should mean nothing to you, since I'm not a prospective bridegroom."

"Won't you need an heir someday?" she asked. "Won't that require a wife?"

"Maybe. Someday. But you'll already be an old married lady with a half dozen children sitting at your knee when that day comes."

Lark frowned. She'd had no idea Seaton was so opposed to marriage. She couldn't resist asking, "Why?"

"What?"

"Why don't you want to get married?"

"You saw what your brother went through with Fanny. He barely survived the pain of it. I don't think I could bear to lose a wife and child."

"Not every wife dies. Or every newborn, for that matter."

"Enough do die to make loving a wife—and having her bear your children—a risky business. I refuse to do it." He heaved a sigh. "How did you get me started on this?"

"I asked you to share my bed."

He pursed his lips. "Yes. An invitation not to be refused, if I were a dishonorable cad. Or if I had aspirations of becoming a married man. Which I don't. So I'll be spending the night downstairs. Have a good sleep, Lady Lark. I'll see you for breakfast in the taproom in the morning."

A moment later he was gone, and Lark was left alone in the bridal suite. What had she expected?

Of course he hadn't stayed in the room with her, when there was no room for either one of them to sleep on the floor. He was a gentleman. Not to mention a good friend to her brother. He wasn't going to take the chance of ruining her and forcing the two of them into marriage, especially when he had such a fear of the institution.

So where did that leave her? Should she give up and spend the rest of the week with the Courts' servants? Or should she fight for the man she loved?

With the very last of her energy, Lark prepared herself for bed, pondering the task ahead of her. How did you convince a man that loving a woman was worth it, despite the chance of losing your loved one at some point in the future? How did you convince a man that the risk of a wife dying in childbirth was worth it for the joy of holding your child in your arms?

Lark didn't get a great deal of sleep over the next several hours. She was miserably hot and, for some reason, itchy, and got up to open the window. Then she was thirsty and got up to pour herself a glass of water from the pitcher, which turned out to be empty. She was too tired to call someone to bring her water, so she went back to bed thirsty, and more tired than she could ever remember being.

She tossed and turned under the covers, as her troubled mind tried to figure out a way she could possibly convince the man she loved—a man who had no intention of ever getting married—that she was the one woman he had to have in his life.

Chapter 32

SEATON HAD SPENT a miserable night trying to sleep in a ladder-back chair near the fire in the tap-room. His discomfort at sitting upright was nothing compared to the misery he felt at the thought of being obliged to marry his best friend's little sister. But he didn't see any honorable way to avoid a leg-shackle, not once Blackthorne heard about the events of the past twenty-four hours.

The situation was made far worse by the fact that Lady Lark was exactly the sort of woman he found most attractive. She possessed physical beauty, of course, but she also happened to be charming and determined and smart enough to beguile him into the situation in which he found himself. He could easily fall in love with her.

He knew better. That way lay madness or, at the very least, the prospect of a great deal of pain. He would simply have to keep himself from loving her. That was all there was to it. Even if he was eventually forced into marriage with her, he would guard his heart with ax and sword and a very strong shield.

Early the next morning, Seaton rented a private

parlor where he could change his clothes and shave, then waited for Lady Lark to appear downstairs until long past the time he thought she should have been up and dressed. "Spoiled brat," he muttered. Several patrons had already come downstairs and were eating breakfast. The innkeeper offered him food and drink, but he waved him off. "I'm waiting for—" He caught himself in time and finished, "My wife."

"Isn't that always the way of it," the man commiserated.

An hour later, Seaton's mood had passed from annoyance to concern. He headed up the stairs and knocked on the door to the bridal suite. He kept the aggravation he felt out of his voice, thinking that, if she was playing games, he didn't want her to know that she'd managed to win. "Lady Lark? Are you awake?"

His alarm increased when there was no answer. "Lark? Are you in there?"

He tried the door and discovered it was locked. He was tempted to break it open, but he wasn't sure what sort of dishabille she might be in, and he wanted to be able to shut the door again, in case she wasn't decently dressed. He took the stairs down two at a time and caught the innkeeper by the shoulder, as he was setting down a plate of kidneys and eggs.

"Is there a problem, milord?"

"Do you have an extra key to the bridal suite?"

The innkeeper chuckled. "Locked you out, did she? Can't say it hasn't happened before." He left the taproom and located a key behind the front desk. As he handed it to Seaton he said softly, "Mayhap a mite more gentleness is called for."

Seaton didn't stop to defend himself, simply took the steps back up three at a time. He stopped for a moment to catch his breath, knocked one more time, and said, "Lark, I'm coming in. Cover yourself."

Then he unlocked the door and stepped into the room. The curtains were being blown around by the cold wind coming in through the open window. He could see the outline of a figure snuggled under the covers. The chit was still sleeping! He closed the window and turned back to the bed. Lady Lark hadn't moved. If it was Lark. He wasn't quite sure.

Seaton crossed to the bed and carefully drew the covers back to reveal a head of black hair and the recognizable profile of Lady Lark Wharton. Her skin looked flushed and dewy, as though she were too warm. She tossed and moaned but didn't open her eyes.

His concern mushroomed to something more akin to fear. He sat down beside her on the bed and lifted her up so his arm could circle her shoulders. He brushed a damp strand of hair from her cheek and realized her skin was fiery hot. "Lark?"

Her eyes fluttered open. "David?"

"How do you feel, little one?"

She pouted her lips and said in a throaty voice that sent shivers down his spine, "I'm not a child. I'm a woman."

"A very young woman. Who seems to be ill. What's wrong, my dear? Can you tell me?"

She brushed her nose with her hand, before her eyes slid closed again. "Don't know. So hot. So thirsty."

Seaton settled her head back on the pillow and headed for the ceramic pitcher in the corner. It was empty. He raced back down the stairs and back up again a few moments later with the pitcher full of water. He poured a cup for her and brought it to the bed, lifted her shoulders again, and held the cup so she could drink from it.

She gulped thirstily, grabbing the cup out of his hands. But she was too weak to hold it, and water spilled onto the sheet. To his surprise, as he rescued the cup from her, she grabbed the wet sheet and held it to her cheeks.

"So hot."

It was clear that she was ill and needed a doctor, but Seaton didn't want to leave her alone. He felt dreadful for thinking Lark had been acting like a spoiled child, sleeping in and making him wait on her, when she'd actually been indisposed.

He pulled the wet sheet off the bed, revealing a pair of trim calves and ankles peeking out from a modest nightgown, then quickly covered Lark with a dry blanket, which he tucked around her. "Rest," he said. "I'll be right back."

He ran pell-mell down the stairs for the second time and inquired of the innkeeper where he could find the closest doctor. He returned a half hour later with a quack who'd told him it was likely his wife would get over whatever it was, if she was simply allowed to rest. Seaton hadn't been satisfied with that explanation. "She's young and healthy.

There's no reason for her to have a fever unless she's ill with some disease. I expect you to examine her and figure out what's wrong. And fix it!"

Seaton hadn't planned to stay in the room while the doctor examined Lark, except he didn't quite trust the man. He barely stopped himself from pummeling the physician when he began unbuttoning the front of Lark's nightgown. "What are you doing?"

"Examining the patient," the doctor retorted.

"Is that necessary?" Seaton demanded.

"Ahh," the man said as he spread the two sides of the nightgown to reveal Lark's chest, so that her breasts were exposed almost to the nipple. "I should have guessed."

Seaton took one look and turned his head away, but he was unable to keep his body from reacting to that brief glimpse of female flesh. Lark had been right. The doctor's examination was leaving no doubt that she was a woman. Seaton kept his gaze averted as the doctor continued his examination. "You should have guessed what?" he asked the man through tight jaws.

"Measles."

Seaton's heart sank. It took him a moment, when he turned back around, to realize that the doctor had bared Lark's entire chest, all the way to her belly. He felt ashamed, because he was looking at Lark's person without her permission or awareness. But he was also choked with desire, despite the fact that she was covered with bright red spots. He croaked, "Measles?"

"I wanted to check her belly for the rash, and

you can see for yourself, she's got measles, sure enough. We've been having an outbreak here in the north."

"But we've just come from London," he protested. Although, when he considered the matter, he realized it was entirely likely that one of her friends, visiting London from the North, had given Lady Lark the measles. "Will she be all right?" Seaton asked, keeping his back turned, but peering over the doctor's shoulder, as the man rebuttoned Lark's nightgown.

"Should be. She'll need rest and whatever liquids you can get down her throat."

"How long till she's well?" Seaton had visions of Blackthorne arriving in Berwick-upon-Tweed, when Lady Lark didn't return home after the week she was supposed to have spent visiting with the Court family, and finding Seaton staying with her at the Black Swan as man and wife.

"Ten days ought to do it," the doctor said.

"Ten days!"

"Could be longer," the doctor said. "Depends on how strong your wife is and how bad a case of measles she's caught."

Seaton sank onto the end of the bed. "Good lord."

"She'll need someone to nurse her, to wash her body down with cold cloths to keep the fever at bay, and to make sure she takes nourishment," the doctor said. "Have you had measles, milord?"

Seaton stared at the doctor in bewilderment. "What?"

"Complications of measles for a gentleman your age can be quite serious."

"I had the measles when I was a boy," Seaton said, still stunned at the turn of events.

"You can hire a nurse to care for your wife, if you don't think you can manage it yourself," the doctor assured him.

Seaton wasn't sure he wanted anyone from Berwick-upon-Tweed taking care of Lady Lark, in case she revealed something in her fevered state that might compromise her further. "I'll take care of my . . . wife." It was getting easier to say the word. And more certain that Lark would become his wife, whether he liked the idea or not.

He supposed his visit to Tearlach Castle would have to wait. Blackthorne's American waif had been a prisoner there for two years. She would just have to remain one a few days longer.

Chapter 33

BLACKTHORNE FOUND HIMSELF facing a footman dressed in his grandmother's livery. Had she had an attack? Was she dying? He swallowed down the bile at the back of his throat and croaked, "Is the dowager duchess—"

The footman thrust a missive in his hand and said, "It don't concern Her Grace."

Blackthorne felt his knees wobble with relief and pressed his palm against the door to keep himself from falling down.

He wasn't surprised that the footman knew the contents of the message he'd been sent to deliver. Servants often knew as much—or more—about what was going on in a household than the occupants themselves. But something was wrong, or his grandmother wouldn't have sent a message to be delivered in the middle of the night.

Ignoring the fact that he was dressed in his nightshirt, he stepped outside onto the cold stone, where there was more moonlight, rather than take the time to light a lamp in order to read the message.

My dearest grandson,
  I have the most dire news to import.

Blackthorne's heartbeat ratcheted up, and the blood began to rush in his veins. He forced himself to continue reading whatever bad news his grandmother had thought deserved a midnight messenger.

You will doubtless think me the most foolish old woman when you hear what has happened. Had it not been for the veriest accident, I would never have discovered the truth. I take full responsibility for what has occurred.

What disaster could have befallen a houseful of women in the middle of London? he wondered. He wished his grandmother would get to the point. He tried skipping to the end but found himself gasping for breath when he read the words: *She is gone.*

Someone had died? Who had died? He skipped back up to the body of the letter and forced himself to read every word.

The Courts attended your wedding breakfast, and Lark asked if she might be allowed to go home with them for a visit. Since they are good friends, I agreed. Lark left one week after your wedding to travel north with them on the train. Imagine my consternation when I met Mrs. Court while shopping on Bond Street—after she had supposedly left London with Lark in her care.

It seems Stephanie contracted the measles, so the Courts were forced to remain in Town until her recovery. I naturally inquired about Lark, since, as you know, she has never had the measles. I discovered, to my horror, that Lark had never been invited to spend a week with the Courts in Berwick-upon-Tweed, and that Mrs. Court had no idea where Lark was.

I hurried home to question Lindsey as to her twin's whereabouts, but she was also under the mistaken impression that her sister had been invited to spend time with the Courts.

I subsequently discovered that Lark's maid is not with her! She has gone home to visit her mother. Your sister has simply disappeared—by herself—to heaven knows where.

She is gone.

The only person of Lark's acquaintance who left London at the same time is the Earl of Seaton.

Could they possibly have eloped? I swear I never saw a romance developing between them, but I don't know what else to think.

I hope you will forgive me for not keeping a closer eye on the girl, but she deceived her twin as well, so I'm certain something havey-cavey is afoot.

I regret the necessity of interrupting your honeymoon, but I believe your presence in London is required immediately.

Your Grandmama

Blackthorne swore, unable to believe the words he'd just read. Lark gone? Simply disappeared? And Grandmama thought she might have eloped? With Seaton, of all people? Impossible.

Or was it?

It was odd that Seaton hadn't told him where he was going or how long he would be gone. Not that they were always in each other's pockets, but in the general course of things, they spent enough time socializing together that, if Seaton had planned to be gone for any appreciable time, he would have said something.

Blackthorne considered whether it would be faster to take a coach to London tonight or wait for the train in the morning. The train made far more sense, especially since he had no intention of leaving his wife on her own, now that he'd learned who she really was.

"Tell Her Grace that my wife and I will be there by noon tomorrow. You can exchange your horse for one in the stables."

"Yes, Your Grace," the messenger said. "Thank you, Your Grace." Then he was gone. Likely the messenger would only make it back to London an hour or two before Blackthorne and his wife arrived on the train, but he wanted his grandmother to have the solace of knowing that he was on his way.

He stepped back inside the house, closed the door, and tensed when he heard someone breathing heavily in the darkness behind him. "Who's there?"

"Who was that? Is something wrong?"

Blackthorne turned to find his wife standing wide-eyed in the moonlight. She looked so beautiful, with her golden hair tumbled around her shoulders, that his breath caught in his throat. "Lark has disappeared."

"What do you mean?"

"She said she was going to visit friends, but those friends are still in London, and Lark is nowhere to be found."

"How awful! You must be beside yourself with worry."

Josie's mild description didn't begin to describe the terror he felt. His innocent sister was lost somewhere in—or perhaps out—of London, and he didn't have a clue where to start looking for her.

"Are you leaving now to find her?" she asked.

"You and I are both going to London on the train in the morning."

"I don't see how I can be of much help in searching for your sister," his wife protested.

"I don't want to lose track of you while I'm hunting for Lark," he said in a sharp voice.

He saw the anger flare in her eyes before she said, "You don't trust me to stay here?"

"No."

He couldn't tell in the moonlight if Josie's face had flushed, but a muscle worked in her jaw, before she lowered her eyes to the floor.

A moment later, she raised her gaze to meet his and said, "You're not being fair."

"*I'm* not being fair? I'm not the one who concealed my identity."

"I told you my name," she retorted. "Can I help it if you didn't recognize it?"

"I never saw you again after I left the ship," he shot back. "Where did you go? What happened to you?"

"You're the one who broke his promise to send me home," she accused.

"Your Grace? Is something wrong?"

Apparently they'd been shouting at each other loud enough to wake Harkness. "We'll be leaving for London tomorrow," he said.

"Is there anything I can do for you tonight?" Harkness asked.

"Go back to bed!" Blackthorne snapped.

Harkness raised his eyebrows, but having been a duke's butler all his life, that was the extent of the expression he allowed himself.

"I'm sorry," Blackthorne said immediately. "I'm not upset with you. Lark has disappeared."

"I can remember a time when you and your brother went missing," the old man said. "You turned up safe and sound. I'm sure the same will be true of your sister. Good night, Your Grace."

As the old man disappeared down the dark hallway, Blackthorne thought back to the time he and Monty had run away. It didn't offer much solace. They'd been caned once too often by their father for some slight infraction and had decided they would search out a camp of gypsies and travel in their caravan as far from the duke as they could get.

He couldn't imagine Lark leaving for such a reason, especially since he couldn't remember the last time she'd experienced any sort of corporal punishment. Had she felt too hemmed in by the dowager? Was that what had happened? Did she need more freedom than she'd been allowed? His grandmother was a strict taskmaster, and to his shame, he'd allowed the burden of his sister's care to fall entirely on her for the past year.

He felt Josie's hand on his arm, her offer of comfort surprising.

"She'll probably already be home by the time we get there tomorrow," she said.

Which reminded him he had a train trip with his wife to endure in the morning. He didn't think he could sit in civilized silence with her for the length of the journey, if he didn't have answers tonight to the questions that had been raised by his knowledge of who she was.

He saw her feet were bare on the stone floor, and he knew from his own bare feet that the stone was cold. He swept her into his arms and said, "We need to talk."

For a moment he wasn't sure whether she was going to fight her way free or allow him to hold her, but her arm slid around his neck, and she rested her head against his shoulder. He wasn't sure what that sort of surrender portended. Was she going to tell him everything at last?

Blackthorne headed for the library, wondering how the woman in his arms could make him feel strong and protective, and annoyed enough to wring her neck, all at the same time. When they reached the library, he carefully set her down in one of the chairs in front of the fireplace. He felt her fingertips caress his neck as her hand slid away, sending shivers down his spine. He wished he'd thought to sit down with her in his lap. But it was too late now.

He turned and built up the fire, then settled in the chair beside hers. He didn't light a lamp, since he thought he could better conceal his disconcerting attraction to her in the shadows.

She spoke before he could say anything. "I have a few questions of my own to ask."

"I have no secrets."

"We'll see." She took a deep breath and asked, "Why didn't you arrange to send me home as you promised?"

"But I did! I asked Seaton to make the arrangements immediately after I left the ship."

She frowned. "And you trusted him to do as you asked?"

"Of course. He was, and is, my best friend. At the time, he was soon to be my brother-in-law."

"Is there any reason you can think of why he wouldn't do as you asked?"

"Are you telling me he didn't?" Blackthorne said incredulously. "That you haven't been in the bosom of your family in America for the past two years?"

"Answer my question," she persisted.

"No," he said, shaking his head. "I can imagine no reason why Seaton wouldn't have done as I asked."

"Did you ever confirm with him that he'd followed your instructions?"

He started to say yes and stopped himself. He'd never asked Seaton about the girl, because he'd assumed his friend had followed his wishes. He hadn't wanted to know where she'd asked to go, for fear that he might be tempted to seek her out. "No," he admitted at last. "I never asked for confirmation."

"Am I to presume that you had no idea where he arranged for me to be sent?"

"You may presume that, yes." He hesitated, then asked, "Where did he send you?"

"Tearlach Castle."

Blackthorne came out of his chair and stood facing her. "What? That property is *mine,* not Seaton's. Where would he get the audacity—or the authority—to do such a thing?"

"Are you calling me a liar?"

"I'm saying it's impossible."

"Would you like me to describe the place?" she said in a stony voice. "I know it well, having worked there for the past two years as a maid."

"*Worked* there? As a *maid*?" Blackthorne was appalled. "I don't believe you." What she suggested was ludicrous.

"Why would I lie?" she asked, rising from her chair, her hands fisted, to confront him barefoot toe to barefoot toe.

"Why would Seaton leave you there? It makes no sense." Blackthorne could imagine no circumstances that would cause his friend to divert the American he'd rescued to one of someone else's properties, let alone force her to take employment as a maid.

"It's true."

Then Blackthorne remembered that his bride was extravagantly wealthy. "You obviously had the financial means to leave. Why would you stay?"

"I didn't learn of my inheritance until a few days before I came to London and met you. In fact, I was on my way home to my family—who'd finally located me and provided the funds for the journey—when I heard of your need for a bride to save Blackthorne Abbey."

"Am I to believe you knew exactly who I was—what I had done for you in the Sioux village—when you married me?"

She nodded.

"So you married me to repay me for saving your life," he said scornfully.

She didn't confirm his statement. But she didn't contradict him, either.

"I didn't want your charity," he said harshly. "And it was no kindness to put me in your debt, when I have no way to repay you."

"But there *is* a way you can repay me, Your Grace."

He arched a brow at her use of his title. "I'm listening."

"You can place your nephews in my care."

It suddenly dawned on him that at one point, she'd pretended not to know he had nephews, when she must have spent the past two years in their company. That was odd, but it also made a kind of sense, since she'd been concealing the fact that she'd spent the past two years in England. "I have no objection to bringing Spencer and Clay to live with us here at the Abbey, as soon as enough repairs have been made to make it livable."

She opened her mouth but shut it again without speaking. "Thank you. Is that everything you want to know?"

He had more information than he could easily digest. Some of the things he'd learned only left him with more questions. It was just dawning on him that she must blame him for having been relegated to working as a servant. And that his best friend had, for some mysterious reason, put her there—and left her there—for the past two years. And through it all, Seaton had never said a word to him!

He thought back to all the times he'd been caught by his friend mooning over the missing American girl. Seaton must have been laughing up his sleeve. It was humiliating. It was infuriating.

What if Josie hadn't come into her inheritance? Had Seaton planned to leave her there forever after? Blackthorne needed to hear from his friend's own mouth what had possessed him to divert the girl to Tearlach Castle in the first place.

But Seaton was missing. Along with Lark.

Blackthorne suddenly wasn't as willing to discount his grandmother's suspicion that Seaton and his sister might have eloped. If his friend could conceal such a terrible secret as his kidnapping of Josephine Wentworth, then what dastardly intrigue might he have planned for Blackthorne's missing sister?

He needed to find his friend and demand answers, after he located his sister, of course. Or maybe one would lead him to the other.

Blackthorne felt sick to his stomach. Why had Seaton never said anything? What motive could he possibly have had for what he'd done? Blackthorne tamped down his growing rage. He would need all his faculties about him, when he finally confronted his friend.

Chapter 34

JOSIE HAD SAT in utter silence beside her husband for the entire train ride to London, an oppressive hush which persisted as they began the brief coach ride from Paddington Station to his grandmother's townhome. Blackthorne had given her a great deal of food for thought the previous evening. It seemed the duke was not quite the villain she'd presumed him to be, but rather a dupe of his friend, the Earl of Seaton. Although, it was still a mystery why Seaton had done what he had.

Even so, she didn't consider Blackthorne blameless. He'd made a promise to her, then delegated it to someone else, who'd proved unreliable. Furthermore, if he'd come even once to visit his nephews at Tearlach Castle, he would have discovered Seaton's deception. She gave a small, rueful smile as she thought of the reasons Blackthorne believed she'd married him. Because he'd been *kind*. Because she felt *obligated* to him.

The primary emotion that had survived their encounter last night was relief that her husband still had no inkling of why she'd actually married him, or that she intended to take his nephews and flee to America.

She wondered why she was suddenly "fleeing" rather than merely "returning home."

Because you're starting to like the Dastardly Duke. You love what happens with him in bed. And you're afraid that, if you don't get away soon, you'll never leave. He's agreed to bring the boys to the Abbey when it's repaired. You could stay in England and—

"Shut up!" Josie muttered to silence the treasonous voice in her head. She didn't realize until Blackthorne's head turned sharply in her direction, that she'd spoken the words aloud.

"Pardon me?"

Since her husband hadn't said anything, the words obviously hadn't been directed at him, but Josie nevertheless replied, "I wasn't speaking to you."

He glanced languidly around the otherwise empty carriage. "Then to whom were you speaking?"

She hesitated, then admitted, "I was having a conversation with myself. In my head," she added unnecessarily.

"Ah. And doubtless did not like what you had to say."

Josie bristled at his suggestion that he wouldn't have liked what she had to say, either. "If you must know—" She cut herself off. "It's no business of yours what I was thinking."

"Your thoughts couldn't be happy ones, if you spent the past night as sleepless as I did. Where would you have gone, if you were my sister?"

Josie was surprised at the change of subject, but she considered the idea seriously before saying, "She must have planned her escape, in order to disappear without her maid and without a soul knowing where she was going, including her twin."

"That's what worries me." He added, "Along with the fact that Seaton is missing at the same time."

"You believe your best friend has something to do with your sister's disappearance?"

"He managed your disappearance."

"But I never saw him again after I left London," she pointed out. "He doesn't seem the sort of man to kidnap a female."

"Unless he eloped with my sister, as my grandmother suggested."

Josie thought back to her trip to the zoo, and her suspicion that Seaton was attracted to one of Blackthorne's sisters, who also seemed to be attracted to him. "Have you noticed Seaton paying particular attention to her?"

He shook his head. "None at all. And Seaton has more than once mentioned his aversion to the married state, which makes him an unlikely bridegroom."

"How does your sister feel about him? Maybe she's the one seeking to put him in a compromising situation."

The duke's eyes widened. Apparently, he hadn't considered the possibility that his innocent sister could be engaged in such manipulative behavior.

The carriage stopped, and Josie saw Blackthorne shoot a worried look at the front door of his grandmother's townhome. She laid a hand on his arm in comfort, something she'd also done the previous evening without thinking.

When Blackthorne had swept her up in his arms last night, she'd rested her head against his heavily beating heart and slid her arms trustingly around his neck. At the time, she hadn't understood her willingness to offer comfort to a man she believed had wronged her so terribly.

Later, in the wee hours of the morning, alone in her room with her feet tucked under her, safely away from any roving mice, she'd realized that she'd offered succor to Blackthorne to repay him for the succor he'd offered her—when she'd run to him, so terrified of the mouse in her bed. His lovemaking had been another rescue of sorts, a willingness on his part to hold her close and take away the fearful memories from her past.

And then there was that incident in the stable loft. She'd known he wanted to make love to her, but she'd denied them both. She still wasn't sure exactly why she'd run from him.

Josie blushed at the memory of the very long, very deep kiss they'd shared while lying in the hay. She looked up to find her husband's gaze focused on her rosy face.

"I'd give a great deal to know what you're thinking right now."

"Shouldn't we go inside?" she countered, avoiding his suggestion that she bare her soul.

He tapped on the side of the coach and a footman opened the door and let down the steps. The duke stepped out and reached up a hand to help her down. He pulled her close and slid her arm through his, as they headed up the stairs. Somehow she knew he needed her support again, for whatever they discovered inside, and she willingly gave it.

The butler opened the front door before they reached it and stood back to let them in, announcing, "Her Grace is in the drawing room, Your Graces."

Josie felt herself tugged along as Blackthorne strode down the hall. A footman opened the drawing room door and closed it after they entered.

The dowager duchess evidenced none of the unflappable dignity she'd possessed when Josie had met her two weeks ago. A strand of silvery hair had come loose at her temple and her once-fierce blue eyes looked haunted. She rose, leaning heavily on her cane, and reached out a shaking hand to her grandson.

"It's worse than I imagined," the dowager duchess said.

"What have you heard?" Blackthorne asked, releasing Josie and hurrying across the room to take his grandmother's hand.

Josie watched the old woman crumple into her grandson's arms. Blackthorne held her close, his hand soothing its way down her rigid back.

"Tell me all," he said.

"She left on the same train as Seaton," his grandmother replied in a frail voice.

"How do you know?"

"I put a Bow Street runner to work, of course," she said with asperity, raising her head to glare at him.

Josie saw the smile appear on Blackthorne's face at his grandmother's spirited reply.

"Very well, my dear," he said. "Did the runner find out where they were bound?"

"North," the dowager said in a stark voice. "To Berwick-upon-Tweed."

"How is Lindsey?" Blackthorne asked. "I expected to find her here with you."

"She hasn't come out of her room since she discovered her twin lied to her," the dowager said.

"Perhaps I should speak with her."

The dowager seemed torn. "I'm not sure that would be productive. Lindsey knows nothing to the point."

But she might need the sort of comfort an older brother could provide, Josie thought. "You should at least let your sister know you've come," she said to the duke. "Maybe she's remembered something that might help you in your search."

"I questioned her most straitly," the dowager said. "If Lindsey knew anything, she would already have divulged it to me."

Josie looked Blackthorne in the eye. "If you were my brother, I would appreciate a hug and a word of support. Lindsey must be feeling guilty at not having somehow divined what her twin was planning."

"And you know this because . . . ?" the duke said.

"I have twin sisters of my own."

The duke's eyes widened, but he quickly recovered and said to the dowager, "It won't hurt to check on Lindsey, to make sure she's all right."

He caught Josie's hand on the way past and pulled her along behind him, as he headed up the stairs to the next floor. He hurried down a long hallway, until he reached a door near the end. He knocked on it and called out, "Lindsey? Are you in there?"

"Marcus?"

Josie heard the hopeful sound in Lindsey's voice, and two feet hitting the floor and running to the door. It was pulled open and Lindsey threw herself into her brother's arms, sobbing so pitifully that Josie thought her own heart would break.

She met Blackthorne's troubled gaze over his sister's head and, since he already had his arms around Lindsey, hugging her tight, mouthed the words, "Say something."

"Everything will be all right, Lindsey. There's no need for tears," he said in a gruff voice.

"How do you know that?" his sister accused, raising a tearstained face to glare at him. "Lark might have been ravished. She might be lying dead in a gutter. We might never see her again!"

He took his sister firmly by the arms. "I thought you had more gumption than to fall to pieces like this. Imagine what Lark will say when she hears what a widgeon you've been."

"I don't care what Lark thinks, since I never intend to speak to her again," Lindsey shot back. "How could she, Marcus? Why would she lie to me? She's my other half. We've never kept secrets before. Why now? Why was she so desperate to get away that she kept her plans a secret from me, her very own twin?"

"I don't know, dearest. We'll have to ask her when she returns home."

"Will she be coming home? Have you discovered where she is?"

"Not yet. But I promise you I'll find her and bring her back. I'm certain there will be a good explanation for her bizarre behavior, and I have no doubt she'll beg your pardon."

Josie watched the duke pull a handkerchief from his pocket and dab at the tears on his sister's cheeks.

"Go wash your face, and then join Grandmama downstairs. She could use your company."

"I'm sorry, Marcus. If I feel this guilty, I can only imagine how badly grandmother is taking Lark's disappearance."

"Do you have something to be guilty about?" Blackthorne asked. "Is there something you know that you haven't yet told Grandmama?"

Lark kept her eyes lowered as she admitted, "Lark asked me not to say anything to Grandmama about her invitation from the Courts until all the wedding guests were gone. I realize now she didn't want Grandmama to be able to question Mrs. Court about the invitation and discover it didn't exist.

"I believed Lark when she told me she'd agreed to meet the Courts at the station to catch the train to Berwick-upon-Tweed, because she'd never lied to me before."

"Why do you think she lied to you this time?"

"I don't know!" Lindsey said in an agonized voice.

"Have you ever seen Lark alone in company with Seaton?" Blackthorne asked.

Lindsey blotted at the last of the tears on her face, which was scrunched up in thought. "Seaton? No."

"Has she ever evidenced a preference for him?"

Lindsey shook her head, looking confused. "She would have said something to me, if she had a tendre for him."

"Would she?" Josie interjected.

Both Whartons turned on her, Blackthorne with a black brow arched in question and Lindsey with both black brows arrowed down.

"Are you suggesting—" Lindsey began.

"I'm only saying that affairs of the heart are usually conducted in private—even between twins," Josie interrupted. "At least, that was my experience with my twin sisters, Hannah and Henrietta."

"Your twin sisters kept secrets from each other?"

"They were closer than two peas in a pod for their entire lives—before they began their courtships. But when my sister Hannah married, she told Hetty nothing of her experiences with Mr. McMurtry. And when Hetty fell in love, she refused to share her feelings with Hannah."

Josie realized she was stretching the truth a bit to suggest that Hannah had been *courted* by Mr. McMurtry. She'd found her husband by answering an advertisement in the *Chicago Herald* for a mail-order bride. And Hetty had been so resentful of Hannah's interference in her love life, that she'd ignored her sister's admonitions, and ended up causing two jealous men to kill each other over her. But Josie could honestly say that, before they'd allowed a man—or two—into their lives, her twin sisters had been as thick as thieves.

Precisely because Lindsey had been kept in the dark by her twin, Josie would have wagered every penny she had left of her inheritance that Lark's adventure involved a romance with some gentleman. And because of how closely Lark was watched, that gentleman was most likely someone in whose company she often found herself, like Blackthorne's best friend, the Earl of Seaton.

A maid arrived in the hallway and said to Josie, "You have a visitor, Your Grace."

"Me?" Josie didn't have a single friend in London and couldn't imagine anyone calling on her, especially at the dowager duchess's home. "Who is it?"

"He won't give his name. The gentleman just says you should come at once."

Blackthorne turned to his sister and said, "Dry your tears and come downstairs. We'll see you shortly."

Then he took Josie's hand possessively in his and started down the hall. "I suppose we'd better see who's come to visit you."

Chapter 35

"MR. THOMPSON? WHAT ARE you doing here?" Josie exclaimed.

"You know this man?" Blackthorne said.

Josie was so surprised, she answered with the truth. "Yes. He's a Pinkerton detective." She clasped her hands together to stop their trembling and asked, "Has something happened to Spencer and Clay? Was it scarlet fever, and not measles after all?"

"It was measles," Mr. Thompson replied. "And the Lords Spencer and Clay are recovering apace."

Josie put a hand out to steady herself, and it landed on Blackthorne's sleeve. "Oh, thank goodness!"

He pulled his arm free, as though she were some foul thing, and said in an icy voice, "You hired a Pinkerton to spy on my nephews?"

"No. Yes. Not really," Josie stuttered, seeing a look on her husband's face that did nothing to help the state of her quivering knees.

"Which is it?"

Josie realized she was in deep water and wasn't sure she could swim back to shore on her own. She shot a discomfited look at the Pinkerton, who stood waiting patiently in his long black duster, his black bowler hat in hand.

To her relief, Mr. Thompson turned to the duke and said, "I'm aware of your current dilemma, Your Grace. I came because I have information that might be of help."

"Who are you?" Blackthorne demanded.

"As your wife said, I'm a Pinkerton detective. I was hired by Miss Wentworth's—excuse me, the duchess's—sister Miranda, that is, Mrs. Jacob Creed."

"For what purpose?"

"To locate Miss Wentworth, advise her of her inheritance, and make arrangements for her safe return to America," the Pinkerton replied.

"You seem to have failed in your objective," the duke pointed out. "Miss Wentworth—the duchess—is still in England."

The Pinkerton's mouth twisted wryly. "That is true, Your Grace."

The duke's eyes narrowed perceptively. "But you're still here. Why?"

Josie was afraid the Pinkerton would reveal her plan to abscond—now she was *stealing* them?—with the boys, so she said, "I care dearly for your nephews and wanted to be sure someone was looking after them, once I left Tearlach Castle."

"My nephews, who have both a governess and a housekeeper to look after them?"

Josie bit her lip to stop any further explanation of her behavior.

Blackthorne eyed her speculatively, and she knew

he was remembering her probing questions at the Abbey about his nephews, her desire to bring them to the Abbey to live, and her original pretense that they were strangers.

She lifted her chin and said, "I asked Mr. Thompson to keep an eye on Spencer and Clay to make sure they were doing well, until they could join us at the Abbey."

"Why wouldn't they be doing well?"

Josie hadn't expected the question, and she wasn't sure how much she should say about the two boys being caught up in the ongoing feud between his housekeeper and the children's governess. "No reason," she said, deciding discretion was important if it became necessary, as it still might, to make her escape with the children. She wasn't happy with that choice of words, either. *Escape*? From what, pray tell?

She forced her thoughts back to the necessity for some sort of answer the duke would accept. "Mr. Thompson has been able to reassure me that Spencer and Clay are fine."

"Except for having the measles," Blackthorne said, his eyes narrowed suspiciously.

"Yes. Except for that," Josie said lamely. "And they should be over them very soon, if they aren't already."

"How did you get here so quickly from Northumberland?" Blackthorne inquired of the Pinkerton.

"I've been in London taking care of business," the Pinkerton explained. "I have an associate in Northumberland watching over your nephews."

His lips twisted wryly as he said, "A Pinkerton never sleeps." He cleared his throat when Blackthorne scowled and continued, "Which is how I came to discover the whereabouts of your sister Lady Lark Wharton."

Blackthorne clamped a strong hand on the Pinkerton's shoulder, his face grim. "Where is she? What's happened to her?"

"According to my man, she's staying at an inn called the Black Swan in Berwick-upon-Tweed." He hesitated and added, "As the wife of the Earl of Seaton."

Blackthorne's shoulders bunched. "Are they married?"

"Not unless they were married before they left London," the Pinkerton replied. "According to my associate, they registered at the Black Swan late last night as man and wife—without a trip to Scotland beforehand. I could make inquiries, if you like."

"Damn and blast," Blackthorne muttered, his hands knotting into dangerous fists. "I'll kill him." He focused his gaze on the Pinkerton and said, "How soon can you arrange for your man to find her a chaperon and escort her back to London?"

"I'm afraid that won't be possible for some time."

"Why not?"

"Your sister has contracted the measles."

"Oh, dear," Josie said.

"Who's taking care of her?" Blackthorne asked.

"A doctor has seen her, Your Grace. But she is apparently being nursed in the bridal suite at the Black Swan by the earl himself."

Blackthorne's lips compressed to a very thin, very angry line. "I suppose I shall have to go and fetch her myself."

"I'll go, too," Josie said, adding, "She'll need someone to be with her, once Seaton has been sent on his way. And I've already had the measles."

The duke opened his mouth to say something but snapped it shut again. "Very well."

"There is a train to Berwick-upon-Tweed leaving this afternoon, Your Grace," the Pinkerton said.

"Go fetch whatever you require for the journey," Blackthorne said to Josie, "while I apprise my grandmother of the situation."

"Don't you think we should wait until we have a chance to see whether your sister and Seaton are married? Or not?" Josie asked.

Blackthorne's face looked grim. "If they aren't, they will be soon. Go! Get what you need. We don't have much time to catch the train."

Once Blackthorne was out of hearing, Josie turned to the Pinkerton and said, "Thank you for not revealing my plans."

"What plans are those, Your Grace?"

Josie realized suddenly that she'd never spoken directly to the Pinkerton about her desire to rescue the boys—who were now her nephews-by-marriage—from the clutches of the Dastardly Duke and take them to America. But she would never have a better chance to steal them—that word again!—and disappear than she would while Blackthorne was distracted taking care of his sister and dealing with Seaton. Presuming she still wanted to leave her husband, something she wasn't at all sure of anymore.

Blackthorne had seemed willing to bring his nephews to live at the Abbey when the renovations were completed, but she still had no satisfactory answer for why he'd abandoned them for two long years. The safer course was to take the boys with her when she left.

Was she still leaving? Josie missed her family. She wanted to see them, talk to them, hug them, and kiss them. She couldn't imagine Blackthorne leaving the Abbey in the midst of all the work being done to go with her—or willingly allowing her to travel on her own. Nevertheless, she was determined to visit her family—and soon. The only issue was whether to take Spencer and Clay with her when she did.

She wished she hadn't promised to nurse her sister-in-law. She would feel obliged to do exactly that, at least until Lark was feeling more herself. She would have to watch for an opportunity to scoop up her nephews and take ship from Berwick-upon-Tweed on a vessel headed to America. Or, if not to America, at least to someplace she could find a ship to America.

In Lark's situation she had one more example of how badly Blackthorne was managing those in his care. Naturally he was worried about his sister now. But where had he been before she'd run away?

Even so, Josie's stomach knotted at the thought of walking away from her marriage. Maybe, before she acted, she should speak more frankly of her concerns to her husband and delve more deeply into his feelings about his nephews—assuming he would share them with her. Surely he would rescue them immediately, if he realized the direness of their situation.

Then again, maybe he wouldn't. Maybe Blackthorne would plead the necessity of spending months repairing the Abbey without having Spencer and Clay underfoot. The two young boys couldn't help getting into trouble. It was never anything vicious, but the results were occasionally disastrous. But when push came to shove, she wasn't going to allow them to suffer any more than they already had.

Josie missed her sisters and brothers. She missed . . . She thought the word *home,* but the truth was there was no home to go back to—just the bosom of her family. And even that no longer existed, now that her sisters were spread out across the West from Texas to the wilderness territories of Wyoming and Montana.

Here. Home could be here.

With the Dastardly Duke?

He isn't quite as dastardly as you painted him in the beginning. In fact, he's seemed quite reasonable lately. Surely, if you explained the boys' circumstances to him, he would remedy the problem. After all, he helped Harriet reunite with her sisters.

But helping Harriet hadn't required him to be personally responsible for two young boys who would be constantly underfoot. He might simply hire another governess, rather than bring Spencer and Clay to live at the Abbey. What if she got along

as horridly with Mrs. Pettibone as Miss Sharpe
had? Then where would the boys be? As unhappy
as they were now, that's where!

No, she must move quickly and surely, once Lark
was feeling better, to grab the boys and run.

*You're actually going to kidnap them? Won't
the duke come after you? Won't he have you ar-
rested and put in jail?*

It wouldn't actually be kidnapping. I'm their
aunt.

*Tell that to an English judge when the plaintiff
is a duke of the realm.*

Josie chewed on a hangnail, then realized the
Pinkerton was still standing there, and dropped her
hand to her side.

"I have some business I need you to do for me."
She quickly explained what she wanted, before she
could lose her courage.

The Pinkerton listened and nodded. "Yes, Your
Grace, I can handle that. But won't the duke—"

"Blackthorne is to hear nothing of this."

The Pinkerton raised a skeptical brow but said
nothing.

"Once I married Blackthorne, I became Spencer
and Clay's aunt. As far as anyone is concerned, I'll
merely be taking my nephews for a holiday in
America."

Chapter 36

DESPITE THE FACT that his sister had died of a lingering illness, Seaton had virtually no experience nursing a sick female. Fanny had insisted on having a nurse take care of her, and he'd only been allowed into her sickroom to visit. Seeing Lady Lark, someone he cared about far more than he was willing to admit, suffering with measles was his worst nightmare come to life. Someone as healthy as she was normally didn't die from the disease, but terrible complications could occur, and one never knew who would fall victim to them and end up blind or crippled . . . or dead.

More than once during the past day, Seaton had been tempted to find someone else to care for his patient. But the grateful look in Lark's eyes when he pressed a cool, damp cloth against her fevered face, and the need to provide a clean handkerchief for her runny nose and wretched cough, kept him sitting beside her bed. He'd even applied a baking soda concoction the doctor had recommended to the painful rash that covered her neck and arms and chest and belly. That had been a torment, because he could see how beautiful she would be without the spots, and experienced firsthand just how miserable she was because of them.

He thought it odd that Lark didn't seem self-conscious when she'd been unclothed in his presence, but he decided that her illness kept her from being aware of the inappropriateness of the situation.

In between treatments she slept, tossing and turning so fretfully that he spent a great deal of time untangling the sheets and blankets and pulling them back up so her bare calves and ankles—and occasionally her naked thighs and buttocks—were decently covered.

Oh, he'd been well and truly caught in parson's mousetrap. There was no getting out of marriage to the girl. The only question was whether he should manage the deed himself or wait for her brother to demand it. Seaton was physically attracted to Lark, of course, and he admired her spirit, which had been evidenced by a great many wild pranks he'd witnessed over the years, as she was growing up. But that was part of the problem. It would be all too easy to fall in love with her. And then where would he be?

He'd be a dead duck. A tortured, unhappy man, frightened to make love to his wife for fear of getting her pregnant and killing her. To make matters worse, Seaton felt sure that Lark would object to his keeping a mistress. He foresaw a long life of appalling celibacy.

And what about Lark? How did she feel about him? He knew she'd finagled that meeting on the train, but had she merely been hoping for an adventure? Or had she intended to lure him to the altar? Unfortunately, Blackthorne would likely be on the doorstep of the Black Swan before Seaton had a chance to speak to the sick girl about her feelings.

Lark moaned and turned over, twisting the covers down to her waist. Seaton rose from his chair beside the bed and rearranged the blanket to keep her from getting a chill, brushing her silky hair aside so he could feel the back of her nightgown to ensure it wasn't damp with sweat.

Lark had been wearing a cotton gown when the doctor arrived that morning, but it had become sweat-soaked during the day, and it had been necessary to get her into something dry. Seaton had searched through her bags until he located another nightgown, while he sent the one she'd been wearing downstairs to be laundered.

He'd been shocked when he realized Lark was wearing absolutely nothing under her gown. He'd expected to be protected from seeing her completely naked by the presence of female underclothes. Apparently, she didn't wear any to bed. He found himself imagining what it would have been like to discover that fact on his wedding night.

Seaton made a disgruntled sound in his throat. He was gaining far more intimate knowledge about his best friend's sister than was good for his heart rate. Lark's skin might be covered in a bumpy red rash, but it did nothing to conceal her figure, which was something out of the ordinary. He'd been forced to handle her hair to move it out of his way, when he took a cool cloth to her face and neck, and he'd marveled at its thickness and texture. He didn't have to wonder how it would look spread out on a pillow, because he'd seen it so.

Seaton fed Lark soup, and since what went in had to come out, and she couldn't leave the room, he'd provided a chamber pot, and given her a few moments of privacy to use it.

He wondered how soon Blackthorne would locate them. He was torn between wanting this interlude to continue and being desperate for it to end. He wondered how many more hours he would be alone with the girl, totally responsible for her wellbeing. He couldn't help feeling protective. He couldn't help caring about her, even though he didn't want to feel anything. He wondered how much he was going to resent being trapped into marriage this way.

He suppressed his feelings of umbrage when he thought of what Lady Lark would have to contend with when she was herself again. How would she react when she'd recovered enough to realize that a single gentleman—her older brother's friend—was the one who'd been nursing her? He somehow thought the grateful looks she'd been giving him would disappear in a flash. Would she be embarrassed? Ashamed? More likely, she would be angry. Finally, what would she think when she realized they were going to be forced by circumstances to marry?

"David?"

Seaton was surprised to discover Lark was awake and staring up at him. It was another sign of how sick she was that she'd addressed him by his given name. Although, to be honest, ever since they'd arrived at the inn, propriety seemed to have gone out the window.

"Yes, sweet—" He stopped himself just in time from calling her "sweetheart." It was a term he might have used with an adorable child, but he knew in his heart that he'd been saying it in an entirely different context. How could she have slipped beneath his defenses so suddenly? When had she become someone special to him, when he was so determined not to care?

"What is it, Lady Lark?" he asked in a quiet voice appropriate for a sickroom. And why was he addressing her so formally, when she'd been merely Lark to him, every time he'd thought of her, all day long?

Her wary eyes searched the room. He saw her distress when she recognized it as the bridal suite at the Black Swan. He watched her pick at her cotton nightgown in confusion, as though she couldn't understand why she was wearing it. Then she spied her hand and saw all the raised red spots on it. Her eyes closed, and she moaned before whispering, "Measles."

"Yes, you have the measles."

"So the sniffles on the train were more than the sniffles, and the cough was more than a cough."

"It appears so."

Her eyes opened wide in fright, and she tried to sit up. "How long have I been ill? My brother—"

He put a hand to her shoulder to force her back down. "Rest easy, my dear." He gritted his teeth as another blasted endearment slipped out. "This is only the evening of the first day you've been ill."

"How long does it take to get well from measles?"

"The doctor said perhaps ten days."

"Ten days! I can't be gone that long. My deception will be discovered, and my brother will kill me."

After he kills me, Seaton thought. Lark still had not woken up enough to note, with inevitable maidenly alarm, that she was dressed in a nightgown and lying in a bed upon which a single gentleman—he, himself—was seated. Suddenly, she figured it all out.

Her eyes went wide with dismay. "Oh, lord. Oh, heavenly angels. Oh, dear."

All in all, he decided, she was taking it pretty well.

"What are you doing here?" she demanded.

"Nursing you."

"Without a chaperon? Or a lady's maid? Or anyone to provide the proprieties?" she shrieked.

She wasn't actually shrieking, but the anguish in her voice raised the hair on his neck like fingernails on a chalkboard.

"What were you thinking?" she railed.

"If you will recall," he said in a calm voice, "we registered as man and wife. When you didn't come down for breakfast, I came here and found you ill with a fever. I summoned a doctor, who assumed we were married. He discovered you have the measles. Since there was no one else in attendance, he gave me instructions on how to care for you."

She put a hand up to stop him from saying anything more, a horrified look in her eyes. "Are you telling me that you've been in this room all day long, *alone,* taking care of me?"

He discovered his throat had swollen closed with some emotion, preventing speech. He swallowed over the painful knot, but that did nothing to solve the problem, so he simply nodded.

She closed her eyes and muttered, "I want to die. I want to fall into a hole and cover myself over with dirt and disappear forever. My grandmother. My brother. My sister! They'll be so disappointed in me. I can't bear it!" She wagged her head from side to side on the pillow. "What an idiot I am! How will I ever live this down? How did I let this happen?" Then she forced herself up on her elbows and asked, "Have you sent news of my illness to anyone?"

"Of course not."

She let out a breath. "Then we should be able to carry this off without anyone becoming the wiser."

"Carry what off?"

"You can arrange for my transportation to the Courts' home, where I can recuperate on my own. I'll send a note to Grandmama telling her that I've contracted the measles, and it will delay my return home. Problem solved."

"Except that I've spent the day here alone with you." He took a deep breath and added, "And have seen everything of you there is to see."

He wouldn't have thought one could see a blush on a face so full of puffy red spots, but he did. "So you see, my dear—" He paused, closing his eyes in mortification at his apparent inability to keep that sort of affectionate expression out of his speech to the chit, then continued, "We've been trapped. We must marry. Neither of us has any choice."

He realized what he'd said and barely repressed a groan. Did he have to remind her that he felt "trapped" at the same time as he called her "my dear"? Had he really been so insensitive as to suggest that neither of them "had any choice"? That was no way to go into a marriage that he could see no way of avoiding.

Her jaw jutted, and she tipped her chin up. "*You* may feel trapped, but *I* don't."

He was shocked into blurting with blunt rancor, "For the past several hours, I've been handling your body as though I had the same rights to it as I would if you were my mistress. You are compromised beyond redemption. You *must* marry me."

The blush was back but her chin was still tipped up and a martial light gleamed in her bleary blue eyes. "I'm sorry for your discomfort."

He snorted.

She continued doggedly, "But no one who knows us is aware of the situation. Why should we be forced to do something that would make us both unhappy?"

"You would be unhappy married to me?" He was aggrieved that his offer was being so soundly rejected. And, he admitted to himself, a little hurt. She should be grateful, not argumentative, when he was willing to give up his freedom to save her good name.

"I don't believe you would be happy in a marriage not of your choosing. And I certainly would not."

He made a face. He was the one who'd used the word "trapped." He had no one to blame but himself for her resistance. "You do see how impossible it would be for you to go on, if we didn't marry?"

"Why? Because you've seen my body?"

It was his turn to flush. He'd never heard such plain speaking from a gently raised female. He was learning things about his intended bride's backbone that he'd never suspected.

"You're too sick to be traveling anywhere. And I can't believe the Courts would welcome someone with the measles into their home."

"Nevertheless, that is where I'm going, as soon as it may be arranged. Don't you see? We must salvage what we can from this disaster. Once I'm back home in London, if you have any desire to seek my interest or affection, you're free to do so."

Seaton scratched at the day's growth of itchy beard on his chin. Had he ever encountered such a pestilential female in his life? He didn't think so. He watched her shoving the covers aside, as though she intended to get out of bed and get dressed. "What are you doing?" he asked to confirm his suspicion.

"I must dress."

"You're sick. You should be in bed."

"I confess I don't feel at all well. But I think I can manage to dress. Once I'm in a carriage on my way to the Courts' home, I can stretch out on the seat and sleep."

"You intend to travel alone?" He heard the concern in his voice, but it seemed there was no stopping himself from caring about her.

"I couldn't very well show up on the Courts' doorstep without a maid and in the company of a single gentleman. What would the servants think?"

"It's a little late to worry about appearances."

"Please, David. Don't argue. I'm not feeling well enough to do battle with you. Leave me alone to dress—"

"You will need help," he said. "You're not well enough to manage by yourself."

"I can call a maid to help."

"You have the measles. No one will come near you. Sweetheart— Damn and blast!" he muttered, disgusted with himself for addressing her so familiarly, and then, realizing that he'd compounded his mistake with profanity, he snarled, "Just let me help you dress!"

She crossed her hands over her breasts as though she'd suddenly noticed how thin the cotton nightgown was. Her modesty had arrived far too late to keep him from remembering quite clearly the delicate pink nipples he'd seen with no covering at all.

"I would be mortified to have you see me in a state of dishabille."

"It's too late for embarrassment. I've already seen every inch of you. Make up your mind."

"Very well," she said, her lips forming a petulant pout that only emphasized how kissable they were. "But you may not use this encounter to force the issue of marriage. Promise?"

He gritted his teeth so hard a muscle in his jaw jerked. She wanted him to promise that he wouldn't pursue marriage after he'd helped put clothes on her naked body? Surely he was destined for Bedlam. "After you're dressed, I'll be happy to send you on your way without another thought to your reputation, if that's what you want."

"It is."

He saw her arms, which she was using to hold herself up, begin to shiver. "Are you all right?"

"I'm feeling a little woozy. I just need to lie down for a moment." As she slid back against the pillows, her eyes drifted closed. "Give me a moment," she murmured. "And I'll be fine."

Seaton saw the flush on her face and knew the fever had returned with a vengeance. Her plan might have worked, if she'd been well enough to dress, well enough to travel. But Lady Lark wasn't going anywhere tonight. He rose to find the cool, wet cloth he'd been using to ease her fevered brow, then seated himself beside the woman he was somehow going to have to convince, for her own sake, to become his wife.

Chapter 37

JOSIE WAS JOLTED so hard by the train's sudden stop that she would have landed on the floor, if Blackthorne hadn't thrown out an arm to stop her forward momentum. Her fashionable straw hat had fallen over one eye, and she shoved it back with one gloved hand while she groped for the edge of the wooden seat with the other. She shot a fearful look in Blackthorne's direction and asked, "What just happened?"

"At a guess, the engineer saw a hazard on the track and stopped the train."

A murmur of voices in the train car suggested that everyone else felt as confused and anxious as Josie did. Blackthorne seemed completely calm, unlike many of the passengers, who were chattering and frantically racing around, peering out the rain-splashed windows—a futile endeavor, since it was pitch black outside, except for the occasional flash of lightning.

Fortunately, within a few minutes, a conductor stepped into their car, held up his hands for silence, and announced, "We've been flagged down. A train has gone off the tracks north of us and been wrecked. This train will remain here until the rails are cleared."

"When will that be?" a passenger asked.

"Not today. Probably not tomorrow. Perhaps in a day or two," the conductor said.

Josie glanced at Blackthorne. His jaw tightened, but otherwise there was no sign of the distress she knew he must be feeling. She was wondering how far they were from the closest town when the conductor said, "Arrangements will be made to take you to the village of Ashington, where you can find accommodations."

Josie turned to Blackthorne and asked, "Are we close enough to our destination to finish the journey by carriage?"

He steepled his fingers beneath his chin and pursed his lips in thought. "It's about fifty miles from Ashington to Berwick-upon-Tweed. I could probably make the trip in a very long day on horseback, but considering the lightning, the rain, and the mud, the journey will have to begin tomorrow."

Josie saw the tension in his shoulders at the knowledge that his rescue of Lady Lark would have to be postponed. "What if we took a carriage and left tonight?"

"Depending on the weather," he continued, "and the condition of the roads, even if we travel by carriage, we'll need to spend at least one night on the road."

Which would mean the overnight delay would be necessary no matter how the trip was made.

"You should go on tomorrow without me," she

said. "I'm sure I'll be fine waiting by myself in Ashington, until the train can take me the rest of the way."

Josie watched the struggle on Blackthorne's face, knowing he was torn between his duty to his sister and his duty to his wife. She was traveling without a maid, just as he was traveling without his valet. Both servants would be following in a day or so, scheduled to arrive after Blackthorne had rescued his sister, to avoid their discovering Lady Lark in any sort of compromising situation.

"Taking a carriage makes more sense," he said at last.

"Or we could wait for the tracks to be cleared."

He shook his head. "It may take longer than the one or two days the conductor estimated. Or there might be another obstruction between here and Berwick-upon-Tweed."

She raised a questioning brow, and he explained, "The coal miners in Darlington aren't happy with the wages they're being paid by the colliery. Sabotaging the railroad that hauls the coal is one way of making their feelings known."

"Then a carriage it is," she said.

Except there were no carriages to be had. Ashington wasn't a large town, and the best they could do was a wagon with a team of plow horses. Josie eyed the wooden bench seat, considered the steady rain, and said, "I think we should spend the night at an inn and rent saddle horses in the morning. If you're right, and we're lucky," she added with a rueful smile, "we can make the journey in a day."

"Can you ride so far?" Blackthorne asked skeptically.

"I expect I'll be sore, but it seems the only solution."

Having a duke for a husband had its advantages, Josie discovered. They were offered the finest room to be had at the nicest inn in Ashington. Unfortunately, that wasn't saying much. It was also the *only* room to be had.

As she surveyed their room, where she'd been sent to refresh herself before supper, an anxious knot formed in her belly. The dip in the middle of the small, lumpy bed suggested it was going to be difficult, if not impossible, to stay on her side, if they shared the bed. And there was no dressing screen, so unless Blackthorne left her alone at bedtime, she would have no privacy to undress. She hadn't given Blackthorne a chance to inspect her back again after he'd made his discovery of who she was, and she had no intention of giving him a better look. The moonlight had kept him from seeing the true awfulness of her scars. There was no sense subjecting him to another look. If they shared the room, she would have to be sure to be in her nightgown in bed before he joined her.

And it was only fair that they share the room. They had a miserable journey ahead of them, and it wasn't fair to ask Blackthorne to sit up all night in a chair.

Josie felt unaccountably breathless as she sat across from her husband nibbling on a piece of bread, while they waited for the main dinner course to be served. The fact that they would shortly be going upstairs to sleep in the same bed probably had something to do with her agitation.

For his part, Blackthorne kept rearranging the cutlery and straightening his napkin in his lap, his lips pressed in a grim line, which probably had something to do with the awkward silence that had fallen between them.

"She'll be all right, you know," Josie said as she dipped her spoon into the last of a bowl of oxtail soup.

"How can you possibly know that?" he snarled.

It was a sign of just how troubled he was that he'd lost the savoir faire he'd exhibited as they'd made their way to this inn, secured a room, and finally ended up in this private parlor eating dinner. Apparently, he'd reached his limit.

Josie extended her hand across the table, and Blackthorne gripped it so tightly, she struggled not to wince.

"I never figured Seaton for the blackguard he's turned out to be. First hiding you away like that, and now stealing Lark away right under my nose. I can't believe he's been lying to me all these years. I can't believe he'd do something as monstrous as ruin my sister. Why would he do it? I trusted him!"

The words seemed wrenched from him. Josie realized it wasn't only his sister's precarious circumstances that had Blackthorne so distraught. It was the knowledge that his best friend had betrayed him. She knew a great deal about how that felt, based on her own experience with a certain unkept promise made by the English gentleman sitting across from her.

"Seaton must have some rational explanation for his actions toward me," she said. "I'm sure you only need to ask him to discover the truth."

"I can't imagine what possessed him," he mused, his gaze turned inward. "I told him I wanted you sent home. He promised he would see to it. If he decided to do otherwise, he should have said something to me sometime over the next *two years* when I brought up the subject."

Josie's eyes widened. "You discussed a woman you'd only known for a matter of days for *two years* afterward?"

Blackthorne looked shocked, when she replayed his behavior in words, and lowered his gaze, as though he were embarrassed. He murmured, "I wondered what had happened to you." He met her gaze and added, "And I wondered why I never heard from you."

"You really never received any of the letters I wrote?"

He pulled his hand free and sat back in his chair. "What letters? How many letters?"

"I sent at least a dozen letters to your address in London, asking why I was being kept a prisoner at Tearlach Castle." She bit her lip before she could add that she'd also asked him to come to the rescue of his nephews. She didn't even want to hint at the possibility that they needed rescuing, since she intended to abscond with them as soon as possible.

He shook his head. "No one would dare to intercept my correspondence. A dozen letters simply disappear? Impossible."

"Is everyone at your home in London so reliable

that no one could have been bribed to destroy them?"

He frowned, apparently running through the list of servants in his mind to determine if one or another could be corrupted. At last he said, "More likely your letters never left Tearlach Castle. Are you sure Seaton didn't arrange for someone to intercept them there?"

"He might have. But the castle wasn't the only place from which I posted letters. I sent several through other means and by other routes. Surely one must have gotten through."

"None made it to London," he insisted. "Seaton had the free run of the house, but he wasn't there often enough to check every letter coming in."

"Who else wouldn't want you to know I was still in England? Who else would believe you might seek me out, if you knew I was still here?"

He was silent for a moment before he said, "I can't think of anyone. Nor do I understand why Seaton did what he apparently did."

"I suppose you'll have to ask him when next you see him."

Josie bit her tongue when she saw Blackthorne flinch and realized that thinking of Seaton only reminded him that his best friend was up to no good with his sister.

A meat pasty and some roasted chicken with vegetables had come and gone while they'd been talking. Josie was surprised to discover she was so full, she couldn't eat another bite.

As she shoved an untouched bowl of apple cobbler away, Blackthorne said, "I'll join you in half an hour."

Josie felt a quiver of something that might have been fear as she rose from the table, but she refused to give in to the feeling. She wasn't sure what to think of the man she'd married, but it was becoming clear that Seaton, rather than Blackthorne, was the villain who'd abandoned her two years ago. Blackthorne had had no inkling, indeed, had never imagined, that his friend could deceive him in the way he apparently had.

That still didn't explain why the duke hadn't come to Tearlach Castle even once during the past two years to check on Spencer and Clay. He might not be guilty of abandoning her, but he'd certainly been guilty of forgetting the very existence of his nephews. He'd shown no inclination to visit them on this trip, either.

During the train ride, when she'd mentioned visiting the boys at Tearlach Castle, and the possibility of bringing them back to the Abbey to live, he'd said in a brusque voice, "Spencer and Clay are the least of my worries right now. They're fine where they are."

Blackthorne might be innocent of one wrong. But not of the other.

As she trudged up the stairs toward that small, lumpy bed, the persistent voice in her head piped up again.

Are you going to let him make love to you? What if you get pregnant? You're planning to leave. Would that be fair to him? Or to the child? Or even to you?

Josie shook her head to silence her conscience. She had no idea whether the duke would follow her if she took Spencer and Clay to America for a "visit" and simply didn't return. But she was certain he would show up breathing fire, if he learned she'd taken his heir with her as well.

Once she was back in their room, she undressed quickly, slipped under the covers, and waited. And waited. And waited.

Chapter 38

BLACKTHORNE FELT OVERWHELMED by the unfamiliar emotions bombarding him. He had no experience with betrayal, unless one counted what his uncle had done to his father.

It was the elder son who inherited in England, so even though Blackthorne's father, Randolph, had been older than his twin brother, Alexander, by only a few minutes, he was the heir. According to Alex, his mother had assured him on her deathbed that *he* was the elder son, that she'd done her best to persuade their father that he was mistaken in thinking Randolph was born first. But the duke had attached himself to his younger son and refused to accept the truth.

Alex had fought his brother in court to prove his right to the dukedom. But neither their father nor their mother had been alive to attest to anything. In the end, a nursemaid had been brought in, and she'd sworn that Alex was the younger. His uncle had left London and never been heard from again.

Had his father felt this awful emptiness? Had his father wondered how someone so close to his heart could want to hurt him so badly? Had his father felt this growing rage that threatened to erupt in violence? If so, it was no wonder Uncle Alex had run away and never come back.

His best friend had been the raft that kept Blackthorne afloat as Fanny's illness worsened. Seaton had provided a shoulder to cry on—something Blackthorne had actually done—which had made the difference between mere agony and total madness, as he watched his beloved wife dying before his eyes. Having Seaton there to reassure him that life must go on had kept him from putting a pistol to his head. And after his wife was gone, sharing his memories of Fanny with his best friend had made it possible to move on with his life.

It was devastating to learn that Seaton had been lying to him all along. That his friend had been manipulating him behind his back. That his friend had never been his friend at all.

Blackthorne felt a terrible ache in his chest, as though his heart was being squeezed by rough, uncaring hands. He wanted . . . He needed . . .

He found himself blindly taking the stairs two at a time to reach his room. Something was there, *someone* was there who promised surcease from pain. He opened the door and saw by the light of the lantern that the rumpled bed was empty. He searched the small room for his wife and found her standing barefoot in the corner, her tangled curls flowing over her shoulders, her mouth open wide in shock. She was wearing a chemise and tying the ribbon on a pair of pantalettes. It was unclear whether she was dressing or undressing.

He crossed to her without speaking, hauled her

into his arms and held her tight, as though her physical presence could keep his thundering heart from beating out of his chest.

"Where have you—" she began.

He pressed her face against his waistcoat, cutting her off, and said, "Let me hold you."

She stood rigid in his embrace for a moment, before he felt her arms slide around his waist and her body align itself with his. He nudged her chin up with a forefinger and found her mouth with his. His tongue surged inside seeking comfort and found a sweet haven. He angled her head to find better purchase and plundered the treasure he discovered within.

His wife was no passive partner. Blackthorne felt her tongue in his mouth, tasting, touching, seeking. She caught fire in his arms, tugging at his cravat and tearing at the buttons on his waistcoat. He let go of her long enough to help her, yanking the silk cravat over his head and sending waistcoat buttons pinging across the wooden floor, as he tore off coat and waistcoat and threw them aside.

She shoved his shirt up out of her way, her hands greedy with the need to touch, as he stripped it off. He pulled her close again, pausing only long enough to tear her flimsy chemise in two, so that he could feel warm flesh against flesh.

His hands found their way to the scars on her back and he groaned as he tenderly traced the marks. She froze and pressed her forehead against his chest, her breathing labored.

"Don't look," she begged. "Please don't look."

"I don't need to look," he whispered in her ear.

"I see these marks in my dreams. I've never forgotten you, Josie. Not for one moment of one day."

She lifted her face, and he saw the wonder in her eyes, before he lowered his mouth to capture hers. Her arms circled his neck and held him tight, as his hands caressed her.

It never occurred to him to wonder why Josie wasn't fighting him, why she seemed to need him as much as he needed her. He only knew that merely kissing her and holding her was no longer enough. He picked her up and tossed her onto the bed, stopping only long enough to tear off his shoes and socks and trousers and smalls before joining her.

His eyes flared with desire as she wriggled out of her pantalettes and kicked them away, presenting a brazenly naked feast before him. Her arms were open wide, welcoming him as he covered her body with his own, pressing her knees wide and plunging inside her, making them one.

He slid his arms around her, but as he pulled her close, gravity sent him rolling with her into the deep trench at the center of the sagging bed, so that she ended up on top, their bodies still joined.

She looked astonished, as she pushed herself upright, her golden hair tumbling across her naked breasts, her knees bent on either side of his broad chest.

He arched his body into hers and watched as her eyes closed, and her mouth fell open in ecstasy. Her hands slid across his chest, and she looked down at him with passion-glazed eyes, apparently surprised to discover that his nipples had turned into buds as tight as her own. He pulled her close enough to reach her breast with his mouth and suckle, causing her to moan.

Their bodies arched and swayed, the pleasure ebbing and flowing like waves on the seashore. Watching Josie's face, seeing her wonder and delight, eased the ache in his heart. Then her face changed, and he saw a pleasure akin to pain. She threw her head back as her body began to convulse, and a raw, animalistic sound emerged from her throat. Her breathing became ragged, her body boneless, until at last, she fell forward and lay in a trembling heap on his chest.

He closed his arms around her and turned her under him, his body still pulsing within hers. He held his weight on his arms as he looked into her heart-shaped face, waiting for her eyes to open, waiting for her to come back to herself. She opened half-lidded eyes, and a satisfied, cat-with-the-cream smile curved her lips.

He moved inside her and saw her eyes go wide with amazement. He felt the corners of his mouth curve upward in the beginning of a smile, as her hands threaded into his hair and drew his mouth down to hers. Her eyes slid closed again, as her hips thrust upward, and her tongue came searching. She slid her fingernails down his nape, as her body arched against his. He made a guttural sound as he thrust deep, deeper, until he spilled his seed, and they became one body, one soul, finding a haven of bliss.

Blackthorne slid onto his side next to her, and she rolled into him. He reached for the sheets and covered their sweat-slick, heaving bodies. He pulled her close to his pounding heart, then reached over and extinguished the lamp on the table beside the bed.

He was nearly asleep when she said, "I was worried when you didn't come back. I thought you might have gone without me."

He kissed her forehead and hugged her tighter. "I think it's what I should do tomorrow morning. Leave you here, I mean, while I go ahead on horseback. You can come on the train, once it's repaired."

He wanted time to deal with whatever he found when he arrived at the Black Swan, without his wife there to ameliorate the situation. He wanted the chance to yell at his sister like a big brother, rather than treat her with the calm expected of the head of the family. He wanted to confront Seaton with all the fury he felt toward a man who'd been his friend and confidant for most of his life, before betraying him so heinously.

"All right," she said, snuggling against him. "I'll wait here. I know you'll do what's right, whatever you find when you get there."

He hugged her close, but he said nothing. His throat was too swollen with emotion to speak.

Chapter 39

LYING IN BED alone the next morning, Black-thorne having departed sometime during the night for Berwick-upon-Tweed, Josie stretched, groaning as she raised her arms high and extended her toes toward the foot of the bed. Then she snuggled back down under the warm covers, pulling them close and smelling the disconcerting scent of the man she'd made love with last night.

It had been a strange interlude, but no stranger than most of their marriage so far. She'd felt Black-thorne's need and responded to it by holding him close. In the dark of night, after they'd made love, she'd felt his hands trace the scars on her back, before he'd turned her in his arms and kissed the length of each weal, where the lash had bit her flesh. Between kisses, he'd whispered, "You should be proud of these scars. Each one is proof of your courage."

It was something Josie had never considered. It made her see herself differently. Not as the coward who'd hidden under the bed and kept her parents from escaping the fire, but as someone who had the ability to be strong for herself and for those weaker than herself, like Spencer and Clay.

Josie might have the courage to escape with Blackthorne's nephews, but after the night just past, she no longer had the will. She didn't want to leave the Dastardly Duke. She wanted the chance to see whether he could ever come to admire her as much as he did her single act of valor. She crossed her arms behind her head and settled more comfortably into the valley in the center of the mattress.

More importantly, did she have the courage to stay?

Why did she suddenly yearn to be loved by a man she'd hated for years? How had everything changed in such a short time? She wasn't going anywhere until she'd figured it all out, even if that meant spending the entire day in bed.

After her ordeal over the past two years, it was a luxury to be able to simply do nothing. Unfortunately, although her body was relaxed, her mind kept spinning out of control, like a child's top gone wild.

Josie wondered if her three married sisters had ever felt as confused, after marrying perfect strangers, as she felt this morning. She wished they were closer, so she could talk to them. She missed them terribly. Maybe they could make some sense of her feelings for her husband. It was hard to believe she still hadn't told them she wasn't on that ship bound for Charleston, but she'd thought she'd be long gone by now. She supposed she'd better get a telegram off today to let them know she was going to be delayed for . . . How long?

She had no idea.

Blackthorne's property in Northumberland was close enough to Berwick-upon-Tweed that she believed she could get him to visit his nephews, after he'd dealt with Seaton and his sister, and see their situation for himself. Josie thought it would take a harder heart than Blackthorne had shown so far to keep him from bringing them back to the Abbey to live.

Unless . . . Josie was forced to admit there was a very real possibility that Blackthorne had ignored his nephews because he simply didn't want the daily responsibility for taking care of two rambunctious children.

Josie growled low in her throat with frustration. Her thoughts kept going around in circles. She had no way of knowing the truth, since she'd been married to the man for too short a time to really know him.

If Blackthorne agreed to bring his nephews to live with them at the Abbey, it would assuage her concern for the boys. But Josie still felt torn in two, because she missed her family and wanted to see them again. It had been so long! She needed to hug her sisters and laugh with them and share stories of everything that had happened to everyone over the past two years.

What should she do? Stay? Or take the boys and go? Which choice was the right one?

Josie was startled by a knock at the door and got caught in the covers trying to leap out of bed to answer it. Blackthorne wouldn't have knocked, so it wasn't him. It might be the innkeeper wanting to know when she would be leaving, although she thought Blackthorne had probably given him that information, since he'd said he would pay in advance for the room, until the tracks were cleared and the train was running again. Or it might be a maid coming to clean the room. It was even possible the Pinkerton had found her, with news about Spencer and Clay.

She scrambled out of bed and grabbed the quilt to wrap around herself before she opened the door.

"Good afternoon, Your Grace. I got worried when you didn't come down for luncheon."

Josie stared at the innkeeper, shocked to realize how much of the day she'd worried away. "I was resting." It was the best excuse she could come up with.

"I wouldn't have bothered you, but I thought you should know the track has been repaired. The damage wasn't as bad as they thought. The wagons and coaches will be loading up shortly to take everyone back to the train."

Josie thought of the grueling ride Blackthorne was making to reach his sister, when a few hours' delay would have allowed him to arrive in an hour or two, depending on how many more stops the train had to make before it reached Berwick-upon-Tweed. It was possible she would be there before him, which would give her time to sneak in a visit with the boys and discover whether they were over the measles.

"I'll be ready shortly," Josie said. "Would you

send someone up here to collect our bags?" Black-thorne had left everything except a single change of clothing with her.

It took very little time to dress, and because the rain had stopped, the trip back to the train was made without even getting wet. Perhaps because of the delay, or a fear of further sabotage, the train steamed straight through to Berwick-upon-Tweed without stopping.

Josie wasn't even surprised when the first person she saw when she stepped off the train was Miranda's Pinkerton detective.

"Mr. Thompson. Why am I not surprised?" Josie said with a smile. "How on earth did you get here before me?"

He winked and said, "A Pinkerton never sleeps."

"Why are you here?"

"I have news that couldn't wait."

Josie's heart jumped to her throat. "Black-thorne?"

She saw the surprise in the Pinkerton's eyes and realized that her first concern had been for her husband, not for the two boys she loved as much as her brothers. That told her something about herself that she wasn't sure she wanted to know. "Does it have to do with Spencer or Clay?"

"No, ma'am."

Josie's heart began pounding hard enough to break her rib cage. She realized she'd grasped the lapels on the Pinkerton's black duster and forced herself to let go. "Please, don't keep me in suspense."

"It's your sister Miranda, ma'am. She's very ill. She may be dying as we speak."

Josie thought she might faint. She reached out a hand and caught the Pinkerton's arm for support. "Dying? Miranda?"

"Her babe came early. She has childbed fever."

"I have to get to her. I have to see her. She can't die before—" Fear choked off Josie's voice. "How fast can I get to her? How many days will it take?"

Josie felt frantic, panicked by the thought that she had been found at last, only to arrive too late to thank her sister for never having given up the search. "Oh, God. It might already be too late. I should have gone home. I should never have stayed and married the duke. And now . . ."

She crossed her arms over her body to hold herself together, when it felt like she might fly into a million pieces. "If you knew I would be on that train, then you must have known I would want to go home immediately. Are the travel arrangements made?"

"Almost."

"What's causing the delay?"

"I didn't know whether to buy passage for one. Or for three."

Josie gave a cry of anguish. It was too late to ask Blackthorne why he'd never visited his nephews. Too late to be frank and honest and probe his heart for the truth about his feelings for Spencer and Clay. What a fool she'd been! She should have broached the subject sooner. She should have told Blackthorne exactly how much she loved the boys—and worried about their happiness. She should have made it clear that she wanted his nephews to come and live with them—not sometime in the future, but *right now.*

She'd done none of that. During the brief time she'd spent with the duke, she'd skirted the subject. She wasn't sure she could trust Blackthorne to do the right thing where Spencer and Clay were concerned. And since she didn't know her husband's true feelings about the two boys, she didn't dare leave them behind after she was gone. However mistaken she'd been about Blackthorne when it came to her own incarceration at Tearlach Castle, the same might not be true regarding his abandonment of his nephews.

Josie had no idea exactly when Blackthorne had left Ashington, no idea when he might be arriving in Berwick-upon-Tweed. She had no choice. Even a day's delay might result in her reaching her sister too late. She had to leave with the evening tide, and she had to take Spencer and Clay with her.

Chapter 40

BLACKTHORNE WAS COLD and wet and tired, but his journey was nearly done. His horse hadn't thrown a shoe—or him—and he'd made good time from Ashington to Berwick-upon-Tweed. But despite leaving in the middle of the night, the journey had taken him the entire day. It was late in the afternoon by the time he hit the outskirts of town and found his way to the Black Swan. He'd been grinding his teeth for the better part of the past hour, imagining Seaton's bones between them.

The blackguard! Where did he get the gall to steal Lark from under my nose? Why did he keep Josie in England against her will? Why did he pretend to be my friend, when his actions were those of a scoundrel?

Blackthorne made sure his mount was comfortably bedded down in the stable, before he headed into the Black Swan. He half expected one of Mr. Thompson's agents to be waiting to greet him, but he didn't see anyone wearing a black duster and bowler hat on the porch of the Black Swan or inside the taproom. Thompson's man likely hadn't expected Blackthorne to arrive as soon as he had. The ride had been brutal for man and beast.

Blackthorne rang the bell at the counter, and when the innkeeper showed up, announced, "I'm looking for the Earl of Seaton. I believe he's staying here."

The innkeeper smiled. "Yes. He's here with his wife. But you don't want to go up there."

"Why not?"

"The young lady has contracted the measles."

"I've had measles. Which room is it?"

"Why don't I send for the gentleman—"

Blackthorne grabbed the innkeeper by the throat. "Which room?"

"The bridal suite. Last door on the right at—" He stopped speaking abruptly when Blackthorne let go and headed for the stairs.

When he got to the bridal suite, Blackthorne didn't knock on the door, he simply put a booted foot to the area near the knob and kicked it open. He wasn't sure what he'd expected to see, but it wasn't what he found.

His sister's hands rose to the throat of her nightgown. She was sitting on the edge of the bed, her elbow perched on a table that had been situated nearby with a chessboard on it. Several pieces had already been moved from the board to the table. Seaton leapt up from a chair that had been squeezed into the space between the wall and the table. Both of them stared at him with frightened eyes.

"Marcus! What's wrong?" his sister cried.

"What's wrong?" he roared. "Are you purposely

trying to drive me mad? Your being in this room in your nightgown with Seaton is what's wrong!"

"Let me explain," Seaton said.

Blackthorne sneered. "I can see for myself what's going on here."

"It isn't what it looks like," Lark said.

Blackthorne lifted an aristocratic brow. "You're married to him? And this is a friendly game of chess between husband and wife?"

"Well, no, I'm not," Lark said. "But we will be when—"

"When hell freezes over!" Blackthorne turned to his *former* best friend and said in a deadly voice, "I demand satisfaction."

Blackthorne watched all the blood drain from Seaton's face. His sister's face might have blanched as well, but since it was covered in red spots, it was hard to tell.

"None of this is David's fault," Lark protested, crawling across the bed toward him. "I'm the one who left home without telling anyone where I was going. I took the train to Berwick-upon-Tweed without David's knowledge or consent."

"David? Now Seaton is *David*?" Blackthorne jeered.

Lark winced. "I wanted . . ." She lifted her chin and looked disdainfully down her nose at him, a pose he'd seen his grandmother use to great effect. "If you must know, I wanted an adventure. It isn't David's fault the train arrived so late in the evening. All he did was try to protect my reputation."

Blackthorne focused his gaze on Seaton. "By

bringing an unmarried lady to an inn and registering as husband and wife?"

The blood rushed back to Seaton's face. "Lark wasn't feeling well, which turned out to be measles. It was too late to take her to the Courts' home, so I thought—"

"You thought you'd take advantage of an innocent girl?"

"You know me better than that," Seaton shot back.

"Do I? Tell me about Josephine Wentworth."

"What?"

"Don't play dumb. I know you took Josie to Tearlach Castle and kept her confined there for two long years."

Seaton's mouth dropped open. "That was Josie? The girl I took to the castle was the heiress you married?"

To give him credit, Seaton appeared genuinely astonished, but Blackthorne wasn't going to be fooled again. "You're a better actor than I thought. Of course it was Josie!"

"Good lord," Seaton said, running a nervous hand through his hair. "No, that's not possible."

"Josie said you arranged for her to go to Tearlach Castle."

"I arranged for *the girl you rescued* to go to Tearlach Castle. Or rather, my sister did. Are you saying Josie and that girl are one and the same?"

"Wait a minute. Just wait!" Blackthorne's mind was whirling. "Are you suggesting *Fanny* is responsible for Josie spending the past two years as a maid at one of my properties?"

"Who else would do something as fanciful as hide the girl away somewhere so you could meet her again at some point in the future? That was Fanny from start to finish. She used my solicitor to arrange everything. I never knew the girl's name. I made it a point not to find out, so I wouldn't slip when I was in my cups. Fanny kept you from visiting Spencer and Clay so you wouldn't discover the American's presence before the time was right.

"And I didn't say anything in the year after Fanny died, because I knew you needed to marry an heiress to save Blackthorne Abbey. I thought I was doing you a favor."

Blackthorne was stunned into speechlessness. He sank onto the bed and stared out the window. He felt Lark's hand on his shoulder and turned a blind eye to her.

"Are you all right?" she asked.

Blackthorne took a deep breath and let it out. "Not really. What am I to do with you?" His gaze shifted from his sister to his friend. "With both of you?"

Seaton took a step forward, reached for Lark's hand, and held it in his. "I've gotten a special license, but we have to wait for Lark to recover from the measles before we can say the words to a cleric."

"You planned to marry without her grandmother or her sister or me, *the head of the family*, present?"

"I realize it wasn't a well-thought-out plan,"

Seaton conceded, "but it was all I could think of to prove my intentions toward Lark are honorable."

"You *want* to marry my idiot sister?"

"I'll thank you not to speak of my fiancée in those terms," Seaton said, his shoulders squaring.

"Thank you, David," Lark said. "And I'm *not* an idiot, Marcus. I'm in love with David."

"And I'm in love with your sister," Seaton said.

Blackthorne shook his head in disbelief. "You are?"

"I have been these past six months," Seaton replied.

"Oh, David," Lark said. "Why didn't you let me know?"

"Because he wasn't in any hurry to get married," Blackthorne said sardonically. He quirked a brow and asked his friend, "Why the sudden change of heart?"

"I'll admit the situation forced my hand," Seaton said. "Lark and I have had time while we've been in this room together to talk—just to talk—about how we feel. Your sister can be very persuasive."

"Don't I know it," Blackthorne muttered.

"As it turns out," Seaton finished, "I'll simply be marrying Lark a little sooner than I might have arranged the matter on my own."

"My sister will recuperate here with my wife as her chaperon," Blackthorne said. "You will return to London posthaste. At the appropriate time, you will call on me to ask my permission to court Lark.

You will become affianced in due time, and will marry at St. George's in London, with the entire ton in attendance."

Lark threw herself into her brother's arms. "Oh, Marcus, thank you!"

Seaton reached out a hand, and Blackthorne took it. He was still in shock, but his wounded heart was somewhat comforted by the knowledge that his friend hadn't betrayed him, that Fanny had arranged everything. Fanny! He wouldn't have believed it of her. She must have known him better than he'd known himself. In an amazing twist of fate, her machinations had resulted in his marriage to the girl he'd rescued. As for the falling in love part, he thought maybe that had happened, too. At least, on his side. He was never quite sure what Josie was thinking.

Seaton grasped Blackthorne's hand in both of his and said, "I'm looking forward to being a part of the family." He grinned and added, "Especially now that I know it includes your American waif. Speaking of which, where is she?"

"In Ashington, waiting for the tracks to be repaired."

Seaton frowned. "Really? The train from London arrived at noon."

"Are you sure?"

"Everyone on the damned thing showed up at the Black Swan wanting something to eat and complaining about the delay overnight in Ashington."

"And my wife? Did she come looking for a meal?"

"I don't know. You might want to ask the inn-keeper."

Blackthorne stopped at the door he'd kicked off its hinges and said, "Sorry about the door. I'll have someone sent up to fix it."

Then he was gone to find his wife.

Chapter 41

JOSIE HAD KEPT her distance from the Black Swan after stepping off the train, because she didn't want to take the chance of running into Seaton. Instead, she took a room at the Duck & Goose, where she changed into an expensively tailored dress that made her look more like the Duchess of Blackthorne and less like the maid-of-all-work she'd been the last time she'd seen Miss Sharpe and Mrs. Pettibone. Then she set out in a rented carriage with the Pinkerton for Tearlach Castle.

"What if they won't let me take the boys with me when I leave?"

"Remember who you are," Mr. Thompson replied. "As the young lords' aunt-by-marriage you have the authority to take them anywhere you choose."

"What if Miss Sharpe and Mrs. Pettibone don't believe I'm the duchess?"

"Word should have reached them by now of the duke's marriage, including the name of his bride."

Josie bit the inside of her cheek. She could imagine Mrs. Pettibone's outrage at discovering that the bane of her existence was now married to her employer. She was afraid that Miss Sharpe might feel she had to defend her charges against an upstart like Miss Josephine Wentworth, if Josie had the temerity to suggest that she would be relieving the governess of her duties.

But there was no help for it. The only way to rescue Spencer and Clay was to act as brave as Blackthorne seemed to think she was. She must arrive on the doorstep as the imperious, must-be-obeyed Duchess of Blackthorne and issue orders to the two women as though she'd been born to the title.

The carriage drew to a stop, and a footman opened the door and lowered the stairs. She waited for Mr. Thompson to step down. When he didn't, she asked, "Aren't you coming in?"

"You don't need my help, ma'am. I would only be in the way."

Josie had assumed the Pinkerton would be by her side, lending her story credence, if necessary. She hesitated a moment, then rose and took the footman's hand to help her down the steps. She turned back and said, "I won't be long."

The footman ran ahead of her and lifted the ancient iron ring that served as a door knocker and let it fall with a resounding clang, as the rusty iron ring hit the rustier iron plate behind it. When the door was immediately opened, Josie realized that one of the shepherds in the field must have seen the fancy carriage and run to tell those in the house that the duke was on his way.

The butler's eyes turned into saucers when he saw Josie dressed so fashionably, from the feathered hat perched jauntily on her head, to her dark-blue princess sheath, to her gloved hands, all the way down to her black patent-leather high-button shoes.

"Why, hello, Miss—" He cut himself off, flushed to the roots of the few white hairs left on his head, and said, "I mean, Your Grace."

That was one question answered. If the butler knew she'd married the duke, everyone else did, too. "Hello, Morton. How is your gout?"

"It's fine. Thanks for askin', Your Grace." He peered past her toward the figure sitting in the carriage. "Is the duke comin' in?"

Josie realized the coach curtains kept the interior too dark for Morton to see who'd arrived with her. She took advantage of the butler's misapprehension and said, "Perhaps later. I'm here to collect the boys for an outing. Where are they?"

"I believe they're in their rooms."

"On a warm, sunny day like this? Why aren't they outside playing?"

"You'll have to ask Miss Sharpe," Morton replied, taking a step back when he saw the look on Josie's face.

Josie bit her tongue. It was either that or blurt the abrasive word that had come to mind. She clenched her hands into fighting fists, then said in a calm, rational voice, "I believe I will."

She was on her way upstairs before Morton got the door closed. Her heart was pounding by the time she got to the third floor. She went straight to Spencer's room, because she knew she would need his help keeping Clay from getting overexcited before they managed to make their escape from the house. With any luck, she could avoid seeing Mrs. Pettibone entirely.

She knocked lightly and opened Spencer's door before it was answered. She found him lying on his bed with his back to her. "Spencer?"

When he lifted his head, she saw his face was tear-streaked. He sat up abruptly and shifted around until his feet were on the floor. "Josie? Is that really you?"

When she held out her arms, Spencer came flying into them so hard he nearly knocked her down. She expelled an *oof* when his head hit her solar plexus, but her arms closed tightly around him.

"I'm so glad you've come," Spencer said between pitiful sobs. "It's been awful without you!"

"How is Clay?"

He lifted his face to hers, and his features crumpled. "You won't believe what they've done to him."

Josie's heart leapt to her throat and threatened to choke her. She lifted Spencer's chin so she could look into his tear-drenched eyes. "What? What have they done?"

"They've tied him to his bed. Miss Sharpe didn't want to at first, but Mrs. Pettibone insisted, because Clay kept sneaking out of bed when he had the measles and running down to the kitchen. Mrs. Pettibone said he was going to infect the entire staff. So Miss Sharpe agreed to tie Clay down until he was well."

"Are you telling me Clay is tied to his bed right now?"

Spencer nodded. "And he's been over the measles for two whole days! He calls out to me to set him free, until he gets tired and finally falls asleep. Miss Sharpe caught me untying him and said if I interfered again, she'd tie him tighter the next time. She said it's for his own good, but it's not! He hates it. I didn't know how to reach you, and Uncle Marcus might as well be on the moon."

Josie's resolve to rescue the two boys firmed, not that it had ever wavered. Or maybe it had, a little. But it was clear they desperately needed rescuing.

"Get dressed. We're leaving."

Spencer stared at her without blinking. "Where are we going?"

"You're coming to America with me."

"I heard you married Uncle Marcus."

"I did. Which makes me your aunt Josie. And I'm taking you and Clay for a holiday in America. Right now."

"Whoopeee!"

Josie clamped a hand over Spencer's mouth. "We don't want to give Miss Sharpe or Mrs. Pettibone any excuse to hamper us. As far as either of them will know, I'm taking you and Clay on a picnic."

Spencer's mouth thinned. "I'd like to see the look on Miss Sharpe's face when she realizes we're gone for good. We are leaving for good, aren't we?"

"Absolutely. Dress and pack a bag with whatever you might want to take with you, while I go get Clay."

Josie opened the door between Spencer's and Clay's rooms as quietly as she could. Clay lay flat on his back with one ankle tied to the iron railing at the foot of the bed. He had his thumb stuck in his mouth, something she hadn't seen him do for a full year before she'd left. It took her another moment to realize that one of his wrists was tied to the rails at the head of the bed. Miss Sharpe was nowhere to be seen.

Josie crossed to the foot of the bed and untied the knot that held the rope to Clay's ankle. He stirred and moaned but didn't waken. Then she sat beside him and reached for the knotted rope around his wrist. Josie's stomach clenched when she realized he'd pulled hard enough on the rope to chafe his skin red and raw.

"You poor baby," she murmured as she untied the knot. "You will never, ever be subjected to this treatment again. Never," she whispered.

When she had Clay free, she lifted his limp body into her arms. He was hot, and she wondered if he might not be completely recovered from the measles. Whether he was or he wasn't, they had to leave. There was no time to waste.

She brushed his sweat-damp hair from his forehead and said, "Clay, sweetheart, wake up."

His eyes drifted open and he stared at her, looking confused. "Josie?"

"Yes, it's me, darling. How are you feeling?"

"I had the measles. I was covered all over in red spots. But they're gone now. I want to go out and play, but Miss Sharpe says I have to rest."

"Would you like to go on a big ship with me and Spencer?"

Clay smiled, and she saw he'd lost one of his two

front teeth in the short time she'd been gone. "Sailing on the ocean? You and me and Spencer?"

"Just the three of us."

"No Miss Sharpe?"

"Absolutely not!"

"No Mrs. Pettibone?"

"They're both staying right here."

Clay seemed to be making a miraculous recovery. The feverish glaze disappeared from his eyes, and he sat bolt upright in bed. He started to scoot off the edge and froze. He looked at his wrist and then at the foot of the bed, where his ankle had been tied. "I wished and wished for someone to come and untie me. And you came! Let's go, Josie."

Josie laughed at his childish exuberance. "Let's pack a few of your things to take with us, shall we? What's your favorite toy?"

Clay made a face. "Miss Sharpe took it away, because I'm a bad boy."

Josie's teeth clenched. She would like to have a half hour with Miss Sharpe and the bullwhip the Sioux had used on her. How could anyone be so cruel to a child as sweet and innocent as Clay? "Never mind," she said. "We'll buy lots of toys for you to play with when we get to America."

"Where's America?"

"Across the ocean. Let's go get Spencer. It's time—past time—to leave this place."

"And never come back?"

"Never."

Chapter 42

BLACKTHORNE WAS BESIDE himself with worry. He'd discovered that Josie had met a man dressed all in black on the train platform—likely a Pinkerton—and left with him. After that, there was no sign of her. She'd simply disappeared. Desperation sent him to Tearlach Castle, where he thought she might have gone to visit those she'd known as a maid-of-all-work. When he arrived, he discovered a calamity far greater than he could have imagined.

"Your Grace? You forgot somethin'? You're back for another visit?" the butler said as he opened the door.

"Back? I haven't been here for two years."

"But you was here earlier today," Morton protested. "You stayed in the carriage while Her Grace collected the young lords. You all drove away within a half hour."

"I tell you I haven't been near Tearlach Castle—" He cut himself off, because it was clear someone posing as him—the Pinkerton?—had come with Josie. "You say she took Spencer and Clay with her when she left?"

"Said you was all goin' on a picnic, Your Grace.

She had Mrs. Pettibone prepare a basket of food. The housekeeper wasn't too happy about that, I can tell you."

"I thought preparing food was part of her job," Blackthorne said.

"Oh, Mrs. Pettibone didn't prepare it herself. She had Cook do it," the butler confided. "It was takin' orders from Her Grace that was the problem, if you don't mind my sayin' so."

Blackthorne did mind, but he kept his mouth shut in order to find out as much information as he could, before he started asking some hard questions. "Why would Mrs. Pettibone mind taking orders from my wife?"

"'Cause Mrs. Pettibone used to be the one *givin'* orders to your wife," the butler said with a chuckle.

"Did she prepare the food basket as my wife requested?"

"Certainly, Your Grace. Her Grace waited, foot tappin', till it was done. She wasn't none too pleased with the housekeeper for keepin' her standin' there waitin', I can tell you."

"Where were the boys when all this was going on?"

"Right there by Her Grace's side. She had each lord's hand in one of her own. Wasn't lettin' 'em go for nothin' or nobody."

"Where was their governess?"

"Standin' right there in the kitchen, steamin' like the potatoes boilin' in the pot for supper," he said with a grin.

"Miss Sharpe didn't approve?"

"Said those boys was just gettin' over measles

and shouldn't be taken outdoors. Her Grace said a child gettin' over measles shouldn't be tied to a bed, neither."

Blackthorne stiffened. "What did you just say?"

The butler looked away guiltily. "Shouldn't of repeated none of that."

"You said the boys *had* measles?"

The butler looked up. "They're better now."

"So why were they tied to a bed?" Blackthorne had a hard time controlling the violence he felt toward whoever had treated his nephews so badly.

"It was only Clay."

"*Only* Clay? Why was Lord Clayton tied to anything, let alone a bed?"

"You'll have to ask the governess. But it was the housekeeper made her do it."

"*Made* her do it? The woman doesn't have a brain of her own?"

"The two of them don't exactly see eye-to-eye about the young lords. Or much of anything," the butler added under his breath.

Blackthorne headed for the stairs without another word.

"I don't think either of them ladies is up there," the butler called after him.

Blackthorne ignored him. He headed to the third floor, looking for the nursery where Clay had been the last time he'd visited him. He cringed at the thought of how long it had been. Two years. Josie was right. His behavior toward his brother's children had been inexcusable. He should have brought them to live with him a long time ago. He only hoped it wasn't too late. He opened the door to

Clay's room and saw the ropes that lay on the mussed-up bed, one tied to the foot, one to the head rail.

Bile rose in his throat at the thought of his nephew tied up like some wild animal. Especially Clay, who was all the more precious, because he would always remain an innocent child.

Blackthorne hurried through the connecting door to Spencer's room and breathed a sigh of relief when he saw no ropes or anything else that might have been used to bind the boy. He also saw no toys. Or books. Or anything else to indicate that a vital and intelligent boy of eight inhabited the room.

What the bloody hell is going on here? No wonder Josie thinks so little of me. What uncle allows his own flesh and blood to be treated this way? I don't blame her for taking them away. But why didn't she simply confront me? Why didn't she tell me how badly Spencer and Clay were being treated?

He remembered how blithely he'd answered her questions, how certain he'd been that the boys were well cared for. He tried to remember her exact words.

Have you hugged them? Have you told them you loved them?

Blackthorne felt a searing flush of shame at what he'd allowed to happen to his nephews. He couldn't remember another time in his life when he'd felt such a heavy, almost unbearable, burden of guilt. He hoped it wasn't too late to make amends. First, he had to find the two boys. And, of course, his wife.

He slammed his way out of Spencer's room and raced back down the stairs. He headed for the place he was most likely to find the housekeeper and the governess. Sure enough, he found both ladies sitting at a table in the kitchen with a cup of tea and a plate of biscuits in front of each.

Both shoved their chairs back noisily and rose when he entered the room, each dropping a respectful curtsy.

"Who told you to tie up my nephew with ropes?" he demanded.

"It was her!" The governess pointed at the housekeeper.

He turned on the housekeeper. "You suggested that atrocity?"

"The boy had measles. He was going to infect the whole house."

"I don't care if he would have infected the entire neighborhood," Blackthorne railed. "He didn't deserve to be tied down like some wild animal."

"But, Your Grace—"

"Your Grace, I—"

He held up a hand to cut off whatever defense each woman was going to make of her behavior. "As of today, you're both dismissed. I will provide enough severance pay to keep you from starving, but you may be sure I'll relate this unpardonable behavior to whoever might be foolish enough to employ you in the future. Now get out of my sight."

When both women—along with the cook and her helper—were gone from the kitchen, Blackthorne sank into a chair and dropped his head in his hands. He'd fired the women responsible, but

he was really the one responsible for his nephews'
plight. Their poor treatment was all his fault. And
only he could make it right. He had to find Spencer
and Clay and bring them to live at Blackthorne
Abbey with him and his wife. If he could find
her . . . and she still respected him enough to continue living with him.

Blackthorne made a frustrated sound in his
throat. It wasn't only his wife's respect he wanted.
He wanted her love.

First, he had to find the three of them. Then he
could apologize. For everything. And promise to
do better in the future. And hope that words would
be enough to convince them to forgive him—and
to come home with him.

He wondered where Josie might have taken the
boys. Had they really gone on a picnic? He doubted
it. If he was sure of anything, it was that she wasn't
coming back here. No, she was headed . . . Where?
Where would she go?

Blackthorne felt a shiver run down his spine. She
wouldn't dare leave England. Not without asking
his permission.

*Yes, she would. It's exactly the sort of thing
she would do. She has a whole family in America that she's been separated from for two years.
She's Spencer and Clay's aunt-by-marriage. And
Berwick-upon-Tweed is a port where ships leave
every day for ports around the world.*

His throat constricted painfully. Now, when he
might have lost her forever, the truth hit him like
an arrow to the heart.

Dear God in heaven. I love her.

He had to find her and beg her to stay. If it wasn't too late. If she was willing to hear what he had to say. He headed back to Berwick-upon-Tweed at a gallop, his heart in his throat, wondering whether his wife's ship was still in the harbor or had sailed away with the tide.

Chapter 43

THE INSTANT THE ship left the docks, Josie realized she'd made a terrible mistake. She grabbed the arm of the closest sailor and cried, "I have to get off this ship. Please, we have to turn around and go back!"

"Sorry, miss. Once the captain sets sail, there's no turnin' back."

Josie fought back a sob of regret, as she staggered to the rail. What had she done? She hadn't realized how she truly felt about Blackthorne until it dawned on her that she might never see him again. She loved him. And she'd left without even telling him goodbye.

She rubbed her thumb across the gold band that held the Blackthorne ruby on her finger. There hadn't been time to leave it safely behind. It was coming with her to America. If Blackthorne wanted it back, he would have to come after her to get it. She wondered if that was why she'd kept it on her finger, to give him a reason to come after her.

She'd made her escape with the duke's nephews, all right, but she felt sick at heart as she watched the flickering lights of the town receding from view.

The two boys were sleeping soundly in tiered bunks in a stateroom belowdecks. For them, sailing to America was a great adventure. Her only uncomfortable moment had come after she'd settled them both in bed, when Spencer asked, "When is Uncle Marcus joining us?"

Josie had hesitated only a moment before telling the truth. "He isn't coming."

"Why not?"

He wasn't invited. "He's very busy fixing up Blackthorne Abbey. It's been neglected for many years and needs a great deal of work."

"What you mean is *we're* too much work," Spencer muttered.

She'd tucked Clay in, then rose and stood next to Spencer's head, speaking in a voice only he could hear. "Your uncle loves you. I'm sure he does. He's been very sad at the loss of his wife. And very unhappy because it seemed for a long time that everything he valued, all the Blackthorne lands and properties, would be forfeited because his father—"

She cut herself off as she was about to say "and your father." Instead she finished, "Had run up a great many debts. That's why Uncle Marcus left you so long at Tearlach Castle, not because he didn't love you."

"So why didn't Uncle Marcus ever come to see us?"

Josie didn't have an explanation or excuse for Blackthorne's behavior, so she didn't make one. "The good news is that I was able to use my fortune to help your uncle pay his debts and begin repairs at the Abbey. Now there will always be a place for you and Clay to live, whenever you're in England."

"So why are we going to America?" Spencer asked.

"Because my eldest sister is very sick, and I want to see her before . . ."

Josie didn't complete her sentence, because she didn't want to put into words what might happen to Miranda. She kissed Spencer's forehead and said, "You need to sleep. When you wake up in the morning, you and Clay can come up on deck, and we'll watch the wind fill the sails and blow us across the sea."

"Good night, Aunt Josie."

"Good night, Spencer. I love you."

"I love you, too."

She'd waited until both boys were asleep before she'd gone up on deck, arriving just in time to see that they were underway, to panic at what she'd done, and to make a fruitless plea to turn the ship around.

Josie stepped to the rail and listened to the wind in the flapping sails, speeding them on their way. She shivered, and wrapped her wool scarf more tightly around her against the cold.

Except it wasn't the night air that had chilled her to the bone. It was the knowledge that she'd left her heart behind in England. She heard Blackthorne's whispered words lifting her up, telling her how strong she was, even as his protective arms held her close.

He wasn't an easy man to love. Too proud. Too

used to getting his own way. But somehow she'd fallen, deeply and surely, in love with him.

Her heart sank at the thought of what she'd left behind. And sank even further when she imagined what she might find when she got where she was going. She folded her hands on the rail, closed her eyes, and prayed, "Please fight to live, Miranda. Don't give up. I need to see you again. I need to talk with you again. I need—"

"I need a wife. And you were about to rob me of her."

Josie whirled at the sound of the beloved—and furiously angry—voice. "Marcus?" She clutched her scarf to her throat, suddenly frightened at the sight of a tall figure wearing a black cloak that whipped around him in the wind. It couldn't be Marcus. She'd left him behind in England. "Who? What?"

"Don't panic, my dear. It's only me. Your wayward husband."

"Marcus? Is it really you?" Josie felt a rush of joy so strong it brought tears to her eyes. "What are you doing here?"

"I think I should be asking you that." He reached out and rescued a stray curl that had blown across her face, tucking it, as he always did, behind her ear.

She held herself still, aware that his angry voice was at odds with the tender gesture. "My sister Miranda is desperately ill. There wasn't time to consult you before I left."

"So you decided to grab my nephews and steal away on the first ship headed for America without a word of warning? Without saying goodbye or even good riddance?"

She ignored the pain she heard in his voice and asked, "How did you know I brought Spencer and Clay—"

"I know a great deal, my dear. I visited Tearlach Castle. Why didn't you tell me what was going on there? I would have—"

"What would you have done, Marcus?" she interrupted. "Brought them to live with you?"

"I might have."

"But you didn't. In all the time I was at Tearlach Castle, you never once visited them. Why did you leave them to languish for so long? I've seen that you're a caring man. What happened? Why did you abandon them?" She met his gaze, surprised by the pain she saw in his eyes.

"To my shame, I have no excuse. Fanny discouraged me from visiting, but as it turned out, she simply didn't want me to discover you were there."

"I don't understand. How did she know where I was?"

"Fanny was the architect of the Machiavellian scheme that resulted in your being held captive at the castle."

Josie stared at him wide-eyed. "Fanny put me there? But why?"

He tightened the knot on the wool scarf she'd wrapped around her shoulders. "Because she knew how I felt about you."

"How you felt? How did she even know I existed?"

"Because I told her how much I admired your

defiance of someone who was determined to whip you to death. I made no secret of the fact that I was enchanted by the girl I'd rescued. She also knew she was dying. So she made a plan."

Blackthorne's eyes caressed her, while his hands found excuses to touch her.

Josie was entranced and spoke without being quite aware what she was saying. "A plan?"

"Fanny tucked you away at Tearlach Castle for safekeeping, so there would be a way for me to find you after she was gone. Seaton was supposed to tell me you were there, but when he realized I needed to marry an heiress, he decided to save me from myself and kept your whereabouts a secret."

"Then the Pinkerton found me, and I came to London hoping there was some way I could rescue Spencer and Clay, and met you and—"

"Married me," he finished. "Fanny was right about one thing."

"What?"

"That, given a chance, I would fall in love with you."

Josie shook her head. "You can't love me. We barely know each other."

"I've loved the idea of a woman like you for two years. It's taken me only two weeks to fall in love with the woman I married."

Josie's heart skipped a beat. "You love me?"

"I do."

She suddenly felt terrified of the choice she might be forced to make. "I'm still going to Texas to see my family. And I'm taking the boys."

"How would you feel about my coming along?"

Tears of relief and joy brimmed in her eyes. She laid a hand against his chest as a way to reassure herself that this was really happening, that he was here and wanted to come to America with her. She opened her mouth to tell him how happy she was, but what came out was, "There's no place in the stateroom for you to sleep."

He twined one of her curls around his finger. "Spencer and Clay can share the stateroom. The captain loaned me his cabin, so we can finish our honeymoon." He hesitated, released the curl, and said, "Assuming you care enough for me to want to finish our honeymoon."

Josie was surprised that Blackthorne was giving her the choice. She lifted her chin and said, "I suppose you expect me to forgive you for your treatment of Spencer and Clay."

"That would be nice. I don't deserve their forgiveness—or yours—but I promise to take better care of them from now on. With your help, of course."

"I suppose you expect me to say I love you. That you've turned my world upside down. That I'm head over heels for you."

His lips curved in a cautious smile. "That would be even nicer." He closed the distance between them and clasped her cold hands in his warm ones. "Do you? Have I? Are you?"

"You're too arrogant."

"Guilty."

"And toplofty."

"Guilty."

"And stubborn."

"Guilty."

"And I love you more than—"

His mouth captured hers, as his arms bound them together. She was a prisoner once more, but this time, Josie had no wish to escape.

"I love you, Marcus."

"I love you, too, darling. But I think I'm getting a little seasick up here on deck."

Josie laughed. "You? The great Duke of Blackthorne? Seasick? I don't believe it."

"Laugh all you want, but I suggest that if you don't want to see a demonstration of the matter, we retire to the captain's cabin."

Josie put her arm through Blackthorne's and tugged him away from the rail. "Just keep saying 'I will not be sick. I will not be sick.' That's been working for me."

"I will not be sick. I will not be sick. I think it's working."

"Good. I don't want to miss even one night of my honeymoon."

"I will not be sick. I will not be sick. I will make love to my wife, instead."

Josie laughed. "Faker!"

Blackthorne swept her in his arms and headed for the captain's cabin.

Chapter 44

"UNCLE MARCUS, WHAT is that?"

Josie followed Clay's pointing finger to a brown-and-black brindle steer with horns that had to be six feet from end to end. It was proof, if she needed it, that they were nearing their destination, Jake and Miranda's cattle ranch, Three Oaks.

Clay was sitting between Blackthorne and Josie on the bench seat of an open wagon they'd hired in San Antonio, while Spencer sat directly behind them on a keg of nails they'd agreed to deliver to the Creed ranch, because it would save a trip for the local dry goods merchant.

"Those cattle are called longhorns," Blackthorne said, slipping an arm around the boy's shoulder. "Can you guess why?"

Clay looked uncertain, but ventured, "Because their horns are so long?"

"Right!" Blackthorne said, pulling the boy close for a hug.

"That was a good guess, Clay," Spencer said, adding his praise to their uncle's. "I have another one for you, Uncle Marcus."

"I'm listening."

Josie never heard the question or the answer. All she heard was the trust in Spencer's voice, and the love in Blackthorne's. Even though they'd made the journey from England as fast as humanly possible, it had taken far too long. Long enough for Blackthorne to show her that he intended to be a better caretaker for his nephews than he'd been in the past. Long enough for her to fall even more deeply in love with him. Long enough for him to plant the seed for another generation of Blackthornes that was growing in her belly.

And more than long enough for Miranda to either succumb to childbed fever or recover completely.

Josie hadn't tried to get in touch with anyone at the ranch during the journey, because she'd feared hearing bad news, and good news could wait. She'd merely prayed every day that her sister would get well and hoped that Miranda would be waiting with her new baby to greet them when they arrived.

In the distance, Josie could make out a large white house with columns and a second-story porch, the sort Southerners had built before the Civil War. The house was surrounded by live oaks. Three live oaks, to be precise. She could see people sitting in rockers on the lower porch. They had glasses in their hands. Iced tea? Lemonade?

She was suddenly aware of how long they'd been traveling since they'd left San Antonio, how hot it was, and how thirsty she was. And how there was no way she'd be able to swallow even a sip of anything cold, because her throat had swollen completely closed with fear.

"I think we're here, Aunt Josie," Spencer said, bouncing up and down in excitement in the back of the wagon.

"Sit down and sit still!" she said in a sharp voice.

Blackthorne shot her a questioning look, before he turned to Spencer and said, "You're going to end up tumbling off this wagon before we get there, if you're not careful."

Josie was too anxious to apologize to Spencer. Too worried that the seemingly idyllic scene on the porch would turn out to be something entirely different. Like a wake.

"Can you see their faces?" she asked Blackthorne. "Can you tell if they're happy?"

"They're smiling!" Clay said. "They're happy to see us."

Josie put a hand above her eyes to shade them from the sun, since her stylish hat provided no protection. "Are they really smiling, Marcus? Can you tell from here?"

"They're grinning, sweetheart. From ear to ear."

"They wouldn't look like that if anything bad had happened, would they?" she asked anxiously.

"I don't think so. But I'm English. Who knows what an American will do."

Josie swatted him on the arm. "Don't be mean."

"I guess that bruising hit means you're going to relax and enjoy the rest of the ride."

Josie shot him a questioning look. "What do you mean?"

"You've been coiled up like a metal spring all

morning. I was afraid you were going to shoot off that bench seat into the clouds at any moment."

Josie laughed and realized how strange the sound felt. She tried it again, and it sounded more natural. Suddenly, she was laughing so hard tears were squeezing from her eyes.

"What's so funny, Uncle Marcus?" Clay asked.

"Your aunt is imagining herself shooting off that bench into the sky like a firecracker."

Clay joined in the laughter. "Aunt Josie is a firecracker!"

"No, she just sparkles like a firecracker," Spencer quipped.

"She kisses like one, too," Blackthorne chimed in.

"Stop picking on me," Josie said, but she was laughing along with everyone else.

That happy picture was what her family saw when Josie arrived at Miranda and Jake's front door. She sobered as Blackthorne drew the team to a halt, her gaze flitting from one familiar face to the next, skipping the strangers who stood or sat beside them.

Miranda was sitting in a rocker wrapped up in a blanket, even though it was a warm day, a babe in her arms. A stranger sat beside her in a matching rocker. Nick sat on the porch rail with Harry—no longer the sickly four-year-old she remembered—perched beside him. An old man in a wheeled chair sat with a young girl in his lap, neither of whom she recognized. Those must be Miranda's new relatives.

Her glance skipped to a broad-shouldered man sitting on a hanging swing, with Hannah beside him. Hannah had a redheaded little girl in her lap, and she was pregnant. Beside them stood two people Josie didn't recognize, but the man had features similar to Hannah's husband, and the woman was stunningly beautiful. Josie's gaze shot to Hetty, who'd been badly wounded the last time she'd seen her. Hetty was sitting in a woven, fan-backed chair with a baby in her arms. A plain-faced man stood with his arm possessively on the back of the chair. A younger woman and a young man Josie didn't recognize sat on the porch steps nearby, along with a teenage boy.

Tears blurred Josie's vision as she croaked, "I've missed you all so much!"

A moment later, she was off the wagon and running for the porch. Her family didn't wait for her to come to them, they met her halfway and crowded around her. She hugged any part of them she could reach—arms, heads, bodies cradling babies—everyone babbling unintelligible words of greeting and holding tight, as though to assure themselves that this was really happening.

It took Josie a moment to realize that Miranda wasn't part of the circle. She freed herself and took a step back, eyeing everyone again, letting herself enjoy the sight, and the familiar idiosyncracies, of each family member. Then she pulled free and crossed the porch to where Miranda still sat, with Jake standing beside her holding her shoulder, apparently to keep her from rising.

"Miranda?" A second look at her sister revealed that, although she'd obviously survived the fever that had threatened her life, she was not completely well. Josie dropped to her knees before her sister and rested her head on Miranda's knees. Her eyes slid closed, as she felt Miranda's hand gently remove the silly hat she'd worn and caress her golden hair.

"I'm so glad to see you," Miranda said in a low, hoarse voice.

Josie felt a tear slide down her cheek. They were all here, alive and well. She hadn't realized how much she blamed herself for the breakup of her family. She was the one who'd found Jake's advertisement for a mail-order bride in the Chicago newspaper. She was the one who'd written to him on Miranda's behalf. And she was the one who'd urged Hannah to marry Mr. McMurtry, because she couldn't stand even one more beating from Miss Birch.

She'd lived for two long years with the knowledge that she was personally responsible for splitting up her family. Only somehow, despite the long separation, they'd all not only survived but apparently thrived.

Josie lifted her tear-streaked face and searched her sister's features, finding the warm glow of happiness in her eyes, despite her recent illness.

"I'm so glad you're all right," Josie said. "I was so afraid . . ."

"I'm well and the baby's well and you're here and we're all back together again. Everything really has turned out happily ever after."

Josie gave a happy sob, and then Hannah and Hetty became watering pots, as they all gathered around Miranda's rocking chair. The men shuffled their feet and rearranged their Western hats, while the Wentworth children held each other tight and bawled their eyes out. Well, except for Nick and Harry, who watched the girls slobber over each other with looks of disgust.

At long last, Josie swiped at her eyes, and stood, searching for the three people she'd brought with her to Texas. She ran back to where Blackthorne waited by the wagon and hauled him onto the porch, along with Spencer and Clay.

"This is my husband, Marcus," she announced to everyone. "And these are my nephews, Spencer and Clay."

It took more than a little while for everyone to greet everyone else and for Josie to finally sort everyone out. Their family had grown so much! The two young people standing on the porch turned out to be Hetty's stepdaughter and her husband, and the beautiful woman was married to Jake's youngest brother, Ransom Creed. The Creed men were the sons of Cricket Creed, who'd married an Englishman named Alexander Blackthorne after her first husband, Jarrett Creed, had died in the Civil War.

"Do you suppose that Blackthorne fellow is any relation to you?" Josie asked her husband.

"I had an uncle named Alex *Wharton*," he replied. "But he disappeared a long time ago."

"You look just like Alex Blackthorne," Miranda said. "Doesn't he, Jake?"

Jake made a face. "Sorry to say, he does."

"Jake doesn't care much for his stepfather," Miranda explained.

"I wouldn't mind if I never see the son of a bitch again," Jake muttered.

"Jake!" Miranda chided. "Watch your manners. And your language."

"If your Alexander Blackthorne is my uncle Alex, then I couldn't agree with you more," Blackthorne said.

"Speak of the devil," Jake muttered, his gaze focused on four riders headed for the house. "Meet my stepfather, my mother, and my twin half brothers, Noah and Nash."

Josie stared in disbelief at Alexander Blackthorne. "I can't believe it," she whispered. "That man looks exactly like the painting of your father at the Abbey."

"That's because he's my father's twin brother. The one who tried to steal the dukedom," Blackthorne replied.

"That sounds like the son of a bitch, all right," Jake said.

"Jake, stop it," Miranda said.

As Alexander Blackthorne dismounted, he approached his nephew and said, "I'd know those features anywhere. You must be the latest Duke of Blackthorne."

"That would make you the bastard who tried to steal my patrimony," Blackthorne shot back.

The transplanted Englishman laughed, but it wasn't a mirthful sound. "I decided if Randy wanted the dukedom enough to lie through his teeth for it, he could have it. We both knew the truth."

"Are you saying I'm not the rightful duke? That

you are?" Blackthorne challenged. "My father proved in court—"

"That he had the funds to pay a nurse to perjure herself. But, as I said, I've got a new life here in Texas that suits me a lot better than my life in England ever did. I prefer to stay as dead as I'm sure my brother believed I was."

"Are you suggesting my father—" Blackthorne began.

"I'm saying I have no intention of returning to England. Ever. You're welcome to every moldy old stone in Blackthorne Abbey. They're yours with my blessing."

"That's good. Because I have no intention of ever giving up a single one of those moldy old stones to anyone. Ever."

"Are you two done?" Josie asked, her hands on her hips. "Because we have a celebration to start." She turned to Jake and said, "I'd like a little of whatever is in those cold glasses. And please get something for my husband and his uncle—your stepfather—while you're at it."

"I'd do it, if I were you," Blackthorne said with a chagrined smile. "These Wentworth women can be hell on wheels."

"Don't I know it!" Jake replied with a laugh, as he disappeared into the house.

"Wait a few months, and we'll have our own little hellion on wheels," Josie whispered in her husband's ear.

Blackthorne looked stunned for a moment, then picked her up and whirled her in a circle, as he announced to the gathered crowd, "We're going to have a baby!"

His announcement was greeted with a host of whoops and hollers.

Josie looked down at the smiling face of her husband, then at the joyful faces of her family, and knew she'd never been happier than she was at this very moment. She took Blackthorne's face between her hands, kissed him tenderly on the lips, and said, "Thank you for bringing me home."

Epilogue

BLACKTHORNE WAS BESIDE himself. His wife was being torn in two, and there was nothing he could do to save her. In fact, he was the one who'd subjected her to such punishment. If only he could take her pain on himself!

"Owwww," he muttered. Josie was squeezing his hand so hard, he thought she might break his fingers. He'd had no idea she was so strong. But then, it took a great deal of strength to push a babe out of one's belly, and she was working very hard at it.

They'd come to the glass summer house for a picnic and sent the carriage away so they could be alone. He'd felt perfectly safe doing so, because the carriage would only be gone for two hours, and it was a full two weeks before the baby was due to arrive.

He'd spread out a soft blanket inside the glass house because clouds were threatening rain, and began setting out the picnic lunch he'd had Cook prepare for them.

Josie had wandered down to the pond to listen to the frogs and watch the turtles plop into the water from their warm stones. She returned just as he finished arranging everything. She leaned a shoulder against the doorway, rested a hand on her belly, and said, "I think it's time."

"Yes, lunch is ready. Come sit down."

"I mean time for the baby."

He'd felt a small spurt of panic and tamped it down. "That's ridiculous. It's another two weeks before—"

She closed her eyes and breathed slowly for several moments.

He was on his feet beside her by the time her eyes reopened. "What's wrong?"

She smiled wanly. "My water broke when I was down at the pond. I was having a few twinges when I woke up this morning, and a few more throughout the day, but they seemed too inconsequential to be labor." She soughed out a long breath, her eyes bleak. "I guess I was wrong."

He stared at her with disbelief. "But the carriage isn't coming back for two hours!"

"I know."

"You can't have a baby out here in the middle of nowhere with only me for a midwife."

"Maybe it won't come to that," she said, laying a comforting hand on his arm. "Maybe the carriage will be back in time for us to return to the house and summon the doctor."

"Maybe it won't."

"Everything will be fine, Marcus. Women deliver babies every day."

"And die doing it!" He immediately regretted suggesting that such a disaster might befall his wife. But his memories of Fanny's difficult delivery and subsequent death had never been far from his mind during Josie's pregnancy.

"Let me help you clear off the blanket," she suggested. "I'm going to need a place to lie down."

"I'll take care of that. You . . ." He couldn't think of a thing to suggest that she do.

"I'll remove my undergarments." She must have seen the shock on his face, because she explained, "Because they're wet. Not because I believe I'll be delivering a child anytime soon."

He did his best to create a comfortable bed for her, taking off his coat and waistcoat and balling them up to make a pillow for her head, but she seemed unwilling to settle in one place.

"I'm feeling fine," she assured him. "I'd rather walk than lie down."

So they walked—and talked—for the next two hours, and drank lemonade, and talked some more, while he searched the darkening clouds on the horizon for any sign of the carriage. He checked his grandfather's gold watch often, watching the minutes tick by with a sick feeling in his stomach.

The Pinkerton who'd bought his gold watch from the Sioux had delivered it to Miranda, and she'd returned it to him when they'd traveled to Texas. His whalebone-handled knife was gone forever, but he would have willingly given it up a thousand more times to rescue the woman who'd become his wife.

He was checking his watch again, noting that three hours and ten minutes had passed since Josie's water had broken, when she announced, "I think I'll lie down now."

Another hour passed while he sat on the blanket by her side, watching her face to see how much pain she was enduring, as the contractions came and went. She bit her lip until it bled, trying not to cry out. He'd never admired her more.

"Where in bloody hell is that carriage?" he muttered when another thirty-four minutes had passed. She was more restless now, unable to find a comfortable position, moaning pitifully when the pains came and grasping his hand like a lifeline.

"This is all your fault," she muttered.

"Yes, my dear."

"You're the Dastardly Duke. I never should have married you."

His brows rose at the appellation, but he merely replied, "You're right, my dear."

"I'll never forgive you for doing this to me."

"No, my dear."

"You're a beast."

"Yes, my dear."

"It hurts, Marcus," she cried, her eyes pleading for some surcease from the pain.

"I know, my dear," he rasped.

"Make it stop! Please, make it stop!"

"Soon, my dear." He dampened one of the numerous table napkins Cook must have thought they would need and dabbed the silky cloth against her forehead.

She shoved his hand away and said, "That's not where it hurts!"

"Whatever you say, my dear."

Blackthorne was fighting his terror in the only way he knew, by acting calm and rational and unflappable. He felt anything but. He'd made it through the nine months of Josie's pregnancy without collapsing with fear, because she'd always been so cheerful . . . and so healthy. Now her face looked wan, and beads of sweat—no dewy perspiration for his Josie—had formed in the space above the lips he loved to kiss, and on her worried, furrowed brow.

She suddenly began to grunt and growl, like an animal fighting to escape an inescapable trap.

"Josie? What's happening?"

"I need to *push*!"

This *was* all his fault. Who took a nine-months-pregnant woman for a carriage ride to a glass summer house in the middle of nowhere, with a fierce thunderstorm threatening to erupt at any moment, and then sent the carriage away, so they could have the illusion of being entirely alone?

He'd felt so sure there was no possibility of danger to his wife. He'd been told it usually took a *whole day* for a woman's first baby to be born. Besides, it was two full weeks before their child was due to arrive.

Except it had decided to be born today.

Something terrible must have happened to delay the coachman this long. Four hours and fifty-two minutes had come and gone, and now his wife was going to bear their first child on a blanket on the floor of the summer house, with the Duke of Blackthorne playing midwife.

"If you have to push, then push, my dear."

"Will you stop calling me that?"

"But you are, Josie. The dearest thing to my

heart. I love you, and I won't be able to bear it if you leave me. So you're going to bear down with all your might, and push our child out into the world. That's an order! Do you hear me?"

His wife laughed. It was a huffing sound, but it was definitely laughter.

"Did you just *laugh* at me? After all I've been through today?"

She laughed again. And then groaned and made an awful grinding sound in her throat. And then, to his astonishment, she began to swear like a drunken sailor. He listened in awe to the foul words coming out of his precious wife's mouth. Where had she learned such coarse language?

Suddenly, she yelled, "It's coming!"

Blackthorne looked at the items he'd collected in preparation for this moment. He'd laid out a table napkin in which to wrap the newborn, and he had the sharp knife Cook had sent along to slice the ham sandwiches, with which to cut the cord. Finally, he'd brought the *London Times* to read, imagining himself with his head lazing on Josie's thigh down by the pond. He planned to use that to wrap up the afterbirth.

He'd never been more grateful than now for the fact that the hostler at Blackthorne Abbey had allowed a young boy of ten to watch the birth of a foal, explaining each step of the way what was happening. At least he had some clue how to help his wife. But he'd never imagined the terrible pain she would have to endure.

And he had no idea what he was going to do if there was some complication.

"I can see the head!"

His wife said nothing, merely grunted and growled like some dangerous, helpless beast.

"And now the shoulders," he said.

A moment later his tiny, perfectly formed daughter slid into his hands. She lay there for a moment without a sound, and then opened her eyes and looked at him.

"Is the baby all right?" Josie asked anxiously. "I don't hear anything."

"She's perfect. She's just staring at me with very wide blue eyes."

Josie pushed herself up on her elbows. "I want to see her. Hand her to me, Marcus."

Before he could do as she asked, her eyes widened and she said, "Oh. There's more."

"I know, my dear," he said quite calmly, because he knew the worst was over, and that this was merely her body pushing out the birth sac, which was no longer needed. He quickly swaddled the baby in the waiting table napkin and laid her at Josie's side, then grabbed the newspaper he knew he would need.

Except, what came out next wasn't the afterbirth.

"Oh, my God!"

"What's wrong, Marcus? Am I dying? I must be. The pain is back!" She began panting and grunting and groaning again, and pushing and straining and . . .

"It's another baby! It's twins!"

Between huffing and puffing, Josie said, "We shouldn't be . . . surprised. Twins run . . . in both our . . . families."

A moment later, another perfect little girl slid into Blackthorne's hands, but this one was yelling her head off—which set the other one to crying. He quickly wrapped his daughter in a second table napkin he'd hastily shaken free of crumbs and laid her on the blanket on Josie's other side. Then he retrieved the newspaper for the second time, as both afterbirths made their appearance. He set the newspaper aside, then washed his hands with left-over lemonade, which made them cleaner but left them sticky.

Blackthorne swiped his hands on his trousers, which were already a lot the worse for wear, before clasping them together, so his wife wouldn't see how badly he was still shaking. Unfortunately, she was looking right at him, and he realized he wasn't fooling her.

"It's all over, darling," she said, smiling and reaching out her hand to him. "Come here. We're all fine. Both of our daughters seem to have very strong lungs."

Blackthorne felt like crying. With relief. And with joy. Then the heavens did it for him, releasing tor-rents of rain that pounded on the glass roof. The rhythmic sound seemed to fascinate the two babies, who suddenly stopped crying.

Blackthorne lowered himself to the floor beside his wife and stared down at their twin daughters. "They're as beautiful as their mother."

"They look like you."

"Heaven help them." He stared at the water streaming down the walls of the glass house. "It feels like we're encased in some strange, watery world."

"I've always loved this glass house," Josie said. "Now it will be an even more special place."

"Which you're never coming within a mile of the next time you're pregnant." He kissed her brow, and then each cheek, and finally, her mouth.

She laughed. "Oh, Marcus. Sometimes you're so funny."

"I'm a duke. Dukes are never funny. They're top-lofty and arrogant."

She laughed at him again, a trilling sound that made his heart sing. Her laughter was interrupted by the sound of the carriage finally returning.

"You're safe at last," his wife said. "The cavalry has arrived."

He made a disgusted sound in his throat. "Far too late to be of any real assistance."

She raised a brow. "You were planning to *carry* the three of us back to the Abbey?"

"There is that," he conceded.

"Uncle Marcus! Guess who's come for a visit!" Clay yelled from the carriage window. Without waiting for Blackthorne to guess, he added, "It's Aunt Lark and Uncle David."

"And Grandmama and Aunt Lindsey," Spencer shouted from beside him. "They're all waiting at the Abbey for us to bring you home."

"Good lord," Blackthorne muttered. "No wonder the carriage was late returning. They must have needed a ride from the train station. They weren't supposed to arrive for another two weeks. I suppose Grandmama wanted to be sure she was here for the arrival of the heir."

"She's going to have a bit of a wait," Josie said ruefully, pulling her twin daughters close.

The moment the coachman opened the door and let down the steps, the two boys came tumbling out and scampered through the rain into the summer house.

"We have cousins!" Spencer said upon spying the babies lying on either side of Josie.

"Slow down and be careful," Blackthorne admonished.

"Can I hold one?" Clay asked.

The word "no" was on the tip of Blackthorne's tongue, when Josie said, "Of course, but sit down beside me first."

Blackthorne's heart was in his throat. What if Clay dropped the newborn? Or let her head fall back too far?

The simple-minded boy dropped down with crossed legs and seemed to hold his breath, as Josie lifted the twin on her left into his waiting arms. He held the newborn as though she were made of breakable glass and looked up with a smile that made Blackthorne's heart swell with love.

"You're doing a good job, Clay," he said.

"I want to hold one, too," Spencer said, plopping down on Josie's other side.

She shifted the second girl into Spencer's careful hands, and he looked up at Blackthorne and beamed with pride. "I think she likes me, Uncle Marcus."

"Let's see if you still feel the same way about her

in a few years, when she's tagging along after you everywhere you go."

"Aw, it'll be great," Spencer said with the naïveté of the ignorant.

"How come you had your babies out here, Aunt Josie?" Clay asked.

"For some reason, our carriage was late returning to pick us up," Blackthorne said sardonically.

"Oh. 'Cause we had to pick up everyone at the train station," Spencer said. "Wow, Uncle Marcus! I never knew you could deliver babies."

"Neither did I," Blackthorne said. "Mostly, your aunt did all the work."

"Thanks," Josie said with a laugh.

They sat quietly together for a long time, sharing this very special moment.

"The rain has stopped," Josie said at last. "I suppose we should load everyone into the carriage and get back to the house. After all, we have a very anxious grandmother waiting to see the new additions to the family."

Blackthorne took the baby from Clay so he could stand, and then very carefully placed her back in his arms.

"What's her name?" Clay asked.

"We only decided on one name, because we weren't expecting two babies," Josie said.

"I suppose the first-born girl should be Elizabeth," Blackthorne said.

Josie focused her gaze on Spencer and asked, "What name should we give the baby you're holding?"

"I like Emma," Spencer said.

"I like Emma, too," Clay said.

"Then Emma it shall be," Blackthorne said.

"Hello, Emma," Spencer said, trying out the name.

"And this is Beth," Clay said, using a shortened form of Elizabeth.

"Sounds perfect," Josie said.

Once both boys were standing, each holding a baby, Blackthorne carefully wrapped his wife in the blanket and scooped her into his arms. "Gentlemen, it's time to take our ladies home."

While he waited for the footman to help the boys get settled with the newborns in the carriage, Blackthorne felt Josie's fingers caress his neck and leaned down to kiss her tenderly on the lips.

"Thank you for our daughters," she whispered.

He grinned and said, "The pleasure, I assure you, was all mine. Anytime you would like a repeat performance, I—"

She cut him off by pressing a hand over his mouth. "Whoa, there, Your Grace. Let's take a little time to enjoy these two, before we start on two more."

"I love the way your mind works, my dear."

Josie laughed.

Acknowledgments

I want to thank my editor, Shauna Summers, for bringing out the best in me as a writer, Lynn Andreozzi for the amazing covers she puts on my books, Gina Wachtel for her support of me and my work, and all the folks at Penguin Random House who help make my books available to the reading public. I am eternally indebted to you all.

I would never find the time to write without the help of my assistant and personal marketing manager, Nancy Sloane, to whom this book is dedicated. In the three years we've worked together, she's been an enormous asset, keeping my website updated, running contests, formatting newsletters, and generally doing all the business of writing and promoting books that is so necessary these days.

I want to thank my sister Joyce for her knowledge of English grammar. She's always there when I have a question and always has the right answer!

Finally, I want to thank all the readers who write to me begging for the next book. Your joy in my work makes it all worthwhile.

LETTER TO READERS

Dear Faithful Readers,

So many of you wrote to ask for Josie's story that I had to put it down on paper! I hope you've enjoyed reading *Blackthorne's Bride,* the final book in my Mail-Order Bride series, which also includes *Texas Bride, Wyoming Bride,* and *Montana Bride.* This series has become one of my favorites.

I've already started work on the third book in my contemporary King's Brats series, which began with *Sinful* and *Shameless* and continues with *Surrender.* An excerpt from *Surrender* follows this letter. Enjoy!

You can contact me, sign up for my e-newsletter, and enter contests through my website, joanjohnston.com. You can also like me at facebook.com/joanjohnstonauthor or follow me at twitter.com/joanjohnston. I look forward to hearing from you!

By the way, if you enjoyed this novel, it's connected to more than thirty-five other books in my Bitter Creek series, beginning with my contemporary novels *The Cowboy, The Texan,* and *The Loner.* If you'd like to read more about Cricket and Jarrett Creed, check out my historical Sisters of the Lone Star series, *Frontier Woman, Comanche Woman,* and *Texas Woman.*

Take care and happy reading,
Joan Johnston

Taylor and Brian's story heats up in the next installment of *New York Times* bestselling author Joan Johnston's sizzling contemporary Western romance series, where power, money, and rivalries rule—and love is the best revenge.

Surrender

Coming soon from Dell

Continue reading for a special sneak peek

DOES YOUR LIFE *really flash before your eyes when you know you're going to die?* Taylor Grayhawk was a great pilot, but there was nothing she could do with both engines flared out. A whirlwind of fire had engulfed her Twin Otter as she flew over Yellowstone National Park dropping smoke jumpers to fight the raging inferno that had been burning for the past two weeks. She turned to stare over her shoulder at the single smoke jumper who hadn't made it out of the plane.

"You can still jump," she said over the eerie rustle of the wind in the open doorway at the rear of the plane.

"Not without you," the jumper called back.

"I don't have a parachute."

"We can share mine."

Taylor calculated the odds of getting to the ground hanging on to Brian Flynn by her fingernails—and whatever other body parts she could wrap around him. He was wearing a padded jump jacket and pants made of Kevlar, the same material used for bulletproof vests. It was bulky, to say the least. She imagined herself falling—sliding down his body—into the crackling flames below and shuddered.

"I'll take my chances on getting the plane to the ground in one piece," she said, turning back to the control panel to see how much lift she could manage without the engines. Not much. She searched in vain for a meadow—any opening in the trees— where she might crash-land the plane.

The spotter, who was required on all flights to gauge the wind, fire activity, and terrain, hadn't shown up, so Brian, who'd already been dressed in his smoke jumping gear, had served as the spotter instead. Unfortunately, he hadn't been able to steer her away from what turned out to be a catastrophic encounter with fire. Taylor doubted anyone could have anticipated the sudden tornado of flame that had shot up hundreds of feet into the air from the forest below.

"This plane's headed straight into the fire," Brian said from the doorway. "We need to jump now, while there's still time to hit a safe clearing. Get over here, Tag. Move your butt!"

The use of her nickname, which came from her initials—Taylor Ann Grayhawk—conjured powerful, painful memories from the past. Brian had dubbed her with it when he was a junior and she was a freshman at Jackson High.

Taylor felt the plane shudder as the right wingtip was abruptly shoved upward by a gust of hot air and knew that time was running out. In a voice that was surprisingly calm, considering the desperation she felt inside, Taylor reported their position on the radio, along with the fact that she'd been unable to restart the engines.

"I'm putting us down in the first clearing I find," she told the dispatcher.

"Roger," the dispatcher replied. "Good luck."

The problem was she didn't see a clearing large enough to allow her to land without going in nose first. Survival was questionable. Disaster seemed imminent.

Two words kept replaying in her mind: "What if . . . ?"

What if their fathers, King Grayhawk and Angus Flynn, hadn't been mortal enemies? What if Brian's elder brother, Aiden, hadn't caught Brian making love to her after the junior prom? What if her fraternal twin sister, Victoria, hadn't made it clear that if Taylor didn't stay away from Brian, who was just one more of "those awful Flynn boys," she was never speaking to her again?

Brian had become a firefighter and married someone else. She'd become a corporate pilot and gone through several futile engagements. They were both free now, but Brian's divorce a year ago had left him so heartsore and gun-shy that he was likely never to fall in love again.

None of that mattered now. Very likely she and Brian were going to die in the next few minutes. What made her heart ache was regret for what her life might have been like if only . . .

"Tag?"

She looked over her shoulder at the tall, broad-shouldered man who'd been forbidden fruit when she was a teenager. She'd run her fingers through his thick black hair, holding on tight as they made love. His piercing blue eyes had seen past her movie-star-beautiful, confident, blond-haired, blue-eyed exterior to the abandoned child inside, who desperately wanted to be loved.

She'd grown up with an older half sister as a mother, after the mother who'd borne her had run off with one of her father's cowhands. Her wealthy father had been mostly absent, serving two terms as Wyoming governor in Cheyenne, while he left his four daughters back home at his ranch in Jackson Hole.

Because of the animosity between the Grayhawk and Flynn families, she'd started out determined to seduce Brian Flynn—and dump him. It would be fair repayment for all the nasty things he and his three brothers had done to her and her three sisters. *His* heart was supposed to end up broken, not *hers*. She hadn't planned on liking him. Brian was the first boy to offer affection in return for the sex she'd been offering to any boy who gave her a kind look—and some whose looks weren't so kind— hoping to find someone who would care about her.

"I'm not leaving without you, Tag," Brian said. "Get out of that seat and get your beautiful ass over here!"

Their eyes met, and she felt the past flooding back. All the things she should have done . . . and hadn't. All the things she shouldn't have done . . . and had.

The thought of a future with Brian almost had her rising. But there was too much water under the bridge. Or water over the dam. She'd been disappointed too many times by too many men. Some people were lovable, and some were not. She was just one of those people who wasn't destined to find a man who could love her. Brian Flynn had had his chance. She no longer believed in the possibility of any kind of happily ever after. Her life was liable to end in an altogether more gruesome way.

"You go," she said turning back to search through the windshield for the clearing she knew had to be there somewhere.

A moment later she felt a strong hand grip her arm, yanking her out of her seat.

"I am not, by God, going to take the blame for leaving you behind, you stubborn brat!"

The plane shuddered, and the wings tipped sideways.

"Let me go!" she cried, reaching back to the control column in an attempt to right the plane. But he pulled her inexorably toward the door, which was already tilting upward at an angle that might keep them both from escaping.

Taylor jerked free and rushed back to her seat, grabbing the control column and bringing the plane back to level flight. She glanced over her shoulder and said, "Just go, Brian! Someone has to keep the plane steady so you can get out the door."

"I'm not going anywhere without you, Tag. Get that into your head. So you can either join me in getting out of this plane, or we can both go down with it in flames."